THE
AENEID

VIRGIL

THE
AENEID

A New Verse Translation by
Len Krisak

With Introduction and Notes by
Christopher M. McDonough

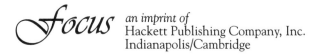

focus an imprint of
Hackett Publishing Company, Inc.
Indianapolis/Cambridge

A Focus book

Focus an imprint of
Hackett Publishing Company

Copyright © 2020 by Hackett Publishing Company, Inc.

23 22 21 20   1 2 3 4 5 6 7

For further information, please address
   Hackett Publishing Company, Inc.
   P.O. Box 44937
   Indianapolis, Indiana 46244-0937

   www.hackettpublishing.com

Cover design by Brian Rak
Interior design by E. L. Wilson
Composition by Aptara, Inc.
Map: Adapted from Rcsprinter123, after QuartierLatin1968. CC BY-SA 3.0.
https://creativecommons.org/license/by/3.0/deed.en.

Library of Congress Control Number: 2020906508

ISBN-13: 978-1-58510-964-7 (hardcover)
ISBN-13: 978-1-58510-963-0 (paperback)

∞

Contents

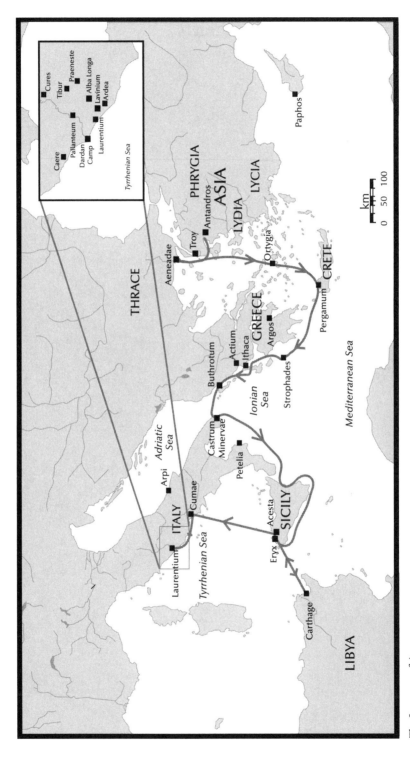

The Journeys of Aeneas

Introduction

In the ruins of Pompeii, there are places where you can still decipher *arma virumque cano*—the opening words of the *Aeneid*—scribbled out on the walls in the years just before the volcano erupted and covered the city in ash in A.D. 79. Time and the glaring Mediterranean sun have almost bleached out the ancient graffiti, but the Roman masterpiece those markings quote endures, an inspiration to poets, artists, leaders, and readers from antiquity to the present day. What is it about Aeneas's story that so deeply resonates, the story of one civilization destroyed while another rises, of gods above who smile while others nurse undying grudges, of shades below who wail while others wait to be born?

Publius Vergilius Maro (70–19 B.C.) is known to the English-speaking world as Virgil (or Vergil). His *Aeneid* is, among many other things, a tale of two cities, Troy and Rome, and the mythical hero whose fate binds them together. By the time Virgil was writing in the mid-first century B.C., the Trojan War was already the ancient world's best-known story, familiar from Homeric epic, Greek drama, allusions in prose, and depictions in art. Hardly anyone, literate or not, could have been unfamiliar with how the Trojan prince Paris stole Helen, wife of the Greek king Menelaus, and how the Greeks sailed to recover her; or how the Greek hero Achilles quarreled with Agamemnon and quit the Greek campaign but ultimately rejoined it and killed the Trojan champion Hector in battle. The story of Troy's tragic fall, clinched not by battlefield heroics but by Odysseus's (Ulysses's) brilliant scheme of hiding armed Greeks within a seemingly harmless wooden horse, is told in Book Eight of the *Odyssey*. But it is re-told and elaborated upon in the *Aeneid* with startling originality. Here, for example, not only does a hollow wooden offering to the gods monstrously belch forth warriors and destruction upon the too-trusting Trojans, but no less treacherously, the gods themselves destroy both the Trojan priest Laocoön—who had warned his countrymen about the trap—and his innocent sons, for good measure.

Aeneas is a refugee from the Trojan War and new to Italy. As future father of the Roman race, he is also the Trojan hero of Virgil's poem. In the final lines of the poem, Aeneas kills the native hero, Turnus, king of the Rutulians (an indigenous people established near Rome), who thus dies as an Italian version of Hector. Turnus's death, like that of Hector, the poet indicates, is a blood sacrifice necessary for the foundation of Rome. The tale of an even greater such sacrifice is one that is related earlier in the poem—that of the Carthaginian queen Dido, a host to the wandering Aeneas. The two leaders become lovers, though her own feelings for him are manipulated by the goddesses Juno and Venus working together. Juno, who loved Carthage but hated Aeneas more, lets Dido die in order to foster eternal enmity between Dido's city and his. The wars with Carthage were an important touchstone of actual Roman history, and the defeat of the African enemy more than any other helped to define the national character that Virgil celebrated in his mythological poem. For Virgil, Rome's historical confrontations with Carthage can be seen against the mythical backstory of the single, beautiful, noble queen, whose destruction Juno allows out of hatred but which, in the larger scheme of things, the chief god Jupiter allows for the sake of fate.

When asked to relate the story of the sack of Troy in Book II, Aeneas tells Dido and her court that while his own city burned he was visited in a dream by a vision of Hector, a ghost still gory from his deadly encounter with Achilles. "The enemy has Troy," he tells him. "Troy topples with its spires" (II.291). And so, against his every instinct and after long, futile combat in the streets, Aeneas flees. He shoulders his father, Anchises, and leads his young son Ascanius (also called Iulus) by the hand as he leaves, but in the melee loses his wife Creusa forever. The diaspora of the Trojans was a mythical one, but the *Aeneid*'s depiction is based on the real-life stories of peoples defeated and uprooted all over the classical world who took what they could carry and mourned what they could not. That torched cities and forced wanderings often resulted from the conquests of Rome was a point grimly recognized by its greatest poet. In the epic's second half, Virgil brings Aeneas to Italy, a "promised land" to his hero but to the Rutulians and others who occupy it, a homeland to be defended against invasion. By the *Aeneid*'s end, however, the wheel of fortune is just completing its inevitable turn, and Aeneas becomes the conquering hero he once fought against and fled.

The mythological lynchpin between Troy's fall and Rome's rise is, as already noted, Aeneas. But just as significantly, the *Aeneid* creates a bridge between the Roman future and the Greek literary past. Without doubt, much of Virgil's poem is patterned after Homer: the classicist Brooks Otis referred to Books I through VI as the "Odyssean *Aeneid*" and Books VII through XII as the "Iliadic *Aeneid*," for good reason. It was never Virgil's intention to deny his debt to the older poetic tradition. "It is easier to steal the club of Heracles," he is reputed to have said, "than to lift a line from

Homer." The brilliance of the *Aeneid* as mythology lies not in reduplicating beloved ancient myths but in adapting them in the service of later political realities. Many instances might be given, but one will suffice. At his most despondent—at the poem's dead center in Book VI—Aeneas descends into the Underworld. It is a scene modeled after Odysseus's own journey to the dead, in Book Eleven of the *Odyssey*. Where the Homeric hero visits with ghosts from his past, Aeneas meets with his deceased father who unveils for him the souls of his posterity waiting to be born. Before the hero's eyes rise up the generations who will exercise power over the known world. It has not happened yet but will, and Aeneas, here at the very beginning, can see it all. Over the great horde of Roman souls, Aeneas's father utters the famous words, "Remember, Roman: *you* / Will rule the nations with your might (*that* is your due, / Your art), imposing on their peace, law's blessèd crown— / With mercy (fight the haughty till they're beaten down)" (VI.850–53). They are lines that might as well have served as the motto of the Roman Empire.

The scene in the Underworld is brilliant in its exposition, a daring—even postmodern—inversion of the Homeric prototype that casts tumultuous events long past as things yet to take place. But some have rightly taken issue with Virgil's mythicizing as ideology. "No, Virgil, no," W. H. Auden had written of this moment in the *Aeneid*. "Not even the first of the Romans can learn / His *Roman history in the future tense*, / Not even to serve your political turn" ("Secondary Epic"). The glory of Rome is on full display in the *Aeneid*, it is true, but those politicians who thought to draw inspiration from it—Auden was thinking of the use and abuse of classics by fascist pro-pagandists when he wrote—had only bothered to hear half the story. Aeneas gazes upon the conquering Romans below, but he also sees the souls-to-be of those who will devolve into brutal civil war against each other. Born in 70 B.C., Virgil saw the civil wars firsthand—he was in his mid-twenties when Julius Caesar was assassinated—and the living memory of a society tearing itself apart provided the immediate political backstory to all his work. But the horror of the atrocities, Virgil seems to say, is necessary for the achievement of victory: the greater the degradation, the greater the glory—the kind witnessed under the triumphant reign of Julius Caesar's adopted great-nephew, Caesar Augustus, during which the *Aeneid* was written. Small wonder early Christians, and later ones as well, took up Virgil as a sort of proto-Christian, a forerunner of their own sacral point of view.

"How can we know the dancer from the dance?" Yeats once asked, and the same question might be put about Virgil and the *Aeneid*: How can we know the singer from the song? Behind the war (*arma*), behind the man (*virumque*), there is a singer who self-consciously sings (*cano*), a fact of which Len Krisak's supple new translation reminds us in its opening line, "My poem sings of one man forced from Troy by war." The *Aeneid* is a masterpiece of mythology and of politics—and both topics have kept scholars busy for generations with explication and elaboration—but it is, above all, a consummate work of art. "The stateliest measure ever moulded by the lips of man," was how Lord Tennyson described Virgil's poetry, and there is no doubt that, even if you can read the *Aeneid* in Latin, you will sometimes find yourself at a loss for words. When Aeneas looks upon the walls of Juno's temple in Carthage, for instance, he sees piteous depictions of the Trojan War and wonders aloud at their evident ability to arouse feelings of sorrow in others. *Sunt lacrimae rerum et mentem mortalia tangunt*, he famously intones. "Here too, men's griefs touch others with *lacrimae rerum*" (I.462). The overwhelming sadness of the moment comes through without question, and the near impossibility of putting it into words is a mark of the poet's genius. To his credit, Krisak leaves the poignant but famously untranslatable phrase *lacrimae rerum* untranslated, leaving intact what Virgil meant us to feel but not be able to articulate. In the *Aeneid*, we find set pieces and individual lines that have become standard points of reference and allusion for generations of poets, from antiquity through the Renaissance to the present day. When Dante is in despair in the *Inferno*, it is Virgil who comes to him. When Milton's Satan rails against God, it is Virgil's Juno he is channeling. But let us remember that it has never been only the literary elite who took delight in the works of Virgil. Many years after having studied it in school, there are leagues of students who can still recite passages of the *Aeneid* by heart. And let us not forget, either, those petty vandals in an Italian vacation spot who, finding themselves with a writing implement and a little time on their hands, tagged the ancient walls with lines Virgil had written a century before.

Christopher M. McDonough
University of the South

Suggested Further Reading

Dyson, Julia. *King of the Wood: The Sacrificial Victor in Virgil's* Aeneid. Norman: University of Oklahoma Press, 2001.

Galinsky, Karl. *Augustan Culture: An Interpretive Introduction.* Princeton: Princeton University Press, 1996.

Gransden, K. W. *Virgil: The* Aeneid. 2nd ed., prepared by S. J. Harrison. Cambridge: Cambridge University Press, 2004.

Frazer, James G. *The Golden Bough: A Study in Magic and Religion,* abridged edition. New York: The Macmillan Company, 1922.

Hardie, Philip R. *Virgil's* Aeneid: *Cosmos and Imperium.* Oxford: Clarendon Press, 1986.

Jenkyns, Richard. *Virgil's Experience: Nature and History, Times, Names, and Places.* Oxford: Oxford University Press, 1998.

Johnson, W. R. *Darkness Visible: A Study of Vergil's* Aeneid. Berkeley: University of California Press, 1976.

Knauer, Georg Nicolaus. *Die* Aeneis *und Homer: Studien zur poetischen Technik Vergils mit Listen der Homerzitate in der* Aeneis. Göttingen: Vandenhoeck & Ruprecht, 1964.

Le Guin, Ursula K. *Lavinia.* Orlando: Harcourt, 2008.

Lyne, R. O. A. M. *Words and the Poet: Characteristic Techniques of Style in Vergil's* Aeneid. Oxford: Clarendon Press, 1989.

Mac Góráin, Fiachra, and Charles Martindale, eds. *The Cambridge Companion to Virgil.* 2nd ed. Cambridge: Cambridge University Press, 2019.

O'Hara, James J. *Death and the Optimistic Prophecy in Vergil's* Aeneid. Princeton: Princeton University Press, 1990.

Otis, Brooks. *Virgil: A Study in Civilized Poetry.* Oxford: Oxford University Press, 1964. Reprint, Norman: University of Oklahoma Press, 1995.

Perkell, Christine, ed. *Reading Vergil's* Aeneid: *An Interpretive Guide.* Norman: University of Oklahoma Press, 1999.

Putnam, Michael C. J. *The Poetry of the* Aeneid: *Four Studies in Imaginative Unity and Design.* Cambridge, MA: Harvard University Press, 1965.

Thomas, Richard F., and Jan M. Ziolkowski, eds. *The Virgil Encyclopedia.* 3 vols. Chichester-Oxford-Malden, MA: Wiley-Blackwell, 2014.

Wiltshire, Susan Ford. *Public and Private in Vergil's* Aeneid. Amherst: University of Massachusetts Press, 1989.

Translator's Preface

The *Aeneid* is an epic Latin poem in twelve books, written in the standard meter of epics both Greek and Latin: dactylic hexameter. Because classical meter is based on the value of *quantity*—length of syllables, whether by position or by the inherent nature of the vowel of that syllable—and not, as in traditional English prosody, by the stress or accent on syllables, translators through the centuries have tended to substitute equivalent feet in English for Latin feet. In practice, this means that where a Latin poet would treat a dactylic foot of three syllables as *long-short-short*, the English-language poet would create dactyls out of a *stress-unstressed-unstressed* triad. This is so primarily because attempts at writing English verse in quantitative feet (and there have been a number of historical attempts to do so, by Robert Bridges among others) have yielded disappointing results. The subsequent lines of verse in English seem to offer no recognizable pattern to the ear of the listener or reader, whether of *Beowulf* or *A Shropshire Lad*. The result reads like prose. At Virgil's death, the *Aeneid* was not finished. Some fifty-five lines were never completed, and where these appear I have offered correspondingly short lines.

But there is a further problem in carrying over Latin feet into English equivalents: How does the modern poet sustain almost nine thousand lines of dactyls created by stress or accent? Tennyson famously experimented with possible solutions to this problem and wryly concluded it was next to impossible. And here are the first four lines of Byron's "Bride of Abydos":

> Know ye the land where the cypress and myrtle
> Are emblems of deeds that are done in their clime?
> Where the rage of the vulture, the love of the turtle,
> Now melt into sorrow, now madden to crime?

Immediately apparent is the considerable degree of metrical finagling needed to keep these lines dactylic.

For these reasons, I have rendered Virgil's dactyls as iambs—that ancient standby metrical foot of the great preponderance of English poetry. Hence, iambic hexameters—six-foot-long lines in the pattern most readers of

English verse will recognize immediately. I make no pretense as to the originality of this decision, but merely confess that any other prosodic choice would have been beyond my skill as a poet.

This brings us to a last—and most important—decision: to rhyme my hexameters in couplets. I fully realize that there is almost no rhyme in Latin verse, and that true scholars may well be appalled to see Virgil dressed in the robes of Yeats and Frost and Wilbur, but I also feel strongly that the *Aeneid* is a *poem*, and I wanted to find some way to make the readers of this work feel that they were in fact reading a true poem in English. Virgil's verse is musical and supple, with principles of sound and rhetorical figures in full play, from alliteration and consonance and assonance to chiasmus and adynaton and beyond. That I am no Dryden or Pope is too obvious even to mention, but I did want to stake a modest claim on the attention of my contemporaries, who will, as always with any poet, be my final judges.

For the Latin text of the *Aeneid*, I followed the Loeb Classical Library edition, which records in its footnotes numerous variants from the eight main manuscripts. What follows is a line-for-line translation of Virgil's text.

Len Krisak

Acknowledgments

I wish to especially thank Brian Rak for his constant support of this project; Christopher McDonough for his scholarship, hard work, and sound advice on many matters; Liz Wilson for her steady shepherding of the entire text through production; and Emily Williamson, without whose skill and energy this translation of the *Aeneid* would never have come into being.

I also wish to thank the editors of these publications, in which portions of this translation first appeared, sometimes in slightly different form:

I.1–33 appeared in *The Partisan*
II.1–56 appeared in *PN Review*
VIII.18–25 appeared in *Arion*
XI.490–497 appeared in *Arion*

Len Krisak

For their helpful thoughts on the notes, many thanks to my students Kathryn Hicks, Samuel Jones, Virgina McClatchey, Hannah True, Hpone Myint Tu, Jackson Yates, and Munford Yates.

Christopher McDonough

for Ruth

THE AENEID

Book I

My poem sings of one man forced from Troy by war.
Fate harried him to find a home on Latium's shore—[1]
On some Lavinian littoral. By land and sea,
Driven by loss, by gods who would not let him be,
By unrelenting Juno's[2] lack of any pity,   5
He made his gods a home at last, founding the city
Of ancient Alba, then the battlements of Rome.

Speak, Muse.[3] Speak out, and say where Juno's rage came from.
Tell me why great heaven's queen hounded this man
So marked by righteousness[4] through such hard labors. *Can*   10
Such savage indignation grip a deity?

There was an ancient city, far from Italy
And Tiber's mouth, called Carthage. Colonized by Tyre,
It was resourceful, rich, and storied in war's dire
Arts. They say that Juno loved it even more   15
Than Samos. Here was her armor (she set such store
By Carthage); here, her chariot. Even now, she aimed,
If fate allowed, to make this city feared and famed,
Ruling the world. But she had heard Troy's progeny
Would one day topple Punic towers. Supremacy   20
World-wide would come from this, a war-proud people winning
Libya's ruin (that's how the Parcae planned their spinning).

Anxious, and mindful of the war she once had waged
For her belovèd Argos, Juno—still enraged
By what began that war, and bitter in her soul   25
Still; nursing hate at just the thought of Paris' role

In judging her, and of her beauty meanly spurned,
And of that race, and stolen Ganymede's unearned
Honors—burned hotter still, and shook the storm-whipped main
For men the Greeks and cruel Achilles had not slain.   30
She kept them out of Latium for so long that they
Despaired the fates would ever let them find their way.
Such massive effort: that's what founding Rome entailed.

Now sanguine on the sea, the ships had scarcely sailed
From Sicily, their brazen bowsprits ploughing spume,   35
When Juno, nursing endless hate, began to fume:
"Am I to give in now? Give up my cherished plan,
Thwarted in turning back a Teucrian king—one man—
From Italy? No doubt the Fates say so! But *she*
Could burn the Argive fleet or drown it in the sea,   40
Could Pallas, just because one guilty man went mad—
Ajax. She pitched Jove's lightning from the rack, and bade
The whipped-up winds rip through the sails and shrouds to maim
That man who while his breast still billowed smoke and flame,
Found out a jagged rock that spiked him all his life.   45
But I, the queen of gods, Jove's sister and his wife,
Must all these many years wage war against one race.
Who then will worship Juno's godhead? Who will place
Their little sacrificial offerings on my altars?"

So Juno's furious fire flares and never falters.   50
Aeolia's where the goddess flew off next—there where
The storm clouds breed in caves. King Aeolus rules there,[5]
Deep-grottoed jailer, subjugating with his chains
The willful winds and howling storms and drenching rains.
Indignantly, they growl as one while mountains groan.   55
They rumble round their barricades. High up, alone,
The sceptered Aeolus commands them from his throne,
Tempering their rage. (He *has* to soothe them or they'd flay

The sea and land, and heaven would be swept away.)
Jove, Father Filled with Power—lest this should come to pass— 60
Penned them in pitch-black caves, and piled a mountainous mass
On top, and named their king, who by Jove's iron bull
Knew when to slack the reins, and when he had to pull.

Juno came begging now: "Lord Aeolus: Jove, who
Is King of Men and Father of the Gods, gave you 65
The power to use the winds to calm—and stir—the sea.
Sailing the Tyrrhene now, a race that maddens me
Carries its conquered Lares from Troy to Italy.
Whip up your winds till all those ships are drowned.
Sink them! Destroy them! Scatter corpses all around 70
The ocean. I have fourteen nymphs—all beautiful;
Heavenly bodied—and the loveliest of all
Is Deiopea. She is yours for marriage, yoked
Forever if you do this. Once you two are locked
In wedded love, you'll be the father of a breed 75
Of perfect children."

                    He replied, "You only need
To state your wish, great queen, and that is my command.
I owe all this to you: the scepter in my hand;
My kingdom; Jove's good will; a place at heaven's board.
As for the clouds and tempests, *you* made me their lord." 80

These were his words. Then with his spear he smashed the hollow
Mountain on its side. The winds like shock troops follow,
Burst through the breach, then blast across the world in gales,
Covering the churning sea, which, *de profundis*, flails.
Winds from the northwest, east, and south combine to force 85
The giant breakers juggernauting toward the shores.
Hard on, the shrouds and rigging shriek, as grown men cry.
Suddenly, thunderheads have palled the daylight sky

From Trojan sight. Black night lies brooding on the main,
As thunder rolls and lightning flashes out, again   90
And then again—sure signs of sudden death for all.

Aeneas buckles at the knees, prepared to fall.
Shivering, he cries out, with palms turned up to cup
The stars, "They're three and four times blessed who rendered up
Their lives as Trojan fathers watched them from some wall.   95
O Tydeus' son, greatest Danaan of them all,[6]
Why couldn't I have fallen on the Ilian plain
And gasped out life's last breath, your right hand having slain
Me, there where Hector lies (killed by Achilles' spear),
Sarpedon, too. The Simois saw disappear   100
So many brave men, bodies sucked down with their helms
And shields"—his words.

                    Just then the North Wind overwhelms
The ragged, flapping sails; it's smacking, raising waves
To heaven, snapping oars. Prows spin as the sea staves
In the sides. Ocean cliffs as broad as they are steep   105
Crash down. Some sailors briefly crest; some see the deep
Go gaping, opening to seething sands below.
The South Wind slams three ships on hidden crags; down go
The victims on the Altars (mid-sea rocks named by
The Latians; backbone in the sea, they loom mile-high).   110
The East Wind drives three more on reefs, each stove-in ship
Now smashing on the shoals, held in the sandbanks' grip—
A sickening sight.

                    Orontes and his Lycian craft,
Aeneas now sees sundered: one surge hits it aft,
Shaking the helmsman out headlong. Right there, that bark   115
Corkscrews three times, gulped by the maelstrom in the dark.
Storm-strewn, the swimmers ride the sucking whirlpool. Men

And planks and armor sink, and never seen again,
The Trojan treasure spends itself on wind and wave.
Ilioneus's sturdy ship, as well as brave   120
Achates', Abas's, and old Aletes', sinks
Before the storm, as all their planking's jointed links
Come loose. The torrents flood through gaping seam and flaw.

But all this pandemonium King Neptune saw—
The swells let slip; still waters ripped from Ocean's bed—[7]   125
As angrily he scanned the sea, raising his head
In majesty. He surfaced in one blue summation
To view Aeneas' fleet, the scattered desolation,
The heavens raining ruin, and the waves that beat
The Trojans down.

           So Juno's fury and deceit   130
Lay patent to her brother. Calling East and West
Winds to account, he speaks: "Could you be so impressed
By where you come from that you dare to flout my rule?
To fuse the sky and earth and make yourselves the tool
Of trouble? I *rule* you! But first I'll still the sea.   135
You'll pay stiff penance later, answering to me
For what you've done. Now fly back to your lord and say
My trident rules the waves; by Fate, he must obey.
Eurus, the caverns where you live—that's his domain,
So Aeolus may strut and play the suzerain   140
There only, in the windy jail that shuts you in."

So Neptune spoke, and then the swells die, and the din.
He sweeps the clouds away and ushers back the sun.
Cymothoë and Triton, shouldering as one,
Set loose the ships. The god himself now pries them free   145
With his trident and clears the sands and tamps the sea
Down. On the waves, on weightless wheels, he skims; he hums.

Sometimes, in noble nations, vile sedition comes,[8]
As raging crowds go raving mad, and stones and brands
Go flying (fury puts the weapons in their hands).   150
But if they notice someone they respect for years
Of honored service, then they pause, with pricked-up ears.
He masters them with words that calm their boiling passion.
Well, Neptune quelled the roaring swells in just that fashion.
Their Sire saw the sea, then drove beneath blue sky;   155
Wheeling his mares, he let his eager chariot fly.

Exhausted, the Aeneans sought the nearest land,
And found that they were headed straight for Libyan sand.
A quiet, island-isolated inlet lies—
A banked-in bay where Ocean's blue summation dies,   160
Thinning through ever-finer fingers. Here and there,
Twin peaks and walls of cliff, foreboding in the air,
Brandish their points. Below, the broad bay lay subdued.
And high above, there stood a backdrop's shimmering wood,
Beetling a brow where gloomy-shadowed copses clung,   165
While at the cliff base gaped a hollow cavern hung
With rocks. Fresh water rilled there. In the living stone:
Ledge-benches—for the nymphs. Here, ships were left alone,
Unfettered where they wrecked, no anchor biting down.

Aeneas, with just seven ships that didn't drown,   170
Limped in here. Disembarking, longing for the land,
The Trojans finally embrace its saving sand,
Their brine-soaked bodies prostrate. Good Achates, though,
Rose quick to strike a spark from flint. Then to and fro
He waved the stalks of tinder in the air until   175
They took, and kindled flame, and burned away the chill.
The spent crew lugged ashore the brine-soaked grain gone bad,
And using any cereal-sifting tools they had,
Prepared to parch, and crush by stone, the remnant grain.

Meanwhile, Aeneas climbs a peak and tries to gain   180
Perspective on the scene, in hopes that he might find
Antheus' Phrygian ships the storm has left behind,
Or Capys, or Caicus' armor, set stern-high.
He cannot see a single ship, but he can spy
Three stags that graze near shore, leading some deer that trail   185
Them in a tenuous column, straggling down the vale.
Arrested by the sight, he notches to his bow
Three shafts in turn (Achates bore these), then lays low
The leaders, with their noble racks that prong the light.
Aeneas' darts next put the common rout to flight   190
(They race through greenwood as his arrows start to bite).

This overpowering archery goes on until
His seven ships have one each of the massive kill.
On shore, Aeneas divvies up the giant forms—
And good Acestes' stone-cold jars of wine that warms   195
(His noble gift the Trojans later stored on leaving
Trinacria).

          Aeneas tries to soothe their grieving
Hearts with these words: "We few—till now, unhappy few—⁹
This band that's borne so much: the gods will end this, too.
You tempted Scylla at her limits and you tested   200
The howling fury of her boulders; you have bested
The Cyclops' stones. Recall that courage; rout your fears
And grief. It may be you will glory, one day years
From now, at how you came through such calamity,
Such suffering. Latium waits, where we will find our see,   205
Our peaceful fate. There, Troy will rise again. Endure!
Make ready for the better days ahead for sure."

Though overcome with care, Aeneas used such language,
Pretending hope, but stifling in his heart his anguish.

The remnant prepare for the feast the game provides,   210
Baring the guts when they have stripped the ribs of hides.
Some cut the flesh to bits, spitting what's barely dead,
While others fill and fire cauldrons. When they're fed,
The party get their strength back. In this benison,
They stretch out on the grass, all filled with venison   215
And wine, their hunger quelled. And as the feasting ends,
They clear the board and speak in hushed tones of the friends
They've lost.

        From fear to hope, they sway: Are some alive?
Or will they never come again? Could they survive?
But most of all, Aeneas grieves Orontes, shakes   220
For Amycus, brave Gyas, brave Cloanthus; takes
To heart the awful fate of Lycus. Then, a stop,
As Jupiter looks down from Mount Olympus' top
And spies the sail-winged sea, the shores, the land spread out,
The world-wide nations. Poised up on the sky's redoubt,   225
He fixed his gaze on Libya, while he thought about
The troubles of the Trojans.

        As he did, her glistening
Eyes brimful of tears, sad Venus spoke, Jove listening:
"You rule the cosmos with undying power: under
Your reign, all gods and kingdoms learn to fear your thunder.   230
What vile lèse-majesté has my Aeneas done?
What did these battered Trojans do who've undergone
Such suffering, kept from Italy by being barred
From every land? Some day to come—you gave your word—
They'll sire Romans, Teucer's line restored as ocean   235
Masters and land commanders by decree. What notion
Swayed you? Troy's ruin left one hope for me: its throes
Would balance with imperium, one fate oppose
The other. Now, just one disastrous fate pursues them—

These men so cursed by evil that almost subdues them.   240
Great King, when will their struggles end? Antenor got
Scot-free of the Achaeans, managing to plot
A safe course through the inlets of Illyria
And past Timavus, in Liburnia's interior
(Timavus' springs gush from nine mountain mouths, then roar   245
In spate, to flood the ploughlands on the valley floor).
And yet he founded Padua, where Teucer's race
Came home—a town where Trojan arms could find their place.
He rests now, settled in a placid peace, while we—
Promised the skies, and called your special progeny;   250
Stripped of our fleet (unspeakable is Juno's rage!)—
Fall short of Italy by leagues? *This* is the wage
Paid virtue? *This* the way you'd have Troy rise again?"

He smiled on her, the Father of the gods and men—
That look that calms a storm at sea—then with a kiss[10]   255
Upon her trembling lips, he told his daughter this:
"Dear Cytherea, have no fear; your children's fates
Are fixed. One day, you'll see the pledged Lavinian gates,
And set great-souled Aeneas in the sky that waits.
No 'notion' 'swayed' me, and in fact, because your soul   260
Is troubled, I'll unroll the future's secret scroll:
There'll come a day your son will fight a fierce campaign
In Italy, obliterating peoples vain
And fierce. He'll build walls for his children, write their law
Three Latian summers later (when three winters draw   265
Their cycles closed, and mark defeat of the Rutulians).
Ascanius then, he who now is called Iulus,
The boy once Ilus (while the Ilian state was standing)
Will sit in power and greatness thirty years, commanding
Through the reeling days. Then he will shift his throne   270
From its Lavinian capital, hewing the stone
For Alba Longa, which will stand three hundred years,

Peopled by Hector's race, till Ilia appears,
A priestess-queen who'll bear two boys to Mars. One twin,
Called Romulus, exulting in the she-wolf skin   275
His mother wears, will carry on this line and raise
The walls of Mars and call the Romans after his
Own name. I set no bound on them, no time to come,
But grant them endless rule. And their imperium
Will win at last my furious wife who plagues them, sea   280
And land and sky. She'll come to love them just like me,
On second, better thought—the togaed[11] Romans, ruling
The world. I pledge this. Then, one day, the lustrums rolling
By, Assaracus's house will master Phthia
And bright Mycenae. Vanquished Argos then will be a   285
Roman dominion, and a Caesar will arise
From Troy. He'll bound his glory by the star-gemmed skies,
His power by the sea—a Julius from the line
Of Iulus. At ease, you'll greet your heir divine
At last, and see his eastern spoils, and at his shrine   290
The world will pray. Then wars will cease, peace smooth the ages.
Old Faith and Vesta and Quirinus (Remus' rages
Calmed), will legislate. The dire Gates of War
Will shut their iron bars on Wrath within. No more
Will Furor sit on stacks of swords; hands chained   295
Behind (a hundred brazen knots), his mouth blood-stained,
He'll shriek insanely."

                Saying this, Jove sends the son
Of Maia from on high, so Carthage can be won,
To show the Trojans welcome, and lest Dido, kept
From fatal knowledge, close her ports. The broad air swept   300
By wings like oars, he races to the Libyan shore,
Alights, and carries out Jove's will. The Tyrians' war-
Like hearts relent. But most importantly, their queen
Warms to the thoughts of Trojans—thoughts that are serene.

Yet good Aeneas, worried by *his* thoughts all night,   305
Decides to rise the moment that he sees the light,
And scout these places—strands to which the winds have blown them.
What fauna haunt these unploughed lands? What people own them?
(He means to bring his friends reports.) First, he decides
To mask the ships with canopies of trees. He hides   310
The fleet below a cave that's arched by lambent shade.
And with Achates only, and a broad steel blade
On each spear cradled in his hand, Aeneas strode
Forth.

     Mid-way, in the darkwood path, his mother showed[12]
Herself—a virgin's weapons and a virgin's face   315
(Spartan, or like Harpalyce, the girl who'd race
Her Thracian mares or make swift Hebrus seem too slow).
For from her shoulder she had slung a ready bow
In huntress mode, and lent the scattering winds her hair.
Her fluent robes were knotted and one knee was bare.   320

Before Aeneas speaks, she hails him: "Young men, say
If you have seen my sister wandering this way,
A quiver round her, and a mottled lynx hide, or
Full-cry in hot pursuit to spear some foaming boar?"

Thus Venus. Then the son of Venus spoke this word: 325
"Your sisters, Lady, I have neither seen nor heard.
But how should I address you? Yours is not a human
Face, your voice not human. Goddess more than woman,
You must be Phoebus' sister. Are you of the line
Of nymphs? Whoever, lift our burden; be benign.   330
What coast have we been cast up on? Tell us what sky
We wander under, errant, ignorant; the high
Waves and the winds have blown us to this unknown land.
We'll feed your altar victims from a grateful hand."

Then Venus said, "I am not worthy of such honor;   335
All Tyrian virgins wear the quiver. Each binds on her
Calves the tall cothurnus, Punic-purple. We
Have built Agenor's city—Tyrians, you see.
But Libya bounds us—people warlike, free of pity.
Queen Dido rules, whose brother drove her from that city   340
Of Tyre, and it would take a maze-like tale of wrong
To tell it all. What matters most, though, won't take long.
Sychaeus married her. Phoenicia's richest lord,
He was a man poor Dido ardently adored.
Her father gave her chaste to this Sychaeus, two   345
United in love's rites. It was her brother who
Was king, the worst of Tyrian men: Pygmalion.
Then rancor came between them, and that wicked one,
Gold-blinded, killed Sychaeus, caught off-guard before
The altar. Wickedly, he stained his steel with gore,   350
No thought of Dido but to hide the deed and trick
That bride with empty hopes—to put off one half-sick
With love. But then her still-unburied husband came,
A pallid ghost who showed his face to her in dream.
He bared his stab wounds, told the tale that would unravel   355
All: the bloody altars' crime; the house's evil.
He urges her to hurried exile, and, to speed
The plan, tells where to find the wealth that she will need:
An ancient hoard of buried gold and silver. Stirred
To act, she readies friends for flight; they heed her word,   360
Assembling—those with ardent hatred of their prince,
Or acrid fear. They seize on ships supplied by chance,
And cargo them with all Pygmalion's gold. The riches
He grasps at sail away—a brilliant action which is
A woman's.[13] Here they landed, where the citadel   365
Of Carthage you see rising, and high walls as well.
This land was *bought* outright, so *Bursa* is its name

(The ground a bull's hide compassed, all that they could claim).
Now, who are you, and where have you come from? What shore?
Speak up, and say what country you are sailing for." 370

Questioned like this, he sighed, then found his voice down deep
Within: "O goddess, had you time, my tale would keep
You up till Heaven closed and Hesperus ended day—
Were I to trace our sorrows *ab origine*.
From Troy (if you have heard of Troy), the tempests tossed 375
Us over seas that landed us on Libya's coast.
Aeneas is my name—called *pius* from the love
The gods have shown me—and my fame they know above.
With salvaged gods, I sail to find my destiny:
A people come from Jove; a home in Italy. 380
With twenty ships I set out on the Phrygian sea—
My mother guiding—searching for what Fate had given.
Just seven ships remain, wave-battered, Eurus-driven.
Deserted, destitute, I tramp these deserts, spurned
By all Eurasia."

            Venus heard, but now concerned 385
Lest he go on, broke in and said, "No matter who
You are, I know the heavens haven't hated you.
You breathe life still, and here our Tyrian kingdom waits.
Aeneas, go straight on to Dido's palace gates,
For I have news: your people live. Your fleet's surviving 390
Remnant has found its haven, having braved the driving
Winds—unless my home-schooled augury's in vain.
You see that sky? Twelve swans have formed a daring skein[14]
Jove's eagle had been scattering (down from the ether
It had swooped in broad daylight). Their long 'V' either 395
Scouts for refuge now or scans some landing place.
Swinging back on extended wings, with hearts that race,

They chant, still circling the skies with sturdy grace.
In just that way, your ships and crew are safe; or near
The harbor mouth, their bellied canvas will appear   400
Soon. Go now. Let the road more traveled lead you on."

She spoke, and as she turned, her pink neck brightly shone,
Her head's ambrosial tresses breathing goddess-scent.
Down to her feet, the goddess' fluent raiment went.
She stood a true divinity; he knew her tread—   405
His mother's.

            Then his words pursued her as she fled:
"Cruel as well, you mock me. Why? Again, again,
With empty images, you lead me on in vain,
Hands never touching. It's true words I wish you'd speak!"

And so accusing her, he heads toward what he'd seek.   410
But Venus, as they move off, cloaks them in a shroud
Of dark mist, and—a goddess—pours thick, mantling cloud
Around them. No one now can see or touch them, no
One challenge them or slow them down. He sees her go
Skyward to Paphos, heading home in happy flight.   415
Her temple's hundred altars breathe out, in her rite,
Sabaean incense, rising; fragrant wreaths exhale.

Meanwhile, they hurry on to take the leading trail,
Ascending soon the hill that looms above the town,
Fronting the battlements on which its brow looks down.   420
Dazzled, Aeneas sees huge forms that once were huts;
Dazzling are gates, and din, and broad streets once mere ruts.
The ardent Tyrians, hard at work, now raise a wall,
Now build the city's citadel with stones they haul
By hand. Some choose a site and mark it off with ground   425
Lines; others make up laws, name magistrates, or found

Their sacred senate. Harbors get dredged out here; there,
The theatre's first course is laid, as masons tear
Great columns from the cliffs to grace the stage that's coming.

Like that, the early summer bees work on, while humming   430
In sunshine in the flowering meadows, as they lead
Their own kind, just matured, or pack their combs with mead-
Sweet nectar till the liquid nearly bursts its cells;
Or welcome burdened workers as their troop repels
The herd of lazy drones inside the hive. Work went   435
Like that, and thyme made fragrant honey redolent.[15]

"Blessèd are those who right now watch their cities rise!"
Aeneas cries, seeing where rooftops stab the skies.
He enters in a cloud—a miracle—with many
Crowded round him, but he moves unseen by any.   440

Mid-city stood a grove, luxuriously shaded,
Where the Phoenicians, blown by storms, first excavated
The sign that Juno showed: a fiery horse's head
(That's what that race became so famous for, and led
Ages to come to know them by: their wealth and war-   445
Like spirit). Here, Sidonian Dido laid the floor
Of Juno's giant temple—gift-rich, great with numen.
The beams were plated bronze; with brazen steps the limen
Rose, and bronze doors closed on groaning hinges. Here
There first appeared that wonder that allayed his fear,   450
And here Aeneas' hopes for safety first took shape,
Beginning in a surer trust in Troy's escape
From its misfortune.

                    There below that lofty shrine,
As he awaits the queen, he surveys every sign
Of craft, and marvels at the city's luck, and all[16]   455

Its work. He sees his war adorn the walls!—the fall
Of Ilium—battles famous everywhere. He sees
King Priam and the two Atrides (all of these,
Achilles fights against!).

                 He stopped, and sobbing, cried,
"Achates, what land *doesn't* know how we've been tried?   460
Here also, righteousness still wins respect (see Priam?).
Here too, men's griefs touch others with *lacrimae rerum*.[17]
No sorrow now; your wretched tale of grief well-known
May win our safety."

              Pondering then the bloodless stone,
He sighs too much; huge tears begin to wash his cheeks.   465
For here he saw the fight for Pergamum, with Greeks
In flight as Trojan youths pursue, or Phrygians racing
From that chariot, with plumed Achilles chasing.

Nearby, he sees (as he goes on to sigh and weep)
The snow-white tents of Rhesus (still in shallow sleep,   470
He died, Tydides' gore-stained victim—there were more).
That killer drove the fiery horses back before
One taste of Trojan grass, one sip from Xanthus' shore.

Elsewhere, Troilus has thrown his arms away in flight,
A star-crossed boy who picked Achilles for a fight.   475
His empty chariot's horses drag him as he sprawls
Back, clutching reins; on through the dust, his long hair trawls.
His spear, wrong end around, indites the Trojan ground.

Meanwhile, *their* tresses streaming, Ilian women bound
For hostile Pallas' temple run to offer up   480
Her *peplum*—suppliants come to beat their breasts. They cup

Their palms; she looks away who should be their protector.
Three times round Ilium's walls, Achilles drove with Hector
Inscribing dirt, then sold the lifeless trunk for gold.

Oh, then Aeneas summoned up a groan deep-souled,   485
Seeing those spoils, his comrade's corpse, the chariot, and
Defenseless, unarmed Priam reaching out his hand.
He saw himself, too, closing with Achaea's best;
Troops from the east; the armor on dark Memnon's breast.
Penthesilea rages; her Amazons wield,   490
One thousand warriors strong, a lunar-crescent shield.
That fierce virago battles men, her gold sword-hanger
Baldricked beneath her bare breast as she welcomes danger.

Amazed Aeneas stares in wonder; what is seen
By that Dardanian astounds. Meanwhile, the queen,   495
Beautiful Dido, who's attended by a throng
Of youths, progresses toward the shrine, the way along
Mount Cynthus' ridges, or beside Eurotas' banks,
Diana leads her choral dancers, in whose ranks
A thousand Oreads will gather, left and right.   500
She wears a shoulder quiver as she goes, her height
A regal goddess's. Joy swells Latona's pounding
Heart.

    So Dido walked, her happiness abounding.
The center of all work, she urged her kingdom come,
Then entered at the temple doors; beneath its dome,   505
Ringed by armed guards, she claimed her throne—the lofty place
From which she legislates, and rules the Punic race,
Assigning work in equal shares, by choice or chance.

It's just then that Aeneas sees a crowd advance:
Antheus and Sergestus; brave Cloanthus and   510

The black-storm-battered remnant of his Teucrian band—
Those driven overseas to these so-distant climes.

Aeneas stands amazed; his friend's amazement rhymes.
Achates quakes with fear and joy. Both burned to shake
Their comrades' hands, but these uncanny happenings make   515
Them pause. Remaining cloud-cloaked, both look on. What fate
Will greet the men, their fleet? Why have they come to wait
On Dido? Chosen men from each ship came to plead,
Seeking the temple (and her kindness) in their need.

Inside, and granted royal audience, the senior,   520
Ilioneus, spoke up with a courteous demeanor:
"O Queen whom Jove has tasked with founding Tyre again,
And curbing haughty tribes with justice: we are men
From Troy, made hapless by the winds on every sea.
We beg you: keep our fleet untouched by fire. We   525
Are goodly people; help us in our misery.
We have not come to Libya with sword in hand
To pillage, driving captured booty to your strand;
No vanquished people would. We nurse no thought of that.
There is a place Greeks call Hesperia—a fat   530
Land, known for fertile soil and war. An ancient folk,
Oenotrians, inhabit it, but Rumor spoke
Of some new tribe that calls it Italy, from one
Who leads them. Going on,
We met Orion's sudden gale, whose battering   535
Surges dashed us on the reefs. By scattering,
Austral winds, our ships were flailed, through waves and through
The mazing rocks. Yours are the shores we've drifted to.
What sort of men are these? What country, to encourage
Such barbarous ways (and keep us from your beach's anchorage)? 540
They will not let us land, your guards, with their alarms.
But if you scorn both human kinship and men's arms,

Then fear the gods at least, who weigh both wrong and right.
Aeneas was our king, and when it came to might
Of arms and piety, he could not be surpassed.   545
If he evades Fate still, and has not breathed his last
Of heaven's air, and cheats death's shade by his survival,
Then we are not afraid. Nor should *you* be, to rival
Others in kindness. Sicily has cities, too,
And fields, and famed Acestes, once of Troy. If you   550
Would only let us beach our gale-wind-pummeled fleet,
And work your woods to cut new mast, plank, oar, and cleat!
That way, if we recover king and friends, then we
Can make for Latium gladly—sail for Italy.
But if that hope is lost, and if the Libyan sea   555
Has drowned that best of Teucrians, and there's no chance
Iulus lives, we still can sail the sea's expanse
For Sicily, from which we came. There, home awaits
Us, and a king—Acestes—by Messina's straits."

As one, the Trojans hail the case he states.   560
Then Dido, looking down, speaks briefly: "Pay no heed
To what you fear or grieve for, Teucrians. Harsh need
And this our infant kingdom force me to these hard
Measures. We have long borders, too, that we must guard.
Who doesn't know Aeneas' race; who doesn't know   565
Of Troy; her brave men; what she's had to undergo
By war and fire? Our Punic hearts are not so slow,
Nor we so distant from that team whose reins Sol wields.
Choose great Hesperia, with its Saturnian fields,
Or Eryx, for Acestes' rule. No matter which is   570
Your choice, you'll sail with escorts, sped by Punic riches.
Or choose this place I build, and we'll live peer-to-peer.
Anchor your ships if you would rather settle here,
With Tyrian and Trojan given equal claim.
I wish your king, Aeneas, driven by that same   575

South Wind, were here. In fact, I'll send out men of worth
To scout the shores and scour the far-flung Libyan earth,
Lest he be wandering shipwrecked in the town or wood."

Both men long eager to escape their cloud for good,
Achates and Aeneas thrill to all that she has   580
Spoken. Achates breaks the silence with Aeneas
Pater: "O goddess-born, what plans and what ideas?
You see that all are safe, with fleet and friends restored
But one whom we saw drown when he fell overboard.
All this, with what your mother said, is in accord."   585

He'd barely spoken when that cloaking nimbus cleared;
It broke apart, sky-high-ward, till it disappeared.
And there Aeneas stood, resplendent in the light,
In face and form a god (his mother's touch: the bright
Eyes and a hero's hair; the ruddy glow a boy   590
Wears when he shines with all the luster of his joy;
Like hand-buffed ivory; how silver work will get—
Or Parian marble—when its carving has been set
In gold).

          Then, unforeseen by all, he hails the queen
With sudden words: "I stand here now, the one you mean   595
To seek: Aeneas—Trojan ripped from Libyan seas.
You pitied our unutterable miseries,
The only one to offer us your home; to share
Your city with what Greeks have left, worn out with care
On land and sea, burdened with every lack. To pay   600
You back, Queen Dido, is beyond us. There's no way
That Dardans, scattered through the world, could give such thanks.
But if respect remains in the celestial ranks
For what is good, and if there's justice anywhere,
May gods who know what's right honor you with their fair   605

Rewards. What happy age, what parents, bore you? While shadows
Drape the slopes, and streams run seaward, and the meadows
Of the sky still feed the stars, your honor, name,
And praises will live on, whatever land lays claim
To me."

      His speech was done, and so Aeneas shook   610
His cherished friend Ilioneus's hand, then took
Serestus by the left, then all the others: good
Cloanthus and brave Gyas.

               Sidon's Dido stood
Stunned, first by him, then by his woes. She asked, "What fate
Has chased you, goddess-born, through jeopardy so great?   615
What violence has steered your fleet here to our shore?
Are you that same Aeneas gracious Venus bore
By Phrygian Simois to Anchises of Troy?
I remember well: at Sidon, as an envoy,
An exile driven from his home, he sought our realm   620
With Belus' help, when Belus sought to overwhelm
Rich Cyprus with an iron grip—my conquering sire.
And ever since, I've known of Troy—its trial by fire—
And of your name, and of Pelasgian kings. Your own
Enemy praised you Teucrians much, and wished it known   625
That he descended from your ancient stock. So come
Ahead, young men, and walk the hallways of our home.
A fate like yours drove me through many hardships, too,
Ordaining that I come to rest and start anew
Here. Not immune to woe, I learn to ease the toil   630
Of others."[18]

      Done, she leads Aeneas to the royal
Halls, where she announces temple sacrifices.
And careful not to leave his friends to their devices

Back at the beach, she sends them twenty bulls; a hundred
Mammoth feral boars; a hundred lambs un-sundered   635
From their ewes—rich banquet fare.

Inside the palace, luxury is everywhere,
As regal splendor lights the tables men prepare.
Tapestries boast in artful purple; silver plate
Covers the boards; the exploits of the ancient great—   640
Dido's forebears, gold-graven in a long line—trace
From far back, countless deeds of her heroic race.

Aeneas (for a father's love could not ignore
His son and friends) soon sends Achates to the shore
(Aeneas loves this boy he could not cherish more),   645
To bring Ascanius back when he's been told of Carthage,
And to fetch as gifts things snatched from Ilium's wreckage:
A mantle stiff with golden forms; a veil whose selvage—
Yellow acanthus—once dressed Helen (she had salvaged
It from Mycenae, fleeing Argos for that "marriage"   650
She sought in Pergamus)—rich marvels she had kept, her
Mother Leda's treasures; and there was a scepter
That Ilione, Priam's oldest daughter, bore
Once, and a priceless necklace strung with pearls she wore
To grace her coronet studded with gems and gold.   655
Achates raced back to the ships, as he'd been told.

But Cytherea[19] has new plans, new tricks, new schemes:
How Cupid, soon transformed to what he only seems,
Might come as sweet Ascanius, with a flaming arrow,
Maddening the queen and firing her very marrow.   660

In fact, she fears both Dido and her Tyrian lies.
At night, it's Juno's anger propping Venus' eyes

Wide open, red with care; she tells her wingèd boy,
"My son, without you, I've no power to employ.[20]
My son, undaunted by great Jove's Typhoean darts,   665
I turn to you to beg you; use your godly arts.
You know Aeneas has been battered, shore and sea,
Your brother cursed by Juno's fierce hostility.
And many times, our grief has been your grief. Right now,
Phoenician Dido holds him back with soft words. How   670
I fear Junonian 'hospitality'—dread thing
To come. She will not wait at such a fateful hinge,
So I intend to charm and cheat her, and to ring
The queen with fires of love; no goddess then can change
Her, but—all mine, held fast—she'll crave Aeneas' love.   675
Consider this, and in your time: how you can move
My scheme to work. Aeneas' son, my one great care,
Prepares to heed his father's call for gifts he'll bear
To the Sidonian town, gifts saved from sea and Trojan
Fire. I'll lull the boy-prince with a sleeping potion   680
And hide him high on Cythera, to keep him from
Perceiving my intrigue—or in Idalium,
My shrine. For this one night, a boy yourself, put on
That boy's familiar face. The countenance you don
Will by your feigning fool the helpless Dido, happy   685
And lost in the rich food and drink. Then, on her lap, be
Sure, when you are wrapped in hugs and sugared kisses,
That you inspire secret fire, and—absent hisses—
Pretty poison."

          Love hears, and so obeys. He strips
His wings, and gleefully, Iulus' double, skips   690
Along. But Venus pours the dew of soft repose
Over Ascanius's tired limbs, then hugs him close,
Bearing him to Idalium's lofty groves, where he

Lies drugged in marjoram and shade so flowery
It breathes.

       Meanwhile, obedient to her words, and taking   695
Achates' hand, the happy Cupid soon is making
His way with royal gifts on toward the Tyrian town,
Arriving where the queen, in state, is lying down
(Rich tapestries; a golden couch). Aeneas here,
Young Trojans there, recline on purple. Men appear,   700
Pouring from ewers over hands. They serve out breads
From baskets, bringing towels napped with close-cut threads.
And fifty fetching maids within are tasked with serving
A plentiful array and lighting fires, observing
Hearth rites.

       Tables groan with bounteous food, as yet   705
A hundred more—girls matched with boys the same age—set
The cups. And happy Tyrians, too are there; they throng
The chambers, summoned by their queen, and sprawl along
Embroidered couches, wondering at the gifts brought by
Aeneas, marveling at Iulus' looks and sly,   710
False words, the robe, the veil in saffron, yellow-stitched
Acanthus.

       Even more, the doomed and love-bewitched
Phoenician cannot sate her soul, but as she gazes,
Thrills to boy and gift alike. Her dry heart blazes.

When Cupid's done with hanging on Aeneas' neck,   715
Hugging that loving father (though it's all a trick),
He finds the queen, who with her eyes—and all her soul—
Now fondly dotes on him whose "love" will take its toll
On Dido so deceived (a great god hugs her). He,
Obeying Venus, works on Dido's memory   720
Of her Sychaeus. Bit by bit, sly Cupid tries

To substitute a living love, and thus surprise
A heart long fallow, long unused to love, now numb.

A lull to clear the board, then brimming wine-cups come;
Commotion fills the halls through which loud voices boom,   725
While ceiling cressets hang from each gold-coffered room
And torches conquer night. The gold libation cup
The queen commands is thick with gems. Wine fills it up,
An heirloom handed down to Belus for his chalice.
Then silence settles down throughout the noisy palace.   730

"Jupiter, you have decreed the rites, they say,
For host and guest. Then let this be a happy day
For Tyrians and for these exiles come from Troy.
May children keep this day. Let Bacchus Who Brings Joy
Be here, and Juno. Tyrians, grace this collocation."   735

Her toasting done, she poured out wine as a libation,
And was the first to raise the cup to wet her lips,
Then challenged Bitias, who scorned to drink in sips
(He drained the brimming, foaming gold; the cup was bare).

The others drank, too. Then the bard who wore long hair,   740
Iopas (Atlas-taught), begins: the great hall rings;[21]
His golden lyre hymns first errant moon, then sings
The sun's work; where mankind came from, where beasts, and where
The rain and fire, Arcturus, and the Little Bear
And Great Bear twins; the showery Hyades; why winter   745
Suns run fast to die in Ocean; what stars hinder
The tardy nights.

       The Tyrians clap; the Trojans, too.
Yes, Dido—who was doomed—with sparkling discourse, drew
The night out, drinking deep of love, and begging so
To hear of Priam, and of brave Hector, laid low;   750

To hear of Dawn's son and his armor, and the fillies
That Diomedes drove; to hear of great Achilles.

"My guest, start from the start, speaking of Greek deceit,"
She said—"of Greek betrayal and of Troy's defeat.
And tell us, now the seventh summer is at hand,   755
Of all your desperate wanderings over sea and land."

BOOK II

A SILENCE FELL AS THEY INTENTLY WATCHED THAT MAN,
Father Aeneas.[1] From his high couch, he began:
"You ask me, Queen, once more to dredge up grief beyond
All telling: Troy destroyed, dead in its black despond;
Danaans with its stolen wealth; cruel things I saw   5
And played my part in. Name a man these wouldn't draw
A tear from—Myrmidon, Dolopian,[2] or fierce
Ulyssian. Already, dewy night careers
Down from the sky, and setting stars cajole our sleep.
But if your need to hear our ruin runs so deep—   10
A brief redaction of that crushing final wrack—
Then though the mind recoils to call such sorrow back,
I will begin.

        Fractured by war and blocked by Fate,
The Greeks are watching years melt at a glacial rate.
They build a horse with Pallas' help—a giant thing   15
Cross-ribbed with firs—as if it were an offering
For safe return. (Or so the rumor flies around.)
But secretly, their choicest fighting men are bound
Up deep inside the horse's dark, capacious womb,
Its bowels crammed with soldiers waiting in the gloom.   20

The isle of Tenedos[3] lies just in sight, well-known
And rich when Priam's kingdom still stood on its own,
Now just a bay unsafe for anchoring any ship.
The Greeks hide on its forlorn beach's rock-strewn strip.
We thought Mycenae was their course before the wind—   25

That Teucria was free, our troubles left behind.
The gates swing open wide. We go to view the Doric
Camp and the abandoned shore. We are euphoric.
Here, Dolopian troops were stationed, here the brutal
Achilles, here their fleet. Here we grew used to futile   30
Combat. As for Minerva's lethal gift, some gape,
While others stare at the colossal horse's shape.
Thymoetes first cries, 'Drag it to the citadel!'
(Fell treason or Troy's certain fate? No man could tell.)
But Capys and the prudent, wiser heads exhorted   35
Us: 'Heave it headlong in the sea, these Greeks' purported
Gift. Or torch it on a pile of kindling. Lance
It! Probe that hollow gut.' But given half a chance,
The indecisive people splinter in their stance.

Then, followed by a giant mob, and fierce as hell,   40
Laocoön comes racing from the citadel,
And still far off, cries, 'Citizens, you've lost your mind!
You think they've *sailed*? Could any gift they've left behind
Not be a trick by Greeks? Is *this* Ulysses' fame?
Either Achaeans lurk inside its wooden frame,   45
Or else this horse was built to be an engine at
Our walls, for spying, or to crush our houses flat.
Some ambush lies inside it. Trojans, smell this rat!
Whatever gift Danaans bring, I doubly fear.'4

His admonition done, he launched a massive spear   50
Into that timbered horse's hollow, bentwood womb.
It stuck there, quivering, and echoing our doom;
The vaulted cavern shook, resounding with a groan.
Had gods not spoken—if our minds had been our own—
We would have heard, and fouled with swords that Argive lair.   55
Troy would be standing still—and Priam's keep still there.

Meanwhile, imagine: Dardan shepherds full of noise
Were dragging to the king a stranger, with that boy's
Hands tied behind. He'd *meant* his capture. Just a boy,
He'd *meant* to do this very thing, and open Troy   60
To the Achaeans. Confident, prepared to meet
With certain death, he hoped to win by sheer deceit.

From all sides, eager Trojan youths rushed in to see,
Streaming around and vying in their mockery.
Listen—and learn from *one*, the faithless treachery   65
Of *all* Danaans.
For as he stood unarmed within the gawking crowd
And scanned the Phrygians nervously, he cried aloud,
'Oh, now what land or sea would take me in? What waits
For all my misery at last? The Dardan hates   70
Me, while the Greek abandons me, and even worse,
Would scourge me—or destroy me with his bloody curse.'

At such a wail, our feelings changed, and we grew calm.
We begged him to explain his race, where he was from,
What news he brought, and why he thought that we should trust 75
A captive. Feeling safe, he spoke. This was the thrust
Of what he said: 'Indeed, great king, I will not lie
No matter what. My Argive birth I won't deny.
That's first. Dire Fortune may have shaped Sinon⁵ for woe;
Her cold caprice won't make him false and lying, though.   80
You may have heard of Palamedes, Belus' son?
Maybe the glory of his fame, as rumors run,
Has reached you? The Pelasgians, by perjury
And wicked witness, sent him down to death, for he
Opposed their war. They *mourn* that innocent who's slipped 85
The world of light! That Palamedes might accept
Me (we were kin), my father sent me young to learn

To fight. And while that kingship stood secure, in turn
We thrived: kings asked his counsel, and we had a name.

But when Ulysses' malice (he of bitter fame)   90
Had driven Palamedes from the shores of life,
I dragged my shattered soul along in pitch-black grief,
Enraged at how my friend had died in innocence.
Mad as I was, I spoke up. If by any chance
I came home conqueror to Argos, that dear land,   95
I swore I'd come back threatening vengeance by my hand—
And war.

      That day then marked my destiny's first taint
Of evil. From that day, Ulysses worked to plant
Black rumors, scaring me with charges to incite
The mob, and guilty—as he knew—dared me to fight.   100
In fact, he worked with Calchas till . . . but why do I
Unwind unwelcome tales? Why stall? If "all Greeks lie"
Is all you need to hear, then right here, let me die;
The Ithacan would love that, and the Atridae
Would buy it dear.'

        Well, *then* we burned to learn his whys   105
And wherefores, vulnerable to Pelasgian lies
And evil. Trembling, Sinon spun, his heart a whore:
'So often the Danaans, worn down raw by war,
Had longed to sail away, spurning the Trojan shore.
Oh, if they had! Each time, harsh winter gales would thwart   110
Them. Auster threatening wrack, their ships remained in port.
Especially while that maple-timbered horse stood there,
The rumbling thunderheads resounded through the air.
Perplexed, we send Eurypylus to Phoebus' priest,
Who brings these dismal words back from that shrine: "You
     pleased   115

The black squalls once with virgin blood, Danaans, when
You came to Ilium's coast, and you'll need blood again
To get back home. An Argive life must satisfy
The winds." The crowds were thunderstruck, and, wondering why,
Could feel their very marrow chill. Which man was Fate   120
Preparing, which Apollo? Here, that reprobate
From Ithaca produces vatic Calchas—great
Acclaim—and in their midst, demands to learn Apollo's
Will. What *is* it? Many seem to know what follows:
Scheming Ulysses' bloody crime. Mouths shut, they read   125
The signs, as Calchas sulks ten days, and will not heed
Their call to say who dies. But then (as they've agreed),
Ulysses bellows, and at last the seer contrives
(Barely) to speak my name.

                Men whet the altar knives,
And all agree. What they have feared is borne with grace—   130
As long as someone else's death supplies their place.
And then the day was come, the rites all ready now,
The salt meal, and the holy ribbons round my brow.
I snatched myself from death, and yes, escaped unchained,
Lurking all night in muddy fields that hadn't drained,   135
And hidden in the sedges till they'd sail. (If only!)
I'll never see my homeland. Hopeless now . . . and lonely.
My loving children and my sire, I'll never see;
The Greeks may even torture them because of me,
To expiate, by death, this so-called crime of mine.   140
Poor souls! But I beseech you by the powers divine;
By deities who know the truth; by what remains
Of honest trust in men; by faith still free of stains:
Pity such burdens. Pity undeservèd grief.'

For just such tears, we pitied him and spared his life.   145
Priam himself first orders they untie those binding

Rope cuffs. 'As to who you are,' declared that kind king,
'Forget them now, those Greeks whom you have "lost." You'll be
A part of us. But speak the truth: explain to me
The purpose of this massive, timbered horse. Who built   150
It? Why? Is it an offering to atone for guilt?
Some war machine?'

                         He stopped, and Sinon, schooled in plots
And in Pelasgian guile, his raised hands freed from knots,
Addressed the stars: 'Oh, witness, endless fires. Numinous
Inviolable ones; O swords and holy, ominous   155
Altars I fled: be witnesses, with sacred bands
I wore as victim: I was right to break those bonds
And hate the Greeks; right, too, to bring their perfidy
To light. If they are hiding evil, loyalty
To law and home won't hold me. Troy, stand by your vow,   160
The promises you made, and, you yourselves safe now,
Keep faith if I prove right and bring you great rewards.
Danaans counted on what Pallas' help affords:
All chances of their winning, and trust in their beginning.
For ever since the foul Tydides and that sinning   165
Fiend Ulysses dared to rob her holy fane
Of the Palladium,[6] leaving its guardians slain,
And snatched that holy image with their bloody hands,
And fouled the virgin goddess' sacred victim-bands,
The hopes of the Danaans started to recede.   170
Their strength lay shattered, and Minerva paid no heed
(Tritonia's auguries and omens left no doubt).

The image barely placed in camp, flash-flames shot out
From upraised eyes on fire, as salt sweat sluiced its members.
And then—*mirabile dictu*!—like billowing embers,   175
Pallas herself appeared, with shuddering spear and shield.
Quick-thinking Calchas chanted flight—to leave the field,

Sail off. No Argive arms will rake up Dardan walls
Till Argive signs are found and Argos re-installs
The goddess they have cargoed in their curve-prowed ships.   180
And though they run before a wind their fleet outstrips
To reach Mycenae, find new troops and deities,
They'll land here suddenly when they've re-crossed those seas—
So Calchas says. They hope this offering will atone
For the Palladium's theft, foul sacrilege they've done—   185
Lèse-majesté. Still, Calchas said we should devise
This mass of woven wood, building it to the skies
(Too big for Ilium's gates, or dragging it inside,
It couldn't guard your people through their ancient creed).
For if your hands should violate Minerva's gift,   190
Then—may the gods turn on him first!—destruction swift
And sure as omened falls on Priam's realm and on
The Phrygians. But, if by brute force it could be drawn
Through Troy, then Asia might advance as far in war
As Pelops' walls. Our children's fate: to suffer for   195
Our crimes.'

       So artful, perjured Sinon filled our ears,
And lying guile won our belief with actor's tears.
Achilles of Larissa; Tydeus' son; ten years;
A thousand ships: all failed! Yet now we were laid low.

Here, one more portent—worse by far, filled with more woe   200
And wretchedness—bewildered minds that had been lulled.
Laocoön, Poseidon's priest that chance had culled—
Was slaughtering a bull at the appointed altars,
When look!—from Tenedos, across the tranquil waters
(I chill to tell it), huge-coiled twin snakes crest the sea,   205
Heading for shore in tandem, threatening equally.
Their trailing tails drive through the waves, as blood-red crests
Surmount a sea that yields before their surging breasts.

Sea-serpentine and huge, backs arch in monstrous sines,
While foaming waters hiss. And now they're at the plains,   210
With blazing, blood-tide eyes aflame. Our courage failed
As hissing maws were licked with rattling tongues: we paled,
Then ran, all scattering. They kept their dead-sure course,
Making straight for Laocoön.[7] Both lashed the torsos
Of his little sons, then fanged their helpless flesh.   215
They choked Laocoön as well, bound in their mesh
As he came racing with his spears to save the boys;
They snatched him in a stranglehold of giant coils
Wound twice around his waist, and twice around his throat.
Their scaled backs tower there, with arching necks that float   220
Above him. All this while, torn hands claw at the knots,
His headbands drenched in blackened gore and poisoned clots,
As horrid cries rise to the stars—the bellowing
A wounded bull makes as it gallops, trying to fling
The axe some priest has buried (badly) in its withers.   225

Gliding away, though, that draconian tandem slithers
Shrineward, twins seeking fierce Tritonia's stronghold, there
To rest beneath her feet and shield, the goddess' care.
Then panic ran for real; fresh terror shook our souls.
The mob's 'Laocoön deserved this fate!' now rolls   230
From man to man. 'His lance defiled the sacred oak;
His spear profaned what's holy'—so the people spoke,
And begged to drag the horse to Pallas' seat. 'Invoke
The goddess' numen!'

We broke the city open then, laid ramparts bare,   235
Preparing for the work. Hooves rolled beneath that mare
On wheels, and hemp reins roped her neck. Machine of doom,
She climbed the city streets with weapons in her womb.
Our joyous boys and nubile girls chant in a ring

Around it—dancing to the holy hymns they sing.   240
They laugh and test its ropes; it glides and climbs . . . to bring
The city down.

                    O Ilium! Our gods! Our home!
Four times before the gates of war-famed Dardanum,
It stalled. Four times its armory-belly clanged and clashed,
And yet we pressed on, mad, blind, frenzied to establish   245
That dire monster on the city's sacred heights.
Cassandra dooms us with the words that she recites
Then, but we Teucrians scoff (because the gods dictate).
This day will be our people's last allowed by Fate,
As city-wide, boughs green the shrines we decorate.   250

And all this while, the world runs round, till Night comes racing
From Ocean—palling earth and sky with black embracing—
And cloaks false Myrmidons. The Teucrians lie asleep
In Troy, all hushed, the *sopor* in their limbs bone-deep.
And now the Argive troops sail in from Tenedos,   255
Under the tacit moon whose silence is their friend.
Heading for well-known shores, the lead ship lit the sign—
A signal flare—and Sinon, shielded by malign
Decrees from heaven, freed the Argives from the pine
That shut them in. The horse now open, grateful Greeks   260
Can breathe again. From fatal wood, Sthenelus sneaks.
Captain Thessandrus, too, and dread Odysseus.

With all of these comes slithering Neoptolemus,
As Acamus and Thoas and Machaon follow,
With Menelaus and with Epeus, the hollow   265
Horse's maker. They take a city soaked in sleep
And wine, killing the men who fail to guard the keep.
Gates gaping wide, fast-forming squads come storming in.

It was that hour when weary mortals first begin
To rest; when sleep, the grace of gods, seeps through
    each limb.   270
That night, I dreamt that I saw Hector: look! It's him—[8]
So pitiful a sight—sobbing a spate of tears.
Grit-black, gore-clotted, chariot-torn, his ghost appears,
With rawhide thongs laced through his swollen feet. Oh, how
Could one who'd worn Achilles' arms look like this now!   275
A Hector back from battle in those spoils he strips,
Or hurling Phrygian fires on Danaan ships?
A Hector now with blood-soaked beard and clotted hair,
He shows the livid wounds that he's been forced to bear,
All won outside the walls of Troy.

                          I dreamt I wept,   280
And called him with pathetic speech: 'Our Light, who kept
Troy and the Teucrians in certain hope, the wait
For you was endless. Name the shores that made you late,
O Hector whom we longed for. All your kin cut down,
And all the sorrows of the people and this town!   285
Yet we, the weary, see you now. What base man scarred
Your perfect face? I see your body cruelly marred!'

Heedless of hopeless pleas, he offers no reply,
But dredges from his deepest heart the gravest sigh,
Crying, 'O Goddess-born, sail now! Escape these fires.   290
The enemy has Troy; Troy topples with its spires.
You've done enough for king and home. If strength alone
Could save it, Troy would stand yet, rescued by my own
Right hand. Her gods are in your trust; they'll share your fate.
She hands you her Penates.[9] Take them; find that great   295
City you'll found when you have sailed too many years.'

Then Hector stops, and from the inner shrine he bears
Great Vesta and the fillets and the timeless flame.

Meanwhile, Troy howls with grief—grief everywhere the same.
And more and more—although the leaf-scrimmed house
   my father   300
Anchises built lay distant from Troy's center—farther
Off, the din grew clearer at the fight's advance.
To gain a vantage point, I shake my sleepy trance,
Racing up stair steps, there to stand and strain to hear.
(The way, when south winds whip the grain, as fires sear;   305
Or rushing torrents from a mountain spate lay low
The fields, the lucky crop, and rows the oxened plough
Has dug, dragging the timber headlong down the river,
A shepherd stands on some high rock, and with a shiver
Hears the roar.)

              Then all Danaan guile was clear.   310
Here, Vulcan burned Deïphobus's house, and there,
Ucalegon's, his neighbor's; fires spread their fear.
The wide Sigean straits reflect the flames as cries
Of men and clangor of the clarions arise.

Half-crazed, I seize my sword, though swords are pointless. Still, 315
I burn to form a squad to rush our stronghold's hill
And take it. Rage and fury drive me on; I sense
The glory of a warrior's death in Troy's defense.
But look! There's Panthus, fleeing from Achaean swords—
Panthus, Apollo's priest, chased from the summit towards   320
Us. Othrys' son, he bears the holy things, the vanquished
Gods, in his hands, and drags his grandson. Frantic, anguished,
He's there. 'Panthus, where should we fight? At what redoubt?'

I'd barely spoken when Apollo's priest let out
A groan: 'Troy's utmost day is come—the final hour   325
Of Dardanum. Troy dies—and all of Ilium's power.
A raging Jupiter has spirited away
Our world—to Greece. Troy burns. Danaans now hold sway.

That high horse gushes soldiers in the city's heart
As Sinon thrills to what his random torches start.   330
There are as many thousands at the open gates
As sailed from great Mycenae. In the cobbled streets
Of Troy, confronting weapons bar the way, in wait
To kill; their cutting edges mass and coruscate.
The outer-gate guards barely offer to resist;   335
Blind battle is in vain.'

                    But since the gods insist,
And by the words of Othrys' son, I'm swept ahead
Toward flame and bloodshed, where the fighting calls, and dread
Erinys beckons, and the cries of death mount. Soon,
I'm joined by fighting friends beneath a blood-dimmed moon: 340
Ripheus, and Epytus, one of the best, bar none;
Hypanis and staunch Dymas and Coroebus,[10] son
Of Mygdon. (As it was, he'd come to Troy on fire
With a passion for Cassandra—crazed desire.
Like Priam's son, he'd come to fight beside the Phrygians,   345
But sadly failed to heed the god-inspired predictions
Of his bride.)

Seeing their close-packed ranks so keen to fight, I sense
My cue, and cry, 'Young men so brave in Troy's defense:
Our cause is lost. So if you mean to die with me   350
In one last fight, ours is a fate you must foresee,
The gods who propped our altars and our shrines have fled.
You fight to save a burning Troy. Though we'll be dead,
Let's plunge into this mass of swords. We've lost the war.
The vanquished have one hope—to hope for help no more.'   355

Their hearts were spurred to fury. From that moment on,
Like beasts in black mist—maddened, ravening wolfpacks gone
Berserkly blind, whose stomachs are their law, as cubs

Wait, famish-jawed—we cut through spears and swords and clubs
And men, in sure and certain hope of death. We fight 360
Deep in, beneath the cover of the vulturing night.

The carnage that befell us—who could tell it right,
Or say what Havoc wrought, or equal with his tears
Our miseries? Ancient Troy, so proud so many years,
Topples. Dead bodies clog the sacred temple doors 365
Of gods, and litter streets and houses by the scores.
But Teucrians aren't the only ones whose blood is shed;
Where valor flares in victims' hearts, proud Greeks lie dead
Who'd thought to vaunt like victors. Grief is everywhere,
With images of death; with panic in the air. 370

What next? Androgeos, backed by Danaans, shows
Up, ignorant of who we are—his mortal foes.
He thinks us Greek allies, but hasn't got a clue;
'Come on! What's stopping you?' he cries . . . without our cue.
'Why wait so long while others plunder, burn, and sack 375
This Pergamus? Debarked just now? Come on! Attack!'

He spoke, but knew at once; no satisfactory
Response had come. He saw we were the enemy.
Smack in our midst and stunned, he stopped short, caught off guard,
Like someone treading thorny ground, who marching hard, 380
Steps on a snake and suddenly recoils in fear.
Enraged, its neck blood-purpled, it will swell and rear.
That's how Androgeos jumped back at what he'd seen.

Bristling with swords, we charge around, through, and between
Them, killing men disoriented; men now seized 385
By fear. At this first effort, Fortune seems well-pleased.
It's here Coroebus, flush with courage and success,
Cries, 'Follow Fortune and the path she deigns to bless;

The way to safety that she first points out, let's take!
Trade shields with these Danaans; marked like them, be fake   390
Greeks. Bravery or cunning: When it's war, who asks?
Our enemies will arm us.'

                        So he speaks, then casques
His head (Androgeos' plumed helmet), grabs the shield
So finely marked, and hefts the sword: he's Argive-steeled,
Like Ripheus, and like Dymas, too, as all the men   395
Exult, and arm themselves with spoils just captured. Then
We race ahead, mixed in with Greeks, and in the sight
Of strange Greek gods.

                     All through the night, blindly we fight
In close-in combat. Numberless Danaans drop
To Orcus. Some Greeks break; seeking their ships, they stop   400
Fighting, and race for shore-bound safety. Some succumb
To cowardice, and climb back in that horse's womb
They know so well. When gods say no, trust in despair:
Picture Cassandra dragged off by her flowing hair—
Priam's daughter stolen from Minerva's fane.   405
She lifts her blazing eyes to heaven, but in vain.
(Her *eyes*: she cannot raise the wrists that ropes restrain.)

Coroebus could not bear the sight, and half-insane,
He panthered on the enemy, resolved to die.
Our whole band follows, brandishing our swords held high.   410
But from the temple roof, the Trojan missiles fly—
Our fellow soldiers'!—in an awful, killing hail
(Greek armor and Greek crests are now of no avail!).
Cassandra's rescue makes enraged Danaans roar;
From everywhere they batten on us: Ajax, more   415
Than fierce; and Atreus' sons; the whole Dolopian swarm.
(They're like the clash of fighting winds, a plosive storm

Of crashing West Wind, South, and East, so glibly proud
Of all his dawn-drawn horses.) Forests groan out loud,
While spuming Nereus' trident stirs the deepest waters. 420

And then—the ones we'd waylaid into shadowed slaughters
All dark night long, and harried through the city are
The first to note our shields and bogus arms,[11] how far
We are from them in speech. Their numbers are too high,
As suddenly, Coroebus is the first to die 425
(Peneleus kills him at the warlike goddess' altar).
Then Ripheus, most just, and never known to falter
Of all the Teucrians; he loved what's right and true
(The gods, though . . .). Hypanis and Dymas die, run through
By Trojan spears. Panthus, what piety might do 430
Could not stop death; Apollo's fillet failed you, too.

My family's funeral flames and Ilium's ashes: here
I swear that as you died, I shunned no Argive spear
Nor any counter-stroke. For if the fates had willed,
My sword hand would have guaranteed that I'd be killed. 435
We're swept from there, with Iphitus and Pelias, grave
And slowed by age, one by a wound Ulysses gave.
Then clamor summons us to Priam's palace. There,
A massive battle rages on as if there were
No other fighting, no one dying anywhere 440
In Troy. We see wild Mars, Danaans fighting toward
The roofs, and doors attacked by a testudo horde
Of shields. The scaling ladders grapple walls, while right
Beneath the beams, men inch their way up. Right hands bite
The walls' stone edges; left hands hold up shields for cover. 445

The Dardans counter, turning topless towers over,
Ripping up tiles for missiles (for they see the end
Is near). Though at the point of death, they now defend

Themselves, rolling down ancient gilded beams—their splendid
Heritage—while others mass below to block   450
The doors with brandished swords and meet the battle shock
To come. We rally then, to save both house and king,
And stir discouraged comrades with the help we bring.

In back of Priam's palace stood a secret door,
Its passageway connecting all the halls. Here, poor   455
Andromache would come, while there was still a Troy,
And visit—unescorted, with her little boy
Astyanax—grandfather and in-laws. I gain
The rooftop heights from which the hapless Teucrians rain
Down futile missiles with their hands. At roof's-edge stood   460
A tower leading to the stars. All Ilium could
Be seen from it—along with the Achaean tents
And the Danaan fleet. With iron implements,
We gouged the higher courses where the mortar crumbled,
And pushed it from its lofty site.

                                        The tower tumbled   465
Suddenly, with ruin trailing in its wake;
It roars, then smashes the Danaan ranks, which break.
But still more troops come on, though all the while, no stone
Or weapon isn't thrown.
Right at the very threshold, brazen Pyrrhus[12] vaunts;   470
He gleams and glories, blazing in his brilliant bronze—
An adder fed on toxic fodder. (In spring light,
He's puffed up, now no longer buried out of sight
By freezing winter. Skin sloughed, how he gleams, so young!
Proud-breasted snake, he rolls his slithering length along,   475
Then towers to the sun, spitting his thrice-split tongue.)

Huge Periphas, with his Automedon, was there
(Who bore his arms and was Achilles' charioteer),

And all the Scyrian youth; the mass of them attacks,
Torching the roof. First in, he grips a two-edged axe;   480
Then Pyrrhus bursts through as he rips the brass-clad doors
From their pivots. To knock a panel out, he bores
Through oak and breaks a gaping hole. There, deep inside,
Appear the naked atria; no wall can hide
The heart of Priam's sanctum, Ilium's ancient pride.   485

The Greeks see soldiers ready for a final stand,
But deeper still within, with chaos now at hand,
Great groans go up as women shriek and scream; their cries
Resound against the golden stars that pock the skies.
Then through the caverned halls those panicked women race,   490
Imprinting with a kiss the doors that they embrace.
Pyrrhus, Achilles-strong, rampages on; no locks
Or guards can stop him. Battered by repeated shocks,
The tottering gate goes down at length, torn from its sockets.

Force finds a way; Danaans storm the jagged breach.   495
They flood and fill, then kill the first men that they reach.
(No river boiling over its banks rages more,
The moment when its massive waters drown the shore.
Their wild summation sweeps the fields and drags each fold
And herd across the plain.)

                I saw myself that bold,   500
Blood-crazed Neoptolemus. Atrides-trailed, he strides
Past Priam's threshold. Hecuba; the hundred brides-
To-be she bore: I saw them. Priam, too, who stained
With blood the sacred altar stones he'd once maintained.
Those fifty bedrooms (Troy's best hope for sons); doors rich   505
With proud barbarian gold: all fell. The prizes which
No fires had got, Greeks won.

                              And what was Priam's fate?
Seeing the captured city fall, the palace gate
Ripped from its walls, the enemy now deep inside,
Old as he was, he shouldered rusty armor, tied   510
A sword on in his palsied haste, and tried to find
Those hostile mobs where sudden death would be most kind.
There in the central court, beneath Troy's naked sky,
An altar stood, and arching over it, close by,
An ageless laurel lent the household gods its shade.   515
Here, close about the shrine, Queen Hecuba had made
A hunkered stand. Her daughters crouched there, too—in vain,
Hugging those statuettes like doves swept by black rain.

But seeing Priam cased in armor worn when he
Was young, she cries, 'Poor husband, what insanity   520
Possesses you to wield a sword? Where will you go?
The moment needs its champions in defense, but oh,
Not arms like these. If Hector were alive . . . but no.
Quick now; come here. This altar will protect us all,
Or else we all together and at once shall fall.'   525

Stopping, she led the old man to the sacred throne.
But look: Polites, son of Priam, barely flown
From Pyrrhus' sword, through hostile missile, stone, and blade,
Comes racing, wounded, down the lengthy colonnade,
Crossing the open court, with Pyrrhus drawing near   530
In hot pursuit. Now! Now he's there, and plants his spear.
At last, Polites, right before his parents' eyes,
Pays out his fund of blood to smear the stones, then dies.

And at that fall, though it is in death's hand he lies,
Priam now spares no rage, but loud as thunder, cries,   535
'Oh, may the gods repay you for a crime like this,
For such a deed—if heaven deals in righteousness.
What proper thanks are yours? What do gods owe to one

Who makes a father view the head-on death his son
Dies? Death-pollution now defiles a father's face.   540
Not so the man whose son you claim to be! With grace
Achilles treated me, his enemy. Respecter
Of suppliants' rights, he sent the bloodless corpse of Hector
Back for burial; I came back safely, too.'

His words done, agèd Priam impotently threw   545
A pointless spear. Repulsed at once, it clanged and hung
Without effect from Pyrrhus' bronze shield-boss's rung.
Pyrrhus to Priam: 'Go, you *messenger*, and tell
Great Peleus' son what I have done. Quidnunc[13] to hell,
Relate *degenerate* Neoptolemus's deeds.   550
Now die!' Then done, he snags the trembling king and leads
Him altar-ward, trawling through blood Polites spilt.
His left a-twist in Priam's hair, his right hand filled
With blinding steel, he drives it home up to the hilt
In Priam's side. So Priam fell, so was he fated: 555
To see Troy ruined, Pergamus incinerated.
(The king of Asia, with its countless tribes and lands!
His vast trunk, headless, lies on lone and level sands:
A corpse without a name; a severed, trunkless head.)[14]

Then for the first time paralyzed by mortal dread,   560
I froze. My dearest father's form seemed to appear
As Priam—*his* age—died (life left him where the spear
Had trenched its cruel wound); Creusa, too, sad mate;
Our plundered house; and Iulus—what was *his* fate?
I looked back, counting who was left to stand and fight.   565
I was alone. My weary band had dropped from sight
And sunk to earth, or perished, helpless in the night
Of fire. Now on my own, I suddenly discovered,
Next to Vesta's temple, Helen.[15] There she hovered,
Cowering, silent. As I move, the bright flames light   570
My way to see her; everything's in clearest sight.

Tyndareus' daughter fears the furious Teucrians who
Abhor her for the fall of Pergamus. Greeks, too,
Want vengeance—as does cuckold Menelaus. Troy
And Argos' Fury, there she crouched, the hated toy   575
Of Paris. Fire flared inside me—vengeful rage
That Troy was gone. I meant to make her pay sin's wage:
'No, you will never live to look on Sparta or
Your home Mycenae; never triumph, history's whore.
No husband, parent, home, or child. No Ilian train   580
About you, and no Phrygian slaves. With Priam slain
And Troy ablaze, its shores the place our blood has soaked?
Never! No woman-killer's name will be invoked
In honored memory; there's no renown, no doubt.
Yet men to come will praise me for my blotting out   585
Your infamy and forcing you to pay so right
A price. My full heart flames with vengeance's delight
In knowing I've redeemed the ashes of my kin.'

My words, as on I race, my mind in frenzied spin.
But then my dearest mother, never in a light   590
More radiant, appeared. She shone there in my sight,
Looking the way she looks in heaven, dazzling night—
True goddess gods see, just as tall and fair. She grips
My hand to stop me, and declares, with rosy lips,
'My son, this rage! What awful sense of injury!   595
What wrath! How have you lost your dear concern for me?
Won't you look first for old Anchises? Where is *he*?
Ascanius: Does he live? Creusa: Where is she?
The Greek troops hemmed them in on every side, and yet
My love protected them; their blood would not be let.   600
No fires swept them off. It's not Laconia's daughter
Of Tyndareus, Helen, causing all this slaughter—
Not Paris or her hated face. The gods have done
All this—the ruthless gods. They've leveled Troy and won

Its wealth for Greece. Look now! Dark clouds that pall your sight   605
And keep your mortal's understanding from the light,
I rip away! Fear nothing that I bid you do;
Obey your mother's counsels. Where you see these shattered
Piles, rocks torn from rocks, and smoke that mixes scattered
Dust in billows, Neptune pries the stones and quakes   610
The walls his trident gouges, as the city shakes
To its foundations. Fiercest Juno, leading, takes
The Scaean gates, and girt with steel, in frenzy cries
Out to the ships for more allies.
See there—Tritonian Pallas, planted on the heights?   615
Grim Gorgon-shielded, glowing in her cloud, she fights.
Our Father Jove encourages the Greeks and lends
Them heart; he makes the very gods the Argives' friends,
Against all Troy. Escape, my son! Oh, fight no more,
And at your side, I'll guide you to your father's door   620
In safety.'

     Done, the goddess cloaked herself in night-
Black shadows. Then the awful powers in all their might
Appear—dread images that make their animus
Against the Trojans clear.
That's when I thought I saw it sink—all Pergamus   625
On fire; Neptunian Ilium tumbled from its base.
(Much like a woodsman struggling on some mountain face
To fell an ancient ash. With blow on blow he hacks
Away, till yielding to the strokes his steely axe
Has struck, the tree starts trembling at its leafy top.   630
Then bit by bit, its wounds too much, prepared to drop,
It groans, its roots torn, dragging ruin as it goes.)

I climb down, goddess-led, and dart through flames and foes.
(Their swords gave way; the threatening fires ceased to roar.)
But when at last I reached our ancient house's door,   635

My father, whom I looked for first; my father, whom
I hoped to carry to the hills and save from doom
Now Troy was gone, refused to live a life so long
Or suffer endless exile. 'You whose blood is young,'
He said, 'Who have your vigor and whose hearts beat strong,   640
You must escape.
Had heaven wished me longer life, it would have saved
This house. Too much—to see our Ilium enslaved
Once long ago and live? Too much. Leave me to die
Here; bid my tired corpse good-bye right here, for my   645
Own hand will search out death. Those Greeks who hope to find
Rich spoils will pity me. Unburied, I'll not mind
The loss. For all these useless years, I've lingered, hated
By heaven's father, mankind's king. From fulminated
Winds and lightning's scorching fire, I felt the blast.'   650

That's how he carried on, his stubborn will steadfast.
Creusa begged him, as did I and all our own,
Our flood of tears a plea that he not drag us down
With him in ruin, adding to our crushing fate.
But he refused and stood fast, bravely obstinate.   655
Once more blood calls, as I prepare to fight and die.
(What chance or choice?) 'O Father, did you think that I
Could run—could leave you here? How could a thought like that
Come from a father's lips? If smashing Ilium flat
Is what the heavens want—great Troy reduced to dust—   660
And if your heart is set on this, that our deaths must
Be added to our city's, then that way is clear.
For Pyrrhus, drenched in Priam's blood, will soon be here.
He kills the sons before their fathers' eyes, and then
The fathers at the altars.

              Gracious Mother, when   665
You wove me through those hostile spears and flames, was it
To see Greeks at our hearth? My wife and son's throats slit?

Anchises, too, and all a mutual shambles? Bring
Your swords! Beaten, we'll answer life's last summoning.
Hurl me at the Danaans; let me fight again.   670
A few of us today shall die avenged, like men.'

Once more I buckle on my sword; my left arm slips
Through shield straps and I'm rushing out. Creusa grips
The threshold, though, and *look*: she clasps my ankles, tendering
Iulus to his sire.

              'The end that fate is rendering   675
You is ours as well, if you intend to die.
But if your trust in arms is such you mean to try
Them, guard us first. To whom must Iulus yield *his* life?
To whom your sire?—and I, who once was called your wife?'

Plaintive like that, she made the house moan. Suddenly,   680
A portent rose—a thing that we were stunned to see.
Between our hands and faces so distraught, there came
A tongue of fire above our Iulus' head.[16] The flame
Poured out a light that seemed to burn but did no harm
While licking round his hair and brow. In our alarm,   685
We shuddered fearfully and moved to shake the fire
Out and douse his hair with water, but my sire
Anchises, in a joyous transport, raised his eyes
To heaven as his hands and voice addressed the skies:
'Almighty Jupiter, if any prayer appeases,   690
Look down and show us how deserving reverence pleases.
Send us some omen, Father, to confirm this wonder.'

He'd barely done when on our left, the sudden thunder
Shook us. A streaking comet, falling through the night,
Came plummeting; it trailed an arc of wondrous light.   695
We watch it shoot across the rooftops till it marks

A path that glows in Ida's woods. The trench it arcs
Through, smokes with sulfur, far and wide; the ground burns bright.

Convinced by such a marvel, Father stands upright,
Indeed conceding. Then, saluting godly might,   700
He venerates the holy star: 'Now—*now* there's no
Delay. I follow where you lead—that's where I go.
Gods of our fathers, save this house . . . and Iulus, too.
This prodigy is yours, and Troy belongs to you.
My son, I give in; what you ask me, I will do.'   705

He stopped. Now all through Troy the fire's roar grew clearer
As the blazes rolled in billows ever nearer.
'Dear Father, come; climb up, arms round my neck. On my
Own back, this burden like no weight at all shall lie.
Whatever comes, we'll share one danger. There will be   710
One safety, too, with Iulus walking next to me.
My wife shall trail behind us, only steps away.
You slaves, now: listen, and pay heed to what I say.
Outside the city near a mound, a temple of
Abandoned Ceres skirts a cypress tree. (The love   715
Our reverent forebears bore it kept that tree alive.)
Make sure that it's by varied routes that you arrive.
As for our household gods and Troy's Penates, clutch
Them, Father. It would be defiling them to touch
These gods without ablution; after so much slaughter,   720
Blood cries for water.'

I'd spoken. Then I cloak my bowed neck and my brawny
Shoulders with the mantle of a lion's tawny
Pelt, and stooping to my load, take Iulus' hand
In mine (his two steps, skipping, to my one are scanned).[17]   725
Creusa trails as we negotiate the gloom,
And I—whom just before, no spear could frighten; whom

No squads of threatening Greeks could terrify—I jump
At each breath, every sound; my throat chokes on each lump.
On edge, afraid for boy and burden both, I view   730
The gates at last; could we have gotten safely through?

Then suddenly, a sound came rising toward my ears:
Footsteps! Marching! Scanning the dark, my father peers
Out. 'Run, my son,' he cries. 'They're on us! I can see
Their flashing shields and gleaming bronze.' Some deity,   735
Because of this—my fear, my addled wits—bereft
Me of my last clear thought. I ran down alleys, left
The ways that I had long known well. Oh, had my own
Creusa, fate-accursed and weary to the bone,
Just stopped? Or missed the way? Or strayed off in the night? 740
No answer. Now long gone, she vanished from our sight.
I had not looked back for my lost one—had not thought
To look—until that mound, the holy place we'd sought,
Where deathless Ceres was forlorn. Here, in the end,
All met . . . except for her. For husband, son, and friend,   745
She was not there.

       No god or man escaped my railing
Frenzy. What crueler sight did Troy, as it was failing,
Offer? I gave Ascanius and Anchises and
Troy's gods to friends to hide inside a maze-like stand
Of trees, then headed back to Troy again with sword   750
And shield. Now armed, I run what risk the Fates afford,
Retracing every step. My life a pawn, I brave
Each danger, hunting for the wall and gate that gave
Us our out. Tracking back, and marking how I'd come
Through darkness, I examined every step. And from   755
All sides, the very silences dismay me. Scared,
I head off homeward on the chance my wife has fared
That way (oh, just the chance!). Danaans, though, infest

The whole house. Starving blazes climb the gable's crest
And lick with flames, as fires rise like blasts from hell.   760
I race ahead. There's Priam's house, the citadel
Once more. In emptied courts of Juno's refuge, hand-
Picked guards like Phoenix and the dread Ulysses stand
Their watch of spoils. From all of Troy, its wealth of old,
From ashen shrines; the gods' own tables; solid gold   765
Kraters; rich robes the Greeks have plundered: all in piles.
Mere boys and trembling matrons wait in lengthy files
That stretch in all directions.

But yes, I even dared to cry out in the night;
My clamor filled the streets, while in my wretched plight,   770
I groaned in vain. I called 'Creusa!'—called again,[18]
Again. My frenzied questing never stopped. And then . . .
Her poignant image, like a ghost arose: my wife
Before my eyes, her stature larger than in life.
I was struck dumb, my hair on end, my voice a bone   775
Caught in my throat.

                    These words allayed my fears; her tone
Assured: 'How can it help to yield to agony
Like this, sweet husband? Heaven says this must not be
Your grief. They will that you will never carry me
From here; it is not *fas*.[19] Olympus will allow   780
You only lengthy exile and wide seas to plough,
Until Hesperia—a land that you will find
Farm-rich. There, Lydian Tiber's waters gently wind.
There, kingship and a royal wife and joyous years
Will prove your fate. Creusa needs your tender tears   785
No more. Dolopians or Myrmidons, I'll never
See their haughty homes or serve Greek women—ever.
Not I—a Dardan wife to Venus' dear son. No,

The heavens' Magna Mater will not let me go.
Farewell, then. Cherish him in love, the child we share.'   790

Her words were done; she left me yearning, weeping there,
With much to say, then vanished into thinnest air.
Three times I reached out for her in a failed embrace;
Three times eluding me, she melted into space,
The merest breath before my hands—a pinioned dream   795
Set free. The night now spent, I hurried back. A stream—
A giant throng, I was amazed to find—was there
In countless numbers: men and mothers primed to share
Our exile; huddled masses come from everywhere,
With ready hearts and every little scrap they'd saved.   800
My folk are braced for any sea that must be braved.
And now, past Ida's ridges rises Lucifer,
The Day-star ushering the dawn. Danaans were
At Ilium's sentried gates. Defeat. All hope is dead.
I hoist my father, scan the hills; then, off I head."   805

BOOK III

"WHEN HEAVEN'S DEITIES HAD BURIED ASIA'S POWER,
And ruined Ilium, razed at guiltless Troy's last hour;
When Priam's—Neptune's—city sky was smoke and reeking;
Then heaven's omens drove us into exile, seeking
Out distant lands. So there at Phrygian Ida's feet,   5
Below Antandros, we begin to build a fleet.

Unsure where Fate may carry us when we are done,
We gather there. Though summer barely had begun,
Father Anchises said to spread our sails to fate.
In tears, I left those plains where Troy had stood of late—   10
Our native shores and bays. Exiled, I sail the deep
With son and friends and all the Great Home Gods we keep.

Far off lay Mavors' land of broad fields tilled by Thracians
And ruled by fierce Lycurgus once. Two friendly nations
From of old, with allied household gods, were Thrace   15
And Troy—while Fortune favored us. We set our face
That way, and on a winding coast begin our first
New city, named Aeneadae. Our plans are cursed,
Though. Sacrificing to Dione's child (my mother)
For blessings on our work begun, and to the other   20
Gods—to heaven's lords and their high king—I killed
A sleek bull on the shore. Nearby, a mound was quilled
With cornel shafts and myrtle thick with spear-like shoots.

Approaching one, I tried to yank it by the roots,[1]
To use its limbs to roof the altar stone with green.   25
I find a portent there that's grisly to be seen

Or told of: wrenched out by its broken roots, that tree
Bled drops of black blood fouling earth with gore. In me,
A frigid shudder quakes the limbs; a dire frisson
Congeals my very blood with fear. But I go on   30
To try to tear another tree that clutches deep.
I mean to pluck whatever mystery it may keep,
But from its bark, this second oozes black blood, too.
Deeply perplexed, I begged the wood-nymphs to construe
This weighty sign. To Father Gradivus I prayed   35
(The Getae's lord): What message had this blood conveyed?

I fight the stubborn sand, knees braced for one more try,
But—should I say it or stay mute?—I hear a cry
Of terror from the hummock's depths—a piteous moan
Striking my ears—and then a voice to match that groan: 40
'Why tear a wretch like me? Oh, leave my tomb alone,
Aeneas! No pure hands should touch me. Not unknown
To you, I was of Troy. I bleed, but I'm no tree.
Oh, flee this cruel country's greedy purlieus. Flee!
I'm Polydorus. Here, a steely crop broke through   45
My body; shafts of biting spears are what I grew.'

Then truly, with my mind oppressed by puzzling dread,
I stood amazed. The hair was bristling on my head;
My voice hooked in my throat. Poor Priam once had sent
This Polydorus, packed with gold, to Thrace. He went   50
In secret, to be raised by Thrace's king when ours
Lost hope in Dardan arms and saw Troy's waning powers
Helplessly besieged.

               Then when all Teucrian force
Was broken, Fortune fled. The Thracian king's new course
Was following Agamemnon's winning army, breaking   55
Sacred ties, and killing Polydorus, taking
His gold (a hunger that makes men do anything).

When fear lets go my bones, I find our chiefs and bring
Them (Father first) these portents. This is what they thought:
All say to leave that tainted land and what was wrought   60
There: sacrilege; guest-friendship fouled. Let south winds fill
Our sails. Renewing funeral rites, we build a hill
Heaped high for Polydorus' soul; an altar stands
Upon it, dark with cypress and with somber bands.
The Ilian women free their hair—rite's proper form.   65
We offer up the foaming bowls of milk and warm
Blood cupped from victims. Then we sepulcher his spirit
And loudly call his name—the last time he will hear it.

As soon as we can trust the main—when soft winds call
After the deep, and grant calm seas—our comrades haul   70
The ships down, crowding round the shore. Our anchors weighed,
We sail from port, watching as towns and vistas fade.

Mid-sea, there lies a sacred, dearly cherished isle[2]
That Doris and Aegean Neptune love, which while
It wandered round so many shores, the Bowman tethered   75
In place. (He bound it to high Myconos, together
With Gyaros; there it sits, scoffing at wind and sea.)
In that most peaceful place, our weary company
Finds welcome and safe anchorage.

                                        There, we revere
Apollo's town. King Anius—king and Phoebus' seer   80
Alike—his brow in bands and sacred laurel, meets
Us, noticing Anchises—an old friend he greets.
We clasp hands as his guests, and then are ushered in.

At Phoebus' shrine of ancient stone, my prayers begin:
'O Thymbran, grant: a lasting home to those worn down;   85
A people with a second citadel; a town
Like Troy—the remnant pitiless Achilles and

His Greeks left. Who should lead us? Where does your command
Declare our home? O Father, just one sign! Inspire
Us.'

    At that, the lintels, laurels—the entire   90
Shrine—shook hard; the whole hill quaked. The tripod groaned
As Phoebus' temple opened wide. We hugged the ground,
Submissive as we heard the godhead's dreadful sound:
'Enduring Dardans, that same land your forebears bore
You in will welcome your return. She will restore   95
You to her joyous breast. Seek her, for she is yours,
Your ancient mother. There, commanding distant shores,
Aeneas' house shall rule—his sons, their sons, and theirs.'

So Phoebus. Tumult then, with joy in equal shares,
Arose, and everybody asks, 'What walls are those?   100
Where *is* this Nomads' homeland that Apollo chose?'
My father, pondering old men's memories, cries, 'Hear
Me, princes! Where our hope lies, I shall now make clear.
Crete—island of great Jove; isle mid-way in the sea;[3]
Mount Ida's home—was once our nation's nursery.   105
Men live there in a hundred towns, a fertile place.
From there, if memory's sound, the father of our race
Sailed—mighty Teucer. On the Rhoetean coast he set
His kingdom, Ilium and its fortresses not yet
Established. Men were living in the lowland vales,   110
Great Cybele and Corybants too, in the swales
And cymballed Idan groves (her silent worship came
Here with that lady's chariot and lion team).
Come, then, and let us follow where the god commands;
Let us appease the winds and seek the Cnossian lands.   115
Our course is short. Should Jupiter smile on our fleet,
The third dawn finds us anchored on the coast of Crete.'

He stopped, and at the altars, killed the victims due:
A bull to Neptune and, fair Phoebus, one to you;
Storms get a black sheep; favoring Zephyrs claim a white.   120
Some say Idomeneus is banished, taking flight
From Crete, his father's realm, and that the coast is clear,
Crete's houses free of enemies, and oh-so-near.

We leave Ortygia's port, flying across the sea
And coasting Naxos, with its Bacchic revelry;   125
Pass green Donysa, Olearos, Paros gleaming
White, and all the Cyclades that stud the streaming
Seas. We thread straits, breaking foam on countless strands,
As shouting crews compete: 'To Crete, our ancient lands!'

Companion winds rise at our sterns; we ply the oars   130
And land at last on the Curetes' ancient shores.
Then eagerly I build our brand new city's walls,
Urging its people on (the grateful nation calls
It Pergamum, and loves its hearths and citadel).

Our ships were now in dry-dock and our young folk well   135
Along in marrying and tilling (every sort).
Involved in laws and building, I was brought up short
The day that plague came down—a time of foul disease
Infecting limb and life. All died—men, crops, and trees.
We gave up precious breath or dragged around our weakened   140
Hulks. Then, Sirius struck; fields burned, no longer fecund.
Drought withered grasses; sick crops gave no yield.

                                                    My sire
Exhorts us: 'Back to sea, to Phoebus, to inquire
Of Ortygia's oracle. Beg him to bless
This weary people with an end to their distress.   145
Where should we look for help? What course are we to keep?'

Night came, and every soul lay in the hand of sleep.
The gods'—the Phrygian Penates'—holy shapes[4]
That we had borne from burning Troy in our escapes
Seemed *there*—before my heavy eyes; their forms appear,   150
Made manifest in lunar beams, and all is clear,
As through the slatted window streams the full moon's claire.

Speaking these words, the gods dispelled my anxious care:
'Those things Ortygian Apollo would relate,
He sings now here (he sends us to foretell your fate).   155
With Troy in flames, we came with you and yours, to be
Your friends in ships that measure out the swelling sea.
And we will raise up to the stars your sons to come,
And grant their future city high imperium.
Build mighty walls for mighty men and don't recoil,   160
As you change old for new, from exile's lengthy toil.

The Delian did not mean these shores for you—not Crete.
There is a land Greeks call Hesperia, replete
With power and with fertile soil, an ancient place.
Oenotrians lived there; it's said a younger race   165
Has named it Italy, after their leader. *There*
Is home—where Dardanus began. And that is where
Father Iasius arose, who sired Troy.
Get up! Go tell your agèd father; speak with joy
This certain truth: seek Corythus! Ausonia calls!   170
Jove vetoes these Dictaean fields.'

                  Their speech enthralls,
And thunderstruck by such a sight (I had not dreamed
This true epiphany, but clearly I—it seemed—
Had known their looks, their ribboned locks, each living face.
Sweat chilled my skin.), I rise up from my resting place   175

On my pallet, stretching upturned palms. Prayer lifts
My voice to heaven as I offer perfect gifts
There on the hearth.

     Then when these rites have been fulfilled,
My joy must tell Anchises what the gods have willed.
He understood this two-part ancestry, this double   180
Parentage: the error that had caused the trouble
Was one of ancient lands. 'The fate of Ilium
Has tried you, son. Cassandra told me what's to come,
Cassandra only. She foretold what we would claim—
Our people's due. She often spoke Hesperia's name,   185
And often Italy's. But who'd believe some day
We'd see those shores? Back then, whom could Cassandra sway
As prophet? Yield to Phoebus; take the better way,
Now that we're warned.'

     We hear, and joyously obey.
We quit this 'home' as well (though some decide to stay),   190
And spread our sails, sweeping the desolate seas in hollow
Ships. When land was gone, and we had shed the shallow
Waters—sea everywhere, and everywhere the sky—
The livid, lowering storm-clouds crashed down from on high.
They stirred their gale winds till the still, black ocean trembled,   195
Then rolled its shaken waters into swells that tumbled
Us all over the abyss in giant surges.
Black thunderheads erase the day. Night's rain submerges
Sky, as lightning stabs from shattered cumuli.

Off course, we flail, with nothing left to reckon by.   200
Even Palinurus can't tell night from day.
Amidst the blind waves, he cannot regain the way.
For three whole days, we wander in these blackened shrouds;

For three whole nights the stars are blotted out by clouds.
Then on the fourth day, land at last appears to rise,   205
With far-off peaks, and smoke that spirals to the skies!

Sails struck, we work the oars—no more delay! The crew
Strokes hard, churning the foam, sweeping across the blue.
Relieved, we come ashore first on the Strophades.
Greek-named, those lonely islands stud the Ionian Seas—   210
Islands where Harpies like Celaeno roost (in fear,
When barred from Phineus' house, they left their tables there).
No plague or scourge of gods, no monsters worse than these—
Nothing more savage—ever rose up from the seas
Or Stygian waters. Winged and wearing virgins' faces,   215
They scatter noxious sewage, splattering food with feces.
Their hands are talons and their visages are gaunt
From appetite and want.

Blown there, we'd barely found safe harbor when—a shock—
We see fat, pastured cattle and a helpless flock   220
Of goats unguarded in the grass. With unsheathed swords
We rush them, asking Jove to join in our rewards,
The gods to share such spoils. We set up couches there
On crescent sands and banquet on the savory fare.
Then . . . Harpies![5] Diving from the crags like bolts of thunder,   225
They swoop, thumping their deafening wings, our feast their plunder,
And all our food defiled by their disgusting claws.
From putrid stench, a hideous shriek. Our band withdraws,
Deep back below an overhang ringed round by maples
And lambent, quivering shade.

                              Once more we spread out tables 230
And light the altar fires; once again, from some
New compass point where they've been lurking, Harpies come.
That screeching, caltrop-taloned coven rings its prey,

Their maws polluting. 'Swords!' I shout; the men obey
My orders, ready for a war against that race   235
Of monsters, laying their arms in a high-grassed place
And hiding shields. Then when that sisterhood once more
Swoops down, all screams above the island's winding shore,
Misenus, from his lookout, blows the signal trumpet.
Our band attacks, attempting new and eerie combat: 240
Steel swords to slash these loathsome-omened ocean things.

But nothing wounds their backs or bloods their pinned-back wings;
They scatter to the sky in spiraling retreat,
Dropping their spoor and half of what they'd come to eat.
Only Celaeno,⁶ crooked seer, has clasped a crag   245
High up. These words erupt from that repulsive hag:
'Sons of Laomedon: in trade for slaughtered cattle
And butchered bullocks, you intend to offer battle?
You'd drive us guiltless Harpies from our father's land?
Well, carve *this* in your hearts—so you will understand: 250
What Father Jove told Phoebus and Apollo told
To me, First Fury, I reveal to you. You'll hold
A course for Italy, placate the winds, and reach it.
You'll sail your fleet to Italy, and there you'll beach it.
But you will never gird your town with walls until   255
Hard famine—and this outrage—make you eat your fill
Of plates you dine on, tooth and jaw.' That's what she said.

Down on extended wings then, to the woods she fled.
But suddenly, my brothers' veins ran cold with fear.
They lost all heart, imploring that we give up spear   260
And sword to sue for peace with vows and begging words
(Who cared if these were goddesses or cursèd birds?).

There on the shore, with hands outstretched, Anchises, too,
Invokes the gods and names the rites that they are due:

'O gods, negate these threats; forbid their coming true!   265
Be gracious. Save the guiltless.'

                            Then, 'Cast off all lines'
Is his command. We slip from shore. Each sail unwinds,
As Notus bellies canvas, and we churn the deep,
Where only wind and helmsman know the course we keep.
Soon, forested Zacynthus and Dulichium   270
Appear, then rocky Neritos and Samé come.
We pass the cliffs of Ithaca, a land we curse
Because Laertes' kingdom was Ulysses' nurse.
Soon, Mount Leucata's storm-wrapped peaks rise up.[7] And there's
Apollo's shrine, so feared by sailors.

                         Worn with cares,   275
We head in, closing on the temple's little town.
Ships run up on the berm, with anchors crashing down.
At last on land (unhoped-for land): the cleansing rite
To Jove. Fresh victims smoke the altars that we light.

Then . . . Ilian games on Actian shores. My comrades strip,   280
And glad they've given all those Argive towns the slip,
Relieved at their escape through waters thick with foes,
They oil themselves for Trojan wrestling. Round it goes—
The sun—meanwhile. One year's great circle it completes,
When frigid winter with its blasting snows and sleets   285
Roughs up the waters. At the temple doors, I tack
Great Abas' brazen shield, then add this amphibrach:
Aeneas these arms from victorious Danaans.

I set the men to thwarts, that bay soon in abeyance,
As crews compete to stroke the sea, sweeping it wide.   290
Quickly, we're gone; Phaeacia's heights fall back and hide.

We coast Epirus' shores; Chaonia's port draws near,
And then we climb to high Buthrotum's city.[8] Here,
The rumor of a marvel fills our ears: the son
Of Priam, Helenus, is ruling Greeks! He's won   295
From Pyrrhus, son of Aeacus, both wife and scepter
(Andromache had been passed back! A Trojan kept her
Now!).

     Amazed, I burn to know how all this came
About—to question him's my overpowering aim.
I walk up from the harbor, leaving ship and shore   300
Behind, when just by chance, Andromache, before
The town, within a grove a 'Simois' ran through,
Was offering mourning gifts—a solemn banquet to
Her Hector's ashes—summoning his ghost to come
And bless that empty mound of green that was his tomb.   305
(Twin altars hallowed it—a place to weep.)

                            When she
Had spotted me (and everywhere, Troy's weaponry),
She was confused and frightened, stiffening as she looked.
Then, zero at the bone, she swooned, amazed and spooked.[9]
At last, she asks me, 'Goddess-born, can you be real?   310
Are you alive, and is it true, what you reveal?
Or if life's light has fled, then where is Hector?' So

She spoke, then sobbed, tears flooding all that space with woe
And lamentation. I could barely speak to calm
Her, I was so distraught. These few words were her balm: 315
'My life is real, but dragged out *in extremis*. Do
Not doubt that what you see is true. What fate have *you*
Been dealt, once Hector's wife? Andromache, what new
Fate's worthy of you? Are you Pyrrhus' consort still?'

She dropped her gaze, then spoke, though barely audible: 320
'Oh, you were luckiest of all—the virgin daughter
Of Priam. At a hostile tomb, Greeks sought your slaughter
Below Troy's towering walls. But no one drew *you* for
A prize, and no one chained *you* for some master's whore!
Our homeland burnt, our bodies blown across the seas,   325
We have put up with Pyrrhus's indignities,
Youth's vile hauteur, while breeding slaves. And then he chased
Hermione (to claim a Spartan bride) and passed
Me on to Helenus, as slave-wife to a slave!
Orestes, though, on fire and Fury-lashed to save   330
His stolen bride, kills Pyrrhus (taken unaware
There at his father's altar). By this death, a share
In Neoptolemus's realm—some part that's fair—
Is Helenus's. Giving all the plains the name
Chaonia (while the land itself is called the same,   335
From Trojan *Chaon*) Helenus adds "Pergamus"
(The Ilian citadel).

What were the winds—tell us
The fates—that set your course? What god has forced you here?
What of Ascanius? Does he still breathe the air?
Whom now to you in Troy . . .[10]   340
Does he still love the parent he has lost? And do
His father and his uncle Hector stir him to
Ancestral courage and a manly heart?'

And then
She wept a flood of words, beginning once again
A pointless, long lament, when Helenus, brave son   345
Of Priam, comes from town, followed by everyone.
He knows we're kin, and so he leads us in with joy,
A tear between each word. I see a scaled-down Troy

As we advance, a model Pergamus, and so-
Called River Xanthus, just a half-dry stream. I throw 350
My arms around the portals of a 'Scaean' gate,
As Teucrians, too, enjoy the town and celebrate.

The king receives us in the spacious colonnade
Where Bacchic cup–libations flow, as toasts are made
And bowls are tipped. A feast is served on golden plates. 355
Days drag, until the swelling southern breeze inflates
The canvas it's been crying for. I seek the seer
Helenus with queries. 'Priest-king who makes clear
Lord Phoebus' will; Troy-born diviner of the gods:
You know the stars, the Clarian laurel, the tripods, 360
The tongues of birds, their ominous wings in all their force.
So speak. (The gods encourage us; they set our course,
And with their powers, all command we seek the shore
Of Italy—the distant land we must explore.
Celaeno only, chants her Harpy's prophecies 365
Of threatening, strange, unspeakable new prodigies
Of rage and filthy famine.) Which should I shun first?
Or what should be our course to overcome the worst
Of these?'

      Then Helenus performs the rites appointed
(Begging god-grace), unties the bands from his anointed 370
Brow, and filled, great Phoebus, with your will, escorts
Me by the hand up to your temple's very portals,
Foretelling there, in priestly words, what Fate imports:
'O goddess-born, because it's clear the Powers keep[11]
You on your course (and by great Jove you sail the deep, 375
Who sorts out fate and rolls down change through all its rings),
I'll use few words to tell you of a host of things.
That way, you may more safely sail kind seas and find

Ausonia, for the Fates want Helenus kept blind
To more, and now Saturnian Juno stops my speech.   380

First, this: a way without a way, by a long reach
Of lands, keeps Italy far from you; far from near
Are ports to which you think you are prepared to steer.
Your oars must stroke Trinacrian seas; they must propel
You through the salt Ausonian, by the lakes of Hell,   385
And past Aeaean Circe's isle as well, before
You build your city in a land that's safe from war.
I'll name the signs; preserve them in your memory.
When in distress, you'll find a hidden stream and see
A sow—a giantess—beneath the oaks on shore.   390
A sow surrounded by the thirty young she bore,
She'll wallow there, all white, her nursing piglets white.
Here you'll find rest, and this will be your city's site.

This future eating of your tables, do not fear,
For fate will find a way; Apollo will be there.   395
But shun these lands, and flee this closest coastline limit
Washed by our floodtide. The Italian shores bathe in it,
And vicious Greeks inhabit all its towns. Here, too,
Narycian Locri have erected walls, and you
Will find that Lyctian Idomeneus has filled   400
Sallentia's plains with swords. The Greek Meliboeans build
Little Petelia there, as Philoctetes willed,
High on the hillsides. When your deep-sea fleet has reached
Its haven and you've prayed on altars where you've beached,
Then hood your heads with purple cloaks, lest as you pray   405
While worshipping the gods, some hostile image may
Obtrude itself amidst the sacred fires and roil
The omens. Keep this form of liturgy; be loyal,
You and yours, to rites that help your line stay pure.

But when you leave—when winds have blown you to the shore   410
Of Sicily, Pelorus opening wide its door—
Then head for left-side land, and hold to waters larboard,
Long way round. Stay far off from whatever's starboard.

They say these lands once split apart by huge upheaval—
That some convulsive force that rose in dim, primeval   415
Times (long ages work such changes) made abutting
Lands from one, the sea that came between them cutting
Hesperia from Sicily. A narrow tide
Now washes towns and fields on either severed side,
Where Scylla guards the right, Charybdis, whirlpool-hungry,   420
The left (deep in her seething maelstrom, gulping-angry,
Three times she sucks the waters down, three times she vomits
Them back to flail the stars and lacerate the comets).

A cave hides Scylla in its blind and jagged gloom,
From which she juts her jaws out, dragging ships to doom.   425
A human face and comely breasts are all that show
Above her groin; she is a monster down below,
With lashing dolphin tails that join a wolfish womb.
As for Trinacrian Pachynus, give it room,
Slack off, and round that cape the long way, or you'll have   430
To face misshapen Scylla in her giant cave
(Or else the rocks that echo with her howling, sea-
Green hounds).

                    If there is any vision left in me;
If you can trust me as a seer; if Phoebus fill
My spirit still with truth—then goddess-born, I will   435
Advise you of one crucial thing—just one great thing—
Repeating it again, the warning you must cling
To, first and last: pray to Great Juno in your rite.

Use cheerful vows with Juno, so that with her might
(Won by your gifts), you'll leave Trinacria behind   440
And speed toward Italy.

               When you get there, you'll find
Cumaea's town, the haunted lakes, the rustling trees
Avernus bears. There, you will hear wild prophecies.
Deep-caverned Sibyl chants the Fates, then writes their signs
On leaves, and what she writes she sorts in ordered lines,   445
Their numbers stored within her cave. And there they stay
In place, un-stirred until there comes some fateful day:
Door hinges turn; thin breezes blow those leaves away.
The air flows in; each flimsy *folium* whirls and wafts,
And ever after, as they ride in scattered drafts,   450
She will not catch those verses madly un-collated.
Men leave the Sibyl bitterly; her curule's hated.

Here, do not think the cost of your delay too great,
Though breezes call your sails to sea, and friends berate
You. Though able to fill your folds with favoring gales,   455
Be sure to see that seer and plead (for prayer avails;
She'll mouth the oracles, with such untainted bribes,
Saying what wars will come; she'll tell you Italy's tribes,
Revealing how to flee, or make your burdens light;
You'll win a prosperous voyage if you ask her right.).   460
That's all I may reveal; the rest, high Heaven bars.
Go now, and by your deeds, raise Ilium to the stars.'

After that friendly *vates* spoke these words, he told
His people, 'Take sawn ivory and weighty gold
Down to the ships. Load massive silver in each hold,   465
And cauldrons from Dodona.' Then a breastplate, worn
By Pyrrhus once, was given (golden hooks adorn
Its triple-woven structure), and, with brilliant crest,

A plume-decked helmet. For my father, far the best
Are Helenus's horses and his guides, 470
As well as extra crews and weapons he provides.

Meanwhile, Anchises ordered canvas rigged (to waste
No time when favoring winds arrived). Then Phoebus' priest
Addressed my worthy father with respectful carriage:
'Anchises, Venus honored you in lofty marriage. 475
Because it loves you, Heaven saved you twice from Trojan
Ruin. Look! There's Ausonia. Only sail the ocean
And it's yours. Yet you must quickly pass those shores
(Far off's the portion that Apollo says is yours).
Now go,' he cries, 'blessed with a loving child. Why speak 480
Another word? The South Winds rise. Find what you seek!'

Andromache, now sad that we must finally part,
Brings gifts of robes she's stitched with golden-figured art,
A Phrygian cloak for Iulus, and—all courtesy—
Loads him with woven presents, speaking lovingly: 485
'Dear boy, accept these tokens, too, that I may be
Remembered by this handiwork. Andromache,
The wife of Hector, adds her lasting love, as do
Your kin. Astyanax' sole image left me, you
Are he, who had your eyes and hands and face; who'd be 490
Your age now, just your age, if he had lived—if he. . . .'

Before I sailed, I spoke, shedding tears of my own:
'Blessed are those whose happy destiny is known;
The future calls *us* still; from fate to fate we're blown.
At rest, *you* needn't prow the seas' great plains, or chase 495
Ausonia's long-withdrawing land. You see, in place
Of Troy and Xanthus, versions you have built with your
Own hands (beneath signs happier than ours) and more,
Far-distant from the Greeks, I hope. If ever I

Sail down the Tiber, viewing Tiber's fields nearby,   500
And seeing city walls the gods let us inherit,
Then on that day we'll make one Troy of kindred spirit
From these cities—two Dardanian allies holding
Epirus and Hesperia, and whose unfolding
Fates and founding fathers are the same. Oh, may   505
Our children do this.'

                Past Ceraunia, which lay
Close by, toward Italy, waves showed the shortest way.
Meanwhile, the sun sinks, and the darkened hillsides die.
New oarsmen chosen, at the water's edge we lie
Scattered about, refreshing tired limbs (the dry   510
Sands welcome us; we bathe in sleep).

                  Night's horses, driven
By the Hours, weren't halfway through their course's given
Arc when Palinurus springs from bed to try
Each breeze (his ears catch every whisper). In the sky,
He sees the sum of stars serenely slipping by: 515
Arcturus and the rainy Hyades; both Bears.
He spots Orion by the golden belt he wears.
Then when he's sure that heaven's calm and all is quiet,
He signals from the stern. We break our campsite by it,
Heading out to spread our canvas wings.

                   Now star   520
After star is withdrawn, Dawn blushing as the far-
Off, dim-lit hills appear. The low-set land we see
Is Italy! Achates first shouts, 'Italy!'[12]
And 'Italy!' glad sailors cry in unity.

Our sire Anchises wreathed a krater rim with wine,   525
Then at the ship's stern raised it, crowned, to the divine

Powers he called upon:
'Great gods of sea and land and storm, we pray you send
Us on our way with favoring, gently blowing wind.'

The breeze we need increases. As the coastline nears,   530
A bay—then, on Minerva's Height, a shrine—appears.
Our men furl sails and head the prows toward shore, where, bow-
Like, lies a bending bay carved by an eastern flow.
Its jutting crags spray salty spume (the harbor, though,
Is hidden). Towering walls extend twin, rocky arms;   535
The shrine stands back.

                    Here came the first of our alarms:
I saw an omen of four horses grazing far[13]
And wide, all snow-white on the plain. 'You stand for war,'
Father Anchises said. 'Is this our destiny?
These armored horses warn of war. Yet they might be   540
Irenic signs as well, since sometimes steeds submit
To chariot yoke, and learn to champ on peace's bit.
Perhaps there's hope.'

                    We pray to Pallas' holy powers—
The Aegis-Clasher who first heard those cheers of ours—
Then hood our heads with Phrygian cloaks before the altar,   545
Doing what Helenus had warned us not to falter
In: sacrifice to Argive Juno—vows to pay.
And when these proper rites are done, without delay
We head our sail-rigged yardarms' horns about, to thrust
These Greek homes in our wake—these lands we do not trust.   550

Tarentum's bay is spotted next (it's Hercules's,
They say). Hard over, the Lacinian goddess rises,
Shipwrecking Scylaceum, and the towers of
Caulonia. Then, far off, Mount Aetna looms above

Trinacrian waters; from afar we hear their roar   555
That deafens. Next come crushing rocks, and from the shore,
Great clashing noises. Shoals shoot up in tide-swirled sand.

My father said then, 'This must be Charybdis and
These rocks must be the ones about which we were warned.
Row for it, men!' They did, as Palinurus turned   560
The creaking prow about to port. By oar and sail
Then, all the crews drove portside, hard. As if some gale
Were tossing us, we rode each heaven-cresting swell,
Then with the falling wave, plunged to the depths of Hell.

Three times amidst those crags and caves we dipped our spars   565
To rocky thunder and the ocean's booming jars.
Three times we saw the shattered sea spray drench the stars.
The sun sank then, and our exhausted sailors lost
The breeze; drifting, we found the Cyclopian coast.
A harbor's there, untouched by searching winds, and spacious.   570
But hard-by, Aetna roars, whose crashing is hellacious.
One moment, it sends up a smoking cloud of black
Pitch in an eddy red with ashes falling back,
Or blows up globs of fire that lick the constellations.
The next you know, it vomits rocks in eructations   575
Of torn-off entrails. Then it throws up molten stone,
Boiling its bowels and roaring with a massive groan.
(The story is, Enceladus's body, charred
Half-through by lightning, with huge Aetna pressing hard,
Belches out flame from bursting forges. When he turns,   580
Trinacria quakes; smoke cloaks the sky, as if he burns.)

That night, the forest hides us; we endure the sound
Of monstrous prodigies whose source cannot be found.
For star-shine failed to show, nor were the heavens clear

With constellated light; the cloudy sky grew blear,   585
The moon hard in the grip of misty, dismal night.

Now day was rising with the morning star's first light,
And Dawn had sent the dank shades scattering from the sky,
When suddenly the woods expelled a form: we spy
A man half-dead from hunger, draped in wretched rags.   590
A suppliant, he gestures beachward as he begs.
We look back at a squalid ghost with bearded cheek.
Thorns stitch his clothes, but in all else, he is a Greek—
A soldier sent once, years ago, to fight the war
At Troy, bearing his country's arms.

                        When from afar[14]   595
He saw our Trojan weapons and our Dardan clothes,
He trembled at the sight, and half-a-second, froze,
Steps fear-arrested. Then he sprinted headlong toward
The shore, with tears and heartfelt prayers: 'I beg you, lord,
By all the stars and powers above, and by the air   600
Men breathe, oh, take me. Teucrians, take me anywhere.
That's all I ask. That I'm from the Danaan fleet,
I know. Yes, I confess: I fought for the defeat
Of Ilium's Penates. Well, if that's my sin,
Then drown me; chop me into messes; throw me in   605
The ocean. If I die, to die by men will please
Me!'

    Done, he hugged our knees; he *groveled* at our knees.
We beg his tale then—who he was and whence he came;
What dismal fate had come to hunt him down like game.
Anchises then, at once, in friendship's guarantee,   610
Offered the youth a hand. His spirits heartened, he
Puts fear behind him, finally, then speaks: 'My land

Is Ithaca; star-crossed Ulysses was my friend.
I'm Achaemenides, my sire, poor Adamastus
(Oh, to be paupers still!). I signed for Troy, but fast as   615
My friends could leave behind this grisly shoreline, they
Forgot me—left me in the Cyclops' cave, a prey
To bloody banquets in a house of butchery,
A shambles slick with gore. That towering giant? He
Assaults the stars. Gods, spare the world a plague like that!   620
He can't be spoken to; he brooks no gazing at.
He gulps the viscera of wretched men, his wine
Their livid blood. I saw him snatch two friends of mine
Inside that cave, while one huge hand (he lay supine)
Battered them on the rock, his splattered lair all slick   625
With guts. I saw him chewing leg-joints dripping thick,
Black clots of blood; his teeth tore limb from still-warm limb.

Not unavenged, though! No, Ulysses answered him.
Remembering who he was, the Ithacan struck back
Though trapped in dire straits; we went on the attack.   630
For when we caught that greasy giant, drunk and stuffed
And sprawling all across his cave and nodding off,
Belching up winey vomit chunked with orts of gore,
We pray the great gods' favor, choose our lots, then pour
Around him—armed. We raise a spear-sharp branch, then pierce 635
That eye stuck deep beneath a forehead huge and fierce—
An eye like Phoebus' lamp, or like some Argive shield.
So, in the end, were friends avenged, their spirits healed.

But flee, unlucky men! Oh, cut your hawsers free
From shore, and flee!   640
Like sky-tall Polyphemus, who pens his fleecy flocks,
Milking their udders in that cave cote in the rocks,
A hundred others live here, where their race infests

This winding coast or roams below these mountain crests.
Three times the moon has filled its horns with light since I   645
Began to watch, in woods and wastes, my life drag by
Among the bogs and dens of beasts. From some high rock,
I'd sense the Cyclopes, their cries, and feel the shock
Their feet made. Branches half-supply poor berry-rations
Of cornel stones; plants yield their grim deracinations.   650
Scanning the vista of the sea, I saw this fleet
Approaching shore. And now, to any fate I meet
With, I surrender, happy to escape that race;
Whatever way you choose, kill me—and take their place.'

He'd barely finished when up on the peaks we see   655
The shepherd Polyphemus[15] moving massively
Among his flock and seeking out the shore he knew.
A grisly thing: malformed, immense, and sightless, too,
He grips a pine that guides his steps and firms his stride.
His single joy? His wooly sheep—bound at his side,   660
Lone solace to him, too.
Soon as he reached the deep waves that begin the sea,
He rinsed his socket oozing blood. Tall as a tree,
So but half-soaked, he waded through the waters, grinding
His teeth and groaning.

                            We were terrified. With blinding   665
Speed we worked to get away. We took aboard
That worthy suppliant, then softly slashed the cord,
And swept the sea (the bending crews, contending, oared).
He heard our fading voices and was turning toward
Us, but he couldn't get us in his crushing grip   670
Or match Ionia's waves; we gave his rage the slip.
His mighty bellow rose and raised the quaking sea,
Whose waters shook; the roar rocked deepest Italy,

While up from conic Aetna's core came rumbling thunder.
Then, stirred to leave their woods and peaks, Cyclopes blunder   675
Down to harbor-side, clogging the shore. We spy
Them standing impotent, each glaring from one eye—
Aetnean brothers carrying their heads sky-high.
(A gruesome gathering, it's like the way great masses
Of oaks or cone-cloaked cypresses crowd mountain passes,   680
An Artemisian grove, or stand of Jovian trees.)

Headlong we rush to rig, as acrid terrors seize
Us. *Any* course! The sails unfurl to snatch some breeze.
(Charybdis! Scylla! Weren't the words of Helenus
To steer between them, either side sure death for us   685
If we ignored his warning?) Crazed, we're setting course
For where we started, when . . . look! From the strangled source
Of Cape Pelorus, north winds come. We slip away—
Pantagias' mouth, its living rock, Megara's bay,
Low Thapsus—shores that Achaemenides, befriended   690
By cursed Ulysses, traced again, as they once wended.

Along by the Sicanian bay, an island sprawled
Before surf-washed Plemyrium. Its first men called
It Ortygia, and said that Alpheus, river of
Elis, in secret course beneath the sea above,   695
Mingled with Arethusa's spring in Sicily.
We show that place's mighty powers due piety,
As ordered, passing by the bogs and soil of fertile
Helorus, skirting reefed Pachynus' rocks that hurtle
Skyward. Far Camerina shows next (Fate ordains   700
It never be disturbed). Then come Gelonia's plains,
And Gela, with the torrent after which it's called.
From there, we spy Acragas, high and greatly walled
(And famous once for valiant horses that it bred).
Winds help me leave you, palmed Selinus, as I head   705

Past Lilybaeum's shoals, rocks lurking on its bed.
Drepanum's port next, where we're taken in.

                                   But on
Its dismal sands, to every battering gale a pawn,
I lose . . . I lose Anchises: father, comfort, lightening
Every care and fate. Best father, here—frightening   710
Me—you left me, drained, yet saved from every threat.
For what? No horror Helenus said would be met
With—nothing vile Celaeno croaked of grief—compared
With this last trial, the end toward which I long had fared.
I left that place, and let the god shipwreck us here."   715

Aeneas Pater stopped; he'd spellbound every ear,
Telling the gods' decrees and teaching where he'd wandered.
He ended in a stillness every listener pondered.

Book IV

THE QUEEN HAS LONG SINCE FELT LOVE'S WOUND; IT BLEEDS,
Burning in liquid fires that her life's blood feeds.[1]
Her heart sees just his valor and his noble past,
His perfect lineage. His looks and words stick fast
Inside her breast—a wound that threatens it will last.   5

At dawn, Aurora lit the land with Phoebus' lamp,
Its rays clearing the skies of nighttime's deep black damp,
As suffering Dido found her sister-secret-sharer:
"Anna, strange dreams have thrilled me with a pleasing terror!
Who is this man who lives now where I live? His face!   10
His great heart and his warrior's courage! He *must* trace
His birth from heaven. Oh, I'm sure that that's the case,
Since cowardice would show an ancestry that's base.
Oh, how the Fates have cursed him! What a tale we heard
Of savage war! Had I not pledged my granite word   15
That I would not be wed again to anyone
After my first love died and left me all alone. . . .
If beds and bridal torches had not left me numb,
Perhaps his is the lure to which I might succumb.
Anna, it's true: since my Sychaeus cruelly died,   20
And our Penates fell to foulest fratricide,
Only this man has swayed my wavering soul, my will;
I recognize the embers of that old flame still.
But I had rather pray instead that earth had split
And great Jove's lightning bolt had hurled me to the pit   25
Of shades—the chasm'd shades of Erebus—before

Defiling you, O Shame, and all your laws I swore
To then. The spouse who bound me to him stole away
My heart. Oh, may he guard it to our dying day."

When done, she drenched her breast with tear-on-falling-tear.   30
Anna said, "Sister, dear to me as light is dear,
Will you now waste away your youth in grief, alone,
Never to bear a child or make sweet love your own?
Do you believe that dusty Death will ever care?[2]
I grant, till now, no likely wooer could repair   35
Your heart, in Libya—or back in Tyre. I know
You've scorned Iarbas and those Afric princes who
Were bred by that rich land, but can't some new love win?
Have you forgotten just whose lands you've settled in?
Here, battle-tough Gaetulians live, Numidians spurning   40
The bit, and hostile Syrtis. All surround you. Turning
South? A burning desert waste, Barcaeans raiding
Widely—not to mention Tyre may come invading.
And your brother's menaces!
In fact, I'm sure that favoring gods—and Juno's grace—   45
Have blown the Ilian fleet off-course to find this place.
Oh, what a city, sister—what a realm!—would rise
From such a union, were the Teucrians allies
In arms! *Then* Punic glory would ascend the skies!
Perform due rites for gracious gods to whom you pray.   50
Lavish your welcoming. Find reasons for delay
While winter seas still rage; while drenched Orion storms,
Wild skies crash down on ships and crush their crippled forms."

These words rekindled Dido's heart with passion's flame,
Confirmed her doubting mind, and swept her soul of shame.   55
They hurry to the temple, seeking peace at all
The altars, properly killing an animal

For law-fraught Ceres, Phoebus, and Lyaeus, father—
But to wedlock's Juno, before any other.

Libation dish in hand, the lovely Dido now,   60
Between the gleaming heifer's horns, anoints its brow,
Now passes by the temple columns solemnly,
To sacrifice each day, that she might rightly see
In fat-rich altars' quivering guts what things must be.

O vatic blindness! How can prophets, shrines, or prayers   65
Allay mad passion when the very marrow flares?
Meanwhile, heart-deep, love's tacit wound goes trenching down,
As Dido is consumed and maunders through the town.
Frenzied and madding, she is like some reckless hind
A far-off shepherd's shot. He's left the shaft behind,   70
Inside her; he's a hunter unaware, off in
Some Cretan grove. She crashes through Dictaea's glen
Half-crazed, but still the lethal arrow sticks . . . and stays.³

She leads Aeneas on through all her city's ways;
Shows off Sidonian readiness, its massed displays   75
Of wealth. Each time she tries to speak, she stops, mid-word.
Day ends; she craves again that stirring tale she's heard.
On fire, she demands once more to learn of war
At Ilium, once more the words she hungers for.

When all have left, the fading falling moon sinks deep   80
Its light, as setting stars invite the world to sleep.
Alone, she grieves in vacant halls and falls on his
Now-empty couch. She sees him, absent as he is,
And hears him. Spellbound by Ascanius (image of
His father), hugging him, she tries to lure a love   85
Beyond all words. No towers rise; the young don't drill,
Or build the bulwarked port. Revetment work stands still,

As war-defenses, hugely interrupted, cease.
All threatening salients wait; the sky-cranes stand at peace.[4]

When Jove's dear wife saw Dido in desire's grip[5]   90
(Her good name failed to stand against cruel passion's whip),
Saturnian Juno taunted Venus with these phrases:
"Oh, mighty triumph! How such spoils demand our praises!
You and Cupid: what a glorious victory—
One woman conquered by two gods . . . with trickery.   95
Believe me, too, I've noticed how you've held my Carthage
Suspect, and its lofty houses you disparage.
When will this end? And just how far shall we fight on?
Why not a lasting peace instead, with contracts drawn
For marriage? You've got what your heart was so set on—   100
Dido inflamed, love blazing through her bloodstream—so,
Let's rule this race together, you and I as co-
Divinities, with Dido's dower-men from Tyre,
Her mate from Phrygia."

                              Here Juno played the liar,
Venus knew (she planned a Lybian empire,   105
Stolen from Italy). So Venus, in reply,
Said, "Terms like these none but the foolish would deny
You, and besides, who'd want *you* for a foe in war?
If only Fortune favored what you're striving for!
But fate perplexes me. Does Jupiter desire   110
One city for the Trojan wanderers from Tyre,
Or peoples mixed in federated union? You,
His wife, can probe his mind, what he intends to do.
Ask, and I'll follow."

                              Regal Juno had her say:
"That task is mine. Now I will tell you just the way   115
We'll make this compact work. I won't waste words, so pay

Attention. Wretched Dido and Aeneas plan
A forest hunt at dawn, as one. No sooner than
The rays of Titan Sun pull back the world's dark veil,
While men are setting nets and racing over dale   120
And hill, I'll rain black floods on them, mixed up with hail
From Heaven, waking all the welkin with my thunder.
They'll run for cover like it's night they shelter under.
Troy's prince—and Dido—then will find themselves alone
In the same cave. And if I'm sure that you condone   125
This, *I'll* be there to join them . . . and make him her own—
Their *wedding*." Pleased, Love nodded yes, but with a smile,[6]
Since Cytherea saw right through her rival's guile.

Meanwhile, Aurora rose and left the eastern ocean.
In radiance, from the city gates, out rode its chosen   130
Youth, with wide-webbed nets, with broad-tipped spears and snares.
Massylians gallop out, their hounds all quivering nares,
While Punic lords wait at the threshold for their queen,
Who dallies in her rooms. In purple with a sheen
Of gold, and champing at the foaming bit, her mount   135
Awaits her—and a train too numerous to count.
She wears a fine Sidonian cape with golden hem,
A golden quiver, and a cloak pinned by a gem
Of gold, her tresses plaited with fine golden thread.

The Phrygians attend; Iulus rides ahead   140
Exultant, as Aeneas, handsomer than any,
Combines his followers with Dido's, one from many.
He's like Apollo leaving Xanthus' torrents and
His winter home in Lycia for his mother's land
Of Delos. (There the *choros* is renewed, while crews   145
Of Cretans, Dryopes, Agathyrsians with tattoos,
All shout around the crowded altars. He goes roaming
The Cynthian hills with streaming, laureled hair, and combing

Its golden weaving. Arrows rattle on his shoulder.)
Aeneas moved like that; no radiant face shone bolder.   150

When they had reached the hills and trackless badland crags—
Picture it—feral goats spooked from those rocks and jags
Ran down the ridges. Altogether elsewhere, vast
Herds of wild stags, silently and very fast,
Move across the dusty plains in massive flight   155
As they desert the heights. Ascanius, with delight,
Rides in the valleys on a fiery mount that now
Outraces these, now outstrips those. He prays each vow
Will win a frothing boar flushed from the meeker sort,
Or draw some yellow lion down.

                                   A wild report   160
Of thunder rumbles meanwhile—rain and hail all mixed
In tumult. Tyrians and Trojans scatter. Next,
Venus's Dardan grandson wheels around; he seeks
Out shelter somewhere on the plains. Rains gush down peaks
In torrents. Dido and the Trojan prince[7] arrive   165
At the same cave. Then . . . Primal Earth and Juno give
The nuptial signal. Lightning torched the sultry air;
In wedding witness, keening mountain nymphs were there.

That was the primal day of death—the fountain of
Disaster. Dido, covering sin and shame with "love"   170
And "marriage," and by reputation scarcely moved,[8]
No longer pines in secret passion.

                                   Rumor tears[9]
Through Libya's biggest towns—dread Rumor, than which there's
No evil faster. Speed, quick-feeding on it (though
Unsure at first) adds fuel as Rumor races, so   175

That just a hint of gossip wafts her as she flies.
(She stands in dirt, her head hid in the murky skies.)

The gods provoked our Mother Earth to rage (some say),
Such that she bore this last for Coeus, and to play
The role of sister to Enceladus—huge beast   180
Wing-swift and fast afoot, her countless eyes at least
As numerous as her plumes, and—wondrous to relate—
As many tongues and mouths, and ears that prick up straight.
She flies by night through gloom between the earth and sky,
Screeching. She never sleeps—or shuts one searchlight eye.   185
When morning comes, she sits her watch on roofs, or high
Up on the city's towers; her looks can terrify.
Sometimes she clings to lies; sometimes she tells what's true.

In this case, spreading hydra-headed gossip through
The populace, she sang both fact *and* falsehood: Prince   190
Aeneas, come from Trojan blood, was there; long since,
Beautiful Dido had decided she would pair
With him all wanton winter through, in an affair
Forgetting kingdoms—slaves to shameless passion's whips.
Vile Rumor hung these tales on every subject's lips.   195
Right off, she raced to King Iarbas, kindling fire
With what she said, and fed the fuel of his ire.

He—son of Hammon[10] by a ravished Garamantian
Nymph—built Jove a hundred shrines (in wide expansion
Through his realm; a hundred altars, too) and lit   200
Their holy watchful fires—gods' guards that never quit.
Earth oozed with bloody victim fat, while portals bloomed
With divers wreaths.

He heard the bitter rumor, fumed
And blazed (they say), and at the altars thick with numen,
Pled with Jove, his palms turned up in supplication: 205
"Almighty Jupiter, to whom our Moorish nation,
Richly set, pours out its Bacchic-blessed libation:
Do you *see* this? Father, are your bolts we quake
At pointless? Should that cloud-wrapped, hurtled lightning shake
Us to the soul and stir our murmurs? She who strayed,   210
That woman wandering through our lands? Has she not made
A paltry town? The coastland that she ploughs she paid
For (*we* laid out the terms). She turned me down—said *no*
To me, but takes Aeneas in as lord, as though . . . !
That *Paris*, with his band of eunuchs! Takes *him* in,   215
With his Maeonian ribbons holding up his chin.
That girly curled 'man' wins the prize, while we who bring
You temple victims praise you . . . with a hollow ring."

He spoke to Jove like this (but hugged his altars). Pity
Moved Almighty Jove to view the royal city;   220
Finding there mindless lovers heedless of good fame,
He ordered Mercury to charge them, in his name:
"Go forth and call the Zephyrs, son, to wing you down;
Rouse the Dardan idling in that Tyrian town.
In Carthage, he forgets the cities that the Fates   225
Have promised him. Dive through the winds with my dictates.
His mother did not pledge her son to us for *this*,
Nor save Aeneas from Danaan weapons twice.
He's meant to rule Italia, gravid with empire,
Growling with war. He's to hand down a bloodline higher   230
Than any—Trojans ruling earth with Roman law.
But if such fateful glory cannot wake his awe,
And lasting fame can't make him undertake the task,
Then why begrudge Ascanius *his* Rome? I ask,

What's next? What vain hope keeps him in this hostile place,   235
Far from Lavinia's fields and his Ausonian race?
The sum of all I say is, *sail*! That's all I say."

And so it was. Then Hermes[11] hastened to obey
His mighty father's word, first strapping to his feet
The golden sandals that would give him wings; as fleet   240
As winds, they lift him over sea and land. And then
He takes the wand with which he hales pale souls of men
From Orcus, or consigns them to the dark that lies
In Tartarus (it doles out sleep and unseals eyes
In death)—wind-wand; storm-swimming stick that he relies   245
On in the clouds.

         Aloft, he spies the peak and slopes
Of Atlas, arduous, enduring. Atlas props
The sky, his head of conifers cloud-wrapped in black.
There, constant rains beat on him; fierce storms lash his back;
Snow cloaks his shoulders; torrents gush down off his old   250
Man's chin; the icy stubble freezes, stiff and cold.

Cyllenian Hermes balanced here on wings, and poised,
Dove wholly headlong toward the waves from where he'd paused—
Launched like a bird that circles cliff-bound shores to skim
Above the daunting shoals where schools of fishes swim.   255
Just so, Cyllene's son went plunging down between
The earth and sky toward Libya's sandy shore; sheared clean
The winds in coming from his mother's father.

              When
His winged soles brought him to the huts, he saw at once
New buildings rising at the urging of the prince.   260
Aeneas' sword was starred with yellow jasper fire,

His shoulders cloaked in brilliant purple saved from Tyre—
A gift rich Dido worked in golden thread all through
The weft.

       At once the Trojan prince was spoken to:
"Now founding *Carthage* has become your charge? To hew   265
And lay a handsome city's stones? Uxorious!
You've thrown away your fated realm; how *glorious*.
God-ruling Jove himself, whose power spins both Heaven
And earth, has sent me from Olympus-Bright-with-Levin.
My charge: to fly this mandate through mercurial winds.   270
What plans, what vain hopes, hold you here in Libyan lands?
If fate and fortune cannot stir you, and the fame
You'd earn are not enough to make this task your aim,
What of Ascanius, your hope—your heir—to whom
Italia's owed, Iulus due his Roman realm?"   275

So the Cyllenian spoke, and even in mid-speech
Broke off, speeding from keenest human vision's reach.
Far off, he dwindled out of sight in tenuous air.

Aeneas, stunned by what he'd seen, fell dumb. His hair
Stood up in horror and his voice stuck in his craw.   280
On fire to flee those lulling lands, and filled with awe
At such commands, he knew divine imperium.
But what to do?[12] What were the words with which to come
Before the love-mad queen? What gambit should he try?
From here to there his wavering conceptions fly;   285
Thoughts test out every path, each wherefore and each why.
Then with his wavering done, this counsel seemed the best, as
He called Mnestheus, brave Serestus, and Sergestus:
To rig the ships for sea in secret, call each crew,
And stow their arms, not telling them why they should do   290
This. He himself, meanwhile, since Dido doesn't sense

A thing—no hint he'd kill a love that's so intense—
Ponders the best approach, the most propitious way
To speak. What words will suit his needs? His men obey
Him gladly, doing what he says without delay.   295

But who can fool his love forever? Soon the queen
Gets wind of an upheaval that she hadn't seen
Coming. She's fearful, though still safe, until that same
Cruel Rumor brings her maddening news: the Trojans aim
To arm their ships and plot their course; they mean to leave!   300
Helpless, on fire, she wanders Carthage, starts to rave,
A Maenad shaken by the sacred thyrsis.[13] (When
She hears the two-years' Bacchic cry, Cithaeron's din
That calls her, then its orgy blazes through her heart.)
At last she finds Aeneas, but can barely start: 305

"Traitor! You thought that you could *hide* this? Sneak away
In silence? Neither love nor faith could make you stay,
Nor death—the cruel destiny you'd have me meet?
You even work in winter storms to man your fleet
(With north winds everywhere), prepared to put to sea.   310
Savage! If Troy still stood, would you still flee from me?
If you were not for foreign lands and homes unknown,
Would you sail back to Troy through tempests? By your own
Right hand, and by these tears, I beg you (since by now
I've left my sad self nothing else); and by the vow   315
Of marriage we've begun: if ever I have won
From you a single kindness, or if what I've done
Was sweet: take pity on a house in ruin! If
My prayers can find a place still in your heart, cast off
This plan! Because of you, the tribes of Libya loathe   320
Me; Tyrians and Numidians despise me both.
Because of you, my honor perished with my name,
Which was to be my one exalted claim to fame.

I'm left for . . . whom? I'm dying, Trojan, dying. Guest—
The only name that's left from 'husband'—suits you best.   325
Why linger on until Pygmalion storms these walls
Or Iarbas the Gaetulian captures me and hauls
Me off? At least if you had left a child before
You fled—*my* child, some small Aeneas that I bore—
To play here, then I might not be so desolate."   330

Dido was done. Eyes steady under Jove's stern threat,
Aeneas banked down deep the anguish in his breast,
Then briefly spoke: "O Queen, I never would contest
That you deserve the things you want—the very best.
When I recall Elissa, I won't rue the day,   335
As long as I recall myself and breath can sway
This body. In my own defense, I'll only say
I never dreamed—believe me—I would steal away.
But neither did I offer you the wedding torch
Or promise marriage. Were I freed by Fate to search   340
Out destiny and grieve the way I wished, I'd cherish
Troy—whatever remnant of my kin's alive—
And Priam's lofty palace walls would still survive.
I'd rebuild Pergamus for its defeated souls.

But now, Grynean Phoebus' Lycian oracles   345
Have ordered me to take in hand Great Italy.
There is my love; there is my home. If, when you see—
Phoenician that you are—your Libyan Carthage, you
Feel joyous love, then why begrudge Ausonia to
Us Teucrians, who also seek an exile's realm?   350
As often as the dew-drenched night will overwhelm
The earth; as often as each new-lit star arises,
I'm warned; the troubled spirit of a ghost-Anchises
Comes—and thoughts of Iulus, the injury
I do him by Hesperian lands he's yet to see,   355

Though promised. Even now, Jove's messenger (I swear
This on our lives) has come, commanding, through the air.
I saw the god myself, by the clear light of day,
Enter these walls, and all these words I heard him say.
Your grief's incendiary; leave our hearts alone. 360
I sail; my will is not my own."

But while he speaks these words, she looks askance the whole
Speech through. She scans the man; her eyes, in silence, roll.
Done glaring, she ignites . . . and then explodes: "Faithless!
No Dardanus was *your* forebear, nor was a goddess 365
Your dam. On adamant, spawned by the Caucasus,
You sucked the savage breast of a Hyrcanian tigress.
And why hide what I feel? With worse to come, why wait?
And did he sigh, or look to see my tears in spate?
And did he cry, or pity me, who loved him? What 370
Word should I put before another?

Now . . . now, neither
Juno's eyes—nor the Saturnian father's, either—
Look justly on these things. No faith is sure. I saved
A castaway, a beggar on my shores, then halved
My throne for him! Madness! I saved his ships and men 375
From death. My fury blazes. First Apollo, then
The Lycian priests, then even Hermes, sent by Jove,
Comes bearing orders, winging through the clouds above!
No doubt the gods care how we roil their lofty peace.

I won't debate you, and you don't need my release. 380
Go! Latium lies downwind; *seek* kingdoms overseas.
But how I hope—if the gods can—that halfway there,
Stove in on rocks, you drink my vengeance in despair,
Calling 'Dido! Dido!' Though far away, I'll hear.
With smoking torch, my ghost will chase you till chill death[14] 385

Has severed from your body all your brazen breath.
You'll pay! And I will know, below in Hades."

                                        Done
With words, she breaks off mid-harangue and starts to run,
In agony (she's spurned his eyes and turned away).
In fear, he hesitates, with so much more to say.   390
Girls bear the crumpled Dido to her marble room
And lay her on the bed.

                    Her sorrow's tearful doom
Makes good[15] Aeneas want to soften Dido's griefs
And comfort her. It is a massive sigh he heaves,
But even though a riven soul, Aeneas leaves   395
To do what Jove commands. He hastens to the ships,
Where all down-shore, the Teucrians have come to grips
With launching.

                    Caulked keels slip the sands, as every crew
Prepares to sail. They haul the un-stripped limbs they hew,
The un-planed forest logs, for oars.   400
You'd see them streaming from the town and toward the shores,
Like ants anticipating winter in their pillage,
Piling great hills of grain to cache back in their village.
The black line marches through the grass, across terrain,
Bearing its spoils down thin defiles. Their shoulders strain.   405
Unwieldy grains mean some ants regulate the struggle,
Urging on the stragglers. All is work and bustle.

What must you have been feeling, Dido, at such sights?
What sighs you must have sighed, up on your city's heights,
The long shore swarming there before your tear-filled eyes!   410
You saw the whole wide sea alive with clamorous cries.
Lord Love, what won't you make these mortals do? Once more,
She wails; once more, thinks to assail is to implore,

As love receives the offering of her humbled pride
(To fend off pointless death, she'll leave no course untried):   415

"Anna, you see the shores such enterprise commands.
Men come from everywhere; their sails entice the winds.
Delighted crews strew garlands on the sterns. If I've
Endured seeing this grief would come, then I'll survive
It, too, my sister. Still, for me, do this one thing,   420
Dear Anna: since that faithless man made you his single
Confidante and shared his cherished thoughts with you
Alone (you know the best time to gain access to
Him), go and beg him, sister. Tell my haughty foe
I did not plot with Greeks at Aulis to destroy   425
His Trojan race. *I* never sent a fleet to Troy,
Nor did I desecrate Anchises' ghost or ashes.
With stone-stopped ears, he will not hear my words. He rushes
Off, but where? Oh, he should grant his lover one
Last favor: wait for better winds. *Then* he can run.   430
I do not plead the once-true wedlock he's undone,
Nor ask that he resign fine Latium and his realm.
My frenzy begs for rest and peace, some space and time,
Till Fortune schools my battered soul to grief. My plea
Is for this one last grace (oh, sister, pity me).   435
When he assents, his recompense comes as I die."[16]

Such were the prayerful tears that Anna went to cry
Before him, sobbing, sobbing. But no tears can move
Aeneas. Adamant, he'll hear no words of love.
Fate stands its ground; the god deafens his gentle ear.   440
(Picture the northern Alpine winds, blowing now here,
Now there, contending which will tear an ancient oak
Made robust by its years. A roar comes like a stroke;
Wind shakes the trunk as high leaves scatter till they choke
The ground. But still the tree hangs on. As high as it   445
Shoots heavenward, roots plunge toward Tartarus's pit.)[17]

Such tireless appeals assail the hero, battered
On all sides, deeply grieving as his heart lies shattered.
But still his will stands strong; her sobbing has not mattered.

And then indeed did Dido, shaken by her fortune,   450
Weary of the sight of heaven's dome, importune
Death. And to fulfill her plan to leave this light,
She saw, while altar offerings burned incense-bright
(Awful to speak!), the holy waters turn to black,
The wine pour out as loathsome gore.

                                 She kept this back   455
From everyone, including Anna—each dark sign.
And more than this: there was a marble palace shrine
She tended (with a wondrous honor) for Sychaeus,
Draping it in ritual fronds and snowy fleece.
She seemed to hear his voice, his words, come from that place   460
Each night, when darkness draped the world. The dirge-like song
A lone owl on the rooftop sang complained in long,[18]
Low, mourning notes. Besides, a clutch of prophecies
Of ancient seers now fills her heart with dread, till she's
Convinced Aeneas comes—Aeneas!—to her dreams.   465
He hounds her in her frenzy, as she always seems
To be abandoned. Always left alone, she runs
Down endless desert trails to find her Tyrians
(The way crazed Pentheus sees the Eumenides,
A pair of suns, and two Thebes looming. Or else she's   470
Like Agamemnon's son, Orestes, whipped cross-stage,
Fleeing his mother's torches, snakes, and burning rage,
While vengeful Dirae squat in doorways.

                                   So, when grief
Had conquered her, and death become her one relief,
Mad Dido meant to die, and telling no one, planned   475

The when and how. She went to grieving Anna, and
Disguising death with calm looks and a hopeful brow,
Said, "Sister, wish me joy, for I have found out how
To either get him back or free me from this passion.
Somewhere near the setting sun—the bound of Ocean—   480
Lies Ethiopia. Great Atlas shoulders heaven
There, its sphere all studded with the starry levin.
I've met with a Massylian priestess from there; she's
The warder of the shrine of the Hesperides.
She feeds the dragon tidbits, guards the sacred boughs,   485
Strews dewy honey, and to make the dragon drowse,
Poppies. She claims her charms can free the heart she chooses
Or savage it with agonies the charm infuses.
She dams a river's course. Her magic retrogrades
The stars and stirs the spell-bound nighttime's deadly shades.   490
You'll feel earth rumble underfoot, the ash trees climb
Down from the mountainsides. I swear to you that I'm
Using her skills unwillingly—and by the higher
Powers and your dear life. Now, build a secret pyre
Beneath the courtyard sky, then pile it with that hero's   495
Weapons hanging in my room; heap all his gear,
And with that bridal bed I perished on, I'll rid
Myself of all that wretch's traces, as she bid."

The speech is done, and though her visage drains to white,
Anna cannot conceive that with this devious rite   500
Dido intends her death. She thinks that there will be
Despair no worse than at Sychaeus' death, so she
Prepares to do what she's been told.

But Dido, when that courtyard pyre mounted—heaped
With cut-down ilex and with kindling—wreathed and draped   505
It in funereal fronds. Atop the bed she lays
His clothes, his image, and the sword he wore in days

Now past. She knows what's coming. Altars surround
The thunder-calling priestess with her hair unbound.
Three hundred gods are summoned: triune Hecate,   510
With Erebus and Chaos and Diana (three-
Faced virgin). From Avernus (or supposedly),
Waters are flung; next, herbs searched out, and bronze-cut stalks
Ill-met by moonlight, swollen with poison—black milk's.
She stole a foal's caul (charm to win a lover's vow)   515
Before the mother ripped it from his brow.

With sacred hands and meal, before the altars now,
One foot unsandaled, Dido kneels, her robe untied.
She calls on stars and gods to see that she'll have died
A death foretold. And then, if any just and caring   520
Gods watch over lovers mismatched in their sharing,
She prays to them.

              Then, night—and everywhere, life's sleep
Of peace; the woods lay still, and quiet tamed the deep.
In restful dark, the stars, half through their arc, roll round.
Across hushed fields, the birds and cattle make no sound.   525
(Birds nest beneath the night, both in the tangled brakes,
And far afield, haunting the silent, limpid lakes.)
[There is ms(s). authority for a missing line here—528.][19]

Not the Phoenician queen. Her bed a rack, she lies
Awake, and cannot melt the night deep in her eyes   530
Or heart. Her raging love resurges and redoubles,
Convulsive passions heaving in a sea of troubles.

Writhing within, she thinks how to begin. And then:
"What shall I do? Mocked, taunted, do I test again
My former Nomad suitors? Meekly beg those men   535

For marriage, when I scorned them for so long as mates?
Or follow Ilium's fleet, obeying the dictates
Of Teucrians? Because they're glad I helped them months
Ago? In thoughtful thanks for comfort given once?
But who—assuming that I even wanted to— 540
Would take one so despised? Dido-Perdita, do
You see? Laomedon has spawned pure treachery
And pride. *What*, then? Attend their crews, who with such glee
Now sail off? Gather round me all my Tyrian band
In chase—Sidonian men I barely could command 545
To leave their city once? Tell *them* to hoist their sail?
No. Die, as you deserve, and end all this travail
With steel. Sister my tears won; sister: all these woes
You gave my half-mad heart, then drove me on my foes.
If I could live sin-free—no marriage bed, still chaste; 550
A dumb beast, with no sorrows I would have to taste!
I swore faith to Sychaeus' ashes, but I failed."
So Dido's heart was rent; she moaned and wept and wailed.

Aeneas, meanwhile—plans assured, all ships detailed—
Was snatching fitful sleep, high in his vessel's stern, 555
When there appeared the god. His image, on return,
Was as before, his face the same. Like Mercury
In everything—the god's voice and complexion—he
Was blond and young and boyish-lithe . . . but come to warn:
"How can you sleep through all this danger, goddess-born? 560
Unmindful of your peril, don't you see that from
Now on, you're set about? The breathing Zephyrs hum
For you, while *she* is fixed on death, and tries to fashion
Crime and plot deceit; she stirs storm-surging passion.
Why won't you fly from here, headlong, while you still can? 565
Soon you will see torn planks littering the boiling span
Of waters, burning brands, and shorelines all ablaze,

If you're still here at dawn, still mired in delays.
Break clean—now! Women always change in all their ways."[20]
When done, he melted and dissolved himself in night.   570

That's when Aeneas knew the terror of that sight.
He rips himself from sleep and stirs his slumbering crew:
"Get up! And race to man the thwarts. Quick, men! Undo
The sails, and hear me now: a god came from the sky
To spur us once again to rush to sea, to fly   575
From here. Cut free the hawsers. We will follow you,
O holy god, and do what you command us to.
Be with us; lend your grace until the night sky shines
With favoring stars."

                    He stopped, then slashed the mooring lines,
His broad blade flashing from its scabbard. A like zeal,   580
As all make haste to leave, is what his comrades feel,
Hurrying from the shore. And then their ships conceal
The sea completely. Leaning into oars, they chop
The foam and sweep that deep blue face.

                              Now getting up,
Aurora leaves Tithonus' golden bed of night,   585
Making earth glow. When towered Dido saw the light,
And all the port now stripped clean of Aeneas' fleet,
And all the ships at sea in squared array, she beat
Her lovely breast three times, then four times, as she tore
Her tawny hair and cried, "Shall he escape our shore,   590
Great Jove? An alien sailing off in mockery
Of Carthage? Why do we not chase them down the sea,
Those Trojans? We could rip their ships right from the docks.
Get swords and torches! Pull the dead oars from their locks!
What am I saying! Where am I? Have I gone mad?   595

O Dido, wretched from those things the gods forbade,
Back *then*, when you were offering him the crown was when . . .
Now see his 'faith,' a man (they say) whose gods have been
His burden—one who's borne a sire who'd reached his time.
I could have had Aeneas shredded limb from limb   600
And strewn across the waves, with all his men. Quite able
To, I could have killed Ascanius for Aeneas' table!
And yet . . . that issue might have been in doubt. What then?
Death-doomed, why fear? I should have slaughtered all his men
And torched his camp and burned his decks, extinguishing   605
Father and son—their whole race—finally to fling
My body on the pyre. World-scanning Sun, whose beams
See all, and Juno (you know all my wretched shames),
And Hecate (all cities wail your triple names
At midnight crossroads), and you vengeful Furies, all   610
Elissa's death-gods, hear me! Grant me what I call
For—justice! Look down on my misery. If that
Vile man must reach his haven's shore; if that is what
Great Jove demands, dead-set on that result; then may
Aeneas be beset by war, cast far away   615
From Troy to face a warlike race, and, wrested from
His son's embrace, cry out for help that will not come,
And watch his friends all slaughtered. Then, when he's constrained
By savage peace terms, may the land he would have reigned
In be denied him. Let him die before his day,   620
Unburied, on the sand. With these last words, I pray,
And with this blood I bleed. Then, Tyrians, may you harry
Him and his with hate—yes, all his heirs—and carry
That tribute to my bones. Between us, let there come
No love nor league. And may some nemesis rise from   625
These ashes, torching, killing Dardan settlers all
Through time, at every chance. Gods, hear my dying call—
That Punic waves should clash with Trojan waves; that shores

Should battle with each other in unending wars,
And armies battle. They and theirs shall know no peace."   630

Thus Dido grew impatient for her life's release.[21]
She quickly turned to Barce, dear Sychaeus' nurse
(Since back in Tyre, death's black ashes covered hers):
"Dear Barce: bring my sister Anna here. Quick, scurry!
Tell her to bathe herself in clear spring water. Hurry!   635
Have her bring altar victims and sin offerings.
You, too, must wear the ritual bands. Do all these things,
For I intend to carry out the sacred rite
Of Stygian Jove that I've begun, and end my plight.
I mean to burn that Dardan pile of vain manhood."   640

So Dido said. The nurse sped off (as best she could),
Zealous to please. The queen, though, quaked at what she meant
To do. Her bloodshot eyeballs rolled. Her cheeks, all sprent
With red, went deadly pale and quivered as she rushed
The pyre in the deepest palace room, and, flushed   645
With fury, mounted high, then drew his Dardan sword
(This use for such a gift, she never had implored
Him for). Then seeing one last time his Ilian clothes
And that familiar bed, she faltered in the throes
Of her distress, collapsed upon the sheets, and spoke   650
Her life's last words:

                    "While Fate allowed, I loved this cloak.
Now take my soul, and from these sorrows, set me free.
I've lived; the course is run that Fortune granted me.
My shade will pass down into earth with majesty.
I've built these mighty city walls that all may see,   655
Avenged my husband by the price I made them pay—
My brother and my foe. Oh, happiness; oh, way

Past happiness, if Dardan keels had never touched
These shores!"

        That was her cry, face down upon the couch.
"I may die unavenged, but let me die—my pleasure,   660
Hell. That vicious Dardan's eyes can drink full measure
Of this fire from the deep—and take my death
Sign with him."

        Even mid-word, in her utmost breath,
Her maids saw Dido plunge that sword breast-deep, its blade
All bathed in blood, her hands all spattered. Screaming made   665
The rooftops echo. Rumor riots; Carthage reels
In shock. The palace roars with keenings, groans, and wails
As women ululate. The heavens ring with cries,
As if they watch while ancient Tyre or Carthage dies,
Burned down in ruin before some enemy's attack,   670
As flames run wild, the roofs of men and gods gone black.

Breathless, the frightened Anna ran on through the crowd.
She beat her breast with fists, and with her nails she clawed
Her cheeks. Calling her dying sister's name, she cried
Out, "Dido, what was all this for? Why did you hide   675
The meaning that this pyre and altar stone implied?
O sister, what shall I grieve first? I'm left forlorn
Who should have shared your fate. Dying, why did you scorn
Me when this sword's blade should have done for both, and borne
Us off? And did I build this pyre and call upon   680
Our fathers' gods so you could perish all alone?
Oh, you've destroyed yourself, this place, its people—*me*!
You've ended the Sidonian Senate. Grant this plea,
You gods: may tears now wash her wounds, and lips catch up
Whatever final breath floats over her."

                       She stopped   685
Atop the steps, embracing her near-lifeless sister,
Then wept, her robe soaked red with blood as she caressed her.
Trying to lift her eyes, Elissa sank to rest
Each time, gore from the deep gash frothing from her breast.
She fought to raise herself, but with wild, rolling eyes,   690
Fell back three times as she sought out the radiant skies.
Struggling, she searched for light, and when she saw it, sighed.

Then mighty Juno pitied one so sorely tried
So long by pain, in death's long-drawn-out throes. She sent
Iris to earth to free from life's imprisonment   695
That struggling soul. (For since the queen died not by fate,[22]
Nor by some hard-won death, but long before her date,
In misery, enflamed by passion, Proserpine
Had not yet cut the golden lock that would consign
This corpse to Stygian Orcus.)

                     Dewy Iris flew   700
On saffron wings to Dido, trailing every hue
Before the sun. She stopped and said, "I take from you,
This lock that's pledged to Dis. Your flesh has now been freed."
So Iris cut, and watched the vital life's blood bleed,
And saw the soul rise in the wind and then recede.[23]   705

Book V

Meanwhile, mid-sea, Aeneas kept his ships on track
Before the North Wind, tacking through great waves blown black.
As Carthage burned, he *looked* back, never *sailing* back.
Tragic Elissa's fires glow, their kindling spark
Unguessed at by the Trojans, though the cruel mark   5
Profaned love leaves, and knowing what such stark mad love
Can do—those things a woman is capable of—
Made Trojans dread.

           At sea, no landscape meets the eye,
But water everywhere, and everywhere the sky.
Then overhead, a pot-black cumulus. It loomed   10
Up full of night and storm, waves shuddering, dark, and doomed,
Till even pilot Palinurus,[1] from the high
Stern calls out: "Clouds! What clouds surround the heavens! Why?
Neptune, what do you mean to do?" That was his cry,
And then, with rigging down, he calls all hands to row,   15
Turns from the wind, and speaks:

                    "Great-souled Aeneas: no,
Not even Jupiter, with all his guarantees,
Could show us Italy beneath such skies as these.
The traitor winds now rise against us, roaring loud
Out of the jet-black west; air masses into cloud.   20
Against such gales, we cannot hope to fight or win.
Since Fortune is the victor here, let us give in
By altering course. Sicanian ports are close at hand,

I think, and if I'm right, Eryx, your brother's land.
As I retrace the stars, may memory not fail."   25

Then good Aeneas said, "I've watched us fight to sail.
Change course now, since it's clear the stubborn winds insist.
Why struggle on this way? It's futile to resist.
Where could it please me more to steer this fleet so wearied
Than back to where my sire Anchises' bones are buried   30
In sacred soil—there where Dardan Acestes lives?"—

His words. They run for shore, as favoring Zephyr gives
Their canvas breath and ships slice cleanly through the sea.
At length, they head for well-known sands, and gratefully
Rejoice.

　　　　But far off on a crest, Acestes marvels   35
At these arrivals, runs to greet the friendly carvels.
In Libyan bearskin, he wields spears. (Riparian
Crinisus, from a Trojan mother, was the one—
A god—who got him.) Mindful of that ancestry,
He warmly greets these kin; help, hospitality,   40
And rustic riches greatly ease their weary plight.

When at the next day's early dawn, fresh orient light
Dispels the stars, Aeneas, all up and down the beach,
Summons his men, then from a hillock, makes this speech:
"Great Dardan sons, high heirs of heaven's noble race: 45
With passing months, one sun has circled back in place
Since earth received my godly father's bones and blessed
The altar stones of grief and honor. Now, my best
Reckoning says that day has come I'll always keep
In mournful honor, as God wills. Exiled on deep   50
Gaetulian Syrtes' sands, or caught out on the Gulf
Of Argolis—yes, even if I found myself

Inside Mycenae—still, with rites I would revere
Him as I vowed, and load the altars every year
With solemn offerings.

           Now, beside his very ashes   55
We stand—and not, I'm sure, against high Heaven's wishes
Or its will, blown to this friendly haven. Come,
Then: let us all perform glad sacrifice, with solemn
Honors as we pray for winds, and may he grant
My city's founding. Each year, as his celebrant,   60
I'll do for him his temple rites. Acestes, who
Descends from Troy, gives oxen—two to every crew;
Call your Penates to the feast, and *his* gods, too.
And if a ninth Aurora brings fair light to men,
So that her loving rays discover earth again,   65
I'll sponsor Trojan games.² Our swift ships will compete
First, then those sprinters who are fastest on their feet;
Strong javelin men; then archers boasting 'none can best us.'
Next: boxers bold enough to wear the leather cestus.
Let all step up, contesting for the victor's palm.   70
But wreathe your temples first, and stand in reverent calm."

When done, he wraps his mother's myrtle round his brow.
Then Helymus does likewise, and Acestes, now
An aged man. Ascanius, too, then all the boys.
Aeneas went among the thousands and their noise   75
Then, through the great throng's midst, and reached the burial
   mound.
With proper form, he pours libations on the ground:
Two cups of unmixed wine, two cups of fresh milk, two
Of victims' blood.

           Then sprinkling blooms of red and blue,
He speaks: "Hail, blessed father's ashes saved from fire—   80
In vain. I hail again your soul and spirit, Sire.

Fate would not let *us* hunt the shores of Italy
Or seek 'Ausonian Tiber'—whatever that be."

He'd barely done when from the altar's plinth a slick
Snake, trawling seven giant coils wound seven-thick,   85
Wrapped placidly about the mound and glided through
The altar grounds. His back was flecked with spots of blue,
His scales all spangled gold, like cloud-set rainbows throwing
Their thousand, arcing, shifting hues against the glowing
Sun.[3]

    Aeneas was amazed by what he'd seen.   90
At length, the long-tailed snake went gliding off between
The cups and bowls, sampling the food, then harmlessly
Slid back beneath the tomb, leaving the altars he
Had come from. Quickly starting up his father's rite,
Aeneas doubts: Was that the genius of the site?   95
His father's spirit?

    In due sacrifice, he kills
Two sheep, two black-backed heifers, and two swine, then spills
The flat-bowled wine, invoking great Anchises' shade,
His soul sent back from Acheron. Each comrade made
Glad offerings, too, from each according to his store.   100
(Some slaughter ritual heifers, loading more and more
Upon the altars; others stretch out, having set
Up cauldrons coaled for cooking viscera *en brochette*.)

The longed-for day had come; the steeds of Phaëthon,
Nine days elapsed, had charged in with the cloudless dawn.   105
Their happy numbers filling up the shore, folk came
From all around, drawn by Acestes' honored name.
Some wished to see the Trojans, some to strive for green
Garlands. (Inside the course, fine prizes could be seen:
Talents of gold and silver; purple cloaks deep-dyed;   110

Sacred tripods; armor; palms for those who vied.)
Then from a central mound, the trumpeters proclaim
The games begun.

        First come four ships almost the same
Adjudged for speed. Each heavy-oared, they are the cream
Of all the fleet. Then Mnestheus comes, who gave his name   115
To the Memmians (Italian *Mnestheus* soon to be).
His eager crewmen man the *Monster-of-the-Sea*,
While Gyas drives *Chimaera* (city-huge in bulk).
In triple banks, young Dardan men propel this hulk,
Three rows of rowers for three rows of heavy oars.   120
Eponymous Sergestus stands at the *Centaur's*
Helm (he named the Sergian line). Cerulean blue:
The *Scylla* of Cloanthus. (Cluentius, to
That man, your Roman name is due.)[4]

        Where breaker suds
Swell up, far off, a battered rock lies. Sometimes, floods   125
Gulp it when stars are cloud-cloaked as the North wind scuds.
In calm times quiet, it will rise amid these lulls
To make a sunny, welcome spot for basking gulls.

Father Aeneas set a sailors' marker there:
An ilex frond for green goal, so they'd know just where—   130
On such a lengthy course—to make their home-stretch turn.
Places assigned by lot, each captain stood his stern,
Far-shining in a golden purple glory. Coiled
Poplar leaves crown the crew, all naked-shouldered, oiled,
And glistening.

        They sit the thwarts, arms strained against   135
The oars, and wait the signal—pulsing, anxious, tensed
To win; nerves pump their drumming hearts. And when the sounding
Tucket sounds, each straining ship can't wait, but bounding

Forth, resounds with sailors' shouts that reach high Heaven.
Arms strain to pull.

               Calm churns to foam in furrows riven   140
Equally by all four ships, as all the sea
Convulses, rips, and bursts; the oar-blades bite, and three-
Beaked bows. (Far faster than the two-horse chariot races.
Teams take the field, then pour out from their starting places.
Not half so wildly does the driver crack the reins   145
That curve above his plunging horses as he leans
Forward, whip cracking.) Clapping men exclaim; the cries
Of cheering partisans ring out against the skies
As forest groves and half-moon-harbor sands resound
(Men's voices roll, drumming the hills with giant sound).   150

It's Gyas out ahead; he cuts the waves to skim
Forward amid the roar; Cloanthus chases him
(He's better crewed, but held back by the bulky pine
He sails). Then comes the churning *Monster-of-the-Brine*;
The *Centaur*, too. Both strain to head the racing line.   155
It's now the *Monster*, now the *Centaur* narrowing
The gap, then both bows pulling even, harrowing
The salt deep with their lengthy keels.

                    Now they were near
The rocky turning point, when Gyas, in the clear,
Ahead all through the race, called out, "Menoetes! Steer   160
Us back; you're far too wide to starboard! Why? Hug tight
Against the rocky edge and come around from right.
Our portside blades should almost give the rocks a shearing.
Let others keep to open sea."

                   He spoke, but fearing
For hidden crags, Menoetes wrenched the rudder, veering   165
Out to sea. "Menoetes, watch your course! You're out

Too far. Head for the rocks," was Gyas' anguished shout,
Correcting him, when look!—he sees Cloanthus right
Behind—left, toward the rocks, inside his course.

                                     Now tight
Between, he's scraping by, then suddenly he's past   170
Gyas. He rounds the turn to safe sea, sailing fast.
Then Gyas raged for sure, a fire in the bone.
Cheeks tearing amply, and now careless of his own
Pride and the safety of his crew, he flings the nervous
Menoetes headlong from the stern and moves to serve as   175
His own commander-helmsman.

                         Urging on his men,
He turns the rudder shoreward. But Menoetes—when
At last he'd barely lumbered from the deep, an old
Man soaking in his dripping clothes—finally got hold
Of the dry rock that he had swum for, and sat down.   180
The Teucrians, who'd laughed to see him almost drown,
Laughed now to see him vomit brine.

                         Those in the rear,
Mnestheus and Sergestus, entertaining here
A spark of hope, exult: the wayward Gyas may
Be overtaken! Then Sergestus shoots his way   185
Ahead of Mnestheus as he nears the rocks. He's out
Ahead by half a boat-length as the *Monster*'s snout
Comes nosing closer.

                 Pacing mid-ships through his crew,
Mnestheus urges, "Now! *Now*, Hector's comrades! To
Your oars, you men I chose in Ilium's final hour.   190
You're *my* men now, and now's the time to show that you're
That strong, brave crew that rowed right through Gaetulian sands,
Malea's chasing waves, Ionia's expanse

Of sea. I, Mnestheus, can no longer hope to win,
But, oh! (I pray that Neptune's favorite triumphs in   195
This race), to come in last would be a sheer disgrace.
Avoid that only, countrymen! Fight for third place!"

They lean in, sinews straining. Great strokes shake the stern
Of brass, as sea flies under. Mouths and muscles burn
As rapid panting rocks them; sweat runs down in streams.   200

But then, pure chance provides the glory of their dreams:
For as Sergestus ran in tight with reckless force,
The rock-ward prow committed to this dangerous course,
His luck ran out. The ship struck on a sharp crag—hard—
With oars all splintered as the jutting shards were jarred.   205

The smashed-in prow now hung there as the sailors leapt
Up, shouting at this grim delay. They grab pikes tipped
With iron, wield sharp-pointed poles, or fish the sea
For shattered oars.

                    But Mnestheus, cheered by this debris,
Takes heart. He calls upon the winds, then with his oars   210
At utmost speed, heads for the sloping waves and soars
Off down the open sea. He does this like a dove
That's suddenly been startled from her pock-marked cave.
(She leaves her darling fledglings in their pigeonholes,
And scared away, takes off with beating wings. She rolls   215
Across the fields and soon is coasting liquid air,
Skimming her placid way, as steady pinions shear.)

So Mnestheus. So the *Monster*'s sheer momentum heaves
Her flying down the final stretch, as first he leaves
Behind Sergestus, struggling on the high rock, run   220
Aground in shallows, shouting for help (there is none,

As *he* begins to learn to row with broken blades),
Then huge *Chimaera*. Gyas' hulking vessel fades
Away, bereft of any helmsman.

                              Near the goal
Now (Mnestheus chasing him), Cloanthus' is the sole   225
Ship left to pass. He does his utmost, strives with main
And might. Then all the clamor doubles up again
Against the sky; men cheer the chaser with their din.

Cloanthus' crew would be ashamed should they not win.
Clenching their honor gloriously earned, they'd trade   230
Their very lives for it. Cheered on by progress made,
The other crew is strong because they *think* they're so.

Now neck and neck, they might have won. Cloanthus, though,
Palms to the sea, implored the gods to hear his vow:
"You gods across whose deep-sea realm I race my prow,   235
I'll gladly keep my word by setting on this shore
A bright white bull before your altars, and I'll pour
Your salt sea steaming victim's guts and streaming wine."

He spoke, and every Nereid heard him in the brine.
Phorcus' chorus heard him—chaste Panopea, too.   240
Then sire Portunus,⁵ with his own great hand, half-threw
The ship ahead. Faster than South Wind it sped, even
Faster than feathered arrow, landward to its haven.

And then Anchises' son called all within their hearing,
By herald's cry, and wreathed Cloanthus' brow, declaring   245
Him the winner of the crown of green-leaved bay.
Aeneas tells him he should choose and take away
Prizes for every ship: a silver talent; three
Bulls; wine. He gives each captain special dignity.

The victor wins a golden-threaded cloak, around   250
Which Meliboean purple, deeply double-wound,
Weaves in that royal boy[6] on leafy Ida, spear
In hand and running down the quickly tired deer.
(He's like some eager panter. Jove's bolt—lightning-hooked—
His eagle clasps, then grasps from Ida's crags, in crooked   255
Hands, the boy. *His* agèd guardians plead in vain,
Palms to the stars; dogs bay the skies in savage strain.)

Aeneas gives to second place, to have and hold,
A coat of mail that polished hooks of triple gold
Clip up. (He ripped this prize off Demoleos once,   260
Winning both glory and a soldier's strong defense
That day by Simois, beneath high Ilium. But
The bearers Phegeus and Sagaris could not
Hold up its many folds on struggling shoulders. Wrapped
Inside it, Demoleos drove pell-mell the hapless,   265
Scattered Trojans then.) He makes third prize a pair
Of brazen cauldrons and some cups rough-chased in rare
Silver.

    Now everyone was gifted, trophy-proud,
When, as they went, all being purple-fillet-browed,
The crippled ship got free. Hard work had helped it clear   270
The murderous rocks, though losing an entire tier
Of oars.

    Bringing his ship in as the people jeer,
Sergestus lands shamefaced. The way a snake, surprised
And crushed beneath a brazen wheel, or pulverized
Out on the highway by a traveler's stone and left   275
Half-dead, will writhe in vain, twist strung-out coils, and lift
His hissing neck, his eyes on fire; part defiant,
Part wounded, wriggling lame and slow, he wraps his pliant

Body round itself and struggles on, though crimped:
That's how the oarless vessel of Sergestus limped.   280

Canvas up, though, into the harbor's mouth he sails.
Aeneas gives Sergestus, for his ship's travails,
His due reward (he's pleased the ship is safe, the crew
Home free). He wins a woman, Pholoë—one who
Can weave; a Cretan suckling baby twins.

                                        Now, good   285
Aeneas, with this contest over, climbs where wood
And curving hill compass a meadowland. And at
The valley's very center, on its grassy plat:
The circuit of a theatre.

                        He sits down here,
Amidst his thousands, on a raised-up seat. The hero   290
Challenges any who might want to run a race,
Luring keen sprinters with fine prizes set in place.
Sicanians mixed with Trojans come from everywhere,
Euryalus and Nisus foremost.
(The first was famed for blooming youth and being fair;   295
Nisus for loving him.) Next after these, the fine
Diores, regal, and of Priam's noble line.
Salius then, with Patron, at the same time came
(One Acarnanian and one of Tegean fame,
Arcadian-born). Two young men then, both forest-hearty—   300
Trinacrian Helymus and Panopes, the party
Of old Acestes. There were many more besides,
Whose memory the darkness of the ages hides.

Aeneas spoke out to them: "Take these words to heart
And mind: you all shall have a prize when you depart.   305
To each: two steel-head Gnosian arrows brightly buffed,

And a chased axe with double blades to carry off—
All these for every man. The first three places, though,
Win more (and wear pale olive wreaths about their brow):
A courser well-caparisoned goes to first place;   310
Next earns a quiver full of arrows made in Thrace—
An Amazonian quiver hanging from a wide
Gold belt that's jewel-clasped. Third should be satisfied
To carry off this Argive helmet."

                    So he spoke.
Each took his place, and at the sudden signal, broke,   315
Sprinting from the start line. Like storm-clouds, they burst
Forth. Focused, every man thought he would finish first.
It's Nisus flashing far ahead of everyone,
Though—faster than the winds or winged lightning can run.
Next, but behind by lengths, comes Salius. In third place,   320
Pursuing both, but with an even greater space
Between, Euryalus.
Euryalus is chased by Helymus. And just
Behind, Diores flies, as heel and toe kick dust
And Helymus keeps looking back. A longer race   325
Leaves all in doubt—or else Diores in first place.

But then, the end in sight, and runners panting for
The finish, Nisus slips in sacrificial gore—[7]
The grass and ground all soaked and slicked in slaughtered steer
Blood, slime, and crud. No matter how exultant, here   330
The boy could not hold on; the flailing, tottering steps
He tries to print the ground with fail, and down he slips,
Face down in all the dung-mixed mire of sacrifice.

And yet he thought of his Euryalus. For Nisus
Rose from where he lay, and smack in Salius' way   335
He threw himself. Then Salius tumbled prone, a-splay

On inspissated sand, and by this lucky grace,
Euryalus shoots past . . . and wins. He takes first place,
Jogging on through to cheers. Next, Helymus comes trailing;
Then third, Diores. Then Salius comes up, roaring, railing;   340
Fills the theatre's assembly, dins the front-
Row elders. Where's his prize that Nisus' cheating stunt
Has stolen? Most back Euryalus (his manly grace—
And tears—show finely in his form and handsome face).
Diores backs him loudly, too, for having come   345
In third, he knows he'll lose his accidental palm
If Salius has the highest prize bestowed on him.

It's then Aeneas Pater says, "Your trophies stand
Assured, boys; how you finished, none may countermand.
But let me ease the plight of an unlucky friend."   350

He gives to Salius a great Gaetulian
Cat's pelt (thick hair and golden claws weigh down that skin).
Then Nisus: "If this is the pitied loser's prize,
Then what fit winner's trophy ought to go to Nisus?
By my own merit, shouldn't first prize come to me,   355
If Fortune doesn't fail me in its enmity—
Like Salius?"

    Showing his fouled face all the while,
His arms be-slicked with slime, he won Aeneas' smile.
That best of fathers had a shield brought out (the fine
Work Didymaon did, torn down from Neptune's shrine   360
By Greeks once). This he gives—a prize fit for a lord—
To Nisus.

    Then, the races run and each reward
Doled out, Aeneas cries, "Let those brave men of stout
Heart raise their hands in cestuses to fight their bout!"

So he declares, as double prizes are set out   365
For boxing. There's a ribboned steer that's draped in gold
To win; but with a sword and helmet he's consoled
Who loses.

            First up: Dares, flexing every muscle.
He leaps in for the fight, amidst the murmuring bustle
Of the crowd. Yes, Dares, who alone would fight   370
With Paris—and the very man who at the site
Of mighty Hector's grave knocked Butes out (who came
From Amycus' Bebrycian line), as his huge frame
Lurched forward. Dares left him dead on yellow sand.

And that was Dares—first to raise his head and stand   375
To fight. He preens his yard-wide shoulders, jabbing right
And left while boxing air—blows in a shadow fight.
The crowd yields no opponent; not a man-jack dares
To tie the gloves on and go toe-to-toe with Dares.

So . . . confident that no one wants to win the stakes,   380
He stands before Aeneas, tired of waiting; takes
The bull's horn in his left hand. Here's the speech he makes:
"O goddess-born, if no man's rising to the bait,
Then how much longer do I need to stand and wait?
Let me lead this bull away." The Dardans all   385
Agreed. "Aeneas: clearly, Dares wins this brawl!"

At this, Acestes castigates Entellus, who
Sat by him on a green and grassy couch: "Once, you
Were bravest of all heroes (though in vain). And yet,
Entellus, you'll allow a prize like this to get   390
Away without a fight? *Now* where's immortal Eryx,
Once your famous master? What of your heroics

Known through all Trinacria, your spoils suspended
In your house?"

                    And the response: "Fear hasn't ended
My pride, and still I yearn for fame. In truth, my blood   395
Is cold, my vigor gone, slowed by senectitude.
My strength's worn down. But if I had what I once had—
What reckless Dares brags of; were I still a lad;
Then trust me, neither tempting prize nor handsome steer
Would make me stand and fight, nor trophies either. Here!"   400

And with that word he threw into the ring the pair
Of customary cestuses that Eryx wore
(That daunting fighter), thick hides stretched across his fore-
Arms. Every soul was stunned by seven folds of oxhides
Huge and stiff with iron, sewn with lead for boxing.   405
And dazzled most of all was Dares, who is loath
To fight. Anchises' great-souled scion turns them both
Over, inspecting how their heavy folds are tied.

Then old Entellus, speaking heart-deep words, replied:
"You men: if you had seen the gloves of Hercules—   410
That deadly fight here on these shores! And wielding these,
Your brother Eryx once . . . well, you can see the stains
From spattered blood, and leather flecked with bits of brains
Still. Standing tall, he faced Alcides wearing these.
With these, I boxed—before my blood began to freeze   415
And rob me of my strength; before time's jealousies
Snowed on my temples. But if these our gloves are feared
By Trojan Dares, and Aeneas, who's revered,
Agrees to equalize them, and my friend Acestes
Agrees, don't fear. I won't wear Eryx' cestuses.   420
Untie your Trojan gloves."⁸

Finished, Entellus threw
His two-fold mantle off his shoulders. Huge in thew
And limb and bone, he stood there in his naked brawn
Inside the ring.

Then father-like, Anchises' son
Found equal boxing gloves for both, then tied them on.   425
Quickly, those dreadnought fighters balanced on their toes
And put their fists up high, prepared for deadly blows.
Dodging each punch, they keep their heads aloft, back far,
While hand-to-hand, they mix it up and start to spar.
Relying on his youth, one dances round, dissembling;   430
The other—bulking massive, strong—is slowed by trembling
Knees. His big frame shakes; he gasps and pants in pain.

They launch a hundred hasty blows, but all in vain.
Rib cages rumble; chests drum; down the punches rain,
As fists go flickering around their ears and brows   435
In bunches. Hard rights rattle both their solid jaws.

Entellus stands there stolid in his frozen stance,
Defending, ducking, guarding by his lightning glance.
The other's like the sapper of some mountain town
Besieged; surrounding it, he tries to bring it down   440
By probing here and there for openings and faults;
By pressing everywhere, with varied, skilled assaults.

No use. Entellus, surging up, threw out a high
Right cross, but Dares saw it coming. Slipping by,
His agile, dodging body parried it with speed.   445
Entellus spent his strength on empty air. Indeed,
He fell in bulk, with ponderous force—a hulking crash
To earth, just like a hollowed, root-torn mountain ash
On Erymanthus or great Ida.

Then, a rush
Of startled Trojans and Trinacrians; their shout   450
Assaults the skies. Acestes runs to help him out
First, pitying a friend as old as he. He raises
Entellus, whom no falling nor delaying fazes.
Back in the fight and even fiercer, summoning
That manic force that fury, shame, and valor bring,   455
He rages, driving Dares all around the ring,
Redoubling his uppercuts, first lefts, then rights,
Without a stop. Blows come as thick as hail that smites
A roof; they rain down hard, in dense and clattering flurries.
With either hand, the hero harries rattled Dares.   460

Aeneas Pater, lest rage burn beyond control,
Or furious Entellus drive his frenzied soul
Any further, now saved poor Dares from the fight.
He ended it, then spoke these soothing words: "What might
Have made you wish this match? Consider now your plight: 465
Surely you see Entellus' strength was heaven-sent?
Give in then, to the gods. The fight is done; relent."

With weak knees dragging after him, his good friends led
Poor Dares to the ships, propping his rag doll head
That lolled this way and that. His mouth spat gore all clotted   470
With teeth and blood. His friends collected his allotted
Prize of sword and helmet.

But the palm and bull,
Entellus claims, exulting with a heart that's full
(Winning the beast means glory). "Goddess-born," he cries,
"*And* Trojans: see how strong I was once! Let your eyes   475
Take in the death you spared your Dares!" That was all.

Then staring in that bullock's face and standing tall
Before the matchless prize, he raised his right above
That stunning beast, and brought down hard the leaded glove.
Between the horns, brains scattered from the smashed-in skull.   480
Laid out in lifeless spasms on the ground: the bull.
Over its battered form, he cries out from the heart:
"Eryx, for Dares' life, this victim's better barter.
Time's champion now, I doff my gloves and end my art."

At once, Aeneas starts the archery assizes,   485
Inviting everybody as he sets out prizes.
With others, at Serestus' ship, Aeneas raises
Its mast, and from a cord he's fastened to that pole,
Suspends a fluttering dove to shoot at for a goal.

The men assemble as a fine bronze helmet swallows   490
The lots tossed in, and first, applauded by his fellows,
Hipocöon's is drawn—the son of Hyrtacus.
The recent boat-race winner follows—Mnestheus
(He wears a woven olive green wreath, Mnestheus).
Third comes Eurytion (*your* brother, celebrated   495
Pandarus. Once—ordered to—he violated
The truce with the Achaeans, shooting in their midst).
Deep in the helmet lay Acestes' lot—the last.
Yes, bold Acestes, set to show what young men show.

Then each, by main and might, begins to bend his bow;   500
They draw their arrows from their quivers, notch to string.
The first shot through the air leaves its cord quivering,
As Hyrtacus's arrow cuts the wind that stings,
Then hits its target; in the trembling pole, it clings.
The flustered, frightened dove starts fluttering its wings;   505
Around the crowded audience, the clapping rings.

Then hardy Mnestheus with his bent-back bow stood to,
And aiming high, aligned the arrow that he drew
Along his eye. Ill-sped, that arrow missed the bird
But sliced right through the knots and cut the twisted cord   510
By which her tethered foot hung from the towering mast.
Hunting Notus, she raced toward black-cloud overcast.

But quick Eurytion, his arrow nocked and bow
Long since prepared, now whispered, "Brother, hear my vow."
He aimed—and pierced the sky-free dove that had just now   515
Beaten her happy wings beneath a cloud of black.
She left the stars her life, and plummeting, brought back
The shaft that killed her. Now, despite the vanished prize,
Acestes—he alone was left—aimed for the skies
And launched his arrow high, to show them all an old   520
Man's skill . . . and thunderous twang.

                                              Then something that foretold[9]
The future suddenly appeared before their eyes:
A startling portent understood in later days,
When daunting seers would chant its meaning. Brightly arcing
Through the fluid clouds, the arrow left a sparking   525
Trail of flame, then died, snuffed out in thin blue air
(The way a shooting star, loosed from the sky's great claire,
Will often streak the firmament with streaming hair).

The stunned Trinacrians and Trojans stood stock-still,
Beseeching heaven. Great Aeneas read the will   530
Of Jove. He hugged Acestes, full of joy, then filled
His arms with gifts: "Take these. Olympus' king has willed
You special honors, father, as this sign has shown.
And you shall have such prizes for your very own
As venerable Anchises once possessed: a bowl   535

Bestowed on him by Thracian Cisseus (the whole
Work chased with figures) as a pledge of amity
And fit memento from his friend."

                       Done speaking, he
Takes fresh green laurel, crowns Acestes' brow, then turns
To hail him victor over all. And what he earns,   540
This chosen one, the good Eurytion won't envy,
Despite the fact *he* brought the dove down out of heaven.
Rewarded next: the man who cut the cord. And last,
The one whose speeding arrow stuck fast in the mast.

Aeneas Pater, with the contest barely done,[10]   545
Calls in Epytides, the friend and guardian
Of young Iulus. "Go," he tells this trusted, steady
Man, "and charge Ascanius—if he has ready
His cavalry cadets, and they've been drilled—to lead
Them in Anchises' honor, each boy on his steed,   550
And armed."

             Aeneas tells the crowding throng to heed
His orders—stand back, clear the field, and let the boys
Ride in. Their well-squared ranks gleam in their fathers' eyes,
As bridles shine. Trinacrians and Trojans hummed
Approval as they passed, hair crowned with garlands trimmed   555
Correctly. Each boy bears an iron-fitted spear
Of cornel. Some sling polished quivers; others wear
A golden torque high up around their collars, where
It wraps its pliant, twisted rings.

                     Three mounted groups
Formed out of double *chori* all rode in, their troops   560
Behind three captains, each resplendent in detached
Formations, all with leaders uniformly matched.
One happy battle-rank is led by little Priam,

Who carries on your line (his famed grandfather's name),
Polites—forbear of today's Italian race.   565
He's mounted on a dappled, white-flecked horse from Thrace,
With white socks flashing in its cantering, high-stepped pace,
And a white brow. Atys is next, whose long line wends
Its way down to the Latin Atii (best friends,
Iulus and the little Atys). Last—and best,   570
And riding a Sidonian horse—the handsomest
Of boys, Iulus. (Radiant Dido' gift, this steed—
A keepsake-pledge.) The rest ride horses of the breed
Agèd Acestes raised on Sicily.

The glad Dardanians cheer the nervous boys; they see   575
In these young faces, faces of their fathers. Then
The youngsters ride around the ring. Returned again,
They face their kin—and hear Epytides. His cry
And cracking whip, from far away—the signals by
Which all begins—have been awaited eagerly.   580
The boys peel off in equal ranks that split the three
Squads into *chori*, then at "recall," wheel, and lances
Leveled, charge.

       Next, riding over wide expanses,
They hoofprint shapes and counter-shapes, with circles drawn
In circles, playing rousing war games. Racing on,   585
They feign retreat, their backs exposed, or set their spears
To charge, then side-by-side, ride by in peaceful pairs.

All this is as it was in hilly Crete once, so
They say. The Labyrinth wound blinds, dead ends, and no-
Go paths—a thousand undetectable one-ways,   590
Where hints of exit broke up in an errant maze.

That's just the way the mounted Trojan youngsters weave,
Braiding their tracks in flight and fight, as dolphins cleave

Carpathian or Libyan seas in sport (they sew
The foaming waters, stitching cascades as they go).   595
The walls of Alba Longa built, Ascanius brought
Back cavalry displays like these—mock battles fought.
He taught them to the early Latin tribes, who taught
Their children how he'd done this with the youth of Troy.
Then Albans in *their* turn would train each Alban boy.   600
Ancestral honor guides Rome still, as they revere
Their fathers (Troops are "Trojan"; boys are "Troy"). And here
The games conclude their celebration of Anchises.

For Fortune broke their rites, precipitating crisis.
While sports do reverence at the tomb-site, Juno sends   605
Down Iris from the heavens on her favoring winds.
The rapt Saturnian has her scan the Ilian fleet,
For Juno bears an ancient grudge nothing can sate.

As Iris speeds along her bow—a thousand hues—
She rides its racing arc, a virgin no one views.   610
Examining the great assembly and the shore,
She spots the vacant harbor, noting score by score
Its empty ships. But Trojan women, where they keep
The lonely berm, mourn dead Anchises. As they weep,
Bewailing barren seas, they look out far, in deep.   615

"What waves remain for those worn down!" Their common plea?
A home, to rid them of the labors of the sea.
So in their midst, the troublemaker Iris flings[11]
Herself. Transforming robe and face, all goddess things,
She's Beroë, Tmarian Doryclus' old wife,   620
Who'd once had fame and name and family in her life.
She mingles with the Dardan mothers, masked this way.

"O wretches, whom Achaean hands" (cries "Beroë"),
"Had failed to drag to death beneath our native walls!
What ending for this folk on whom foul Fortune falls?   625
She's saved us seven summers now since Ilium fell,
And still our passage past each shore and through each swell
Doles out its endless stars and hostile rocks from Hell.
Wave-tossed, we chase an always-phantom Italy.
Here's Eryx, and Acestes' hospitality.   630
We want a city for our people. Who says no?
O Homeland!—and Penates rescued from the foe
In vain: Shall no town ever be called Troy again,
And Hector's Simois and Xanthus die to men?
No! Come and help me torch these wretched ships! Last night,   635
In sleep I saw the seer Cassandra's ghost.[12] The bright-
Blazing brand she held, she handed me. 'Seek Troy right here.
Your home is here and now,' she cried. So seize the day.
Neptune's four altars are a sign: no more delay!
The very god provides the flame and points the way."   640

And as she spoke, she grabbed the fire brutally,
And wildly brandished it where everyone could see,
Then hurled it. Minds inflamed, the Ilian women lost
Their wits. But not the eldest. Pyrgo, who had nursed
So many of the princely sons of Priam, cried   645
Out, "Mothers, she's not Beroë; this ghost has lied;
It can't be Doryclus' Rhoeteian wife. Can you
Not see the signs—the flashing eyes, the beauty, too—
That prove divinity? The voice. That goddess-face.
Consider how she moves, with such a stately grace.   650
I left the sickly Beroë behind just now,
Upset because alone she had no gift to vow
Honoring Anchises." So she cried.

The dubious matrons, though, were gazing stupefied;[13]
They gave the ships an evil eye, all undecided   655
Between this land and Italy, where Fate abided.
Then Iris rose on balanced wings up through the blue,
And broke her bow below the storm-clouds as she flew.
Past reason hunted are the brands no sooner had
From hearths, than women stunned by wonders run half-mad,   660
While others plunder altars, piling leaves and boughs
And brushwood on the flames. Unbridled, burning prows
And oars and thwarts, Vulcan devours the painted sterns.

Eumelus runs back, shouting that the fleet now burns.
And at Anchises' tomb, and from their seats, the Trojan   665
Throng look up to see a black ash-cloud in motion.
Ascanius reacts. From joyous leadership
Of "Troy," he spurs toward camp, giving his mount the whip.
The breathless captains can't restrain him. Pulling up
Before the fire: "Have you lost all sanity?   670
Oh, this is not some Argive camp, some enemy.
You burn your own best hope. I'm Iulus; can't you see?"

He threw down at their feet the empty helmet he
Had worn as war-games captain. Racing up, Aeneas
(And the troops—their rushed arrivals simultaneous)   675
Watched the wretched women scatter here and there,
All down the shore, or in the caves and woods, or where
They could. They cringe in shame and hide from daylight skies.
Chastened, they recognize their kin, then exorcise
Their hearts of Juno.

                    Even so, the flames would not   680
Abate. Below the wet oak, tow is blazing hot
And belching billowing smoke. The slow relentless heat
Burns through the frames, a smoldering plague with keels to eat.

Neither heroic strength nor floods of water aid
Them.

      Good Aeneas ripped his cloak off then and prayed   685
The gods for help, raising his outstretched hands: "O Great
God Jupiter, if it's not yet complete—your hate
For every Trojan—; should your ageless pity care
For mankind still; we ask that such compassion spare
Our burning fleet and save our tenuous Trojan state   690
From ruin. If we've earned this, though, then let your hate,
Your lightning, doom what ships remain; destroy us here
And now."

      No sooner said than drenching clouds appear—
Black, instant rain that soaks high hills and plains,
   which tremble
To all the thundering skies. The streaming floods assemble,   695
Roiling hard, and freighted dark with thick south winds.
The ships brim over, oak half-burnt; the fire ends.
Charred planks are soaked till all the smoke is gone and most
Ships saved (the scorching plague has meant four vessels lost).

Aeneas Pater, though, stunned by this bitter blow,   700
Now here, now there, churned through his heavy worries, fro
And to, heart-deep: Ignore his fate and settle down
In Sicily? Or look to found some Latian town?

Then aged Nautes—whom Tritonian Pallas taught
And rendered eminent by much wise art (she brought   705
Him answers: what the fury of the gods portended;
What the disposition of the Fates demanded)—
Consoles Aeneas: "Goddess-born, where destiny
Directs or leads us on, there we should follow; be
What may, the only way to overcome it is   710

To bear it. You've Acestes; forebears who are his,
That Dardan's, are divine. Invite his counsel as
A willing partner; cede to him the men who've lost
Their ships or fear your undertaking's heavy cost.
Select the old men and the women ocean-weary   715
And whoever in your band is weak and fearful.
Here will be the city where they'll find their rest.
With your permission, they can call the town Acesta."

Then truly warming to his old friend's words, he's torn
By all the carking worries that his heart has borne.   720
Now black Night, in her chariot, wore heaven's crown,
When suddenly Anchises' image glided down,[14]
It seemed, and from the sky began to speak: "My son,
More dear than life—when I *had* life—, Troy's come undone,
And you've been wrenched by what's befallen Ilium.   725
But I'm here, sent by Jove, who drove the fire from
Your fleet and pities you at last. Now, you should heed
The venerable Nautes' good advice and lead
To Italy your bravest hearts and best young men.
And you must overcome the Latian people then—   730
A stout race raised in ruggedness. But first, come down
To hellish Dis, and through Avernus, pit-profound,
Search out my counsel, son. I'm not in Tartarus,
With wicked, dismal shades, but rather in my house
In sweet Elysium's meeting-place. The Sibyl, chaste   735
And good, will bring you here when you have sacrificed
A host of black sheep, with their copious blood. Then you
Will learn your people's fate and what's been given to
Them for a town. Now go. Dank Night is half-way through
Her course; cruel Orient's panting team is almost here."   740

A puff of smoke, he'd spoken, wisping into air.[15]
Aeneas cries out, "Where do you rush off to? Where?

Who chases you and keeps you from a son's embraces?"
The words die out; he stirs the dormant fire's traces.
And with a heavy censer and the holy meal,   745
He worships Pergamus's Lares, drawn to kneel
Down humbly there at grey-haired Vesta's inner shrine.

Then quickly gathering all, he tells them Jove's divine
Command (Acestes first, though), then his father's word,
Last, what his heart's resolved. They're quick when they have heard 750
(Especially Acestes), listing women for
The city, with the willing men lined up on shore—
Folk craving no renown. Themselves, they re-equip
The oak thwarts, charred planks, oars, and rigging on each ship.
They're few, but fit to fight. Meanwhile, Aeneas ploughs   755
The city's outline and allots each man a house.
Some sites are "Ilium," others, "Troy," and to applause,
Trojan Acestes founds a forum, giving laws
To senators. Then, near the stars, on Eryx' crest,
He builds Idalian Venus' shrine. A sacred priest   760
And hallowed grove attend Anchises' final rest.

By now—nine days of feasting past, with offerings paid
Upon the altars and the zephyred waters laid—
The South Wind whispers, whispers, calling all to sail.
Along the curving sands, the women keen and wail,   765
As all embrace; they draw things out, one night, one day.

Then all those men and womenfolk who could not say
The names of savage seas are somehow keen to go—
To bear the burdens of poor refugees! Aeneas, though,
Consoles them with his good, kind words, and tearfully   770
Commends them to Acestes. Next, he orders three
Calves killed for Eryx' sake, and to the Storms he vows
A lamb. He orders hawsers cut, and with his brows

Bound up in well-trimmed olive leaves, Aeneas stands
There, distant in the bow, the wine-bowl in his hands.   775
He throws the entrails in the sea, then pours out wine.
A surging stern wind follows as they sweep the brine,
And striving crews contend to send them on their way.

But Venus, meanwhile, fraught with cares, has this to say
To Neptune as she pours her soul out: "Juno's fell   780
Antagonism and insatiate rage compel
Me, Neptune, to descend—to stoop—to every plea.
No healing time or pity softens Juno. She
Can never rest, or bow to fate or Jove's decree.
It's not enough that from the Phrygian people's midst   785
Her wretched hate devoured their Troy; that through the most
Extreme and utter vengeance she has dragged what's left
Of Troy, pursuing still the bones it's been bereft
Of. Only she knows why. But you yourself have seen
Of late the Libyan seas stirred by her sudden spleen,   790
Waves fused with sky. She used Aeolus' storms in vain,
And in your very realm!
See how her crimes have egged the Trojan matrons on?
How foully she has burned their fleet? With those ships gone,
She's forced them to abandon friends on alien shores.   795
I beg you—let what's left of them commit their oars
To you in safety. Let them—if my plea is fair,
And if the Fates will let them build their city there—
Attain Laurentian Tiber."

                    Saturn's sea-lord son:
"It's wholly right to trust me, O Cytherean,   800
Born from my seas—a trust I've earned. For often, I
Have curbed the raging madness of the sea and sky
And land. (Come, Simois and Xanthus: testify!)

I saved Aeneas when Achilles raced to smash
Against their walls the Trojan troops so sore-abashed,   805
And sent his thousands down to death, till rivers choked
And groaned, and Xanthus found his outlets all were blocked
(He could not roll to sea). That's when, as he prepared
To battle Peleus' brave son, I snatched and spared
Aeneas—in a cloud; no god's strength or his own   810
Would have availed. *This*, though I longed to tear Troy stone
From stone with hands that once had built that perjured town.
I'm steadfast still, no fear. You asked, and he shall make
Avernus' haven safe. But one, the sea will take
And you'll not find. For many lives, one man must die."[16]   815

The Ocean Sire sees his words now satisfy
The goddess, yokes his champing team in golden bands,
Snaffles the bits, and lets the reins flow in his hands.
His sea-blue chariot cuts the crests, waves sink, and under
The axle, swollen waters calm to hear its thunder.   820
Seas stilled, the clouds go running from the giant sky.
Then comes his sundry crew: huge whales go swimming by;
Next, Ino's son Palaemon, and old Glaucus' chorus,
With wave-swift Triton, and the company of Phorcus.
To port: Melite, Thetis, virgin Panopea,   825
With Thalia, Spio, Cymodoce, and Nesaea.

Seeing each one in turn, our sire is happily pleased.
Anxious Aeneas orders that the masts be raised
Quickly, the yards stretched full with sheets. At once, men set
The mainsails, left and right the same, and then they let   830
All canvas fall, while yardarms turn and turn again.
The pleasing breezes speed the fleet ahead, and then
The pilot Palinurus leads the solid file,
While all take up his heading, sailing out in style.

Along its path now, humid Night was halfway through   835
The sky. Relaxed and stretched out on their thwarts, each crew
Rested its limbs on hard benches. Stillness was all,
When Sleep slipped lightly from the stars to part the pall-
Dark air, dispelling gloom and hunting you (it bears
You, Palinurus, lethal dreams). All unawares   840
And guiltless!

      On the high stern sat the deity,
Looking like Phorbas, pouring out this treacherous plea:
"Iasus' scion Palinurus, surely seas
Can speed the fleet themselves with just a gentle breeze.
The hour's peaceful. Lay your sleeping head, and steal   845
Your weary eyes from work; I'll spell you for awhile."
Scarcely looking up, the helmsman speaks: "You tell
Me, 'scant the salt sea's placid face and quiet swell
And trust Aeneas to this monster'? Truly, why
Should I commit him to a traitor wind when I   850
Have been deceived so often by a smiling sky?"—

His words. Stuck to the tiller steadfast as you are,
He would not let go, clinging, watching you, bright star!
Then see the god with shaking limb sprinkle his brows.
It's Lethe-soaked, Styx-steeped; their power makes him drowse.   855
Sleep deliquesces Palinurus' swimming eyes
That fight to wake. But just as all resistance dies,
And leaden limbs go slack, the hovering sleep god pitches
The pilot headfirst in the clear black sea (he wrenches
Off the helm and taffrail, falling, calling often   860
On his friends . . . in vain).

      The god himself, on soft
Wings, flies into thin air. And yet they sailed ahead,
Fast, safe, and unafraid, as Father Neptune said.

Borne on, they came up to the Sirens' cliffs, long-known
For danger, bleach-white, with many a beach-strewn bone.   865
Then as the ceaseless surf and raucous rocks roared on,
Father Aeneas sensed the ship was yawing, tossed
Adrift. He took the tiller then, his helmsman lost,
And split the pitch-black waves, death-stunned, soul-sore.
"Oh, too much trust in calm-sky seas! You'll lie," he swore,   870
"O Palinurus, naked on some unknown shore."

Book VI

—Hɪs ᴛᴇᴀʀꜰᴜʟ ᴡᴏʀᴅꜱ. Aɴᴅ ᴛʜᴇɴ ᴛʜᴇ ꜰʟᴇᴇᴛ ʀᴀɴ ꜰʀᴇᴇ ʙᴇꜰᴏʀᴇ
The wind, until it gained Euboean Cumae's shore.¹
Prows turned to sea, the anchors bite the ocean floor;
With ships made fast and raked sterns selvaging the sands,
Young Trojan crews leap out in eager scouting bands.   5

Hesperia! Some run to find the fire-seed
Locked up in flint, while others comb the woods or speed
Through thickets dense with game. Some point out springs they've
    found.
But good Aeneas climbs to take the god's high ground,
Apollo's temple seat. Nearby—a huge, blind cave,   10
The dreaded Sibyl's, where the Delian seer gave
That soul and mind his power to tell the future.² Now
At Trivia's grove and golden roof, they pass below.

Once, Daedalus had dared—or so the stories go—³
To fly from Minos, trusting flashing wings to row   15
The sky. Unused to flight, he drifted north, until
At length he fluttered down on the Chalcidian hill,
His first touch back on earth. Here, Daedalus consigned
His feathered oars to you, Apollo, and designed
Your giant temple doors that limned Androgeos' death.   20

And here he showed the poor Cecropians, punished with
Cruel annual tribute—seven sons (the urn stands there,
Lots drawn. And opposite, from out at sea, there stare
The Gnosian cliffs). They saw the bull, his passion for
Pasiphaë, their furtive spawn, the Minotaur—   25

That thing half-beast/half-man that had been spawned for terror.
Here was that lethal maze, the tomb of deadly error.
(But Daedalus, who pitied Ariadne's love,
Himself resolved the treacherous text the labyrinth wove;
He led the blind footsteps of Theseus by a thread.)   30
And Icarus, you'd have been there, too, if Daedalus[4]
Had not grieved so. Twice he had tried to carve your fall
In gold; his hands fell twice.

                        They would have scanned it all,
Had not Achates brought Deïphobe, the priestess
(Daughter of Glaucus) serving Trivia and Phoebus.   35
They had been sent ahead. Now Glaucus' daughter said,
"The moment does not call for seeing sights. Instead,
Kill seven bullocks from an untouched herd, and slay
As many sheep, all rightly picked."

                            With no delay,
Aeneas acts; she's spoken, and his men obey.   40
Then she summons them inside the towering shrine.
From the immense Euboean rock, a cave is hewn
(A hundred adits lead there; from their mouths have spewn
As many voices, as the Sibyl's answers fly).

They reach the threshold, where they hear that virgin cry,   45
"It's time to beg the god! Behold him!" Suddenly,
Before the doors, her face's color failed, and she
Began to pant and heave. Her hair became a storm.
Her heart grew wild, as she assumed gigantic form.
Speech turned inhuman, for the breathing god drew near   50
With power. "Trojan, are you so slow to vow and prayer?
Aeneas, do you pause? For till you act, its maw
Won't open in this great place filled with sacred awe."
She stopped. Through valiant Teucrian blood, a shudder ran.

Then praying from his deep heart's core, their king began: 55
"O Phoebus, you who've always pitied Troy its sorrow;
You who deftly guided Paris' Dardan arrow
To Aeacus's grandson's heel: you led me on
Through many seas, through mighty lands—the far in-drawn
Massylian tribes, the fields by Syrtes' side. Now we   60
Have won the coast of *ignis fatuus* Italy
At last. May Trojan fortunes follow just this far—
No farther! Now, for Pergamus, it's right to spare
Its race, you gods and goddesses offended by
Dardanian Ilium's glory. You who can descry   65
The future, holy seer: I only seek what Fate
Has promised. Let us Trojans settle down in Latium
With our wandering gods and storm-tossed, agitated
Teucrian powers. I'll build for Trivia and Apollo
A solid marble temple; festal days will follow,   70
All in Phoebus' name. O Sibyl, there shall be
A stately shrine decreed to house your prophecy—
The secret destinies you tell my race—with hand-
Picked acolytes, O Gracious One. But don't commend
Your verse to leaves, or like the playthings of the wind,   75
They'll fly; *sing* them." Lips closed; his speech came to an end.

The priestess, though, will not yet let Apollo take
Her. Storming through the cave, the Sibyl tries to shake
The god inside her; all the more, her voice grows faint.
He tames her raving heart and breaks her with restraint.   80

And now the hundred cave mouths open free and wide,
To bear the seer's answers on the winds they ride:
"Dardanidae, you're done at last with what the sea
Can do, though worse things wait on land. Your port shall be
Lavinium, have no fear. But though you will be free,   85
There'll be no joy arriving, either. War ahead!

Grim wars I see! I see the Tiber foaming red.
A Xanthus and a Simois, and Doric camps,
Will all be yours. Right now, a new Achilles ramps
In Latium, goddess-born like you. The Teucrians can't   90
Escape the wrath of Juno, either. Suppliant
And lacking everything, what tribes of Italy,
What cities, won't you beg, again your misery
Caused by a foreign bride, a foreign bed?
Don't yield to evils; go to meet them straight ahead,   95
Bolder than Fate allows. Your first safe path, although
Hard to believe, a city of the Greeks will show."[5]

All through the shrine, Cumaea's Sibyl, setting free
Her frightening puzzles wrapped in dark obscurity,
Makes hollow thunder. As she raves, Apollo shakes   100
The reins and pricks her tortured breast; the deep spur takes.
Then, when the frenzy stopped, her raving tongue fell still.

Now brave Aeneas speaks: "O virgin, no new ill—
No novel evil—shocks me. I've foreseen this whole
Already, as I've passed it through my pilgrim soul.   105
I ask one thing: they say the gateway to below—
To Dis—lies here, where Acheron in its overflow
Bogs down in dismal swamp. I beg you, let me see
My cherished father. Show the sacred way; teach me.
Through fire and the thousand hostile spears I braved,   110
I bore him on my back, and from their midst I saved[6]
Him. Fellow on my dangerous trek, he sailed its seas
And faced the parlous sky and ocean. Through all these
He went, though weak beyond his strength's allotted years.
In fact, he begged for me to find you. In his prayers,   115
He asked that I approach you as a suppliant,
O Gracious One. And so I beg you, will you grant
Both son and father pity? You're omnipotent,

And Hecate had reasons you should rule Avernus'
Groves. If Orpheus could make his wife return   120
(He counted on his Thracian lyre's plangent grace),[7]
And Pollux ransom Castor, dying in his place,
Making his way at will—*and* mighty Hercules
And Theseus—why not I, the great Jove's scion?"[8]

                                       These
Words said, he prayed, while clinging to the altar. Then   125
The Sibyl: "Troy's Anchises' son, it is for men
No trouble to descend to grim Avernus. Day
And night the doors of dismal Dis await. The way
Back, though—to reach the light—*this* is the work to do,
The hardest task. True, kindly Jove has loved a few,[9]   130
And some there are whose shining worth meant that they could,
As sons of gods. Cocytus rings a mid-way wood
With slippery, murky bends. If love and yearning make
You want to see black Tartarus twice, twice swim the lake
Of Styx; if madness makes you long to do these things,   135
Then hear what must come first. Within a dark tree hangs
A stubborn bough with gilded leaves and golden stem.
Thought sacred to Hell's Juno, Proserpine,[10] this limb
Lies hid; the forest's shadows cloak it in dark dells.
But none may go below Earth's hollows into Hell's   140
Before he's plucked that bough, that golden-foliaged thing—[11]
A gift that lovely Proserpine demands you bring
Her. Tear that limb off and another one will spring
Up, golden metal in its place. So lift your eyes
While searching. When you find it, pluck that fitting prize,   145
And it will come off in your hand with perfect ease,
If you are called by Fate. You cannot otherwise
Succeed, by brute force or by steel. Besides, there lies
The lifeless body of your friend. (I see you did not know!)
Decaying there, his corpse pollutes the whole fleet, though   150

You linger on our threshold, seeking counsel. Carry
Him first to his own place—the tomb where you must bury
Him. Black sheep must be the vow that you fulfill,
Or you will never look on Stygian groves, and will
Not see realms living men don't walk." Her voice fell still.   155

Aeneas, looking mournful, and with downcast eyes,
Leaves the cavern, trudging on in deep surmise
About these cryptic words. With him: his good compère
Achates, burdened also with that carking care.
These two men share concerns both numerous and varied   160
(Which dead friend does the Sibyl mean? Who should be buried?).

And then they saw, as they were coming to the strand,
Misenus' tragic corpse; his fresh blood dyed the sand.
Misenus, son of Aeolus: none could excel
Him stirring men or rousing Mars with trumpet-shell.   165
He'd fought beside great Hector and had shown no fear,
Though honored for his horn as much as for his spear.

But when Achilles ended Hector's life, Misenus
Bravely went to join the Dardan prince Aeneas,
Following one no less heroic. Then, while he   170
Was playing on his hollow shell to make the sea
Resound, he madly dared the gods in competition.
They say that he was snatched up by the jealous Triton,
Who plunged Misenus in the waves that spumed the rocks.[12]
So all bewailed this thousandth of his natural shocks,   175
Especially good Aeneas.

                    Weeping then, they raced
To do what Sibyl said—to pile up wood in haste—
The altar of his tomb that rises to the sky.
To ancient woods they go, the lairs where wild beasts lie.

The pine falls, and the ilex, ringing to the axe,   180
As ashen timber drops; men split the splintering oaks
With wedges. Down the mountains, giant tree trunks roll.

Aeneas joins in, cheers the men with heart and soul,
Taking up the tools they use, and does his share.
But still, he ponders in his grieving heart each care.   185
Scanning the towering woods, he settles on this prayer:
"If only here and now that golden branch would show
Within the tall wood, on some tree. For truly—oh-
Too-truly—has the Sibyl limned your fate, Misenus."

He'd scarcely spoken when by chance twin doves of Venus[13]   190
Came winging from the skies. Before his startled eyes
They landed on green grass, doves he could recognize—
His mother's birds. The grateful hero starts to pray:
"Doves, lead me through the air, if there is any way
To find that grove. And show me where its priceless bough   195
Shades fruitful earth. O Mother, do not fail me now
In this uncertain quest."—his words.

                                        Then, stepping slow,
He closely watched the birds who showed him where to go.
(They'd feed a bit, then flit ahead, but never flew
Beyond the range a keen-eyed watcher could pursue.)   200
And when they reached the jaws of foul Avernus, up
They soared abruptly through the liquid air, then dropped
To perch at last. And from that tree they lighted on,
The golden bough was gleaming; through the dark it shone.

In dismal winter woods the strange-leaved mistletoe   205
Will bloom with yellow fruit (a guest that will not grow
From its own tree, it hugs its host's smooth boles). That's how
The black-barked ilex bore that leafy golden bough,

And how the hammered gold enamel chimed the breezes.
Fast as he can, Aeneas snaps the limb. He seizes   210
It and bears it back beneath the Sibyl's roof.[14]

Meanwhile, and busy, too, the Teucrians are not proof
Against the tears they yield Misenus in his just
Last rites. They pay their sad respects to thankless dust,
Then raise a pyre rich with sawn oak and pitch-pine,   215
While cypresses stand guard and somber fronds entwine
The giant sides. Above it, stacked-up weapons shine.

To wash the body and anoint it, some fire cauldrons
Made of bronze with water hot enough to scald;
All mourn. Then, drained of tears, they couch the corpse, and over   220
It they throw rich purple cloaks, the proper cover.
Some comrades bear his heavy litter shoulder-high—
A mournful office, with their eyes downcast—and by
Ancestral custom, touch their torches to the pile.

Heaped offerings burn: food, frankincense, and olive oil.   225
After the ashes cratered and the flames were doused
With wine that quenched the embers and remains, they housed
The gathered bones, as Corynaeus filled an urn
Of bronze. Then, walking round his friends three times in turn,
Asperging holy water from an olive limb,   230
He purified the men, then, *vale*, one last time.
The good Aeneas builds a huge tomb over him.
Misenus' sword and horn and oar all cover him
By that high bluff (*Misenum*, it is called, named for him
Perpetually, *per saecula saeculorum*).   235

When done, he heeds the orders that the Sibyl gave.
There was a giant, gaping, jagged-surfaced cave

Protected by a tree-thick gloom and dismal lake
No birds on their extended wings could safely make
Their flights above (the arching sky inhaled that maw's   240
Toxic miasma spewing from its throat and jaws).

Greeks called that place *Aver-nus*, where *no-birds* can go.[15]
The Sibyl set four black-backed heifers in a row
Here, pouring wine and plucking bristles from their brows—
The topmost tufts—as first fulfillment of her vows.   245
She burnt them in the offerings' fire, then called the name
Of Hecate out loud, whose power is the same
In Erebus and Heaven.

                          Some slit the throats and catch
The tepid blood in bowls; Aeneas, with dispatch,
Conveys by sword a black lamb to the goddess Night,   250
And to her mighty sister, Earth. Next in the rite,
A barren heifer's yours, Proserpina. For Styx's
King, Aeneas loads an altar he constructs
By night; he gives the flames whole carcasses of bulls,
Pouring the rich and fatty oil on burning bowels.   255

But then, see how the earth began to rumble under
Foot at dawn, treed ridges nearly torn asunder,
Dogs howling through the gloom (for Hecate drew near).
"Stand off! Get back, unhallowed men! Stand far from here,"
The Sibyl cried. "But you, Aeneas, draw your sword;   260
You'll need a brave man's heart, a strong man's courage. Forward!"
She stopped, then plunged into the cave, eyes crazy-wide.
But unafraid, he matched his wild guide stride-for-stride.

You gods who rule the world of souls; you silent shades;
Chaos and Phlegethon; you broad and silent glades   265

Of Night: let me tell what I've heard. And by your graces,
May I show things entombed in Earth's deep, dismal places.[16]

They went on dimly, under lonely night, through gloom
And through the vacant halls of Dis's ghostly realm,
The way a fickle moon's begrudging glow will light   270
A forest path when Jove has palled the sky, and Night,
Black Night, with shadows robs the world of color. At
The very threshold, in the jaws of Orcus, sat
Both Grief and vengeful Care. There, pallid Sickness lives,
And sad Old Age, and Fear, and Famine, too, which gives   275
Bad counsel. There sat loathsome Want and Deprivation—
Shapes horrible to see—and Death and Devastation.
Next, Sleep—the kin of Death, and kin to guilty joys.
And just across the way was War, whom Death employs.
The Furies' iron cells stood there, with frenzied Strife   280
(All through her toxic locks, the blood-soaked cords were rife).

The center held a huge, black, ancient elm, which spread
Its limbs for empty Dreams to roost in (people said).
Dream claws clutch branches under every leaf. Besides
More foul-shaped fiends, a myriad of beasts resides   285
There: twisted-double Scyllas stable by the doors;
Briareus-the-Hundred-Armed, stalls with Centaurs;
Chimaera flames; the beast of Lerna hisses; Gorgons
And Harpies match the triple-bodied shade that's Geryon's.

Here, suddenly, Aeneas, quivering with fear,   290
Presents his blade's steel edge against those drawing near.
And if his wiser guide had not explained that these
Were only ghostly beings flittering through the trees,
He would have charged them, slashing with his pointless sword.

Tartarean Acheron's banks are what the way leads toward   295
From here. A turbid, mired maelstrom vomits sands

Up from its depths; Cocytus takes them in. There stands
The squalid water-warden Charon, grim and fear-
Inducing. On his grizzled chin, a beard; no shear
Has touched its tangled hoar. His eyes are fiery hot.   300
His filthy cloak hangs from his shoulders by a knot.
Sole poler of his boat, he minds the sails and punts.
His dark skiff ships what's left of those who breathed life once.
He's ancient, yes, but ancient gods stay green and strong.

The whole mob crowded to the banks, a streaming throng: 305
Mothers and men and bodies—life-defunct—of great-
Souled heroes; boys and unwed girls; young sons whose fate
It was to burn on pyres before their fathers' eyes;
Thicker than autumn's first-frost foliage when it flies
And falls; more massed than birds that from the roiling deep   310
Come flocking toward the shores when winter's chill winds sweep
Them over seas and send them on toward warmer lands.

They stood there begging, pleading with their outstretched hands
To be the first to reach those farther shores they yearned
For. Surly Charon, though, took some aboard but spurned   315
Others, and fended off still more kept back from shore.
Aeneas, moved—astonished—by that mob's uproar,
Cries, "Virgin, tell me what this river mob scene means.
What do these dead souls seek? Those Charon leaves or gleans—
How does he choose who rows these waters dull as lead?"   320

In brief reply to this, the ancient priestess said,
"Anchises' son, true scion of a deity:
Cocytus' pools and Styx's swamp are what you see
(By these, the gods will fear to swear and be forsworn).
This crowd you gaze at are the graveless and forlorn.   325
That ferryman is Charon, carrying the buried
Only. But they must fill their tombs before they're ferried
From those banks across that raucous stream—a hundred

Years. Before the longed-for pools from which they're sundered
Can be theirs, they're doomed to roam and haunt this shore."   330

Mid-step, Anchises' son then stopped, while this and more
He pondered, deeply pitying their wretched fate.
He sees two souls denied the rites of death's estate:
Leucaspis and the captain of the Lycian fleet,
Orontes. (Both sail stormy seas from Troy; both meet   335
With ruin. Auster drowns them, ships and men the same.)

And look there how the helmsman Palinurus came,[17]
Who lately, out of Libya, while trying to track
The stars, had been pitched from the stern into the wrack.
When he could finally see that figure in the black,   340
Aeneas said, "Oh, what god stole you from our side?
Please, Palinurus: say who plunged you in the wide
And drowning seas. Apollo, who has never lied
To me, has with this one betrayal crushed my soul.
He said that you would reach our shared Ausonian goal   345
Unharmed by sea. Is this how Phoebus keeps his word?"

But he: "Anchises' son, my captain: what you heard
His tripod say was true. Drowned by no deity,
I drank my fate. The helm that had been given me
To guard was torn away while I clung tight to steer,   350
And roughly, headlong with it, in I went. I swear
By the harsh seas that as for me, I had no fear
Like that I had that you might lose an unhelmed ship—
That it might founder in the waves if fate should strip
Its rigging off. Three wintry nights the South Wind churned   355
Me in the endless seas. Then when the fourth day turned,
And I rode—barely—on a wave, I sighted Italy.
Then almost safe on shore (I had been swimming little by
Little), still drenched and weighed down, clinging by my nails

To jagged rocks, I am attacked. A mob assails   360
Me savagely, deceived in thinking I'm some prize.
Winds beach me, pull me back; on waves, I fall and rise.
Now, by the air and by the light of heaven, I
Beseech you; by your rising hopes for Iulus; by
Your sire: redeem me, mighty one. Or else (I know   365
You can), throw earth on me, then seek out Velia; row
To reach that port. Or should your goddess-mother show
Some other way (you never would have tried to do
This—cross the Stygian mere—had gods not aided you),
Then give this wretch your hand, and take me to my peace   370
Across the waves. At least in death I'll find release."

When he was done, the Sibyl started in: "Oh, why
Such mad desire, Palinurus? Though you lie
Unburied, you would see the Stygian waters, or
The Furies' brutal river, or approach their shore   375
Unbidden? Hope that prayer will guard you from your fate
Is futile. Hear me: do not be disconsolate,
For all the nearby tribes, compelled by signs from heaven,
Throughout their towns, will see to it your bones are given
Their due. They'll build your tomb, perform the reverent rites   380
That tomb deserves, with *Palinurus* for the site's
Eternal name." These words allay his cares a bit;
Grief leaves him for that place (he gives his name to it).

And so they travel onward, drawing near the stream.
But when the Stygian ferryman had spotted them   385
Threading the silent grove and heading for the shore,
Pre-emptively he challenged them: "Not one step more!
Whoever you may be who come here armed, explain
The reason where you stand. This inky black terrain
Is called the Place of Shadows, Sleep, and Somnolent Night.   390
To haul the living in my Stygian boat's not right.

In fact, I balked at taking Hercules across
This lake, *and* poling Theseus and Pirithoüs,
Despite their fearsome courage and divine descent.
One tried to drag off Tartarus's porter—pent   395
In chains and trembling—from the throne room of the dead,
While others tried to steal his queen from Dis's bed."

The seer of the Amphrysian answered him in brief:
"There is no trickery here, and you will find you're safe
From harmless swords. That hideous guard, inside his cowling   400
Cave, is free to fright the shades with endless howling.
Chaste Proserpine may safely serve her uncle still,
In Dis's house. Now Troy's Aeneas, famed for skill
At arms and for his piety, comes for his father
In deepest Erebus. Unmoved by this? Another   405
Sight, then: bow to this bough!" (She shows the branch that she
Has hidden in her cloak.)

                    His heart-rage shrinks, till he
Has no more words, but marvels at the long-unseen
And deadly gifted wand. He turns his barge, gloom-green
And glaucus, toward the farther bank, unseats the hordes   410
Of souls bunched on its benches, clears the ramps, and boards
The huge Aeneas. Groaning with his weight, the boat—
A leaky-seamed craft barely sound enough to float,
And taking on a sluice of swampy bilge—he steers
At length across the water, landing both (the seer's   415
Safe, and the man) in mud-sown sedge and mired ground.

Great Cerberus's triple howls make hell resound,[18]
As in his watchdog cave, he crouches, huge. She sees
Snakes bristling on his neck, and tosses him a piece
Of sleep-inducing meal that's honey-drugged—a dag   420
That ravenous hell-hound opens three-fold throats to snag.

The morsel gulped, he lets his giant frame go limp
And lays its length out on the cave floor's filthy damp.
This guard entombed in sleep, Aeneas starts to climb
The bankside of that stream men enter just one time.   425

He hears at once a wall of wailing infant cries.
Souls on the brink of life, they never realize
Existence, kidnapped from the breast; their black day drives
Them down to drown in bitter death. Next came the lives
Of innocent convicted souls who met death's fate.   430
(There *is* assignment, though, by Styx's magistrate,
For Minos shakes the urn. Presiding, he convenes
A silent court to learn men's sins—what each crime means,[19]
Each deed.) Sad souls come next: else innocent, they tossed
Away their lives for death by their own hands, and lost   435
The light of day they loathed. Oh, how they'd dearly love
Both pain and want if they could walk the world above
Now! Fate forbids. Unlovely waves and dismal fen
Have fettered them, the nine-fold Styx their moated pen.

Not far from there, and spreading everywhere, appear   440
The so-called Fields of Mourning; brutal Love worked here,
Who ravaged countless souls that came to waste away.
In stony, lost defiles, they hide their cruel decay,
Covered by myrtles. Even death can't end their pain.
Here Phaedra, Procris, and Eriphyle remain   445
(A mournful ghost displaying wounds her son once made).

Aeneas sees Pasiphaë's, Evadne's shade;
Laodamia's, too. There's Caeneus, once a man,
But now a woman, now her former form again.
There, too, Phoenician Dido, bleeding copiously,[20]   450
Wandered the endless woods. And he? As soon as he
Got near her, recognizing her dim figure deep

In shade (the way one sees the cloud-wrapped moon in steep
Ascent—or thinks he sees it—when the month is young),
He spoke . . . after some tears that tender love had wrung: 455

"O wretched Dido! Then it's true, that message brought
To me? They said that you had died—they said you'd sought
Your death by sword. Was I the cause? I swear by all
The stars above, by all that's holy in the pall
Of darkest earth deep down: O Queen, I left your lands   460
Against my will. I wander by the gods' commands,
Amidst these wraiths, through thorny wastes and pitch-black night,
Imperiously coerced. Oh, had I known you might
Have suffered grief like this when we were cut in two!
Oh, stay and let me look on you again! Whom do   465
You flee? These are the last words Fate will let me speak."

Addressing her like this, tears streaming down his cheek,
Aeneas tried to cool her spirit's blazing eyes.
But Dido turned away; the ground had all her gaze.
And as he tried to reach her with his words, her face,   470
Unchanging as Marpesian flint, showed no trace
Of feeling. Raging still, she fled, and found the shadowed
Copse Sychaeus haunted—he whom she'd been widowed
From—her comforter (love's given . . . and returned).
Aeneas, though, shocked by this fate she never earned,   475
Pursues her from afar, with tears of pity as
She goes.

       From there, he takes the only path there is,
Gaining the far fields where famed warriors abound.
Parthenopaeus', Tydeus', and the war-renowned
Adrastus' pallid spirits meet him. Here, the war-   480
Dead of the Dardans that the quick are grieving for—

The chieftains that Aeneas mourns—stretch endlessly:
Glaucus and Medon and Thersilochus (the three
Sons of Antenor); Polyboetes, Ceres' priest;
Idaeus, with his sword still (still not having ceased 485
Driving his chariot).

On all sides, spirits mill
And throng for more than just one sight; they crowd him still
And match his steps to learn the reason why he's there.
The Greeks and Agamemnon's troops, though, quake with fear
At the sight of him. His armor gleams through the black. 490
Some phalanxes turn tail, and take off, running back,
As once before they'd sought their ships. A few ghosts try
To shout, their gaping mouths mocked by a tinny cry.

And here he saw Priam's Deïphobus, the flesh[21]
All shredded from his face, his body wrenched and smashed— 495
His face and both his hands. Razed temples hold no ears,
And where his nose has been, a shameful hole appears.
In fact, Aeneas barely knew this thing that flailed
And twitched and hid its foul abuse. Now, though un-hailed,
He spoke kind words:

"Deïphobus, whose lineage 500
Was noble Teucer's blood: Who chose to wreak such savage
Punishment? Who had such power? On that last
Night, rumor reached me you'd collapsed on corpses massed
In piles of dead Pelasgians that you'd killed. Then by
That Rhoetean shore, I set your cenotaph. My cry 505
Went out three times to summon up your shade. Your name
And arms now guard that place where it had been my aim
To lay your corpse. But you could not be found, and so
I left our land."

The son of Priam answered, "O
My friend, you left no rite undone, but you have paid   510
Deïphobus all that you should—him and his shade.
My own fate and that Spartan woman's crime combined[22]
To drown me in these woes; *she* had me thus enshrined,
For well you know our joys were false that final night.
(Too well, you know.) Once it had leapt our ramparts' height   515
(One bound brought in that deadly horse), and from its womb
Delivered weaponed men to murder Pergamum,
She 'danced' the Phrygian women round—a Bacchic band—
Then signaled to the Greeks with a great burning brand
From Troy's high citadel, while I, care-worn, asleep   520
Upon my wretched marriage bed, oppressed by deep,
Sweet slumber, lay like death. That wife who had no peer
Meanwhile had stashed away my every bow and spear,
And hid the trusted sword I kept beneath my head.
Hoping her Menelaus, glad to find me dead,   525
Would prize this gift, she opens wide the doors and leads
Him in—to expiate her former evil deeds.
But why say more? They breach the bedroom, egged on by
That wicked Aeolid extolling crime. If I
Pray justly, Gods, pay back the Greeks in kind. But you!   530
What fate has brought you *here* while still alive? And do
You come admonished by the gods? Or driven by
Your travails on the sea? If neither, tell me why.
Tormenting Fate? Why walk these sunless halls, this site
Of murk?"

          But while they talked, Aurora scaled the height   535
Of noon, her pink car cresting its ethereal climb.
And well they might have talked past their allotted time
This way, but for his guiding Sibyl's short, sharp warning:
"Night races on, Aeneas; end this spendthrift mourning.
Two roads diverge within this wood; one, on the right,[23]   540

Beneath great Dis's walls, leads to Elysium's site.
The left one, though . . . *it* punishes the impious
By lashing evil shades to godless Tartarus."

Deïphobus replied, "Great priestess, pardon us.
I'm going back to complement the count of souls   545
In darkness. Go, Aeneas; leave. Some better goal's
Your destiny." When he was done, he turned to go.

Aeneas suddenly looks back; he sees, below
The left-hand cliff, huge battlements, ringed by a three-
Fold wall a river's flames race round in circuitry—   550
Tartarean Phlegethon, which tumbles clashing rocks.
With columns solid adamant, a huge gate locks
It. Mortal men—and deities—may try, but never
Break it down by force.

                    And rising up forever,
An iron tower thrones Tisiphone.[24] Blood steeps   555
The robe of one who guards that gate and never sleeps.
All day and night: groans from behind the door she keeps.
Whip sounds, and grating iron, dragging chains, all scare
Aeneas, who is brought up short and rooted there.
"What kinds of criminals are these? Virgin, the sky   560
Is pierced by cries. What punishments are theirs, and why?"

The Sibyl answered him: "O famous prince of Troy,
No righteous man may step across this dreaded sill.
When Hecate made Avernus subject to my will,
She taught me all of heaven's tortures, one by one.   565
The Cnossian's realm most adamant beneath the sun,
Hard Rhadamanthus hears their guilt, then castigates
Each one who should atone but still procrastinates
Toward death, happy to hide—in vain—his misdeeds back

On earth. Stung by Tisiphone's whiplash attack,   570
Those guilty souls at once discover they must face
The snarling snakes her left hand calls her brace
Of sisters with.

                    And then the dead gates open, hard,
Their hinges shrill. You've seen who sits there as a guard—
Who wards that threshold? Well, more monstrous on her
     throne,   575
The Hydra sits, with fifty black maws of her own.
Then Tartarus itself yawns. Headlong down it dies,
Stretching below to darkness twice as deep as rise
The heights of heavenly Olympus from the skies.

Here lies the oldest *gens* of Earth, the Titan race   580
Thrown down by lightning, tumbling to the deepest place
In Hell. I saw Aloeus' giant offspring here,
Who warred with Jove and tried, with their own hands, to tear
His kingdom down and rule instead. I saw as well,
Salmoneus, paying Jove his awful price in Hell   585
For having mimicked lightning and the thunder of
Olympus. Driving four in hand, he shook above
His head a brandished torch, taunting the Greeks. He drove
Through Elis' city, claiming honors due to Jove,
A madman mimicking inimitable thunder,   590
Bronze cymbals and the horses' horn-hard hoofbeats under
Him. The Omnipotent Father, though, from thick
Cloud threw his bolt—no puny brand or piney wick—
And blew headstrong Salmoneus headlong away.

I looked on Tityos as well, whose body lay   595
Stretched out a full nine *jugeri* (he is the foster-
Son of Earth, our only mother, Mater Noster).

A giant, hook-beaked vulture deep inside his chest
Still crops his liver and his pain-primed guts—no rest
(The tissue grows right back; the vulture gnaws his breast).   600

Pirithoüs, the Lapiths, and Ixion: Why
Describe them? Overhead, a black crag hanging by
A rocky thread seems set to fall—right now! A high-
Table feast lies spread out before their golden couches,
While lurking near, the mother of all Furies crouches,   605
Then sweeps their fingers from the tables as she's looming
With a torch and mimicking the thunder's booming.

Here are those who while alive despised their brothers,
Defrauded clients, struck their fathers or their mothers,
Or brooded lonely on the wealth they'd made. They are—   610
Not sharing with their kin—the biggest mob by far.

Here: slain adulterers; seditionists who made
Vile war and broke all faith with masters, unafraid.
Penned up, they wait a torment that you do not want
To know—not drowning pain or other punishment.   615
Some roll huge rocks, while some are bound upon a wheel.
The wretched Theseus[25] sits down where he sits—where he'll
Be sitting ages hence. Worst off of all, one made
A warning witness—Phlegyas as a vocal shade:
'Learn justice; never slight the deities; uphold   620
Their law.'

        Here's one who sold his *patria* for gold,
Here a dictator-lord. And this one bought and sold
The law: he 'wed' his daughter and defiled her bed.
They all dared monstrous things, and what they dared, they did.
I couldn't, with a hundred mouths and tongues and voice   625

Of iron, describe the thousand forms of crime and vice,
Or briefly list the names of all those pains inflicted."

Apollo's ancient priestess, with these trials depicted,
Spoke: "Come now. Take up the path; do what's required.
Dispatch! I see the built-up battlements forge-fired   630
From the Cyclops' furnaces, and archway gates
Ahead, where we must place the gift the god dictates."

She'd done, and down the dark path, stride for stride
They rushed, and crossed the space between, to end beside
The doors. Aeneas reached the entrance, sprinkled fresh   635
Water, and laid the sacred bough down on the threshold.
This duty done at last—the goddess's command
Obeyed—they reached the green fields of the Pleasant Land,[26]
The Fortunate Groves, the final home of all the Blessed.

Here is where ampler air and rosy light invest   640
The plains that know a sun and stars their very own.
Some athletes wrestling on the tawny sand are thrown,
While others train their bodies on a grassy lawn.
Some beat out dances with their feet, or sing a song.

There, truly, Thrace's priest, appareled in his long   645
Robe, plays. His seven separate notes accompany
Their measures, finger-picked or plucked with ivory.[27]
Here: Teucer's ancient line, the fairest progeny,
And great-souled heroes born in better years gone by—
Assaracus and Dardanus (who founded Troy)   650
And Ilus.

     Marveling at their arms and idle war-
Cars from afar, he sees spears growing by the score,
And everywhere, the horses free to graze the plain.

(Joy felt—in chariots and armor and feeding grain
To sleek steeds—when these men were living, finds them here   655
Below.) To left and right, out on the belvedere,
Aeneas sees men feasting to a joyous paean
In the scented laurel groves that set the scene
Of broad Eridanus's spring. It rushes through
The woods to rise above.

                And here were wounded who   660
Had fought for country, priests who while they lived kept pure,
The poets true to Phoebus, those whose ever-newer
Arts and knowledge made life better. Those who'd won
The hearts of men by all the honest good they'd done
Were here as well. And all were bright-white-ribbon-browed.   665

The Sibyl spoke to all, the tallest in the crowd
Especially—Musaeus[28]—since he holds the sight
Of those around, his shoulders at commanding height:
"You blessed souls, and you, the greatest poet, name
Anchises' place. Through dreaded Erebus we came,   670
Fording its streams, for him."

              That hero then replied
With these few words: "There is no one place we abide,
No fixed site set for us. We stroll the shady woods,
Stream-banks for couches, spring-fed meads our neighborhoods.
But climb this rise then, if your heart's wish tends that way;   675
I'll set you on an easy track." He'd had his say,
And striding on, Musaeus showed them, far below
The mountain heights they'd leave, fresh lucent plains aglow.

Father Anchises, though, deep in that green-valed place,
Was counting spirits waiting in its mild embrace   680
For life above; he brooded on descendants there:

The sum of all his progeny; the grandsons dear
To him, their fates and fortunes as grown men, their ways
And deeds.

        And when Aeneas' progress caught his gaze
Across the grass, he stretched his loving arms out wide,   685
Effusive tears cascading down his cheeks, and cried,
"You've come at last then? And that pious love I knew
Would overcome your arduous road has seen you through,
My son. And now I see you, hear you, speak with you
The way we did? I've counted on it, counting grain-   690
By-grain the hours. I see I did not count in vain!
You're welcome to this teeming shore. So tempest-tossed,
My son, you've sailed great seas. What lands you must have
    crossed!
And how I feared what Libya might do to you."

But he: "It was your poor ghost, father—*your* shade!—who   695
In visiting so often drew me to these gates.
My fleet now standing in the Tyrrhene Sea awaits.
O father, father!—let me grasp your hand. Don't pull
Away from my embrace." He spoke—and tears ran full.
Three times he tried to throw his arm around his sire;   700
Three times that shade fled like light winds blown ever higher,
Or like some thinning wing-flown dream quick to expire.

And then Aeneas spots a shy grove in a dell
Laid back where woody thickets whisper Lethe's spell.
(That river glides past all this country's peaceful places.)   705
All round about, there flittered countless tribes and races,
The way a meadow on a placid summer day
Will hum with bees that grace bright lilies and the gay
Display of blooms. That's how those copses buzzed away.

Aeneas, whom the sudden sight has stirred to wonder,   710
Asks why they're there. What are those distant rivers yonder,
And who are those who crowd its banks in such a mass?
Father Anchises: "Souls whom Fate must soon let pass
To second bodies, drink, at Lethe's wavy streams,
Care-cleansing water—draughts deep as forgotten dreams.[29]   715
Oh, yes—I have for so long wished to show you these
Souls face-to-face; to tell you of my progeny's
Numbers, so we'd enjoy the more your Italy's
Discovery."

        "O father, is it certain then
That souls that leave for life above possess again   720
Dull, muddy bodies? Why such sick desire to see
The light?"

        "I'll tell the truth, son, with alacrity,"
Anchises started, touching each point by and by.
"First, some force deep inside them feeds the earth and sky,[30]
The Titans' star, the splendorous moon, the dewy plains;   725
A principle of reason flows through matter's veins
To stir the sum of things, infusing this great mass.
All creatures come from this, and man, and every race
Of thing—the birds; the beasts below the sea's glass face.
These seeds—their origin's divine and burns gem-hard,   730
So long as no vile bodies enter to retard
Their fires—are not dulled by mortal human frames
And members. Through these, bodies meet desire's claims,
And sorrow's, fear's, and joy's. Trapped in their black, blind cells,
They cannot see the light. Indeed, when almost shells,   735
Still, all the flesh's plagues and evil chains that fetter it
Aren't gone. So many things long grown ingrained, inveterate,
Must harden deep within, in oh-so-many ways.

So every soul is scourged with punishment. Each pays
His price for former sins, some hung and kited out   740
Before the empty winds. The taint is whited out
For others in a giant gulf, or purged with flame,
Each soul its special nemesis—no two the same.
Then we are sent through wide Elysium. A few
Enjoy the blissful fields awhile, till time is through   745
Removing all the deep-dyed stain. It leaves refined,
With purest, blazing ether, an ethereal mind.
All others, summoned by the god, crowd Lethe's shore
After they've rolled time's wheel a thousand years or more,
In order truly to forget, so they may wish   750
To live above again, new-clothed in mortal flesh."

Anchises stopped and drew the Sibyl and his son
Into the crowd convened and murmuring as one.
He chose a mound that let him run his scanning eye
Along their ranks and watch their faces going by.   755

"Come now. I will make plain what glory will pursue[31]
The Dardan race, and that long line awaiting you
From Italy—bright souls advancing in our name.
And I will teach you your own fate and destined fame.
You see that young man leaning on an untipped spear?   760
Chance makes him first in line to rise, the one most near
The light. Of mixed Italian blood, he'll win the claire
Above. He's Silvius (an Alban name)—your heir,
Your last-born, old-age child Lavinia will bear
You in the woods. He'll be a king and father kings   765
Who'll rule all Alba Longa, which shall kiss their rings.
Beside him, Procas stands, the glory of Troy's race,
And Numitor and Capys and one who'll renasce
Your name: he's Silvius Aeneas, righteous as
He's strong (if ever he receives his Alban crown).   770

See what fine young men! They show such might and renown,
The Civic Oak will shade their brows. They'll build Nomentum,
Fidena, Gabii, for you. Their bold momentum
Will set Collatia's citadel upon its heights,
Pometii, and Inus' Fort, and lay the sites   775
For Bola and for Cora—names then, now unnamed.

And Mavors' child—yes, Romulus[32]—will be acclaimed
His grandfather's companion, born of Ilia of
Assaracus's blood. See those twin plumes above
His helmet crest? Mars marks him with his own high worth.   780
And see, my son, how under him Rome rules the Earth,
Fame equal to the world's, her will the will of heaven.
And with one unifying wall she'll bind her seven
Hills, rejoicing in her progeny (the way,
Through Phrygia's towns, her chariot will convey   785
The Magna Mater,[33] turret-crowned and proud with love
For all her hundred offspring, gods who live above,
In her embrace).

        Now redirect your gaze here: these are
Your very Romans—Iulus' offspring.[34] Here is Caesar,
And those to come who'll live below great heaven's dome.   790
So often promised, here's the man—the one to whom
Rome owes its golden age: Augustus Caesar (son
To him who's now a god). He'll reign as once was done
By Latian Saturn through this land. Empire shall run
Beyond the Garamants and Indians—lands that lie   795
Past zodiac and every orbit, where the sky
That Atlas bears upon his shoulders wheels that sphere
Inset with gleaming stars. Right now, the Caspians fear
(Maeotians, too) his coming, cowed by prophecies.
Nile branches are perturbed with dread, all seven trees.   800
And though he shot the bronze-foot deer, not Hercules

Even has crossed so much of Earth, who, done with clearing
The Erymanthian woods, left all of Lerna fearing
His bow; nor conquering Liber, down from Nysa, steering
His vine-reined chariot, driving tigers from its height.   805
And *we* still wait to stretch our strength by deeds of might?
Or is it fear that stops our settling Latian soil?

Who's he, though, in the distance, bearing holy oil
And marked by olive boughs? I know that hair, that white-
Chinned Roman king, who'll found our town by laws he'll write.   810
Called forth from little Cures' meager soil to wield
Imperial power, law-giving Numa next will yield
To Tullus, shattering his country's peace. He'll rouse
Inactive soldiers, troops unused to the applause
Of triumphs.

              Lightweight braggart Ancus follows him,   815
Already far too pleased by each plebeian whim.
You see the Tarquin kings, the proud, avenging soul
Of Brutus, and our fasces back in Rome's control?
He'll be the first to get a consul's power and earn
Those savage blades. For civil strife his sons will churn,   820
Their father calls for death, for precious freedom's sake—
A man to pity though, whatever time will make
Of him, a patriot who craved nobility.

And look far off: the Drusi and the Decii,
And bloody-axed Torquatus! There's Camillus, too,   825
Who brought our standards back. That shining pair that you
See there, like-minded and like-armored, shall remain
That way only while hidden here. When they attain
Life's light, what civil war and carnage they'll incite,
As the father-in-law descends his Alpine height   830
And the Monoecian citadel. His son-in-law,

With eastern troops, will fight him as these generals draw
Their columns up. Sons, never train your souls to war
Like this, your swords plunged in Rome's heart! Instead, abhor
Such blood, Olympian-born of mine.[35]   835
That victor there will drive up Rome's high Capitoline,
For having taken Corinth—famed for Greeks he's slaughtered.
This other one will strip Mycene from un-daughtered
Agamemnon, razing Argos. From the line
Of Troy's avengers of Minerva's blackened shrine: 840
Aeacid Perseus' scourge (Achilles' family).
The Gracchi! Cossus! Cato! And the Scipios! See
Those war-bolts burning Libya. From poverty,
Fabricius struck. And you, Serranus, sowing seed.
You Fabii, I'm weary; tell me where you lead?   845
And Maximus! Alone, you saved us by delay.
Yes, some will hammer soft bronze better (well they may),
Until it breathes, or coax from marble living faces,
Plead cases better, plot with rods the heavens' traces,
And say when stars will rise. Remember, Roman: *you*   850
Will rule the nations with your might (*that* is your due,
Your art), imposing on their peace, law's blessèd crown—
With mercy (fight the haughty till they're beaten down)."[36]

Father Anchises stopped, then, as they marveled, spoke
Again: "See how Marcellus comes, marked by the token   855
Of the *Spolia Opima*. Taller than all,
That victor-knight; he won't let the republic fall
To tumult, but will flatten Carthage, raze proud Gaul,
The third in Rome to hang up captured arms for sire
Quirinus."

          Then Aeneas, straining to admire   860
A handsome youth in gleaming armor (one who strode
Beside Marcellus, eyes downcast, his face foreboding),

Spoke: "Father, who is that who walks with him? His son?
Or in his long-descended line, some other one?
What murmuring surrounds them! And what worth he shows!   865
But all about his head, night's sad black shadow flows."

Father Anchises then, with welling tears, in brief
Replied: "O son, don't ask about Troy's giant grief.
Fate only shows him to the world so long, and will
Not let him stay. The Romans would seem mightier still,   870
You gods, if you should let this gifted life extend
Too long. What wailing will the Campus Martius send
To mighty Rome from men! O Tiber, what rites you
Shall see of death as you glide by Marcellus' new-
Built tomb! No Ilian boy will ever lift so high   875
With hope his Latin line, nor will they magnify
So great a son in Romulus's lands. Oh, cry
Such goodness lost! And cry for ancient faith's right arm
Invincible in war! Who would be safe from harm
While he was fighting—any enemy he met   880
On foot, or roweling deep his charger flecked with sweat?
Poor boy, if only you could burst the fate you're set,
You'd be Marcellus![37] Fill my hands with lilies! Let
Me strew his soul with glowing blooms, at least, and load
That spirit with such gifts. That duty, he is owed . . .   885
In vain."

          So, vagrant everywhere, they walk the wide
And airy plain, inspecting all that can be spied.
Anchises, when he's led his son quite through that land,
And seen to it his love of fame-to-come's been fanned,
Next warns Aeneas of the battles soon at hand.   890
He tells him of Latinus' town, and of the race

Of Laurentines; of trials that he must either face
Or flee.

      Sleep has two gates, one thought to be of horn
(The portal through which all true shades are lightly borne),
The other, white like polished ivory as it gleams   895
(Through this, the Manes—dead souls—send our world false
   dreams).

His discourse done, Anchises leads his son there, sending
Him and the Sibyl through the ivory gate. Wending
His way back to the fleet and friends long waited for,
He coasts straight to Caieta's port. Along the shore,   900
With anchors thrown from prows, the ships' sterns rest once
   more.[38]

BOOK VII

Aeneas' nurse, Caieta:[1] with your death you gave
Our shores your share of endless fame. Today, your grave
Lies honored by our offerings, and your name and story
Mark your bones in Great Hesperia with glory.
Pious Aeneas, though, when done with obsequies   5
(He'd built your burial mound), discerning quiet seas,
Set sail from harbor. On his way, he caught the breeze
That blew all through the night, and took the help a white
Moon offered as it glossed the sea with silvered light.

The sands of Circe's shores are next; to these they come,   10
Where Sol's rich daughter makes the hidden copses thrum
With her incessant chanting in a house the height
Of pride, where perfumed, burning cedar lights the night.
Her singing shuttle runs through warp that's drawn out thin,
While ramping, roaring lions can be heard within,   15
Chafing at chains and groaning through the dark. The din
Of giant howling wolves, and bristling boars that rage
Is heard, as well as fearsome bears who rock each cage.
All these, the cruel Circe's magic turned to creatures,
Wrapping human beings in these beastly features.   20
To keep the flower of Troy from such monstrosities,
In Circe's harbor or ashore, with fates like these,
Neptune raised favoring winds to fill the sails, and gave
Troy an escape route from that shallows-seething grave.

And now the sun's rays blushed the sea, as crocus Dawn   25
Brought heaven's light her dust-pink chariot had drawn,
Until . . . the winds wound down, and suddenly, all breeze

Was gone. Oars struggled slowly through the doldrumed seas.
That's when Aeneas spies from far off-shore a great
Woods through which Tiber's handsome waters agitate   30
Thick eddies all a-swarm with golden sand, then break
For sea. About, above, the bright-plumed flyers make
Their song. Accustomed to the banks and riverbed,
They sing to please the sky as they soar overhead.

Aeneas had his crew change course. They turned their prows   35
Landward with joy, then sailed upstream, beneath the boughs
That shaded Tiber.

                    Erato, come now, and say[2]
Who reigned in ancient Latium's times. Show us the way
Things were when that uncanny fleet first dropped its anchor
In Ausonia; sing the first bloody rancor.   40
Tell its cause. You, goddess: stir me—you! My breath
Will chant the battles and the princes borne to death.
I sing Tyrrhenian troops and all Hesperia driven
To arms. To me, a greater theme has now been given;
I write a greater work.

                    Latinus now had ruled   45
His fields and town in peace till time had turned him old.
(They say that Faunus[3] and a nymph—the Laurentine
Marica—gave him life [and Faunus took his line
From Picus, whose progenitor was Saturnine,
He says, since Saturn was his *fons et origo*]).   50

Denied an heir by fate, his son dead long ago
In youth, Latinus had one maiden child instead,
Who kept his palace and was ready now to wed.
All Latium-wide, men sought her—all Ausonia, too.

But most of all, the noble Turnus came to woo.　　55
Latinus' queen was eager for this high connection—
A son-in-law she viewed with specially close affection.

Celestial omens, though (with varied frights), prevented
This. There was a courtyard that a laurel tented,
Sacred-leaved and always viewed with reverent fear.　　60
It's said Latinus Pater found it in the year
He built his citadel, then made it Phoebus' shrine
(The reason that its citizens were "Laurentine").
Then, strange to tell, a dense cloud formed, of rising bees,[4]
That humming up through liquid air's transparencies,　　65
Perched in that laurel's top. They knit their apian knees,
And in a sudden swarm hung from one leafy limb.
The priest cried out, "There'll come a stranger, and to him
We'll bow! Out of the place he comes from, there'll be grim
Soldiers storming the heights our citadel commands."　　70

But as he lights the altar with some fresh-cut brands,
It seems as though the maid Lavinia,[5] while she stands
Beside her father, sets her long hair all on fire.[6]
(Horror!). Bedizened robes are crackling. Sparks shoot higher
As her regal tresses kindle—jeweled, crowned,　　75
Taking flame. Smoke and sulfurous light now wrap her round;
She scintillates the palace grounds with glinting light,
And all are talking of the shocking, eerie sight.
They prophesy that she'll glow bright in fame and fate,
But decimating war will come. The people wait.　　80

The king sought Faunus to explain this dreadful wonder,
Consulting his prophetic father-seer there under
Towering Albunea's regal woods, which thunder
With that holy fountain's dread toxicity

From dark deep down. Here all the tribes of Italy   85
And of Oenotria sought help. The priest, when he
Brought offerings, and in the silent night found sleep
By lying on the spread-out fleeces of the sheep,
Saw phantoms in their many guises flitting through
The air, heard varied voices, and was talking to   90
The gods. He spoke to Acheron, Avernus-deep.

So here Latinus killed a hundred wooly sheep
By rite. A people's father searching for a clue,
He lay there propped up on the skins of beasts he slew.
Then all at once, from deepest woods, a great voice cried,   95
"My son, don't try to make your child a Latin bride!
O son, don't do this just so tribes may be allied.
Strangers will come to be your kin. Their blood will bear
Our name up to the stars, and their descendants, where
The circling sun views both great oceans, shall one day   100
See all the world below their feet, beneath their sway."

His father Faunus' warning in the silent night—
This hushed reply—Latinus' lips could not hold tight,
When Rumor'd flown it through Ausonia, far and wide:
The issue of Laomedon had moored beside   105
The grassy river banks! Beneath a tall tree's shade,
Aeneas, handsome Iulus, and the captains laid
Their bodies—and a banquet. (There they set down wheat
Cakes on the grass for boards to hold what they would eat—
So Jupiter himself inspired them—adding in   110
Wild fruit with Ceres' gifts.) When that was gone, the thin
Bread "plates" themselves were next, as hunger made them chew
Away, and need instructed mouths what they should do.
Boldly, they tear those fateful discs of Ceres' grains
And eat, until of all their cakes, not one remains.   115

That's when Iulus, joking, asked no more than, "So!
We eat our tables, too?"[7]

                    Hearing that question, though,
Meant all their toil was done. His father, as they fell,
Caught Iulus' words and stopped him. Sensing heaven's spell,
He cried out suddenly, "Fate's made this land our due!   120
Penates, hail—you gods of Troy, faithful and true!
Here is our home, this is our country, for I mind
Anchises' secret, how he left these words behind:
'My son, when driven to some alien shore, you find
Your food is gone, and you must eat your tables from   125
Sheer hunger, then the time to found your home has come.
Though weary, site it there, and build your bulwarks high.'
This was that hunger, this the last task left—that I
Should put an end to all our ruin.
Come then, and gladly, at the first light of the sun,   130
Let's scout out where we are, what men live here, and where
Their city lies. We'll range from harbor, here and there.
Pour Jove's libations now, and summon with your prayer
My sire, Anchises. Once more, set the board with wine."

He stopped, then bound his temples with a leafy vine,   135
Invoked the genius there, then called on Earth, of all
Gods, first. The nymphs—and streams not known yet—heard his call.
He summoned Night and all Night's rising constellations,
Idaean Jove, and Phrygia's Mother of All Nations,
Then last . . . his parents, one in Erebus and one   140
Above.

        Then Jove Omnipotent, when that was done,
Took hold of clear blue sky and shook a burning cloud
With his own hand, then thundered three times. At this loud

Signal, all through the Trojan lines, the word went round:
That day had come once promised them: they were to found   145
Their city! Rivals in the feast, they read that sign
With joy, then set out cups and crowned the rims with wine.

Next day, when dawn lights up the earth with its first torch,
The Trojans scout the coasts and borders, as they search
The city out: here's Tiber, and Numicius' spring,   150
And here's their home, those brave folk of the Latian king.

Aeneas picks a hundred men of every ranking,
With olive branches for Latinus. On the way
To his impressive capital without delay,
They go to win a Teucrian peace. As they obey   155
Aeneas's commands, they step off quickly. He
Himself digs in: a shallow trench that will surround
His campsite (for it marks the walls) soon rings the ground—
The shore's first settlement. Its earthworks form a mound.

Their march soon done, the men could see the towers
    and high-   160
Pitched Latian roofs. Then drawing close, they spied nearby,
Outside the walls, young men and boys amidst the dusty
Horse-breaking and dressage. Some gave sharp spears a lusty
Heave or drew back eager bows, while others vied
At racing or at boxing. Galloping up, a rider   165
Brought the news to old Latinus: men had come,
In alien armor! So he has these great ones summoned
To his court, then sits on the ancestral throne.
(Stately and huge, his hundred-columned palace shone.[8]
The city's crown, and once Laurentian Picus' own,   170
Its grove inspired awe and reverence through the ages.)

Now this was where their kings would meet with good presages,
Accepting scepters; here was where to first assume

The fasces. This place was their sacred banquet room
And senate. When the rams' throats had been rightly slit,   175
Then here, at endless tables, elders all would sit.

And statues of their founding fathers stood in lines
Of ancient cedar: Italus; and Sire Sabinus,
Shown with pruning hook, the grower of their vines;
And agèd Saturn, with the two-faced Janus. All   180
The other founding kings as well stood in that hall,
Along with heroes wounded in their country's wars.

A slew of weapons hung upon the hallowed doors,
With curving-bladed axes, captured battle-cars,
And helmet crests, and trophy-gates with massive bars,   185
And spears and shields and beak-prowed vessels' torn-off sprits.
With his Quirinal augur's staff, here Picus sits,
Trabea-decked, *ancile* in his left hand. (Circe's
Potions poisoned him, this man who broke wild horses:
Love-crazed, she struck him with her golden wand, and he   190
Became a rare woodpecker, wings specked colorfully.)
Such was the temple of the gods and throne of yore
From which Latinus called the Teucrians before
Him.

When they'd entered, he spoke first—in friendly tones:
"Dardans (yes, you and Troy, your city, aren't unknowns   195
To us. And we have heard about your voyage here):
What do you seek? What cause, what exigence or near
Occasion of the blue waves brings Ausonian shores
Your harboring fleet? Whether storm-driven or off-course
(Misfortunes many sailors suffer on the seas),   200
You've breached the river's mouth. Now anchored at your ease,
Don't spurn our friendship. Saturn bred us Latians, who
Are just not just because of all that laws can do
With chains, but *sua sponte*—to that old god, true.

In fact, I can recall (though time has blurred the tale)   205
Auruncan elders saying how, born on this swale,
Dardanus went to Phrygia's cities, to the place
Once Thracian Samos, but now known as Samothrace.
He left from here—from Corythus' Tyrrhenian home—
Whom now the golden palace of the sky's star-dome   210
Receives. He swells the heavens' altars' endless sum."

When he had done, Ilioneus'⁹ answer took this form:
"King, noble son of Faunus, neither pitch-black storm,
Nor straying star nor mis-read, landmarked shore has forced
Us over seas, misled, or thrown us off our course,   215
But willingly, by constancy, we reached your gates—
Exiles from what was once the greatest of all states
The sun has seen in coming from the eastern sky.
Our race comes down from Jove, all Dardans gladdened by
Jove's being ours. From Jove's great line, our own true king,   220
Trojan Aeneas, sends us here. How harrowing
The blood-dimmed tide with which Mycenae overswirled
Idaean plains, and how the powers once one world
(Europe and Asia) fought it out where Fate had hurled
Them, *all* have heard—those countries distant and alone,   225
Where Ocean circles back; those whom a torrid zone
The tyrant sun lays over four *more* zones, keeps from
Us. Out of onslaught, sailing desolate seas, we've come,
Asking if we may give our gods a humble home—
A simple strand, with air and water free to all.   230
We won't disgrace you. Your renown will never fall.
Our deepest thanks, ingratitude shall not destroy.
Ausonia will never rue embracing Troy.
Now by his fate and by that hand no man has bested
(Aeneas' faith—and sword—prove true whenever tested),   235
I swear that many peoples, many nations (do

Not scorn the bands of peace, the prayers, we offer you
Unasked) have sought us for themselves as their ally.
But forced by heaven's will, we sought you, driven by
The gods' decrees. Here, Dardanus was born, and here   240
Apollo calls us back, commanding that we steer
Toward Tuscan Tiber and Numicia's holy springs.
Take now (mere tokens of what was) these offerings—
From burning Troy, a precious clutch of rescued things.
Anchises poured libations at the altars from   245
This gold. And these: the scepter used when all had come
To hear his laws; his robes and sacred diadem,
Work of its daughters, done in Ilium."

All through Ilioneus' speech, Latinus, eyes downcast
And yet intently moving, kept his gaze fixed fast   250
Upon the ground. It isn't Priam's scepter or
The figured purple robe that moves the king. Much more,
He weighs his daughter's marriage and the bed that she
Will fill. He ponders ancient Faunus' prophecy:
"This is that man from far away Fate says will be   255
My son-in-law—the summoned one who equally
With me will rule; whose sons' uncommon power and might
Will occupy the whole known world."

                                    Then, with delight,
He spoke at last: "Now may the gods bless what we've planted
(And they've planned). Trojan, what you request is granted.   260
Your gifts are welcome, and the wealth our country yields
(Along with Trojan wealth) is yours, our fertile fields
As well. But if Aeneas wants so much to be
Our friend—if that is what he seeks so eagerly—
Then let him come; our countenance will be benign.   265
To shake your leader's hand will be this peace-pact's sign.

Now tell your king my answer. I've a daughter whom
The omens out of heaven (and my father's tomb)
Will not let wed a Latian man. Our sons will come
From alien lands, it's prophesied for Latium—   270
Men by whose blood our name, I *hope*—and if my mind
Augurs the truth, I'm *sure*—will rise where men may find
It: in the stars. This is the man the Fates assigned."

When he was done, the father chose sleek steeds from all
His herd (three hundred head, each in its lofty stall).   275
He had one led, by rank, to every Teucrian—
Fast mounts, with purple, finely wrought caparison.
And on their golden breastplates, golden collars sit;
Each courser champs its teeth upon a golden bit.
Absent Aeneas got a chariot with two   280
Yoked horses born of heaven; out their nares they blew
Pure fire, those bastards daedal Circe'd bred, a pair,
From Jove's, by mating them to her own mortal mare.
They mounted up, and the Aeneans' ride was swift:
They went with King Latinus' words; peace was his gift.   285

But look: Jove's cruel wife was on her steady flight
From Inachus's Argos when from a great height
She spied the Dardan fleet. Aeneas, with delight,
Is building homes, she learns, and from Sicilian skies
Far past Pachynus, Juno sees that he relies   290
On Latium now, his ships deserted.[10]

                              Pierced with pain,
She stops and shakes her head and rants on in this strain:
"This tribe whose destiny on the Sigaean plain
Was to survive! Whose Phrygian fate has overturned
My favored race's! Why weren't they made captive, burned   '   295
With Troy? But no, they fought their way through armies, spurned

My flames! I think I must have lost my powers at last,
Or spent my rage, or sunk to rest, my force laid waste.
Why, when they fled their homes, aggressively I chased
Them on the waves and challenged them on all the oceans.   300
But force of sea and sky was wasted on these Trojans.
What use have Syrtes, Scylla, vast Charybdis been?
The Trojans moor in Tiber, where they can't be seen,
Safe now from sea . . . and me. Yet Mars eradicated
The countless Lapiths; Jove himself left antiquated   305
Calydon to Dian's rage. What crime had *they*
Committed, tribe or man, for which they had to pay?
But I, Jove's mighty queen, with every power known,
And turning all to use, must fail! Left on my own,
I'm beaten by Aeneas. If my goddess-strength   310
Can't win, I'll beg for help. I'll go to any length
If I can't sway the gods. I'll stir up Hell!¹¹ I own
I'm not allowed to keep him from the Latian crown,
And Fate won't budge—Lavinia *will* be his bride—,
But I can stall that day, delayed if not denied.   315
And I can still destroy both rulers' races. *Let*
Those two unite; their people soon will pay for it!
Her dowry? Trojan and Rutulian blood and bone.
Her maid? Bellona! Nor did Cisseus' child alone
Conceive a firebrand, becoming fire's mother,   320
For Venus, too, has such a son, and he's another
Paris—one more funeral torch for Troy Renascent."

All passion spent, earthward the dreaded goddess hastened
To Alecto of Affliction,¹² from the murk—
The hellish shadows—where the dire Furies lurk,   325
Hearts full of warfare, brutal crimes of rage, and lies.
Even her father Pluto and her sibs despise
Her down in Tartarus, where monstrously, she takes
Such forms and shows such savage looks, she sprouts black snakes.

These rousing words, Alecto hears the goddess say: 330
"Night's virgin child: to keep my honor from decay,
Make mine this service, lest my glory should give way
As the Aeneans court Latinus with the prize
Of marriage, or Aeneas' people occupies
The land. You prick long-loving brothers with the urge   335
To kill. You shatter homes with hate and bring the scourge
And death-torch. You've a thousand different appellations,
A thousand blood-arts. Search your fecund heart's foundations.
Slash the pact of peace and plant war's accusations.
Let the men, right then, all want and need and seize   340
Their weapons!"

      So Alecto, who's infected (she's
En-Gorgon-venomed), seeks first Latium, then the high
Halls of Laurentium's king, in silence, squatting by
Amata's door (a mother's seething worries boil—
What of the Teucrians? Or Turnus' marriage-royal?).   345

Plucking her head, Alecto flings a blue-black snake;
Amata's deep heart's core receives it like a stake.
It makes her fill her house with hate that never rests.
Gliding between her garments and her silky breasts,
It winds its way unfelt by that half-maddened queen,   350
Injecting her with viper's breath. And then it's seen:
A twisted golden chain; a ribbon to a coiled-
Up headband. Twining in her hair, it slithers, oiled,
All down her limbs.

      And while the fluent poison sickens,
Filling all her senses, twisting fire quickens   355
Round her bones. Her mind has not yet sensed this flame;
A mother's gentle voice, and her voice, sound the same.

And yet she sobs. Her daughter and a Phrygian—wed!
"Lavinia led to warm a Teucrian exile's bed?
Her father, yet no pity for her? None for *you*,   360
Even? Or *me*? One breeze, and you know what he'll do?
Head right for water with his dazzled prize, the way
That Phrygian shepherd came to Sparta—not to stay,
But lead his Lacedaemon's Leda's Helen straight
To Troy. You gave your *word*. And you were wont—of late—   365
To guard your own—and take your kinsman Turnus' hand!
If Latians need a son-in-law from some far land,
And this must be, and Father Faunus's decree
Weighs on you, . . . then I say that every country free
Of us—and distant—counts as foreign. So declare   370
The gods. Besides, track Turnus to his source—that pair
Acrisius and Inachus—Mycenae's there."

But when she sees, despite her words, Latinus still
Against her; when the crazing venom's worked its will,
The serpent seeping deep inside her everywhere;   375
That luckless woman, pricked by horrors huge and rare,
Then truly maddened, rages through each city square.

A spinning top that boys intent on play will thrash
In widening circles round an empty court (the lash
Compels its whirling like a drover's whip) amazes   380
As it spins its loops before dumbfounded gazes.
In innocence, they wonder at that twirling top
Each blow gives life. The queen, as if she'll never stop,
Swirls through the hearts of towns and warlike tribes as well.

Worse still, fled to the woods, she fakes a "Bacchic spell"   385
To spawn a greater madness, launch a greater sin:
She seeks the wooded peaks to hide her daughter in,

Snuffing the Teucrians' nuptial torch and dragging out
The wedding, "*Euhoe*, Bacchus! Only you," her shout.[13]
"This virgin's yours, whose thyrsus is for you alone.   390
Her dance is yours; accept the sacred hair she's grown."

Then Rumor races. Women maddened by the same
Frenzy seek strange new dwelling places. Hearts aflame,
They flee their homes, and in the wind, their heads go bare,
Necks naked. Tremulous ululation fills the air.   395
They drape themselves in pelts and carry vine-wrapped spears.
The raging queen herself burns like the torch she rears,
As turning bloody-eyed, she sings the wedding song
Of Turnus and Lavinia.

                    Fierce then, to the throng
She cries, "O Latian women everywhere, hear me!   400
If poor Amata still can claim your loyalty—
And if a mother's rights affect you yet—set free
Your hair and join me in the ritual's ecstasy."
So, far and wide, Alecto goads with Bacchic rowel,
Spurring the queen through wooded lairs where wild beasts
    howl.   405

And when she saw she'd sharpened quite enough these first
Furies—Latinus' house smashed, all his planning burst—
That grim divinity took ashen wing and fled,
To haunt those brash Rutulian's walls the legend said
Danäe built with her Acrisian settlers, blown   410
There by the harsh South Wind. Ardea, it was known
As by our fathers, and Ardea's name is great
Still, though its glory died.

                    Here, palaced Turnus, late
At night, lay deep in sleep. Alecto doffed her grim
Appearance, shed her fearful shape, shook off each limb,   415

And formed herself an old hag's looks, with hoary hair
And coltered brow and sacred ribbon, twining there
An olive spray—a trick to make herself resemble
Calybe, Juno's ancient priestess of her temple.

She showed herself to that fierce prince with words like these: 420
"Turnus, will you stand by while Dardan settlers seize
Your scepter, rendering all your efforts wasted? So . . .
The king denies your bride and what the Latians owe
You for your blood, to set a stranger on your throne?
Well, then! *Court* danger. *Fight* unthanked. *Be* made a clown.   425
Cut down Tyrrhenian enemies, to pall with peace
The Latians. What I tell you, sleeping on night's fleece
Of calm, the mighty child of Saturn ordered me
To say: rise up! And march your army joyfully
From gates to field. Burn all the painted ships that tether   430
In our cherished river; torch those ships, together
With their Phrygian captains. Jove commands it! Let
Even Latinus bleed if he won't pay his debt—
Your promised bride. Let him at last test Turnus' sword."

He mocked the priestess, giving back in turn this word: 435
"The news that ships have breached the Tiber, hasn't—as
You seem to think—escaped me, and your threatening has
No purchase on my soul, for Heaven's queen has not
Abandoned me; I'm not forgot.
But ancient mother: age, defeated by decay,   440
Devoid of truth, distresses you in vain, the way
It mocks your warnings, in the midst of princes' battles,
With phantom fears. Go guard the gods—their shrines and
    statues.
Men will wage war and peace; it is by men war's waged."

Alecto, hearing this, bursts into flame, enraged.   445
But as that young man speaks, at once his body shakes.

His eyes fixed, as that Fury hissed with myriad snakes,
And then a horrid form appeared.

                                        She rolls her eyes,
Hurling him back. He falters, as again he tries
To speak. She bristles double serpents from her hair,   450
Then snaps those whips, snarling through rabid lips: "Despair!
Am I 'devoid of truth, defeated by decay,
Distressed,' and mocked amidst kings' feuds in all I say?
See *this*! I come here from the Deadly Sisters, and
It's death and war-blood in my hand."   455

With that, she targeted a torch at Turnus, sticking
It in his chest. It smoked with lurid light, flames licking.
A giant terror murdered sleep; sweat poured and shone
From every pore and soaked him, limb and flesh and bone.
Maddened, he shrieks, "A sword!" and seeks it by his bed   460
And through the palace. Sword-lust and war's thirst for dead
Men have him, but pure fury most.

                                        You've seen piled tinder
Crackling under cauldrons boiling from that kindling,
Cauldrons bubbling, dancing to the heat? The spume
Mounts, seething from within; the water spews tall foam   465
Until it can't contain itself. The air turns steam.

That's how the prince profanes the peace. He tells his prime
Young warriors, "March against the king! Prepare to fight
To save all Italy and put her foes to flight!
Our mere advance will do for both the Latians *and*   470
The Teucrians!" That done, he calls the gods to stand
In witness. The Rutulians vie: Who will have fanned
The war-flames most? One thrills to Turnus' youth and handsome

Form, one to his bloodline, one to deeds his hand
Has done.

     While Turnus fills the Rutuli with daring,   475
Hell-winged Alecto dives where Teucrians are snaring
Game.[14] With fresh new plots, she spies the shoreline where
Fair Iulus hunts wild game afoot, with net and snare.
Cocytus' virgin sets the hound-hearts quickly racing,
Their nostrils whiffing blood's old scent. Soon, they are chasing 480
Down a stag.

     This was the first cause of that lust
For war that kindled killing animus in rustic
Hearts. A fine stag—giant-racked; torn from its mother's
Nursing breast—had been brought up by nurturing brothers,
Tyrrhus' sons (since Tyrrhus had the king's herd-care   485
And managed far-flung royal pastures everywhere).
Their sister Silvia gentled it to heed her hand's
Commands; she looped its horns, adorned with silken strands
Of flowers. She groomed it, bathing it in crystal springs.
Hand-tamed, it ate its mistress' food. Wood-wanderings   490
Would end with its return to the familiar sight
Of home (all by itself), however late at night.

When it had strayed far off, Iulus' frothing pack
Started that swimming stag as it was climbing back
Up on the grass-cool bank, to cool its heavy rack.   495
Ascanius, too, was hot—for honor—which he meant
To have. He aimed an arrow from the bow he'd bent.
The goddess did not fail his shaky hand, which sent
Off a twanging arrow that pierced the gut and thigh.
The wounded beast, though, ran home with a piteous cry,   500
To sink down bloody, moaning in its well-known stall,

Where beggar-like, it dragged out life, beseeching all
The house.

      First, Silvia, the sister, beat her arms,
Calling for help from rough-hewn men who ran from farms.
And since Alecto roamed the hushed woods still, they raced   505
To help, with fire-hardened torches, all in haste,
Armed with their heavy, knotted clubs. Rage weaponized
What lay at hand, as Tyrrhus called his men and seized,
By chance, an axe (he had been quarter-splitting oak
By driving wedges, breathing hard at every stroke).   510

The savage goddess saw her chance for doing harm;
She fled her lookout perch and sounded the alarm
For herdsmen, from the stalls' steep roof. The curved horn made
Her Tartarean voice boom, as through every glade
And grove, the woods shook, echoing in deep, out far.   515
The distant Trivian lake and the white river Nar
(All sulfurous waters) hear it, and Velinus' springs.
To every anxious mother's breast, her infant clings.

They raced together with their hasty weapons then,
Answering the deadly trumpet call—those rough-hewn men   520
Who'd heard its signal. Out camp gates, to help the boy
Ascanius, came pouring forth the youth of Troy
As well. The battle lines are drawn up for the sake
Of more than rustic brawls with fire-tempered stake
Or massy club: it's two-edged steel now everywhere—   525
A dark sword crop is bristling, as bronze blinds the air.
Sun-stricken armor throws its gleaming light cloud-high,
The way a whitening billow will, at wind's first sigh
(Little by little, sea-waves surge; they leap and leap
Still higher toward the skies, while cresting from the deep).   530

Young Almo, in the front ranks, here was laid low—struck
Down by a whirring arrow. For the point had stuck
Inside his throat. And Tyrrhus' oldest son died, choked
On blood, the path of liquid speech and frail breath blocked.
The dead lie all around, with old Galaesus, who   535
Had died while pleading peace. Once greatly just and true,
He'd been Ausonia's richest man. (Five flocks had *baa*'d
For him; a hundred ploughs had coltered through his sod.
For him, five herds had shuffled home at end of day.)

They raged across the fields, with nothing either way.   540
Her promise kept, the goddess, when she'd steeped the fray
In blood and fed its early skirmishes with death,
Forsook Hesperia, then wheeled across the breadth
Of heaven.

      Vaunting in a haughty voice, she told
Juno, "Your wish for discord makes black war—behold!   545
Now tell these *friends* that they should all confederate!
I've christened Teucrians with Ausonian blood, and wait
Now on your wish, your word, to do oh, so much more.
I'll drag the neighboring towns into this blood-crazed war.
I'll kindle battle-lust with nothing more than words;   550
They'll come from every field I mean to sow with swords."

Then Juno: "That's enough of fraud and treachery;
The *casus belli*'s set. With blood-wet weaponry
That chance first offered them, they battle hand-to-hand.
Let *this* be their alliance, *this* the wedding band   555
They bless—Latinus and that peerless son of Venus!
But high Olympus' father-regent by no means
Meant you to flitter over-freely through the blue.
Leave here. If by some chance there's work still left to do,

I'll more than manage it." So Saturn's daughter speaks;   560
Alecto raises up her wings, with hissing snakes,
And leaves the skies for home (Cocytus).

                                         There's a site
In Italy's deep core, below a mountain's height—
The famed Amsanctus Vale, well-known in every land.
Woods dense with dark leaves hem it in on either hand,   565
And down its center roars a torrent; rocks resound.
That spate goes circling till its racing flood lies drowned.
A fearful cave here spews out savage Dis's breath;
Here Acheron breaks through the deep abyss of death.
Alecto plunges; plague-jaws gulp that deity   570
Of hate. And so she leaves the earth and heavens free.

Meanwhile, Queen Juno quickly acts to give this war
Its final touches. All the frantic herdsmen bore
Their fallen back from battle. Into town they race
With Almo and Galaesus (wounds have maimed his face).   575
They supplicate the gods and call upon Latinus,
While in the hubbub's heart, amid their cries, stands Turnus,
Redoubling fear of fire and slaughter: "Phrygian stock
To mix with ours? And *Trojan* rule! The Latians lock
Me out?"

                           Then those whose women dance the trackless wood,   580
Half Maenad-mad (Amata's power is understood),
Collect their crowd from everywhere, beseeching Mars.

At once, perversely mad for war, their clamor jars
Against the gods, against their signs. They vie to ring
Latinus' palace, but that mob-surrounded king—   585
An anchored ocean crag—immovably resists,

A mighty cliff amidst the smashing combers' mists;
A rock that plants itself against ten thousand waves
That howl in vain, as spume-and-seaweed-crushing caves
Thunder. Against their sides, the blown-back breakers spill.   590

But when no power is granted him to thwart blind will,
And ruthless Juno rules events, the father pleads
And pleads with gods and hapless winds. But nothing heeds.
"Fate breaks us! Whirlwinds blow us into the abyss!
O wretched race, you'll pay the price yourselves for this,   595
With impious blood. And Turnus, too: the punishment
Your crime deserves awaits you; prayers then heaven-sent,
Will rise too late. For me now, close to dying's door,
I've lost all chance of happiness." He said no more,
But went inside and dropped the reins he now forswore.   600

Hesperian Latium's sacred custom from of yore,
Long held to by the towns of Alba, just the way
Great Rome does now when rousing Mars to any fray
(Whether they mean to take in hand some baleful war
Against the Getae, Arabs, or Hyrcanians or   605
Far India, hunting dawn—or eagles they'll reclaim
From Parthians): twin Gates of War (so people name
Them), holy by religion and by dreaded Mars,
And locked by deathless iron and a hundred bars
Of bronze. Their guardian Janus never leaves their sill.   610

When battle is the city fathers' final will,
The Consul, in his Gabine-bound Quirinal cloak,
Unlocks these screeching doors of warfare to invoke
The battle-gods himself. The other young men show
Assent; hoarsely agreeing, brazen trumpets blow.   615
Latinus, too, was ordered in this way to go

Declare war on Aeneas' people, and to throw
The grim gates open wide. He would not do it, though,
Recoiling at that hateful task, but went off by
Himself.

        So heaven's queen came gliding from the sky,   620
To swing the lingering doors wide open personally.
So Saturn's daughter forced the hard-hinged war-gates free,
And dull Ausonia, once asleep and idle, burns.
Some plan to march across the plains on foot; by turns,
Some, riding horses, stir the dust. All cry at once   625
For weapons. Rich fat polishes the shining lance
And lustrous shield, as grindstones whet dull axes. All
Are glad to wave their flags and hear the trumpets call.[15]

It's then that five great cities forge new arms, renew
Their weapons: strong Atina, and proud Tibur, too;   630
Ardea, Crustumeri, towered Atemnae, who
Are hammering out war's vital helmets. Each town weaves
The wicker ribs for shields. Some beat thin, shiny greaves
Of pliant silver, hammering bronzine breastplates. Here
Is where their pride—in sickle blade, and in the share   635
The plough bears—leads: to fire-forge a father's sword.

And now the bugles sound the signal; war's watchword
Goes round. One grabs a hasty helmet, one rigs trembling
Horses to their harness. Some are fast assembling
Shields or three-ply coats of golden mail, or hanging   640
Swords.

        Now, Muses:[16] open Helikon, and singing,
Say what kings were stirred to fight; what ranks then followed
Each and filled the fields; what men back then the hallowed

Earth of Italy produced; what fiery steeds
Flourished. You Sisters wield a memory that feeds   645
On all, while we have scarcely heard a hint of deeds
They did.

      First, blasphemous Mezentius commands
In war; he leaves the Tuscan shore to rouse his bands.[17]
Lausus, his son, stands by him (no one is more handsome
But Laurentine Turnus). Breaker of wild steeds,   650
Fierce hunter from Agylla's city, Lausus leads
A thousand men on (who will follow him in vain—
A man deserving better than that father's reign
Over him; worthy of a better father than
Mezentius).

      Aventinus follows, son of man-   655
God Hercules. Fine as his father, he displays
His palm-crowned chariot with its team of winning bays.
Over the plain he drives, his father's snake-strewn sign
Drawn on his shield: around the Hydra, hundreds twine.
One born of Rhea on the wooded Aventine,   660
He came in secret to that priestess' shores of life.
(She'd lain with Tiryns' Hercules, a god-man's "wife,"
When he'd slain Geryon, then with his cattle, came
From Spain so they could bathe in Latium's Tuscan stream.)

Bringing grim pikes and javelins for martial arts,   665
His troops are armed with polished swords and Sabine darts,
While with a bristling, frightening, giant lion's skin,
Swung by its mane, he gains the palace, marching in
Like that—his shoulders garbed like Hercules', with white
Fangs round his head.

                    Brave Coras, with his brother right   670
Behind—his twin, Catillus—(Argive youths), leaves walled
Tibur (Tiburtus is the one those folk are called
After). These twins rush to the front ranks, where the spear-
Crop's thickest—like two cloud-born Centaurs who appear,
Down from some crest on Homole, from Othrys' snow.   675
The massed woods yield to rushing Centaurs as they go,
And with a deafening crash, the thickets all give ground.

And Caeculus was there, the king who was to found
Praeneste, and whom all believe was granted birth
In Vulcan's roaming herds (and found upon his hearth).   680
He's followed by an army from the countryside:
Men living on Praeneste's steeps; men who abide
In Gabine Juno's fields, or on cool Anio's banks;
Among the Hernican wet rocks; those who give thanks
To Pater Amasenus or Anagnia. Not   685
Weaponed with sword or shield or rattling chariot,
Most sling their blue-lead bullet-stones; some carry twin
Darts in their hands; some wear a cap of red wolf-skin
For headgear, marching with their left foot bare, their right
Shod with a rawhide boot.

                    Now summoned to the fight,   690
Long-torpid tribes obey Messapus, Neptune's son,
And troops unused to warfare follow one whom none
Can kill with steel or fire; this breaker-in of horses
Takes up the sword again. Some hold Fescennium's forces
Or Aequi Falisci's ranks, while others from   695
Soracte's heights or the Flavinian ploughlands come.
Some claim Capena's groves and some Ciminus' hill
And lake. They march in rows that line-straight columns fill,
Singing their king, the way that Asian meadow's muck

(And Cayster's stream) resound when from far off they're struck 700
By long-necked chords from snowy birds as rains are seeding
Clouds and swans wing home from feeding.
No one would think the bronze-clad ranks massed in that crowd
So vast; they'd think that swarming high, an airy cloud
Of raucous birds was aimed toward shore, their great wings beating. 705

There's Clausus, too, of fine old Sabine blood. He's leading
A mighty host, and he himself's a mighty host.
The widespread Claudian tribe and clan—great Latium's boast—
Came from him, ever since the Sabines shared in Rome.
Quirites' troops, and Amiternum's great bands, come—   710
Eretum's, too. Mutusca, famed for olive trees,
Will fight. Nomentum's townsmen come. From Rosean leas
Beside Velinus, soldiers show; from bristling crags
Of Tetrica; from Severus. Casperia brags
Of joining, and Himella. Foruli, and those   715
Who drink the Tiber and the Fabaris, with frozen
Nursia march, with Ortine squads and Latin folk,
And those the Fate-cursed Allia's cutting waters choke
Off—numbers swelling like the waves on Libya's main
When winter sinks Orion; numbers thick as grain   720
Parched by the sun in Lycia's fields or Hermus' plain.
Shields clang; feet tramp. And terra firma shakes with pain.

Next, Agamemnon's son, who hates the Trojan name:
Halaesus yokes his horses to the chariot frame
And sweeps a thousand martial tribes to Turnus—those   725
Who mattock Bacchus' Massic soil; men elders chose
To send from the Auruncan hills and nearby plains
Of Sidicinum; Cales' men. Volturnus drains
Itself (that shallow stream) of soldiers; by their side,
The rough Saticulans and Oscan bands, who plied   730

Smooth javelins they would sling with pliant thongs of hide.
A small shield guards their left; they fight in-close with curved
Swords.

Oebalus, in these our lines, your name's observed
As well—you whom (they say) the nymph Sabethis bore
To Telon (agèd now) when he reigned once before   735
In Teleboan Capreae. Unsatisfied
With fields passed down, his son now ruled lands far and wide:
Sarrasti's people, where the Sarnus floods the plains;
Batulum's folk, and men Celemna's realm contains;
The Rufri; those Abella's appled walls survey   740
(They like to throw their javelins the Teuton way;
Their caps are made of bark from cork trees that they flay;
Their bronze shields glitter and their sword is glittering bronze).

And you, too, Ufens, sent to fight from Nersae Mons.
(In war, they win, and all the world knows well their worth,   745
This extra-tough folk of the hard Aequian earth.
They've grown inured to rugged hunting in their woods.
Ploughing while armed, and always glad for new-won goods,
They carry off the spoils on which they love to feed.

There was also a priest of the Marruvian breed,   750
Who wore a helmet decked with olive leaves. One sent
By King Archippus, Umbro the most valiant,
Could sprinkle sleep, by touch of hand or magic chant,
On vipers and on evil-breathing hydras; still
Their wrath, and balm their angry bites with special skill.   755
But none of this could heal a Dardan spear-point's wound.
No sleep-inducing charms, or magic herbs he found
On Marsian hills, availed against that injury.
Angitia's grove; Fucinus' glassy inland sea;
The limpid lakes: all sobbed for you.   760

Hippolytus's handsome Virbius went, too—
The worthy son Aricia, his mother, sent.
He grew up in Egeria's groves that circumvent
The damp shores Dian's rich, benignant altar graced.
(For people say Hippolytus, the victim—chaste—   765
Of Phaedra's wiles, when he'd been torn by bolting horses,
And paid his father's bloody debt, reclaimed the courses
Of the stars again, and came to live below
High heaven, called there by the healing of Apollo
And by Diana's love.)[18]

              Then Jove All-powerful,   770
Outraged a man should win the light of life from hell,
Pitched Phoebus' son, the one who founded healing's art,
Headlong to Styx in lightning. But with her kind heart,
Trivia hid Hippolytus away, then sent
Him to the nymph Egeria's secret grove. He spent   775
His life alone there in the woods of Italy,
And was unknown. Now "Virbius" was who he'd be.
That's why we keep all horn-hooved horses far away
From Trivia's sacred groves and temple: for that day,
Sea-monsters spooked the chariot team and driver strewn   780
All down the strand. And yet his son drove on to ruin:
Wild horses pulled his chariot down the plain to war.

And giant Turnus stirred the front ranks as he bore
His weapons back and forth. Taller than all the rest,
He wore a three-plumed helmet[19] boasting on its crest . . .   785
Chimaera! breathing Aetna's flames hot from her throat.
The more the fighting raged, the more those fires shot
Their savagery; the more that battle-blood was shed.

But on his gleaming shield, horns lifted on her head:
Io, in gold, already bristled and already   790

A cow—a rare device—and Argus, set to ward
That maid, and Inachus, who from a chased urn poured
His stream.

       A cloud of infantry came next, then ranks
With shields that filled the plain with Argive men; whole banks
Of the Auruncans and Rutulians; old Sicanians   795
And the painted-shield Labicians, with Sacranians.
And those who plough your clearings, Tiber; those who till
Numicius' banks; who colter the Rutulian hill,
Or Circe's ridge; where Jupiter of Anxur guards
The fields; Feronia, happy with her verdant swards;   800
Soldiers from Satura's black marsh; where Ufens winds
Its chilly way through steep-pitched valleys till it finds
An ocean tomb.

       And Volscian Camilla[20] came,
Leading horsemen and squads whose bronze was all agleam—
A warrior girl with hands Minerva's distaff, wool,   805
And basket never knew. Toughened to take the full
Brunt of battle, she beat the wind in every race.
She might have left the grain tips whole, ears still in place
On unclipped wheat still tender as she flew across
Them in her course; or speeding on the waves that toss,   810
Hung poised above the deep, mercurial soles still dry.

Pouring from home and field, young men, as she goes by,
Stand staring. Marveling crowds of matrons gape in wonder
At how her royal purple drapes in all its splendor
From ivory shoulders; how her gold clasp knots her hair;   815
At how she bears her Lycian quiver full of arrows
And a shepherd's myrtle staff tipped like a spear.

Book VIII

When Turnus climbed the citadel and raised the war
Flag of Laurentium, he made the trumpets roar.
Spurring his fiery mounts as clashing arms are heard,
He rallies Latium's young, and all their hearts are stirred
As one. All swear allegiance in a wilding storm   5
Of rage. Messapus, Ufens, and Mezentius form
The general staff (Mezentius scorns the gods).

                              The wide
Farms left behind, men muster ranks from every side.
And Venulus is sent to Diomedes' town,
For help from Arpi: Teucrians are settling down   10
In Latium! Great Aeneas' fleet—and his defeated
Gods—have come! He calls himself a king who's "fated,"
And peoples everywhere have joined the Dardan side,
That hero's name spreading through Latium, far and wide.
Considering how he's started, what does he intend?   15
Should Fortune smile, how does he want this fight to end?
It's Diomedes, more than King Latinus or
King Turnus, who will know.

                         So Latium seethed. Heart-sore,
The hero sees this all. Tossed on a sea of care,
He anguishes, mind darting here, there, everywhere.   20
He grasps at this plan, then at that, a desperate soul.
He's like the light's moiré on water in a bowl
Of bronze. Reflected by the radiant moon or sun,

It flickers everywhere and bounces back up on
The fretted ceiling.

               It was night, and over all   25
The lands, profound sleep draped earth's creatures in its pall,
Each weary bird and beast. The Father lay his head
Down on the river bank. Aeneas' heart was led,
Beneath the sky's cold vault, to wrestle with the grief
Of war, until at last his body found relief.   30

And then appeared old Tiberinus,[1] deity
Of Latium, rising from the lovely river. He
Had poplar leaves and fine grey linen gauze around
Him for a cloak, and dark green reeds whose shadows crowned
His hair.

           He spoke . . . and banished all Aeneas' care: 35
"O you have brought our Trojan city back, the heir
Of heaven's race; from foes, eternal Pergamum
Is saved! Laurentine soil expected you to come
(*And* Latian land). Now here at last's your certain home,
With your Penates.[2] Don't stop now, war-terrified;   40
The raging anger of the gods has died.
Now—lest you think deceptive Sleep has made me for
Some trick: you'll find a huge sow lying on the shore
Beneath some oaks, with thirty piglets—white the young,
And white the sow. Each teat will boast a piglet's tongue.   45
Your city shall be here; your toil ends on this site.[3]
This means, in thirty years, white Alba sees the light.
Ascanius will found that town whose name shines bright.
I sing with certainty. Now hear these words, attending
As I teach you how to come through what's impending.   50
Arcadians (Pallas' offspring), friends of King Evander,
Have settled on these shores, and following his banner,

Chosen to site their city in the hillside manner.
Named for that Pallas, Pallanteum is a place
That wars eternally with all the Latian race.　　　　55
Invite them to your camp so you can be allied.
Along my banks, through proper channels, I will guide
You so your blades can beat the current back. Now get
Up, goddess-born, and as the first stars start to set,
Give Juno what she's due: true prayers. Let offerings　　　60
Defeat her raging threats, and when my counsel brings
You triumph, honor me. It's me you see full-flood,
Grazing my banks and sluicing acres rich as mud:
Blue Tiber. Heaven loves my noble river best.
Here is my home-spring, watering the towns it's blessed."　　　65

He'd spoken. Then he tombed himself deep in his stream
By diving to its bed. From night and sleep and dream,
Aeneas rises, looking toward the dawning beam
Of Heaven's sun. His cupped hands scoop up water from
The river as he pours out prayer: "O nymphs from whom　　　70
All waters spring; Laurentine nymphs from which they come;
And you, O Father Tiber: with each sacred wave,
Accept Aeneas, stave off danger as you save
Him finally. Whatever fountain keeps you, pity
Us. Whatever soil you flow from in such beauty,　　　75
We'll always honor you and be your true gift-giver;
Always, ruler of Hesperia's streams, horned river,
Oh, be with me. And let your presence show your will."
So he speaks, and from his fleet, armed oarsmen fill
Two hand-picked ships. But then! The sudden wonder of　　　80
A portent greets their eyes: bright-gleaming through a grove
Of trees, a white sow with a litter just as white
Is lying on the lush green river bank. So righteous
Aeneas bears this victim to your altar, mighty
Juno—yes, to you—and slaughters sow and brood.　　　85

Then all night long, the Tiber calmed his swelling flood,
Backing his current so the waves lay stilled, subdued
In silence, spreading waters level like some placid
Mere, so that the oarsmen rowed across a tacit
Pond. Then, on their charted course, ahead they raced,   90
To cheers. The slick keels glide; the waters are amazed.
Unused to heroes' shining shields, the woods watch, dazed
And stunned by painted ships that flow by, crew by crew.

Men spend a day and night in navigating through
The long bends, rowing, cutting glassy-watered tree   95
Reflections. When the burning sun's scaled apogee
Is reached, they see some walls, a distant citadel,
And roofs whose numbers Roman might has caused to swell
Since then, when King Evander modestly held sway
Over an unexalted realm.⁴ Quickly that day,   100
They turned prows landward as they neared the city site.

It happened the Arcadian king was in mid-rite
(For mighty Hercules, and for the gods) beneath
The town walls, in a grove. Pallas, his son, was with
Him—all the chief young men, too, and his humble senate,   105
Burning incense. Altar blood steamed in ascent.

But when they spied the tall ships slipping through the shade
In silence, suddenly they all were half-dismayed
By what they saw, and rose up, leaping from the feast.
Bold Pallas says, "Don't stop!"⁵ Not daunted in the least,   110
He grabs a spear and flies to meet them on his own.
Then from a distant rise, he cries: "What cause has blown
You off your course? Where do you go? Down paths unknown?
Who are you? What's your home? Do you bring peace or war?"

As leader then, Aeneas, holding out before   115
Him peace's olive branch, spoke from the stern's high post:

"You see here Trojans armed to fight the Latian host,
Whose haughty warfare forces us to seek relief
From King Evander. Go and tell him we're the chief
Dardanian leaders, here to ask to be allies."   120

Pallas is dumbstruck by their great name. He replies,
"Whoever you may be, come; meet my father face-
To-face; under our roof, you guests shall find a place."
He clasps Aeneas' hand in welcome. Then, all move
Off from the river, walking on into the grove.   125

Aeneas then addressed the king, his words a friend's:
"Noblest of Greece's sons, to whom my fortune sends
Me suppliant, with ribboned branches I hold out
In peace: though you're a Danaan chief, I had no doubt—
Nor fear of an Arcadian kin to Atreus'   130
Twin sons. My own worth and the signs God's given us;
Our fathers sharing blood; your fame spread everywhere:
All link us. Fate has found me willingly led here.
(Dardanus—Ilium's first father-founder, Greeks
Maintain, and born of Atlas's Electra—seeks   135
The Teucrians, where Atlas fathers her. It's he
Who bears the skies upon his back.) And Mercury,
Conceived by dazzling Maia, your progenitor.
High on Cyllene's frozen peak is where she bore
Him. Atlas fathered her, if what men say is true—   140
That Atlas who upholds the starry sky. So you
And I are shoots branching from one root. That is why
I sent no envoys, but decided to rely
Upon myself. Eschewing statecraft probing, here
I am, myself alone, as humbly I appear   145
Before you. Daunians pursue us both with grisly
Warfare. Drive us out, they think, and they will easily
Bring all Hesperia beneath their sway, and rule
The seas that wash her shores, both north and south. If you'll

Accept our pledge, and pledge in turn, you'll learn we have   150
Courageous battle-hearts; that tried, we've been found brave."

Aeneas finished. All throughout this speech, Evander
Eyes Aeneas' face and form, each feature scanned,
Then answers him: "How happily I recognize
And greet the bravest Teucrian! I see *his* eyes   155
And call to mind *his* voice—your father's—great Anchises!
Laomedon's son Priam, I recall, once came,
En route to Salamis, to Hesione's realm
(His sister). Traveling on, he went to see the chill
Arcadian lands. Back then, my young cheeks yet to fill   160
With beard, I gazed at all the Teucrians, who stun.
Laomedon's Anchises is the tallest one
By far, though. Burning with a young man's need to speak
To an heroic man, and grasp his hand, I seek
Him out, escorting him at once to Pheneus' throne.   165
He gave me, when he left, a quiver of my own—
Noble, with Lycian arrows—and a cloak that's golden;
And two golden bits my Pallas is beholden
To him for. So my hand shakes your hand. A friend,
When dawn comes back to earth tomorrow, I will send   170
You off encouraged by our help, with stores we'll lend
You. Meanwhile, since you come in honored friendship, please
Join us in these, our annual festivities,
Which must not wait. Become accustomed to our board."

He had the food and drink that had been cleared, restored   175
Then, showing guests to grassy seats, reserving pride
Of place for great Aeneas: cushioned by the hide
A lion wore—a maple throne. Young men compete
Then (servers chosen by the priest) to bring the meat
Of roasted bulls; to fill the baskets full with fine-   180
Grown gifts of Ceres, and to pour out Bacchus' wine.

Aeneas and the Trojan warriors then feast,
Devouring the chine and vitals of the beast.

When hunger had been checked, and no one wanted more,
Then King Evander spoke:[6] "It's not that we ignore   185
The ancient gods; no empty superstition laid
These solemn feasts on us or had this altar made
For some great godhead. Trojan guest, this is a rite
Renewed for one who saved us from a dire plight.
But first, you see that overhanging cliff rock there?   190
The way its mass lies shattered? How its mountain lair
Stands desolate, the crags hauled down in giant scree?
There was a cave here, veining to infinity,
Where sunbeams couldn't reach, and where the hideous form
Of semi-human Cacus lived, and earth reeked, warm   195
With new blood. Human heads nailed down on haughty gates
Were always hanging—grisly, pale, in putrid states.
Vulcan had bred this monster who would vomit black
Flames as he dragged his massive bulk along and back.
At last, time brought us longed-for help: Alcides came—   200
Greatest avenger god, and boastful of his fame
(He killed the triune Geryon and drove his spoils
This way—the monster's cattle. Victor in his toils,
He led them here to graze the valley's riverside).
The raging Cacus, frenzied lest he leave untried   205
A single evil, or a devious trick undared,
Drove off four bulls to whom no bulls could be compared;
Four peerless heifers, too, he rustles from their stalls.
But to ensure no forward-pointing spoor, he hauls
Them by their tails into his cave. Thus, every mark   210
Of tracks, that thief wipes out; deep in the stony dark
He hides the bulls. No one could trail them to that cave.
Then as Amphitryoniades prepared to leave,
And led his well-fed cattle from their stalls, the herd

Began to low while shambling out. The whole woods stirred   215
To hear their plaints, which echoed from the hills that they
Were leaving. One lone heifer answered them by way
Of mooing from the cave. So, from her cell she foiled
The hopes of Cacus. *Now* Alcides truly boiled,
Seething black-venomed bile. He grabs his knotted war   220
Club, racing up the lofty mountain slope. Then for
The first time, we beheld this Cacus terrified,
Wide-eyed with panic. Coward-swift, his running vied
With the East Wind, cave-ward. Fear lends his feet their wings.
Shut safe inside, he shatters the suspending links,   225
Dropping a giant boulder hung in iron chains
His father crafted, blocking what the frame sustains.
But look: the raging god of Tiryns comes. He turns
This way and that: How to get in? His jawbone girns;
Teeth gnash. Frenzied, three times he scouts the Aventine   230
All round. Three times he tries the stone door, but in vain;
Three times collapses in the valley, frazzled—spent.
Sheer on all sides, there stood a style of pointed flint
That loomed up, rising from the cavern's ridge, just right
For nests of gruesome birds. Then using all his might,   235
He shook it from the right side, since it leaned out left
Above the river. Tearing till that rock was cleft
From deeper rock within, its stone-roots wrenched asunder,
He thrust it all at once away—a thrust the thunder
Cracked to, heaven-high. The stream banks split; the flood   240
Recoiled in fear. But Cacus' vast cave-kingdom stood
Revealed, and shadowed caverns deep below exposed,
As if the earth now gaping deep below disclosed
The hellish realms some force unlocked—that deathly white
Domain the gods hate—so that vast abysmal site   245
Is visible, the death-wraiths quaking at the light
That rushes in. Alcides, then, at once relies
On any weapon, pelting him in his surprise

At light. A howling target for Alcides' rocks,
He's missile-harassed: branches and huge millstone blocks   250
Rain down. But since he can't escape the fix he's caught
In, Cacus vomits smothering smoke clouds from his throat
(A miracle!). They fill his den with billows, choking,
Blotting all the eye might see. Black night comes smoking
In to flood the cave with mingled flame and ash.   255
Alcides' pride cannot endure this. Headlong-rash,
He leaps down through the fire—where thick smoke's rolling wave
On wave, and black mist's seething through the mammoth cave.
As in this darkness Cacus vomits flames in vain,
The hero clamps him like a knot, a strangling vine,   260
And throttles him—eyes popped out, crop-blood drained. Right
    there
And then, the doors come off; the murky den's laid bare.
The raided cattle, in a robbery he'd denied,
Are plain to see, the grisly carcass dragged outside
Heels-first. We gawk but cannot get our fill: the face;   265
The grim eyes and the coarse-haired torso of a race
Half-beast, half-man; the gullet flames now quenched. Since then,
We gladly celebrate these rites as grateful men,
Keeping the day. Potitius, first founder-priest
(With the Pinarii, who guard Alcides' feast   270
Day), built this altar. 'Mightiest,' we make its name
Forever—always 'Mightiest,' one and the same.
So come, young warriors; wreathe your hair with leaves; extend
Your wine-cups. These are deeds to honor and commend.
Invoke our shared god; freely pour the wine."

                                          When he   275
Had done, then poplar—Hercules' variety
Of grey-green, woven leaves—hung fringing from his hair.
The sacred goblet filled his hand. All, then and there,
Made their libations gladly to the gods, in prayer.

Meanwhile, the night drew nearer down Olympus' sides.   280
Priests shuffled out, Potitius first, all dressed in hides
Traditional in these rites. They carried banquet torches.
The feast began again, with savory second courses;
Under the piled-up platters, every altar groans,
As Salii sing round the kindled altar stones,   285
With priestly temples wreathed in poplar sprays. One chorus
Of young men, one of old, sing Hercules's glorious
Deeds. They laud the babe who crushed that serpent pair
Stepmother Juno sent; the infant who razed, bare-
Handed, two cities both incomparable in war,   290
Troy and Oechalia; then, the thousand toils he bore—
Hard labor King Eurystheus set, but truly, doom
Cruel Juno sent.

          "Unbowed, you slew the cloud-born human-
Horses Pholus and Hylaeus. Never beaten,
You killed Nemea's giant lion and the Cretan   295
Monsters. The Stygian lake fell quaking—Orcus' door-
Dog, too, on half-gnawed bones inside his cave of gore.
No, nothing frightened you—not towering Typhoeus, armed
And looming up. You kept your wits and weren't alarmed
When Lerna's serpent, with its storm of death-heads swarmed   300
Around you. Hail, true child of Jove, god added new!
Come see your rites and bless us with the sight of you."

These are the paeans they sing while crowning all his fame
With Cacus' cave and death, that monster belching flame.
The forests ring; the hills re-sound Alcides' name.   305

Then when the holy rites are done, they all return
To town, and as he goes, Evander walks on, worn
With years. He has Aeneas and his son beside
Him—chatting friends to keep them all talk-occupied

Along the way. Aeneas stares at every sight 310
With wonder, taken by each scene. He finds delight
In asking and learning each story of the men
Of old.

   The founder of Rome's fortress answered then:
"Once, native nymphs and Fauns lived in these groves. A race
Of men as well, born hard, from oaks. They had no trace 315
Of law, no rule of living's art. They knew no lore
Of yoking oxen, reaping crops, or how to store
Grain. Branches fed them, and the hunter's savage game.
First down from the Olympian ether, Saturn came,
Fleeing Jove's weapons, exiled from the kingdom he'd 320
Been stripped of. Gathering these hill folk, he decreed
The laws for untaught nations scattered everywhere.
He named this Latium, since he'd lain safe, *latent* here.
Under his reign, we had that Golden Age men say
Once was. The peoples lived in placid peace. But day 325
By day, a tarnished time succeeded: gold gave way
To maddening war; to love of avarice and bribes.
Next came Ausonian bands, and the Siconian tribes,
As Saturn's Latium often set aside her name.
Then kings appeared, and massive, fearsome Thybris came, 330
From whom Italians drew our Tiber's current fame
(The ancient Albula is called by that no more).
And I, an exile seeking ocean's farthest shore?
Almighty Chance, with Fate no human can ignore,
Settled me here. My guardian Phoebus, with tremendous 335
Warnings from my mother, drove me (she's Carmentis,
The nymph)."

   At once, a few steps on, he shows them all
Her altar and what Romans honoring her call
Her gate: "Carmental"—tribute to Carmentis, seeress-

Nymph who was the first to sing great future years   340
Aeneas' heirs would know, and Pallanteum's glory.
A great grove next (restored to be a sanctuary
By busy Romulus); then, Lupercal ("Wolf's Cave")[7]
In a chill cliff (Parrhasian-style, Lycaeus gave
The place its name, from Pan).

                         Then sacred *Argiletum's*   345
Grove's appealed to: *Argus'* guest-*death* gets related.
Evander moves to the Tarpeian Rock, and to
The Capitol (now gold, but thick with thorn when new).
Even back then, that holy place inspired awe;
Even back then, those rustics trembled when they saw   350
Its rock and woods. "This grove," he says, "this hill's green crown:
A god lives there (which god, who knows?). But we've been known—
Arcadians—to see Jove when with his right hand
He shakes his dark shield often; answering his command,
The storm clouds come. And in these two towns, you can see,   355
Among the ruins, relics of our ancestry.
Our father Janus[8] built *this* fort, and *that* one, Saturn—
Janiculum, one name, Saturnia (per this pattern)
The other."

               Talking so, they reached Evander's house,
A humble place, where cattle could be seen to browse   360
And low inside the Roman Forum and refined
Carinae. At his door, he says, "*He* did not mind—
Conquering Hercules—stooping to enter here
My humble royal house. Scorn wealth, my guest, and dare
To be a god like him. Come, don't disdain our lack   365
Of *things.*" He spoke. Under that almost-shack-
Like house's sloping roof, he led Aeneas where
A leaf-couch waited, covered by a Libyan bear-
Skin. Night falls, folding earth beneath her dusky wings.

But Venus,[9] moved to fear by what this uproar brings—   370
Laurentine threats—has motherly good reason to
Address her husband Vulcan: "Dear, I asked of you,"
(She starts, while in their golden bed, and breathing passion),
"Nothing—no arms or aid your skill and power could fashion.
While Argive kings were devastating Pergamum's   375
Doomed citadel with hostile fires, poor Ilium's
Inhabitants were never pleaded for. I never
Begged you for some forger's work of vain endeavor
Despite the massive debt I owed to Priam's heirs,
And how Aeneas' toils drew down my constant tears.   380
Ordered by Jove, he's landed on Rutulian shores
Now. Suppliant like him, I beg the power that's yours
For arms. Revered one, please a mother pleading for
Her son, like Thetis and Aurora; tears implore
You. See the peoples mustering, cities shutting gates.   385
They hone their steel in hopes that it annihilates
My people."

      Then she stops; he waits. A goddess's
Embrace wraps round him: snow-white arms and soft caresses.
He knew at once that old familiar heat that came
To pierce his marrow, melting bones with liquid flame,   390
No different than when plosive thunder sends a white-
Hot fire-bolt to stab the clouds with dazzling light.
His consort, conscious of her charms, rejoiced: she *knew*.

Then Vulcan spoke, bound fast by endless love: "Why do
You search out ancient pretexts? Goddess, where's your trust   395
In me? Your fear the same, it would have been but just
Of me, back then, to arm the Trojans (neither Fate
Nor Father Jove desired a ruined Trojan state).
Both would have let King Priam live for ten years more.
So now, if you're intent on instigating war: 400

Whatever care my craft can promise you; whatever
Liquid electrum makes, or iron, I'll be clever.
Whatever powers air and fire furnish, never
Doubt *your* powers. Stop your pleading, please."

                                                    He ceased,
Then gave her the desired embrace. On his wife's breast   405
He found sweet sleep, and all his members were released.

When ebbing night's mid-stream, first rest defeating sleep;
When a woman supports the house her chores must keep
Alive with humbling toil Minerva's reign requires
With distaff, and she stirs the hearthstones' sleeping fire's   410
Embers, adding night to day-work, setting slaves
Their lamplight chores (it is her chaste bed that she saves
While raising little sons): just so, it's then the Lord
Of Fire, no later up to work than they, heads toward
His blacksmith shop, leaving the downy bed of sleep.   415

There is an isle of smoking rocks that rises steep,
Hard by Sicania and Aeolian Lipare.
Deep down's a cave, and Aetna's vaults, eaten away
By Cyclopean forges groaning as the anvils
Take their beating. Iron hisses in those caverns: 420
Molten Chalybean masses breathing flame.
It's Vulcan's home; Vulcania's that place's name.

From high above, the Fire Lord descends here. In
The cave, Cyclopes smithy iron with a din:
Bare-limbed Pyracmon, Steropes, and Brontes form   425
By hand a bolt the Father hurls down in a storm
To earth. (It's shaped like all those raining from the sky.)
This bolt's part polished, part undone, of triple-ply.

They'd added three storm clouds, three twisted sleeting wires,
And with the winged South Wind, three braids of crimson fires. 430
Now they were blending frightening flashes in the work,
With noise and fear and flames of fury gone berserk.

Elsewhere, they built Mars' chariot (with wheels that flew):
He uses it to stir up men . . . and cities, too.
Some worked at panic-making Pallas' aegis plate,   435
Burnishing serpent scales of gold with intricate
In-woven snakes, and on the goddess' breast, with severed
Neck and rolling eyes, the Gorgon! "Stop with every
Job you're doing," Vulcan cries. "What work's begun,
Remove it, Aetnaean Cyclopes. Turn to one   440
Task only: armor for an ardent hero. Now
It's strength, now rapid hands, you need. Now show
A master's art, without delay!"

                              He said no more.
All went to work, with jobs shared equally, as ore
Flowed down in streams of wounding steel; of bronze and gold. 445
All melted in the giant furnace. Then they mold
A mammoth shield to stand alone against all Latians'
Weapons, welding layers—seven iterations,
Round on round. Some bellows-blow the air they take
In. Others dip the bronze still hissing in the lake.   450
Weighed down with massive anvils, all the caverns groan;
With awful power, they hammer, raising arms as one,
In rhythm, turning molten metal with their tongs.

While Vulcan worked on his Aeolian shores, the songs
Of birds beneath the eaves, with gentle morning light,   455
Woke up the humbly housed Evander from his night.
In tunic and Tyrrhenian sandals, he then tied

On his Tegean sword, shoulder-hung at his side,
And twisted from the left a draping panther's hide.
Besides all this, a pair of guard dogs exited   460
The elevated threshold, trotting out ahead
Of him, to dog their master's steps.

                                        Evander found
His guest Aeneas' quarters, as his mind turned round
All he had said of promised help. Up early, too,
Aeneas, with Achates, walked with Pallas, who   465
Accompanied Evander. All shook hands in greeting,
Then sat among the lodges in expansive meeting,
Talking freely.

                    First, Evander:
"Greatest Teucrian (while you're still safe, commanding,
I can't admit the heart of Ilium doesn't live):   470
Despite our vaunted name, the war help we can give
Is weak at best. The Tuscan river hems us in
On one side, and Rutulian arms have raised a din
Around our ramparts on the other. On they press.
But I propose to link you with a populace   475
That's opulent and strong, with camps and kings. This aid,
So unexpected, chance shows. Here, as Fate decreed,
You've come. Close by, Argylla built its ancient town
On rocky hills, where Lydians, of long renown
In war, once settled on Etruscan heights. For years   480
It prospered, till Mezentius[10] was king. With fierce
And brutal force, he ruled in haughty arrogance.
(Why dredge up heinous murders, or the virulence
Of all that despot did? Let's hope the gods intend
The same for him and his, who even tied them, hand-   485
To-hand and face-to-face—dead bodies—to the living,

For their torture. So he killed, by unforgiving,
Slow decay, with rot and pus—a death-embrace.
Fed up at last, the townsfolk arm, and siege the place
The arrant madman hides, then kill his myrmidons   490
And set the palace roof on fire. Mezentius runs
From all the slaughter toward Rutulian refuge. There
He flees, surrendering to the warrior Turnus' care.
So all Etruria, in righteous fury, rises.
They want the king sent back . . . or there'll be war's assizes.   495
Aeneas, you shall lead these thousands in this war.
Their vessels clamor, densely moored along the shore.
They cry their standards on. But singing destiny,
An ancient bard restrains them: 'Chosen chivalry;
Maeonia's flower; warriors of an epic race,   500
Whom righteous wrath inflames: Mezentius' disgrace
Rightly enrages you, but no Italian man
May lead your like. No, only someone foreign can.'
Etruscan ranks, then, awe-struck, pitched camp on that plain,
And Tarchon's envoys brought me symbols of his reign—   505
His king's insignia and royal staff and crown—
That I might come, assuming the Tyrrhenian throne.
Years-wearied, though, old age slow-freezes, hour by hour.
And strength now past brave deeds begrudges me its power.
I'd nominate my only son were it not for   510
His Sabine mother's blood. Bravest leader by far
Of all the Trojans and Italians, Fate has claimed
And favored you; for age and lineage, it's named
You. Lead this fight! I'll lend you my son Pallas here,
Our fondest hope.[11] Guide him; teach him to persevere   515
In war's grave work—to learn the disciplines of war,
Look you; to see you fight while he's still young. What's more,
He'll have Arcadian horsemen—two hundred, the core-
Strength of our youth, and he himself will add ten-score."

He'd scarcely done when Aeneas, son of Anchises,   520
And Achates, ever-faithful, pondered crises
To come, with somber hearts and ever-downcast eyes . . .
Till Cytherea sent a sign from cloudless skies:
The whole world seemed to totter when the flashing levin
Came crashing down with sudden thunder from high heaven.   525
And then the air shook to a Tyrrhene trumpet blast,
It seemed.

      They gaze up as the thunder claps come fast.
And in the calm sky, in the clouds, they see forge-cast,
Red weapons glowing, and they hear great clashes pounding.
The Trojan hero knew the sounds all found astounding: 530
The arms his goddess-mother'd promised him. He cries
Out, "Do not ask—no, don't—what all this prophesies;
What fates these signs foretell. Olympus summons me.
My goddess-mother said this was her sign I'd see
If war were near. She said she'd bring me weapons down   535
From heaven—Vulcan's work—to help me.
O gods, what slaughter's coming to Laurentium! What
A price you'll pay me, Turnus: Father Tiber's glut
Of shields and helmets and the corpses of the brave!
He'll drown those treaty-breakers under wave on wave;   540
Let them cry war!"

      When done, he leaves his lofty throne,
Re-kindling Hercules's flame (the altar stone
Now stirs from drowsing). Next, he honors with their due
The Lar and humble house-gods. Then he kills a ewe,
As does Evander, properly, with Ilium's men.   545

He next goes to the ships to see his crews again,
Choosing the very bravest he will lead in war.
The rest slip easily downstream. Untouched by oar,

The current runs to tell Ascanius the news
Of how his father's done. Strong mounts that warriors use 550
Are lent the Teucrians who seek the Tyrrhene plains.
Aeneas gains a fine gift: led out by the reins,
A charger in a tawny lion skin with glittering,
Gilded claws.

       Through the small town then, Rumor's flittering:
Riders are racing toward the Tyrrhene king's frontiers! 555
Now mothers double fearful prayers as danger nears.
Now Mars's image magnifies as it appears.
Evander Pater, clasping Pallas' hand as he
Departs, begins to speak, sobbing insatiably:

"Were Jupiter to make me strong, as at that hour 560
When underneath Praeneste's walls, I killed the flower
Of Erulus's troops, and burned their shields piled high,
And with this hand, contrived to make that tyrant lie
In Tartarus (at birth, Feronia—grim to tell!—
Gave triple lives and arms to one I had to fell 565
Three times to send to Hell. He lost, by this right hand,
Both lives and weapons.), nothing ever could withstand
Our sweet embrace, dear son. And proud Mezentius
Never would have piled his contumely on us,
His neighbors, dealing carnage with his grisly blade. 570
(We mourned our town for all the widows that he made.)
And yet . . . you ruling powers, and Jupiter, your king:
Pity this prince from Arcady and grant that thing
A father prays for. If it is your will; if yours
And Fate's decision jibe; if he comes through these wars, 575
And I live on to see my Pallas still alive;
Then life's my prayer. There is no lot I can't survive.
But Fortune, if you mean some grim catastrophe,
Then now—right now—allow the final end of me,

While fear stands poised; while future hope rides on a knife   580
Edge; while I hug you, Pallas, joy of my long life;
Sole comfort. Let no graver news pierce like a sword."

The father's faint and final parting words had poured
Out. Overcome, he let his servants help him to
His house.

        And now the mounted men had ridden through   585
The gates swung wide. Aeneas and Achates led,
The other Trojan captains next, then Pallas, mid-
Column, conspicuous in cloak and fine-chased armor
(Like Lucifer, the object of Venusian ardor
More than all the other stars. From where he laves   590
His holy head, he lifts it from the ocean waves
To melt the dark.). On city walls, the mothers eye
With fear the dust-clouds as the bright bronze squads go by.
The armed men ride through brush, taking the shortest way.
And then a shout goes up; the galloping array   595
Has formed a column. Thundering horse hooves pound the clay.

There is a giant grove by Caere's chilly stream—
A sacred wood long held in reverent esteem
By all. The round hills hem it in with dark green firs.
They say the old Pelasgians guarding these frontiers   600
Once, sanctified this Latian grove, naming a day
For Silvanus of Flocks and Fields. Not far away
From there, camped Tarchon and the Tyrrhenes, at a site
Defended well. Now all their troops, from every height,
Were visible across the spacious plain.

                   That's when   605
Aeneas Pater, with his picked young fighting men,
Arrives. They rest their horses and their bodies. Then . . .

The lovely goddess Venus, bearing gifts down through[12]
The clouds, perceives the valley he's retired to,
Beside the chilly stream.

                          She shows herself, unasked,   610
And speaks: "These perfect gifts, my husband's skills were tasked
With. Now you see you need not wait, my son, before
You dare proud Turnus or the Laurentines to war."
She sought her son's embrace, as Cytherea spoke,
Then set the shining armor up against an oak.   615

He cannot get enough; each piece enchants his sight.
Such gifts from gods! The honor leads to pure delight.
He turns the helmet round, the better to admire
The crest, with terrifying plumes that jet like fire;
The killing sword; the stiff bronze breastplate, huge and bruise- 620
Red like a looming cloud when sun-rays torch its blues
And make it glow from far away. Then come the greaves,
Refined gold, burnished with electrum-plated leaves.
To match the spear, a shield of peerless artistry.

There on its shining field, he who knew prophecy,   625
The prescient Fire Lord, had set the history
Of Italy and every triumph meant for Rome.
His hands had put there all its people still to come—
Ascanius's heirs, and all the battles they
Would fight. In quite another scene, the she-wolf lay   630
In Mavors' green cave, with twin brothers at their play,
Dependent on her dugs and sucking fearlessly
Their foster-dam. Bending her lovely nape back, she
Caressed her young. Their twin limbs, by her tongue are shaped.

Near these are Rome's Great Games, where Sabine girls are raped—[13] 635
Snatched from their Circus seats. Fresh war! as Romulus's

Sons fight with stern Cures, ruled by Tatius.
The same two kings then, with their quarrel laid aside
Stand armed before Jove's altar, wine in hand, allied
By treaty, as they sacrifice a sow. The just-   640
Built "palace" bristles in its Romulean, rustic
Thatch.

     Close by, two four-horse war-cars tore in two
The Alban Mettus (who had sworn what wasn't true).
Then Tullus dragged that liar's viscera through the wood;
The thorn-choked field lay dripping with a scum of blood.   645

Porsenna showed, who ordered Tarquin taken back[14]
From exile; Rome appeared there, under siege-attack
(Aeneas' sons ran on their swords, for liberty).
And you could see Porsenna's fury—threats that he
Was making after Cocles left the bridge in shivers,   650
And after Cloelia broke her chains and swam the river's
Breadth. On the Tarpeian Rock, and standing by
The temple there, guarding the Capitol on high,
Was Manlius. Through golden columns, cackling loose
(Since Gauls were at the gates), there flew the silvery goose.   655

And Gauls were in the gorse, to take the citadel,
Defended by the dark, by night as black as hell.
Their long hair's gold; their clothes are gold. Each cloak reflects
Sparse light in glittering stripes. Around their milk-white necks
Wind torques of gold. To double lances that they wield,   660
They add, for its defensive use, a man-tall shield.[15]

Here he had hammered naked Luperci, and hopping
Salii with wool-bound caps, and targes dropping
From the sky. Chaste mothers in plush carriages
Were leading through the city sacred images.   665

Far off, he'd set the seat of Tartarus, the mile-
High gates of Dis, and punishments for every vile
Thing humans do. And Catiline,[16] you were there, too,
Dependent from the menace of that cliff where you
Were quaking at the vengeful Furies that you saw.   670
Yet there were pious souls, and Cato,[17] giving law.

In and around: the swelling sea, in gold (though blue
Waves billowed white while silver dolphins scissored through
The waters). Making circles with their tails, they clip
The tide. Shield-center: Actium! where ship on ship   675
Battles in bronze. And you could see all Leucas teeming
With Mars' arrays, as waves ablaze with gold were gleaming.

On one side stands Augustus Caesar[18] on the high
Stern, leading the Italians on to battle. By
His side: SPQR, and all the gods. Two tongues   680
Of flame shoot from his brow. His father's starburst hangs
About his head. Close by, wind-blessed, god-blessed Agrippa
Towers. His brows aglow, he leads his fighting ships,
And crowned with naval prows, displays that honoring sign.

The god had wrought an Antony opposed, designed   685
With barbarous strength and foreign arms. By crushing wars,
He rules the eastern peoples and their blood-red shores.
All Egypt, Bactra, and the eastern powers came
(With Antony's Egyptian "wife"[19]—a mark of shame).
All rush as one; the whole sea foams, ripped by the sweep   690
Of blades and trident beaks.

                  As ships row for the deep,
You'd think the Cyclades torn loose, their bulks set racing,
Or peak had clashed with peak, so huge the masses chasing
Towering sterns. Steel-wingèd missiles mixed with burning

Tow come down, till Neptune's furrows seem all churning   695
Red.

    The queen's ships race to where her sistrum's signed.
(She hasn't yet looked back, to see twin snakes behind.)
Barking Anubis, there with every monstrous kind
Of god, is threatening Rome's deities with weapons
Brandished at Minerva, waved at Venus, Neptune,   700
Mars (engraved in steel amid the battling ships,
With dismal Furies in the sky). Discord, robe ripped,
Exults; Bellona follows with her bloodstained whip.

Seeing this from on high, the Actian Apollo
Draws his bow . . . and Egypt flees. The Arabs follow,   705
Then the Indians and Sabaeans flee the scene,
As calling on the winds to fill her sails, the queen
Herself cries, "Now! Right now, pay out the sheets!" The thin-
Lipped armorer has made her death-pale, deep within
The slaughter. By Iapyx' wind, and over water,   710
She runs. There is the Nile! The great flood mourns its daughter,
Cloaked in his watery robe. Blue adits open wide;
He calls her to these streams, where, conquered, she may hide.[20]

But Caesar in his triple triumph, entering Rome,
Was offering Latian gods, for ages yet to come,   715
Immortal gifts—three hundred temples built throughout
The city. Gladness! Games! as clapping people shout.
Altars in every shrine! In every shrine were found
Rome's matrons. Slain steers populate the blood-slicked ground.

He sits to survey, at the dazzling Phoebus' snow-   720
White sill, the nations' gifts; hung on proud gates, they glow.
The conquered peoples pass in endless lines. They vary
In their clothes, their languages, the arms they carry.

Here Mulciber had set the Nomads and the Carians,
With loose-robed Africans, and quiver-slung Gelonians   725
And Leleges. Euphrates softened as it flowed.
Remote Morini showed. The Rhine curved, double-bowed.
Here were the untamed Dahae; there, Araxes, fretting
About its bridge.

          He marvels at the shield he's getting,
Venus' gift; stares at its art—at things unknown—   730
Then gladly hoists its fame and fate as all his own.[21]

BOOK IX

WHILE ALL OF THIS WAS HAPPENING ELSEWHERE, SATURNIAN
Juno ordered Iris sent to fiery Turnus,
Who at that time was sitting in a sacred vale—
His ancestor Pilumnus' grove. There in that dale,
The child of Thaumas spoke, with soft lips lightly rosed: 5
"See, Turnus? Time, unasked, brings round what you proposed
In prayer, but no god dared to promise: left behind
Are city, friends, and fleet; Aeneas goes to find
Evander's home, the kingdom of the Palatine.
There's more. He's reached Corythus' farthest towns, to mine   10
Their Lydian rustics, arming them as fighting forces.
So why hold back? Call up the chariots and horses
Now! Attack their feeble camp!"

          Then Iris[1] rose
Upward to lightness on extended wings, her bows
Immensely arced below the clouds, as off she flew.   15
And lifting his two hands to heaven (Turnus knew
Her), he pursued her flight with words like these: "Tell who
Has sent you through the clouds, Great Glory, down to me
On earth. Explain this sky's bright sudden clarity,
Iris. I see the sky's been split in two. I see   20
Unveiled the stars that ring the pole; I heed what's meant,
Whoever calls me now to arms."

          With this, he bent
And skimmed some water from the stream, filled up the air
With vows, and called out to the gods with constant prayer.

Now, rich in horses, rich in sumptuous array,   25
Across the plains the gilded army made its way.
Messapus leads the front ranks, Tyrrhus' sons the rear.
Their general, Turnus, heads the center. All appear
Like Ganges' seven placid runnels surging high
In silence, or the flooding Nile-streams as they die   30
Down from the fields, and riverbeds accept them back.

That's when the Trojans spot a gathering dust-cloud, black
As night: above the darkling plain, the nimbus billows.
Caïcus is the first to shout out to his fellows
From the outer ramp: "What's *that*, men? Huge black squalls   35
Of smoke are coming. Grab your swords and climb the
    walls!
Quick, pass the spears out! Run! The enemy is here!"
The clamor is tremendous as they race to clear
The gates. Along the walls, massed Teucrians appear.

That's what the battle-wise Aeneas ordered when   40
He left: if something happened in his absence, then
"Do nothing rash—no forming ranks or fighting in
The open. Guard the camp and walls. Stay safe inside."
So though they wish to fight, prompted by rage and pride,
They bar the stockade gates, obeying his command;   45
They're armed and waiting on the towers, making their stand.

But Turnus rode ahead, outpacing his own forces,
He's at the camp already, twenty chosen horsemen
With him. Astride his painted Thracian mount, he wears
A golden, red-crested helmet. "Let's see if there's   50
A man among you who will be the first to fight!"
He cries. "Now watch!" he shouts, sending a lance in flight

To start the battle, then advances proudly in
The plain.

His men, encouraging with fearsome din,
Now follow shouting, stunned by Trojan "cowardice"— 55
Men loath to take the open field and pay the price
Of battle, clinging to the camp instead. He rides
Wildly around the walls, where Ilium's army "hides,"
But no way in!

A wolf outside a crowded fold
In midnight ambush howls through rain and wind and cold, 60
While lambs bleat, safe beneath their dams. Enraged at prey
Just out of reach, he's reckless in his wrath—at bay,
And tortured by his dry and bloodless maw; by hunger
That's been growing worse each day.

So Turnus' anger
Burns, as that Rutulian scans the stockade walls: 65
Resentment flames inside his marrow, and it galls.
How to get at the penned-up Teucrians inside
And pitch them from the walls and strew them far and wide
Across the plain? He charges at the ships close by,
Bulwarked by river and revetment. Then the cry 70
Goes up for fire from his exultant men. A brand
Of pine that kindles from his fervor fills his hand,
And with a vengeance, all his men set to, hot-spurred
By Turnus, armed with fuming torches they've procured
By looting hearths. The smoldering branches cast a glare 75
Pitch-black, as Vulcan lifts their ash-clouds through the air.

Who were the gods who saved the Trojan ships from flames
Like these? O Muse, who quenched those fires? What were their
   names?

Tell me. The ancient tale is long-believed and famous.[2]
Back when Aeneas first began to build his fleet   80
On Phrygian Ida, readying his ships to meet
The main, they say the Berecynthian,[3] mother of
The gods, addressed great Jove: "My son, I know you love
Your mother. Grant this boon, Olympian lord: a grove
Long dear to me—pine forest on a mountain's rim—   85
Is where men brought me sacred offerings. Dark and dim,
It's planted thick with dusky fir and maple tree.
I gave these gladly to the Dardan youth when he
Had nothing he could sail. Deep fears are troubling me.
Relieve those fears, and grant your mother's fervent plea: 90
That neither shattering voyage nor wild storm destroy
Them. Let their mountain birthright bring them blessèd joy."

Her son, who moves the stars, said: "Mother, what do you
Expect of Fate? As for these ships, what should Fate do?
These man-made keels: You'd grant them immortality?   95
Or have Aeneas sail through every mortal sea
In safety? Powers such as these, what god's been given?
No. Their task complete, in their Ausonian haven,
I'll take away their mortal shape—those ships that lived
Through every wave and bore their Dardan leader to   100
Laurentium's fields—and have them breast the foaming blue
As goddesses, like Nereus's Doto, or
Like Galatea." Done, he nodded "yes," and swore
By brother Pluto's Stygian stream; by banks that hiss
With swirling pitch, deep in their waters' black abyss.   105
Then all Olympus trembled at that nodding vow.

And so the day had come—the Fates fulfilling now
Their hour—when Turnus' torches prompted Cybele
To save her sacred fleet. At first, the watchers see
A spectral, flaring light, and then a giant cloud   110

Scudding out of the east, with her Idaean crowd
In chorus.

      Then an awful voice that chilled their spines
Came down upon the Trojan and Rutulian lines:
"Trojans, don't try to save your ships; don't race to fight
For them. Turnus would have to set the sea alight   115
Before I'd let him burn my sacred pines. Go free
At my command, sea goddesses!" Each deity
Tears loose her moorings from the bank. Each ship
Now seeks the deep like dolphins plunging; noses dip.
Wonder of wonders then, new-virgin figures breach   120
The surface, swimming mermaids singing each to each.[4]
[There is ms(s). authority for a missing line here—122.][5]

The spooked Rutulians blanch; even Messapus shivers,
And his horses rear in panic as the river's
Harsh race stops. The Tiber steps back from the deep.   125
And yet the sturdy Turnus' faith and courage keep;
He stirs the spirits of his frightened troops, but chides
Them, too: "These portents target Teucrians. Besides,
Jove's stripped them of their normal help, which doesn't stay
To face our fire and steel. The seas provide no way,   130
No hope, so half the world's denied to Trojan flight
(The land is ours, ten thousand Latians armed to fight).
These god-sent omens leave me, Turnus, unafraid;
Let Phrygians boast about them. Venus has been paid
Back, *and* the Fates, since Trojans reached the rich black soil   135
Of our Ausonia. I, too, have a fate to foil
Aeneas's: to extirpate the guilty ones
Who stole my bride (a pain not Atreus's sons'
Alone. Mycenae doesn't own revenge.). 'But to
Have died once is enough'? No, *sinning* once should do,   140
To make these men hate almost every woman ever

After—men whose faith in rampart walls that sever;
In nuisance moats and feeble blocks to death, supplies
Their courage! Didn't they observe with their own eyes
The work of Neptune—Ilium's walls—sink, all ablaze?   145
But you, my hand-picked men: Which one of you will raze
These ramparts with your sword and storm their camp with me?
They *cower*! Who needs Vulcan's shields or weaponry?
Who needs a thousand ships to conquer Trojans? All
Etruria can join them; I won't need the pall   150
Of night, or sneaking 'theft of their Palladium,'
Or 'fortress guards with gullets cut,' or hiding from
Them, blind inside some horse's belly. I intend
To ring their walls with fire in broad daylight! They'll end
Knowing we're no Pelasgic youths or Greeks they're playing   155
With—men Hector fought off ten years by delaying.
The best of day is spent, men. Use what light remains
To rest, refreshed by, satisfied with, all our gains.
We're readying for war, I promise."⁶

                              Darkness falls,
And sentries post. Messapus' fires ring the walls,   160
As fourteen picked Rutulian officers now watch
The camp, to which a hundred soldiers are attached,
All plumed in red, all glittering gold. With good dispatch
Fresh guards relieve their counterparts, as some recline
Along the grass, or tip bronze bowls to drink their wine.   165
Guards gamble through the night, while watch-fires brightly shine,
And no one gets to sleep.

The Trojans look on all this scene from where they keep
The high ground. Fully armed and anxious soldiers test
The gates, build catwalks and defenses where they rest   170
Their ready arms. Both Mnestheus and brave Serestus,

Aeneas' deputies in an emergency,
To head up state and army, lead with urgency.
And every man keeps watch by lots. By turns, each stands
His post, on guard for danger where the need demands.   175

The fiercest soldier-sentinel was Nisus,[7] son
Of Hyrtacus. The huntress Ida'd made him one
Of lord Aeneas' train—wizard with lance and dart.
Beside him stood Euryalus, a boy apart
In beauty or in Trojan arms; the loveliest youth   180
Of the Aeneadae; a boy whose cheek was smooth.
Their love was one, these two, and side-by-side they'd fight.[8]
They share guard-duty at the same post on this night.

Nisus: "Is it the gods who set our hearts on fire,
Euryalus, or does each man make his desire   185
His god?[9] I've longed to fight or do some mighty deed;
It's not this torpor, but adventure that I need.
You see how the Rutulians trust the state of things:
Their watch-fires scattered wide, they sleep the sleep wine brings.
And everywhere, this peaceful quiet—boring; bland.   190
But only listen to the exploit that I've planned.
Our soldiers and the senior council all demand
Runners be sent to tell Aeneas of our plight.
Were they to grant you what I ask, I think I might
Slip past that mound and reach the Palantean gates.   195
(The glory due the exploit more than compensates.)"

Replying quickly to his ardent friend, besotted
Euryalus saw glory in what Nisus plotted:
"Nisus, in this great deed, would you make me a stranger,
Content to send you off alone to face such danger?   200
My sire Opheltes, that old soldier, never taught

Me that! In Troy, he brought me up on terrors wrought
By Greeks. And never have I treated you like that,
But followed great Aeneas to his utmost fate.
My spirit scorns the light of day; it's my belief   205
The glory of this deed, if it should cost my life,
Is worth it."

        Nisus said, "If I had doubted you,
That would have been a grievous fault. May Jove, or who
It is that looks on us with favor, bring me back
To you in triumph. But if this should come to wrack   210
And ruin (such things can); if chance or god should drive
Me to disaster—then I pray that you survive.
Your youth deserves to live. May someone bury me,
My body rescued or bought back, or—Destiny
Denying me my rites—pray in apostrophe,   215
And raise my stone. Don't let me cause *your* mother sorrow
Like that, lad. She alone—no other—dared to follow
You, and never cared for great Acestes' place."

But he: "Your wasted wishes plead a hopeless case;
I will not change my mind. Let's hurry on!" He goes   220
At once to rouse new sentries in relief. As those
Come up and take their turn, he quits his post to stand
By Nisus' side and seek the prince.

                   Throughout the land,
All other living creatures, cares forgotten, slept,
Their minds set free from worry. But the Trojans kept   225
A captains' council of their best. What should they do?
Send someone to Aeneas, yes, but who should go?
In center camp, the leaders stand, leaning on spears
And grasping shields. Just then, Euryalus appears
With Nisus, begging for admittance right away   230
(The matter's "grave," and "will repay the brief delay").

Iulus was the first to greet the eager pair,
Asking that Nisus speak.

          "Aeneans, give us fair
Hearing," said Hyrtacus's son. "Don't judge us by
Our ages. These Rutulians are asleep; they lie   235
Dissolved in dreams and wine. But we've identified
An opening for ambush, where two paths beside
The gate that's nearest to the sea divide.
Between the fires, a gap shows black smoke on its way
To blot the stars. If you will let us seize the day   240
To reach Aeneas and the Pallantean town,
You'll see us back soon, booty-burdened, laden down
With slaughter's spoils. The road won't trick us as we go:
From hunting in these shaded vales, we've come to know
The river whole. We've seen that city's outskirts, too."   245

To this, sagacious, grave Aletes then replies,
"Our fathers' gods, under whose numen Ilium lies:
In spite of all, you're *not* determined to erase
Us Teucrians, for"—here the tears ran down his face—
"You've brought us young men brave as those of any race: 250
This steadfast pair."

          He held them by the shoulders then,
And took their hands. "What prize could I award such men
As you? What honor for a deed like that? The best—
The first—the gods (and you yourselves) will give. The rest,
Righteous Aeneas will bestow at once, and—yet   255
Untouched by age—Ascanius, who won't forget
Such service."

        Then Iulus broke in: "Yes, and more:
My fate rests on my sire's return, so I implore
You both, Nisus, by our Penates; by the grey-

Haired Vesta and Assaracus's Lar. I lay   260
My future in your lap. Bring back my father! May
I see him once again. There'll be no grief the day
He comes. I'll give a pair of silver goblets, bas-
Relieved, my father took from conquered Arisba;
Two tripods, too, and two large talents of pure gold;   265
A bowl Sidonian Dido gave, its age untold.
You've seen the golden-armored Turnus in the field;
You've seen his horse. If we win Italy, and wield
The scepter, sharing spoils by lot, then Turnus' shield
And horse and crimson crest are yours, Nisus. I'll set   270
Them all aside as your reward. Besides, you'll get
Twelve of the finest women from my father, and
Male captives, too, with their own armor. *And* the land
Latinus owns, as well. But now, I welcome *you*
With all my heart, most honored boy. You are a few   275
Years older than I am, so I embrace you for
My friend no matter what may come. In every war
I wage, I'll seek no glory if you're not beside
Me. You shall see my firmest trust, when it is tried,
Confirm your words and deeds."

                    Euryalus replied: 280
"The times will never show me less than fit for daring
Actions bold as these—as long as Fate is caring
Rather than cruel. But one gift more than all your others
I beg of you: from Priam's ancient line, my mother's
Come to this, poor woman—neither Ilium nor   285
Acestes' town could stop her trekking to this shore
With me. Of this—my leaving—she is unaware,
And ignorant of the risks I run, because (I swear
By Night and your right hand) I knew I couldn't bear
A mother's tears. Console and comfort her—my prayer   290

To you. Let me believe you'll do this, and I'll dare
All dangers boldly."

                Deeply touched Dardanians wept,
The fine Iulus most of all, so moved he kept
In mind this image of such filial love forever.

And then he spoke: 295
"I promise all things worthy of your great endeavor.
Your mother shall be like my own to me, with one
Exception (that's *Creusa*); bearing such a son
Is no small thing. Whatever fate your raid meets with,
I swear my father's oath, on this my life and death: 300
All things that I have promised you when you succeed
Will be your mother's, too, because of this great deed."

He speaks through tears, un-shouldering the golden-hilted
Sword Cnossian Lycaon made him—gilded
With art. And there's an ivory sheath to keep it in.   305
Mnestheus' present is a shaggy lion's skin
For Nisus, who trades helmets with Aletes. Armed,
The pair march to the gate at once, where they are swarmed
By all the captains, young and old, who offer prayers.
Noble Iulus, thinking like a man, with cares   310
Beyond his years, gave them a clutch of grave dispatches
For Aeneas' eyes. (But when the whirlwind catches
Them, they'll rise in useless shreds against the clouds.)

They seek the fatal campgrounds as the nighttime shrouds[10]
Their sortie. Doomed. Before that fate, though, *they* will be   315
The doom of many bodies lying round; they see
These drunken sleepers littering the ground, here, there,
And all about. Parked chariots line the beaches where
Men doze amidst the wheels and harness, cups and swords.

Then Nisus, Hyrtacus's son, speaks first. His words: 320
"Euryalus, we need a bold hand, now our path
Lies clear; stop any sword raised in our aftermath.
Guard well, and I will kill us here a great wide swath."
He spoke this in a whisper as he rammed his sword
Through haughty Rhamnes, slumbering, who as he snored,   325
Weighed down a pile of rugs. Though Turnus's pet seer,
He was a king himself. But he could not see clear
The death that was upon him.

                              Nisus now killed three
Of Rhamnes' servants, sleeping by their weaponry
But careless. Remus' armorer and driver next—   330
Dead at their horses' feet. A sword sliced lolling necks,
Then Nisus lopped their lord's head off, and left the trunk
Jetting warm blood. Gore soaked the bed; the ground was drunk
With blood. He slaughtered Lamyrus and Lamum, too,
And young Serranus, famous for his beauty, who   335
Had gambled half the night away and lay there drowned
In wine, his veins suffused. (If only he had wound
On through the night, rolling the bones till dawn.) He killed
The way a starving lion storms a pen that's filled
With sheep: a ravening, gnawing hunger makes him tear   340
The feeble flock to pieces as it shakes with fear.
His jaws drool red.

                        Euryalus's slaughter matches
This. Blazing with rage among the host he catches
Off-guard (and nameless and unknown), he falls on Fadus,
Herbesus, Abaris, and Rhoetus. Cowering Rhoetus,   345
Though, sees everything. Scared wide-awake, he hides
Behind a giant wine-jar. Deep in Rhoetus' sides,
As he stands up, the blade is driven to the hilt;

It comes out crimson. Purple vomits as he's killed,
Mixed with wine clots.

                  Then fervidly but furtively,   350
The boy moves on: Messapus' men! There he can see
The last fires flickering, and duly hobbled horses
Grazing the grass. But Nisus senses how the forces
Of sword and bloodlust grip Euryalus, and so
He speaks: "Our enemy the dawn draws near. Let's go!   355
Vengeance enough. We've cut our pathway through the foe."

The corpses' slew of hefty silver arms is left,
With wine-bowls and with hangings of the finest weft.
The youth then snatches Rhamnes' trappings, and his gold
Baldric (the gifts of wealthy Caedicus of old,   360
Once sent to Remulus of Tibur, proxy for
His friendship. Dying Remulus's grandson wore
Them next. *He* died; Rutulians claimed them—battle booty).
He slings them on his valiant shoulders—though it's futile—
Then he dons Messapus' helmet, in its beauty   365
Matching the vivid plumes. They leave the camp and head
For safety.

            Meanwhile, as the army's waiting, ready
On the plain, three hundred riders who've been sent
Out from the Latian city bring a message meant
For Turnus. All have shields, and Volcens leads. Now near   370
The camp, not far below the walls, they spot that pair
Some distance off and to the left, despite night's shade
(Euryalus's gleaming helmet has betrayed
The thoughtless boy—a surface off which moonlight's played).

This sighting isn't meaningless: Volcens exclaims,   375
"You two! Stop where you are! Where to? What are your names?

Why armed and running?" No reply; they speed their flight
Into the forest, trusting to the dark of night.
But mounted guards block every path at every site.
These horsemen thwart escape; they are a noose that chokes.   380

The thorn-thick woods are dark with dense and spreading oaks,
All packed with brambled briars reaching every side.
The path was dimly lit and couldn't be descried,
While shadowed limbs and all his heavy booty tied
Euryalus down. He can't get out!—misled by fear.   385
Already, headlong heedless Nisus has got clear,
Dodging the enemy. He's reached what will be Alba
(From the Alban name; back then, the stately stables
Of Latinus stood there). Here he stops to find
His missing friend:

                "Euryalus—he's left behind!   390
But where? Which way should I re-trace this tangled track
Through all the treacherous wood?" At once, he doubles back,
Looking for sign and wandering in the thicket's hush.
But then . . . men's shouts; the noise of horses as they rush
Their prey. Too soon he hears a cry, then catches sight   395
Of lost Euryalus, betrayed by woods and night.
The uproar has confused him, and the troop's whole train
Is dragging him; now overpowered, he fights in vain.
What sword can Nisus wield to save his dying friend?
Or should he rush them all, headlong, to an end   400
Made beautiful by every wound?

                   Quickly he drew
His spear-arm back, prepared to do what he would do,
And gazed up at the moon, to which his brief prayer flew:
"Latonian glory of the stars: yes, goddess, you:
Grove-guardian, be here now to help me lest I falter.   405

If ever Hyrtacus, my father, piled your altar
With offerings in my name, or if I added game
I'd killed, or hung gifts from your dome, or nailed the same
Below your sacred eaves, then guide this through the air
To rout that mob!"

                          Ending, he tensed, then threw the spear   410
With all his strength. It splits the shadows nighttime makes
And pierces Sulmo's back. Deep in, the javelin breaks
In two, its short shaft shivering Sulmo's heart. He shakes,
Ice-cold, bent over, hot blood jetting from his breast.
The pulsing gasps go throbbing through his ribs and chest.   415

The troop looks all around. There's Nisus! At his ear,
Even more eagerly, he's poised another spear,
Which, while the stunned Rutulians hesitate, goes whistling
Through Tagus' temples, stabs his brains, and sticks there, bristling.

Then Volcens went berserk with rage, but couldn't spot   420
Who threw the lance, nor where to charge in, burning hot.
"You're going to pay the blood-price, though—the penalty
For both these crimes," he cries, and with his blade drawn free,
Charges, driving it through Euryalus's side.

Then Nisus, terrified, can't let the darkness hide   425
Him any more, can't stand such agony. He cried,
"It's me! I did it—me! Rutulian, turn your blade
On me. The guilt's all mine; the boy could not have made
Those throws—or dared. Omniscient stars, prove what I tell:
His only fault? He loved his luckless friend too well."   430

Just as he spoke, with wrenching force the sword
Went through his ribs, leaving the fair white torso gored.
Euryalus rolled over dead. Fine limbs ran red

With blood, and on his shoulders drooped his lolling head.
It's like the way the coulter cuts a shining flower   435
That bows to death—some poppy that has met its hour,
And drops its heavy head beneath a random shower.[11]

But Nisus charges into all of them, and hunts
For Volcens only. Volcens is the one he wants.
The enemy surround him, drive him here and there,   440
But still he presses on, and whirling in the air
His lightning sword, he buries it right through the shrieking
Volcens' face. Both dead: the foe whom he was seeking
And himself. Pierced through, he falls on his dead friend,
Discovering there, in death's still peace, his quiet end.   445

You blessèd pair![12] If power informs my poetry,
No day will ever wipe you from time's memory,
You two. So long lives this, and this gives life to thee,
With Capitol, Aeneas's posterity,
And Rome's imperium (they shall live on, all three).   450

Rutulian victors wept to carry Volcens dead
To camp with all their spoils. For Rhamnes, who had bled
To death, the grief was equal, and so many more
Slaughtered at once—Serranus! Numa! Throngs now pour
In on the dead and dying on the ground still hot   455
From killing. Drenched, the very soil begins to clot.
All recognize the spoils: Messapus' helmet, gleaming,
And his gear, which so much sweat was spent redeeming.

And now Aurora, early from Tithonus' bed
Of saffron, rose. Across the earth, fresh rays were spread.   460
And now, as sun streamed down—now, as its light bathed all
The world—an armored Turnus has the trumpets call
His men to arms. Chiefs form their bronze-clad troops by file

And rank, each man his own. Men whet their anger all the while,
With tales re-told. They stick Euryalus' and Nisus'   465
Heads on up-raised spears—a sight that ices
The blood!—then follow, roaring.

Hardened Aeneadae, formed rampart-left, are shoring
Up their lines (their right ranks bounded by the river).
They hold the broadened trenches as they stand fast, grieving   470
On high-set towers; their comrades' pike-stuck heads are ripping
Their hearts. They know the faces far too well, now dripping
Putrescence.

       Meanwhile, wingèd Rumor's flying through[13]
The anxious town. It speeds the news, which races to
Euryalus's mother's ears. Her trembling bones   475
Go cold; the shuttle drops. Her work stops all at once,
And out the wretched lady rushes, tearing hair
And shrieking with a Maenad's madness—racing where
The ranks are thickest on the ramparts. Heedless of
All danger, men, and darts, she fills the skies above   480
With cries:

       "Are you Euryalus I see, who were
To ease my years? So cruel, how could you leave me here
Alone, and never let your mother say good-bye
For one last time when you were being sent to die?
Oh! Dog and bird prey in this Latian land, you lie   485
A stranger. Nor could I escort you to the grave
In death—your mother, who would close your eyes and lave
Your wounds or shroud you in the robe I rushed by day
And night to weave—for grief I hoped it might allay
In my old age. Where now? Where is the ground your body   490
Lies on, where your butchered limbs, and where your bloody
Corpse? You bring me only *this*? I followed you by sea

And land for *this*? Rutulians, drive your spears through me
If you have any pity—all your weapons! Kill
Me first. Or Father of the Gods, be pitiful   495
With lightning: blast me down to Tartarus, and send
Me where my hateful life can find its only end."[14]

A mournful groan went through them all, their spirits shaken
By her wailing, as their battle spirits weaken.
Ilioneus orders Actor and Idaeus: take   500
Inside this grief-igniting woman. Iulus sobs
Profusely as she's carried in.

                But then the throbs
Of battle trumpets brazen out their awful singing;
Far off, a clamor follows and the sky's soon ringing.
Shield-wielding Volscians charge, in even ranks arrayed,   505
Ready to fill the moat or smash the palisade.
Some ladder-scale the walls or probe an opening
Where scant defenders form a less-than-three-deep ring
The light shines through.

            The Teucrians, well-trained
By endless siege, hurled every kind of dart, which rained   510
Down on an enemy thrust under by thick poles.
They use stones, too, and down the deadly barrage rolls.
(With luck, these might break through those shielded ranks arranged
Beneath their shell and glorying in every danger.)

But now those ranks fail. Now, the Teucrians have set   515
A giant rock, and roll it down to meet the threat
Of massing troops. It lays Rutulians low. It fells
Them far and wide, shattered despite their armored shells.
Those scattered soldiers now no longer care to fight
Like men without their sight,   520

But try to clear the walls with missiles. Elsewhere, scorching
Pine in hand, the grim Mezentius hurls his torches.
Messapus—Neptune's scion, breaker of wild horses—
Claws at the ramparts, calling for more scaling ladders.

Muses, inspire my verse that sings of bloody matters.   525
Calliope, I pray you, say what slaughter Turnus
Made—name those his lethal sword sent through Avernus
Down to Orcus. Help me sing of war and Hell.
You goddesses recall; you have the power to tell.[15]

There was a looming tower with walkways—high above,   530
Well-set—which every Latian, fighting fiercely, strove
To storm and overthrow with all his skill and power.
Defending Trojans fought with stones and darts; a shower
Of missiles rained from open loopholes. First to shoot
A blazing torch was Turnus, and the brand took root   535
Deep in the tower's flank. The gusty wind then scoured
The flames, which burned the planks and left the gate devoured.

Half-panicked men inside who run from this disaster
Fail; they shrink and run from ruin falling faster:
The ponderous tower's suddenly collapsed, and all   540
The sky resounds with what has crashed. Half-dead, they fall
To earth, the massive tower upon them. As they do,
Their chests are pierced; their own defenses stab them through
With cruel splinters. Lycus and Helenor run,
Though. (In his prime still is Helenor. He is one   545
Whom a Licymnian slave bore to Maeonia's king
And sent to Troy with arms they'd told him not to bring:
One light-weight, naked blade; one pale, mean, unmarked shield.

When he sees where he is—how Turnus' ranks have sealed
Him in, their thousands here, their thousands threatening there,   550

Like hunters in a thick ring round some boar or bear
That rages at their spears, and leaps on death aware,
And lands in fury on those weapons—that's how he
Rushes headlong to death, amidst the enemy,
Racing for where he sees their blades are bristling most.   555
But Lycus, faster far, goes darting through that host
Despite their arms. He wins the wall and tries to grasp
The top, where anxious comrades' hands reach out to clasp
His own.

          But Turnus, close behind with spear in hand,
Exults in triumph: "Fool! You thought you could withstand   560
Me?" As he speaks, he grabs him hanging by his nails,
And yanks him down; a huge piece of the stockade fails.
He's like Jove's lightning bird that soaring high, swoops on
A hare with crooked hands, or else some snow-white swan.
He's like Mars' wolf that snatches from the pen a lamb   565
The ewe will seek in vain, a bleating, frightened dam.

Then, shouts all round, as the Rutulians charge. Some fill
The moats; some torch the wall-tops. All begin to kill:
Ilioneus slays Lucetius (with a rock torn from a hill)
As he prepares to fling a brand into the gates.   570
Emathion and Corynaeus meet their fates
At Liger's and Asilas' hands. One is lance-skilled;
The other's long-range arrows leave his victims killed.
Then Caeneus fells Ortygius, but Turnus *him* . . .
And Promolus' and Clonius's deaths are grim,   575
And Dioxippus dies, and Sagaris and Itys
Fall, and as he stood upon a tower, Idas.
Then Capys kills Privernus, whom Themillas' spear
Had grazed. He'd dropped his shield, hand to his wound—a clear
Path for the feathered dart that stuck deep in his left.   580
The lethal wound lay in the lungs that arrow cleft.

And Arcens' handsome son he'd sent was standing, too,
Wearing a bright embroidered cloak of Spanish blue.
He'd been raised by Symaethus' streams, in Mars's grove,
Where Palicus's rich and pleasing altars throve.   585
Dropping his spears, Mezentius whirled a whistling sling
Around his head three times, and from its tight-wound string,
The molten bullet sped and split the youngster's head.
His corpse lay on the sand, felled by a shot of lead.

It's then Ascanius aimed his first swift shaft, it's said—   590
Till now, an arrow used to kill game as it fled.
Then he brought down the brave Numanus Remulus,
Who'd wed the younger sister of Turnus, and thus
Was newly royal. He strode before the foremost ranks,
And shouted words both fitting and unfitting, thanks   595
To his tumescent heart all puffed with pride—words he
Should not have mouthed.

                    Numanus bragged relentlessly:
"Twice-conquered Phrygians, where's your shame? To hide behind
Walls twice now, twice-besieged and hoping death won't find
You! Ha! And *you're* the men who'll take our brides in war?   600
What god—what madness—drove you to our Latian shore?
We're not Atrides or Ulysses, prince of fable
Makers! We're stony stock. As soon as we are able,
We teach our infant sons to stand the bone-cold race;
Our boys wear out the woods and keep watch through the chase. 605
Their 'play' is breaking horses, and their 'sport' the bow.
Hardened by work and used to scraps, our young men hoe
The stubborn earth . . . or shatter cities when they battle.
Iron wears down our life. We goad the flanks of cattle
With a spear butt, but sluggish age cannot impair   610
Our heart-strength, weakening our vigor. On white hair,
We wear our heavy helmets yet, and still take joy

In fresh new plunder from the towns that we destroy.
You wear bright purple and embroidered saffron cloth!
The dance is your indulgence; your delight is sloth.   615
You sleeve your shirts; wear ribboned bonnets on your head.
You're Phrygian girls—not men: the pipe plays, and you're led
On Dindymus's heights, drawn by that double-reed.
Timbrel or Berecynthian boxwood flute, you heed
The call of Cybele. Let men fight wars; leave off   620
The sword."

      Ascanius barely heard Numanus scoff
With warning words, but faced him, fit an arrow to
His horsehair string, and with his straining muscles drew,
Pausing just long enough to offer Jove this vow:
"Almighty Jupiter, bless what I aim for now,   625
And every year, I'll bring rich victims to your shrine—
Before its stone, a young white bull whose brow will shine
With gilding. Mother-high he'll bear his head, aloof,
Already butting, pawing sand-spray with his hoof."

The Father heard his prayer, and where the clouds were reft,   630
Just as the bowstring twanged, he thundered on the left.
The high-strung, deadly, hissing arrow flew and cleft
The hollow temples, splitting Remulus's head
With steel. "Go sneer at valor! What was that you said?
'Twice-conquered Phrygians' send Rutulians this reply!"   635
Ascanius stopped, and Teucrians sent up a cry
Of clamorous joy that raised their spirits to the sky.

Just then, by chance, long-haired Apollo on his throne
Looked down on the Ausonians from his cloudy zone,
Viewing their town and troops. Iulus, he addresses: 640
"Your just-born, conquering valor, boy, my godhead blesses.
Scion of gods and sire of gods, you climb the stars!

Assaracus's house will rightly end all wars
To come; Troy cannot hold you."

Leaping from the sky
When done, he parts the breathing ether going by,   645
And finds Ascanius. He metamorphs his face
To Butes', who once held an armor-bearer's place
And guarded dutifully Anchises' gates at Troy.
(Aeneas later made him squire to his boy.)
Now, wearing Butes' face, and with his voice, the god,   650
With Butes' silver hair and thundering weapons, strode
Up, speaking to the fiery Iulus:

"By your bow,
Aeneas' boy, Numanus dies. Let it be so,
That he lies unavenged. No more. Great Phoebus grants
This honor: use your arrows just like his . . . this once.   655
But no more fighting, boy."

That's how the god began,
But then was gone, mid-speech. So far away no man
Could see him go, Apollo vanished in the blue.
The Dardan princes recognized the god and knew
His weapons when his quiver rattled as he flew.   660
They hold the bold Ascanius back; it's Phoebus' will,
And he has spoken. Eager though the boy is, still
He stops, while they resume the fight, their lives laid bare
To death.

From tower to tower, the war-cries fill the air.
Men bend the bloody bow and whirl the killing sling;   665
Earth lattices with lances. Shields and helmets ring
In clangorous clashes, as the brutal battle surges,
Worse than the western storm beneath the Kids that scourges

Earth with flailing rain, and thick as storm-cloud hail
Showering the seas when Jupiter's grim southern gale   670
Bristles and whirls the storm, rending the heavens' veil.

Then Pandarus and Bitias—grandsons of Jove
And Iaera (who bore Alcanor in the grove
Of Jupiter, and she a wood-nymph)—young men tall
As pine trees on their native hills, fling wide the wall-   675
Gate given them by their commander. Trusting to
Their arms, they bait the enemy now thrusting through.
They plant themselves before the towers, left and right,
Steel-sheathed. On lofty heads, plumes shimmer in the light.
Like twin oaks on the banksides of the Po, they rise;   680
Like trees by lovely Athesis, they brush the skies
With shaggy, nodding, unshorn crowns.

                                        Now that they've seen
Their way wide open, the Rutulians breach it clean.
And Quercens and Aquicolus (so handsome cased
In armor) are, with Haemon, Mars's son, and hasty-   685
Hearted Tmarus, routed. All these ranks now fly
For life or drop there in the gateway, where they die.

Then Trojan fighting spirits grow like fire, until
The men are massed together. Hand-to-hand, they kill
By growing bolder; farther, farther out they dare.   690

But when Rutulian Turnus learns, he's storming where
The far-off Trojans fight in turmoil. Captains tell
Him of those gates flung open by men Hell-
Hot, slaughtering; he turns from killing he's begun,
And roused to burning fury, charges at a run   695
The Dardan gate and noble brothers, killing fast

Antiphates, who crumples from a javelin cast
(He'd been the first to challenge—tall Sarpedon's bastard
By a Theban). Cutting air, the cornel shaft
Stabs through the gut so far the torso's deeply gaffed.   700
The dark wound trench foams red; the pierced lungs warm the steel.

Aphidnus, Meropes, and Erymas then feel
The hand of Turnus. Bitias falls next—fiery-eyed,
Soul raging—not by spear (he never would have died
By spear-blade), but a whirling missile, as it hissed—   705
A bolt that neither two bulls' hides, nor trusty breast-
Plate double-scaled in gold would prove it could resist.
His tottering trunk collapses as the ground groans hard;
The huge shield clangs down on his corpse.

                                             A rock pile jarred
Apart will fall like that on Baiae's Euboic shore   710
Sometimes; built up with stones, it topples with a roar.
The great blocks smash the sea as havoc fills their wake.
They crash the depths ahead of ruin that they make,
With seas in turmoil from the risen, boiling sands.
Inarime's sea-bed and Procida's high lands   715
That bury Typhoeus quake at mighty Jove's commands.

At this, the potent Mavors lends the Latian bands
Fresh courage; goads now gouge their hearts and twist about.
He sends the Teucrians Black Fear and Mindless Rout.
Rutulians mass from every side; there's fighting space!   720
Soul-deep, the battle-god has found his place.

Pandarus sees his brother's corpse: Fate's changing face
Smiles on the Latians; chance is driving everything.
So with a mighty, broad-backed push, the hinged gates swing.

He's locked a slew of comrades out in bloody fighting   725
Beyond the walls; the rest, that he has been inviting
In, he shuts up with himself, as in they rush.
Madness, though—not to see, in all that charging crush,
King Turnus breaking through and locked inside the walls!
They're like defenseless herds on whom a tiger falls.   730

At once, his eyes flash fires afresh. His weapons make
A frightening clang; his helmet's blood-red crest-plumes shake.
His shield shoots out the glinting of a lightning storm.
Aeneas' sons, in panic, know that hated form,
Those monstrous limbs.

                           But giant Pandarus leaps out,   735
Burning with wrath. His brother's death now makes him shout:
"It's not Amata's bridal palace, or mid-most
Ardea's walls here, Turnus; we're a hostile host
Inside this camp—you can't escape, nor can you hide!"
The smirking Turnus, undisturbed by this, replied: 740
"Come on, then, if your heart's so stout. Fight hand-to-hand!
Tell Priam there's a new Achilles in the land."

He'd stopped. The other, straining hard with all his strength,
Launches his spear—barked, crude, and knotted all its length.
Wind took it, and Saturnian Juno's hand deflects   745
The strike incoming. In the gate, the spearhead sticks.

"But here's my strong arm's blade; there's nothing you can do.
I wield a wounding weapon and I'm not like you."
So Turnus cries, who rises high and lifts his sword;
Between the temples, iron splits in half the forehead,   750
Severing beardless cheeks. To call the stroke a *wound* . . .
A quake-sized crash: the mass is huge that shakes the ground.
The slain man's limbs collapse; the breastplate pocked with brain-

Bits slams the earth. His skull, precisely cleft in twain,
Is left to flop atop the shoulders, left and right.   755

The Trojans, now repulsed, race off in scattered flight,
And if their victor'd quickly thought to smash the bars,
And let his shut-out fellow fighters through the doors,
That day had been the nation's last, not just the war's.

But Turnus has the slaughter-lust; half-maddened, he   760
Runs on against his enemy,
First catching Phaleris, then Gyges, whose hamstrings
He cuts. Then picking up their fallen spears, he flings
Them at retreaters. Juno lends him heart and strength:
Halys and shield-pierced Phegeus are laid out at length,   765
Alcander, Noemon, Halius, and Prytanis
Die on the walls (not knowing anything's amiss)
Inspiring troops.

       As Lynceus stirs his comrades and
Heads Turnus-ward, he's struck in close, from the right-hand
Rampart side—one glinting stroke. The severed head   770
Then rolls away, its helmet on . . . and Lynceus dead.
Next: Amycus, that scourge of beasts—none more adept
At arming steel or poisoning his arrows dipped
In venom. Then: Aeolian Clytius. The Muses'
Cretheus next—the Muses' pet. How Cretheus uses   775
Lyred song for joy, with notes and chords on strings
(He sings of horses, and arms and their men he sings)!

At last then, Mnestheus and fierce Serestus hear
Of all this slaughter. Rushing up, they see how fear
Has left their men in shambles, and the foe inside.   780
Mnestheus shouts, "Where do you run? Where can you hide?
What other walls, what ramparts elsewhere, can you hold?

My countrymen! Let one man, penned inside our fold,
Cause carnage such as this throughout the camp and go
Scot-free, sending our best young men to Hell below?   785
No pity for poor Troy? Your love of country slow
To rise? For great Aeneas and your gods, you have
No shame?"

        The words inflame them and they grow more brave.
They stop, then wheel their ranks, as Turnus cautiously
Inches toward the stream whose waves he hopes will be   790
His shield. The Teucrians press on—louder, more fierce—
Massing like crowded hunters leveling hostile spears
To kill some lion snarling hate. (That creature though,
Fearful yet savage still, pads backward, eyes aglow
With wrath. Nor hate nor heart will let him turn his back;   795
He wants to kill, but men and spears rule out attack.)
That's Turnus—tense and taut and cautious, he returns,
While in his cauldron heart, the boiling hatred burns.

And even so, he charged the Trojans twice, twice chased
Them in a flying rout, as down the walls they raced.   800
But rushing from the camp, the whole host masses. Nor
Did Saturn's Juno dare lend Turnus courage for
A further fight, since Jove sent Iris from the sky,
With nothing soft for Juno if he didn't fly
The Teucrians' tall battlements at once. That's why   805
That warrior, beaten down on every side by stone
And spear, could not, with sword and buckler, hold his own.
The helmet on his brow clangs. Ringing echoes back
The endless din, and solid bronze begins to crack
Beneath the stone-storm as his crest rips. Blade-blows beat   810
His shield-boss in. Mnestheus fires a Trojan sleet
Of javelins. Down Turnus' body, grimy sweat

Is runneling, pitch-black. His gasping lungs are aching
As agonizing breaths now set his body shaking.

At length, headlong and fully armored, Turnus leaps 815
Into the flood. The Tiber takes him in and keeps
Him up above its mellow race of muddy yellows,
Laving the blood, then wafts him to his fighting fellows.[16]

Book X

Meanwhile, omnipotent Olympus' opens wide.[1]
The King of Men—the Father-God—calls to his side
His starry council. From this palace, he surveys
On high: all lands; the Dardan camp; the Latian race.

Gods sit down in the dawn-and-dusk-doored hall. Jove starts: 5
"Great sky-gods, why these squabbles in your fickle hearts?
Why do you change your minds? What are you fighting for?
I said that Troy and Italy should not make war,
So why this rush to arms, which I forbade? What fear
Compelled both sides to swords? Was my command not clear?   10
Don't force the time for fighting; it will soon be here—
That day when Rome's high hills will feel the awful carnage
Pouring down those Alps burst through by savage Carthage.
Then it will be all right to hate and fight and ravage.
Leave off now, and be glad to keep our firm decree."   15

Jove's words. But golden Venus' words did not agree
In length—his brief, hers not:
"O Father, Power over men, Judge of their lot
(Whom else may I implore? To whom may I appeal?):
You see the insolent Rutulians? Chargers wheel   20
Prince Turnus through the throngs, the favorite of Mars,
Puffed up with pride. Unsafe behind their stockade bars,
The Trojans fight right on the walls. The ditches flood
With gore. Inside the gates, the dirt lies soaked with blood.
Aeneas, unaware, is gone. Do you intend   25
This nascent Ilium's second siege shall never end?
New menaces arise—a brand new Diomede

Leaves Aetolian Arpi now to make Troy bleed.
Indeed, I think my second wound awaits, and I
Have only days before that lethal lance shall fly.   30
If Troy has come to Italy without consent,
Against your will, then let it piously repent
The sin, and never help it. But, if it's stayed true
To all of Heaven's words—and Hell's—then all that you
Command should be obeyed. What force can make fates new?   35
On Eryx' shores, Troy saw the burning of its fleet.
Must I remind you? Aeolus, need I repeat,
Raised raging gales. And Iris came to intervene.
Now Juno's even raised the dead, so there remain
No realms untried: Alecto's been let loose—scot-free   40
To scourge the daylight-kingdom towns of Italy.
Now empire, which I'd hoped for—till our Fortune failed—
Dies. *Let* prevail the ones you wish to have prevailed.
If Troy can't rise again because your heartless wife
Forbids, then by the smoking ruins of its life,   45
I beg you, Father: let me save Ascanius—get
Him safely from this war. Let him live on yet.
Aeneas can be left to toss on alien seas,
And follow Fortune's signposts, but I beg you, please,
To let me shield the boy and take him from this war   50
To Amathus, high Paphos, or to Cythera's shore.
All three are mine, as is Idalia's shrine, where he
Could lay his arms aside and live ingloriously!
Let mighty Carthage crush Ausonia! Then there'll be
No stopping Tyre's towns. What good was it to flee   55
War's plague through Argive flames; to suffer all the sea
Can do—and desert lands—for some new Pergamum?
He and his Teucrians were seeking Latium?
They might as well have built on embered Ilium—
On Troy's blood-poisoned soil. Give Xanthus back. Restore   60

Their Simois, I beg you. Let them live once more,
These wretched folk, through Trojan woes."

                      Queen Juno cried
Out in her rage, "You show the grievance I would hide
To all the world; why make me break deep silence? Who
Of gods or men compelled Aeneas to pursue   65
This war? Who made him King Latinus' enemy?
'Fate drove him on to Italy'? Though that may be,
Cassandra drove him, too. When he left camp, were *we*
His prompter? Did *we* make him throw his life before
The winds? Or make him leave a boy to wage this war   70
And guard the walls? Or make him spoil the Tyrrhenes' trust
And breach their peace? What god, which powers of mine, have thrust
Ruin on him? Where's Juno here, or Iris, ordered
From the clouds? And yet as infant Troy lies bordered
By Latian flames, and Turnus makes his homeland stand—   75
A man whose mother is divine Venilia and
His ancient sire Pilumnus!—Trojans come with brand
And sword to set their yoke on others' fields and wrest
Their spoils, stealing the hand-picked bride from lover's breast!
They offer peace with one hand while they arm their ships?   80
Your power grabs Aeneas from the Greeks and slips
Them fog and thin air in exchange. Their boats you trade
For nymphs, yet *I'm* some monster for the little aid
I've lent the Rutuli? 'Aeneas isn't there;
He doesn't know.' Fine! *Keep* him lost and unaware.   85
'High Cythera, Idalium, Paphos—all are yours'?
Why roil a town pregnant with bloody hearts and wars
Then? Did I try to topple Phrygia's fragile state?
Did I? Or he who threw the wretched Trojans at
Achaea's kings? What cause had Asia then to rise   90

And war with Europe in betrayal, breaking ties?
And did I draw the Dardan to adultery
And Sparta's ravaging? Or arm his venery
To start a war? *That's* when you should have feared for yours.
This whining comes too late—this bickering, settling scores."   95

So Juno put her case, as all the deities
Diversely murmured, sounding like the forest breeze
That starts to rustle, rolling out its hidden humming
That will warn a sailor of the storm that's coming.

The potent Father starts, Prime Power over all;   100
He speaks, and silence falls in the celestial hall.
Earth tremors from its core; high heaven's hushed and still.
The Zephyrs die, and waves grow calm at Ocean's will:
"Take these my words and fix them in your hearts. I see
No Teucrian-Italian league will ever be.   105
And since your wrangling would go on eternally,
I'll treat both Trojan and Rutulian equally,
Whatever hopes they chase; whatever luck today
May bring—new Troy besieged because she lost her way
Through doubtful prophecies, or since it's Latium's fate.   110
And the Rutulians, too. What each side shall create
Brings its own suffering or success. A *neutral* god
Is Jove. Let Fates do what they may."[2]

                                        Then, with a nod,
He swears by Styx's waves and black banks seething pitch—
His brother's. All Olympus feels that nod, at which   115
It quakes. He's done, and rises from his golden throne.
Gods gather round, and to the threshold, lead him on.

And all this time, Rutulians press at every gate
To ring the walls in fire and thus annihilate

The enemy. Aeneas' men, imprisoned by 120
The pales, see no escape. Forlorn, they hold the high
Towers; around the walls, their scanty forces run.

The two Assaraci, with Hicetaon's son
Thymoetes, Imbrasus's Asius, and old
Thymbris and Castor, front the ranks. Sarpedon's bold 125
Two brothers fight beside them—noble Lycians Thaemon
And Clarus. Big as his father Clytius is Acmon
The Lyrnessian. His brother Mnestheus' size,
He strains, then lifts: it is no little stone, his prize.
Some fight with rocks and some with javelins they fling. 130
Some throw down fire, or nock their arrows to the string.

But look: the Dardan boy himself is fighting there,
Right in the thick of it, in Venus' special care.
A gem in yellow gold, it shines—his fine head—bare,
A jewel for neck or brow, like ivory finely laid 135
In boxwood or Orician terebinth, and made
To glow. His milk-white neck and soft gold band that gleams
In clasping it, receive his tresses' flowing streams.

And Ismarus: your great-souled people saw you, too,
Aiming your poison shafts to see what they could do. 140
You came there from a great Maeonian line of old,
Whose men plough fat fields the Pactolus floods with gold.
Mnestheus was there, whose glory yesterday (when he
Beat Turnus down) exalts him to the empyry.
And Capys—the Campanian city's eponym. 145
So men fought bitterly, the bloodshed stark and grim.

Night now. Aeneas cut the waves, his vessel racing.
(He'd left Evander, found the Tuscan camp, and facing
Him at last, told the Etruscan king his name

And race.) He told him what he sought, and why he came,   150
And what he brought—how Turnus' spirit burned, and how
Mezentius was gathering his forces now.
He warned of men's false trust. When Tarchon heard him plead,
He quickly pledged his men and sealed a pact. Now freed
From Fate, the Lydians embarked, as gods decreed,   155
Trusting a "foreign" prince.

Aeneas takes the lead.

Two prow-carved Phrygian lions help the ship to speed,
Mount Ida carved above—a sight the refugeed
Trojans welcome. There, great Aeneas sits and weighs
The varied issues of the war, as Pallas stays   160
At his left, asking now about the stars that guide
Through midnight skies, now how Aeneas has been tried
On land and sea.

Sing, goddesses![3] Throw open wide

Your Helikon. Sing those he led from Tuscany's shore—
Aeneas, sailing on, and arming ships for war.   165

First, Massicus' bronze *Tiger* cut the waves. It bore
A thousand youths who'd left the walls of Clusium or
The town of Cosae. Light-weight quivers that they wore
Supplied the arrows on their backs for deadly bows.

And next, his troops in worthy armor, Abas rows   170
A ship that's shining with a gold Apollo. Then,
Populonia, mother-city, sent six hundred men,
Her sons, expert in war. From Ilva's island shore
(Land rich with Chalybean mines)—three hundred more.

Priest-seer of gods to men, Asilas is the third.   175
Obeyed by entrail, star-writ sky, and tongue of bird,
He reads their signs, and what the lightning says will come.

He stirs his spear-thick ranks, a thousand men their sum.
Pisa gives him command (it found its Tuscan place,
Although Alphean-born).

                    Then: Astur, fair of face.   180
Astur—hopes pinned on rainbow arms, and on his mount.
Three hundred more who think as one add to the count:
Men out of Caere, or who live in Minio's plain,
In Pyrgi, or Graviscae (fever is its bane).

And you won't be forgot, Cynarus, valiantest   185
Ligurian in war; or, leading few at best,
Cupavo, swan plumes rising from your telling crest
(The emblem of your father's form—Love's mischief and
His mother's. For they say that Cycnus, half-unmanned
For love of Phaëthon, sang in the poplar leaves—   190
Those sister-shades—so music might allay love's griefs.
He drew white age about him—feathers soft and long—
Then leaving earth, set out to seek the stars with song).

His son commands the oars; the *Centaur* rushes forward,
A massive ship, with men of his own age aboard.   195
A high-carved figurehead threatens to hurl a boulder
Into the waves, which take the long keel like a colter.

And Ocnus, too, brings troops from native Mantua's shore.
(The Sibyl Manto and the Tuscan river bore
This boy who gave you, Mantua, your walls and name—   200
His mother's. Mantua: old stock not all the same,
With three tribes there. To each of these, four clans belong.
She heads them all. It's Tuscan blood that makes her strong.)

From here, Mezentius arms five hundred—hating him!
And Mincius born of grey Benacus (sedge its rim),   205
Was leading pine-hewn warships on across the seas.

Surging, with hard strokes on the waves, comes Aulestes;
A hundred oars churn waters into foam with thrashing.
He sails the giant *Triton*, conch-shell horn abashing
Deep blue seas. Its bristling bow displayed a man,   210
Waist-up through waves, but fish below. And on it ran,
The waters murmuring underneath, through whirling foam.
So thirty chosen princes sailed their ships from home
To fight for Troy. Through salt-sea plains, their bronze beaks plough.

The light had quit the day, and kindly Phoebe now   215
Had galloped with her midnight team through half the sky.
Aeneas (care won't let him rest) sat steering by
The helm himself and tending to the sails, when there!—
Mid-course, a swimming troop of his own friends appear
To meet him: nymphs[4] whom gracious Cybele had turned   220
From ships to water-deities. And as they churned
The sea, they swam along beside, behind, before—
As many as the bronze prows that once lined the shore.

From far away they knew him. Dancing, they entwined
His ship. Cymodocea followed from behind,   225
Who spoke the best. Her right hand catching at the stern,
She rises; under quiet waves, her left, in turn,
Is rowing.

      Catching him off-guard, she speaks: "Are you
Awake, Aeneas, Venus-born? Now don't heave to;
Full-sail instead! We are your ships, nymphs of the sea,   230
Once pines on Ida's sacred peak. Reluctantly,
We broke our lines when faithless Turnus drove us hard,
Headlong away. Once harried by his flame and sword,
We seek you on the waves. By Mother's mercy, we
Were turned to goddesses, to live beneath the sea.   235
But now your son Ascanius is penned by moat

And wall and Latian weapons pointing at his throat.
Arcadian cavalry and brave Etruscans hold,
Right now, their fixed positions, just as they've been told,
While Turnus aims his squadrons at them lest they reach   240
The camp. Rise up at dawn! 'To arms!' must be your speech
To all. Take up that perfect shield the Fire-Lord
Has given you, its rim pure gold. If you accord
My words your trust, then come tomorrow's light, the day
Will see huge piles of the Rutulians you will slay."   245

When she had done, well-versed in such a dexterous motion,
She shoved the tall ship as she left. Across the ocean,
Arrow-javelin-fast it flew, to match the wind.
The others sped up, too. Anchises' son, his mind
Amazed, still cheers his heart with what this thing has signed.   250

Then looking to the vaulted skies, he prays, "O kind
Idaean mother of the gods whom city towers
And Dindymus and lion teams with reined-in powers
Please, now lead me in the fight and help make good
This omen. Bless the Phrygians by whom you'll have stood."   255
And as he spoke, returning day brought back the light;
It rushed on in a flood that chased away the night.
He tells his men to keep his signals in their sight,
Prepare their hearts for war, and steel themselves to fight.

The Trojans and their fort in view, he takes his stand   260
High on the stern and swiftly lifts in his left hand
A blazing shield. The Dardans on the ramparts cry
To heaven; fury lives that was about to die,
As javelins fill the air (Strymonian cranes will fly
That way, swimming below black clouds, to say they're there,   265
Fleeing the South Wind, trailing clamor through the air).

This stuns Ausonia's captains *and* Rutulian Turnus,
Till they look behind and spy the shoreward sterns
Of vessels moving in a sudden living sea.
Aeneas' helmet burns, as if its crest might be   270
On fire, the plume ablaze. His shield-boss shoots a flood
Of flame—a dire comet glowing red as blood
In clear night skies. Or Sirius, that scalding torch
That means weak man will thirst through drought and plague
    that scorch.
(It rises in a grieving sky with baleful glow.)   275

The reckless, certain Turnus never doubted though:
He'd seize the shore and beat Aeneas back. What's more,
His words inflame his men with what they're fighting for:
"You prayed for this and now it's here. Be bold! Break through!
Lord Mars himself is in your hands, men. Each of you,   280
Remember wife and home and deeds done by your fathers.
We'll stop this wobbly enemy right at the water's
Edge, while he's still staggering through sand and wave.
Fortune favors the brave!"[5]
Done, Turnus ponders: Whom to lead as he attacks?   285
And who should keep the fort's walls at the Trojans' backs?

Meanwhile, Aeneas lands his men by gangways from
The tall ships. Many wait for waves to ebb, but some
Rely on leaping into shallows, some use oars.
Then Tarchon sees where breakers softly meet the shores   290
And shallows fail to froth and sound. The slipping tide
Glides in, its waves unhindered.

                          Taking this for guide,
He comes about at once, and cries out to his men:
"O chosen band, bend to your heavy oars again,
Make these ships rise and drive against the hostile strand   295

With ramming beaks; colter your keels, and plough the sand!
No shipwreck bothers me if I can seize the land
Of such a harbor."

        Tarchon's crews have heard him speak.
They rise and row their glistening ships until each beak
Has run up on dry Latian ground, and every bow   300
Lies beached unscathed. But Tarchon, not *your* ship! For now
She smashes in the shallows, hangs up on a rough
Rock ridge in dubious balance, beats the waves enough
Until she breaks, men plunging in the waters. There,
The splintered oars and thwarts that swirl around impair   305
Their struggle. Tangled in the debris everywhere,
They fight to stand against the current's undertow.

The swiftly moving Turnus doesn't dally, though:
He wheels his total force about to hold the shore
Against the Teucrians. And then the trumpets roar.   310
Aeneas first attacked the rustics—lucky sign
Of what's to come. He smashed on through the Latian line,
Killing Theron, who'd sought him out. The wound's red wine
Through brazen joints and gold-scaled tunic, quenched steel's thirst.
Then, Lichas—orphaned and untimely ripped, un-nursed.   315
(Your ward then, Phoebus. Why was he, when he was born,
Kept safe from sword? What *point*?) Tough Cisseus next was torn
From life, then giant Gyas, as they bludgeoned men
With clubs. But Hercules's weapons failed them then,
As did their sire Melampus and their own huge hands.   320
(He'd been Alcides' friend, meeting earth's twelve demands.)

Look! Through the braggart Pharus' mouth, Aeneas hurls
His javelin; deep down in, the spinning weapon burls.
You too, unlucky Cydon, with your new heart's joy,
Clytius. Careless of your love—he was a boy   325

To you—you would have lain, dead by the Dardan's hand,
A wretch, had he not met your brothers' fighting band
Of Phorcus' seven children. Of the seven spears
They throw, some bounce off helm and shield, while Venus steers
The rest away, to only graze his body. Venus   330
Is kind!

Then tried-and-true Achates hears Aeneas
Shouting, "Bring me spears! Each one I throw again,
Of those that pierced the breasts of Greeks on Ilium's plain,
Will stick in a Rutulian; none will fly in vain."

And so he grabs a heavy lance. Its spinning mass   335
Goes smashing through the warrior Maeon's shield of brass
And shears his breastplate and his breast in one great pass.
His brother Alcanor comes running to his side,
Propping Maeon with his arm. That arm then died.
(The spear straight through it, too—the weapon's blood-soaked
    course.)   340
The shoulder-tendons hung it, useless, without force.
From the body, Numitor then ripped the lance,
Heaving it at Aeneas—but only to glance
It off the great Achates' thigh: he'd missed his aim.

Now Cures' Clausus comes, who trusts his young man's frame,   345
And still far off, spears Dryops just below his chin;
The heavy shaft goes through the gullet, driven in
With piercing force. Life goes—and voice as well, mid-sound.
As Dryops vomits blood, his forehead smacks the ground.
Three different ways then, Clausus kills three men of Thrace,   350
Three warriors of Boreas' exalted race.

Then three Ismarian heroes fall whom Idas, who
Had fathered them, had sent (their fatherland had, too).
Auruncan bands come with Halaesus and the son

Of Neptune—bravely mounted Messapus. Now one 355
Side, now another, strains to drive the enemy
From off Ausonia's shore. As winds war equally,
Rising in dubious battle in the wide blue fields
Of heaven, all while neither cloud nor storm-wave yields
The fight, so Trojan men and men of Latium's land 360
Press hard in combat, toe-to-toe and hand-to-hand.

But elsewhere in the field—rocks scattered far and wide,
Where floods had torn the bushes from the riverside—
Pallas sees his Arcadians, unaccustomed to
A fight on foot, turn tail to Latians who pursue. 365
(The nature of the churned-up ground convinced them they—
This once—should all dismount.)

                    He starts to chide, to pray;
Their only hope, he uses bitter words to light
Their hearts on fire: "Friends, where to? Don't trust in flight!
By what you've done, Evander's name, the wars you've won, 370
And by my hopes to match my father's great renown,
Our swords must carve through enemies, where we will hack
Our way. Both Pallas and your country call you back
To where the ranks are thickest. Men, not gods, attack
Us! We are mortals pressed by mortals, with as many 375
Lives, as many hands, as they. There isn't any
Place to run to. Look: seas bar escape; they're hemming
Us in. So should we run to Troy or play the lemming?"

—His words. Attacking where the densest ranks await,
He first meets Lagus, drawn by an unlucky fate. 380
As Lagus tries to heft a heavy stone, he's struck;
The spear Pallas has thrown lands mid-spine. There it's stuck
In bone until the hero Pallas runs to pluck
It out. And Hisbo, falling on him in ambush,
Fails in that forlorn hope. Enraged, he'd thought to rush 385

At Pallas to avenge his friend's cruel death, but he's
Received by sword blade, buried in his lungs, which wheeze.

Next, Sthenius, then Anchemolus is found and slain
(Of Rhoetus' line, with his stepmother he had lain).
Then twins died on Rutulia's plains: you, Thymber, fell,   390
The son of Daucus, and Larides, your like, as well.
You sweetly stumped your parents, boys no kin could tell
Apart. But Pallas made that easy, now you're dead,
For Thymber: King Evander's blade has lopped your head,
While Larides, your severed hand sought out its lord,   395
As dying, twitching fingers tried to clutch their sword.
Stirred by the chiding Pallas and these feats they see,
The shamed, enraged Arcadians charge the enemy.

Then Pallas pierces Rhoetus in his war-car flying
By, so Ilus wins a brief reprieve from dying.   400
(The hefty spear had flown toward Ilus, far away,
But Rhoetus took it, halfway there. He'd been *your* prey,
Great Teuthras, and your brother Tyres', till he tumbled,
Half-dead. Heels beat Rutulian earth so hard it crumbled.)

Sometimes a hoped-for summer wind will rise. Throughout   405
The woods, a shepherd kindles fires all about.
Each space between flares suddenly, as Vulcan's bristling
Ranks make one line through the fields. The shepherd, whistling
Victory, sits and gazes at the joyous burning.

That's how your comrades rose as one, all bravely turning   410
To help you, Pallas. But Halaesus, battlefield-
Hardened, hurries toward them, clever with his shield;
Ladon, Pheres and Demodocus will fight
No more. He strikes Strymonius's hand off, right
Before it's lifted to his throat (the sword gleams bright).   415
And then he staves in Thoas' face; the smashing stone

Scatters a mash of Thoas' brains and blood and bone.
(His prescient father hid Halaesus in the wood,
But when the old man closed his greying eyes for good,
The Parcae grabbed the boy, doomed to Evander's steel.)   420
Pallas now hunts him, praying, "Let this weapon feel
Its way, my father Tiber, through Halaesus' breast.
In your oak, these arms—the hero's spoils—shall rest."
The god heard. While Halaesus did his hapless best
For Imaon, the Arcadian's spear went through the chest   425
He'd left defenseless.

                    Lausus, though, a force of war,
Won't let such slaughter daunt his men. There falls before
Him Abas, who's surely the battle's toughest knot.
For Tuscans and Arcadians, that is their lot
As well. You Teucrians fall, too—those Greece did not   430
Destroy. The armies clash, both led well and both strong,
With front and rear ranks smashing, as the crushing throng
Pins hands and weapons tight. Here, Pallas presses; there,
Young Lausus pushes back. They are almost a pair
Equal in age and handsome stature. Fortune, though,   435
Had vetoed their return home. Heaven's King said no—
No valiant battle, face-to-face. Their fate would be
For both to meet soon with a greater enemy.

Meanwhile, Juturna,[6] Turnus' sister, spurred him to
Lausus's aid. His soldier-scything chariot flew,   440
And when he saw his men, he cried, "Stand back![7]
Pallas is mine; no other hero will attack
Him but myself. Oh, how I wish his father here
To see!" And then, as ordered, Turnus' men stood clear.

But when the Rutuli retreated, then the young   445
Man, marveling at that proud contempt on Turnus' tongue,
Eyes his giant figure from afar and scans

Him, answering words with words, and with a glowering glance:
"Either I'll soon be praised for rich spoils taken, or
For my brave death. My father will expect no more.   450
Give up your threats!"

                —His words. Up to the front he stepped;
All hearts of Arcady go cold. Then Turnus leapt
Down from his war-car, set to fight on foot, and hand-
To-hand. The way a high-up lion, having scanned
The plain and seen a bull prepared to make a stand   455
Will rush down on his foe: that's just how Turnus seemed.

But Pallas was the first to move, and when he deemed
His prey in spear-range, hoping chance might aid the try
Of someone weaker, Pallas cried to heaven: "By
My father's welcome, and the board to which you came   460
A stranger, come, Alcides; help me in my aim.
Let me strip his blood-red arms as Turnus dies,
And stand above him as he looks with clouding eyes."

Hearing the boy, Alcides chokes back heart-deep sighs,
Then weeps his useless tears. The Father tries to say   465
A few kind words. His son hears, "Every man's last day
Is marked. His span of life is brief along the way,
The living lost. But deeds can make his fame outlast
Him—that is bravery's task. The sons of gods, in vast
Numbers, fell at the walls of Troy. Sarpedon, my   470
Own son, fell with them. Even now, Turnus must die;
Fate calls. The final goal is reached. His spirit yields."
Words done, he turns his eyes from the Rutulian fields.

But Pallas throws with all the strength he can afford,
Then clears his sleeving scabbard of its glinting sword.   475
The hurtling lance heads for the shoulder-armor joint,

Then drills the shield rim till the weapon's razor point
Has grazed the massive frame of Turnus. With his oak
Shaft, weighed forever, *he* lets fly.

       And then he spoke
To Pallas: "See if my spear doesn't penetrate   480
Deeper than yours!" The steel head tore through every plate
Of bronze and iron, on through every bull's-hide fold—
A shuddering stroke that drilled the boss. The spear took hold
Where it had pierced the mail, sticking in Pallas' chest.
He pulled the burning weapon from his wounded breast— 485
To no avail. By that same path there follow blood
And life. Dying, he falls, and bites the alien mud
With gore-stained mouth. He's stanched his deep wound with a
  thud,
As all his armor crashes down on Pallas, clanging.

Then Turnus taunts the corpse he's hanging   490
Over: "Arcadians, listen! Tell Evander this:
I give him Pallas back. The *merit* is all his.
What honor tombs have, and what comfort burial is,
Are my largesse. But he will pay me dearly for
His 'guest' Aeneas."

     Left foot on that corpse, he tore[8]   495
Off Pallas' massive, dead-weight belt—a prize engraved
With those young murdered bridegrooms, husbands their depraved
Brides killed on one mass wedding night: this had been told
By Eurytus's Clonus all in fine-chased gold,
With blood-drenched rooms.

     Now Turnus thrilled at victory 500
And spoils. O humankind, the doom you can't foresee,
Or how to keep your bounds when you've been lifted high!

For Turnus' time will come when he'll have wished to buy
An unharmed Pallas, never mind how steep the cost.
He'll hate this day and all its booty. Pallas, lost   505
To crowding, moaning friends, is borne back on his shield,
Great grief and glory to his sire. His fate is sealed.
The day that gave you to the war took you as well,
Though you sent heaps of dead Rutulians down to Hell.

Now not just rumors fly of Pallas' death, but sure   510
And certain proof; Aeneas' men may not endure
Much longer. Teucrians face certain death without
His help. He hunts you, blood-drunk Turnus. Through the rout
Of pressing enemies, his sword now scythes a swath.
Aeneas sees Evander in his mind; the wraith   515
Of Pallas, too. And he recalls their friendly feast
To which he came once as a hand-pledged stranger-guest.
And then he took—alive—four sons of Sulmo and
As many raised by Ufens, each a burning brand
Sent to the Manes, each to sprinkle Pallas' pyre   520
With their blood.

　　　　　　　　And next he aimed a deadly spear
At far-off, agile Magus ducking as it sped
Quivering above. Arms round Aeneas' knees, he pled,
A suppliant: "Oh, by your father's ghost, and by
Your hope in growing Iulus, do not let me die   525
To son and sire. In my house, whole talents lie
Buried—chased silver and great gold, both wrought and raw.
Troy's victory won't turn on me; I'm not the straw
Whose life will tip that scale."

　　　　　　　　　That's how he begged. When he
Was done, Aeneas said, "Let all your talents be   530
Your scions' gold and silver. Turnus, long before,

Put paid to all this sort of begging trade in war
When he killed Pallas. That's the way Anchises' spirit
Feels, and Iulus, too: your pleading has no merit."
And then Aeneas grasps the helmet with his left   535
Hand, bends the neck, and plants his sword up to the haft.

Phoebus' and Trivia's priest, Haemonides, was near,
The holy ribbons round his brows. His robes and gear
Were all in gleaming white. But coming face-to-face
With him, Aeneas kills him, having given chase.   540
Astride the corpse, he cloaks it in his giant shade.
Serestus shoulders off the arms, a trophy made
For you, King Gradivus.

                Next, from the Marsian hills,
Umbro, with Vulcan Caeculus, steps up and fills
The ranks. The raging Dardan had already chopped   545
Off Anxur's left arm; with the shield attached, it dropped.
(He'd boasted big before, hoping the words might match
Some deed and stir his soul, perhaps. Or that he'd snatch
A long grey life from this, a promise made before.)

Then Tarquitus (whom Dryope the nymph once bore   550
To sylvan Faunus), boasting in the bronze he wore,
Stood thwarting fiery Aeneas, who, his spear
Poised, pins the heavy shield and breastplate, driving clear
Through both. Then as the youth pleads uselessly and tries
For words, Aeneas strikes: the head falls.

                    Where it lies,   555
He rolls the warm trunk, stands, and has his hostile say:
"Now lie there, fearful man. Your mother will not lay
You in the earth, nor set the family tomb to weigh

Down on your limbs. Kite bait instead, or maelstrom-drowned,
You'll ride the wave where starving fish will suck your wound."   560

Quickly, he catches Lucas and Antaeus, shock
Troops of Turnus, brave Numa, and the tawny-locked
One, Camers, Volcens' son (Volcens—Ausonia knew
No richer, ruling mute Amyclae). Aegaeon, who
Would wield a hundred arms, a hundred hands, men say,   565
And flash his fire from fifty breasts and mouths the day
He swashed as many shields and bared as many sword
Blades all against the bolts of Jove: Aeneas roared
Like him.

      Across the plain he vents a victor's red-
Hot rage now as his sword-point warms. There, see him head   570
Off toward Niphaeus' four-horse team, their breasts turned to
Him. But they saw his long strides as he almost flew
In lethal fury toward them, and they spooked in fear,
Fell back, and spilled their driver in their wild career
Shoreward.

      Meanwhile, Lucagus and Liger, brother   575
With brother, join the battle. Liger drives; the other
Waves his drawn sword madly. Two white horses charge.
Aeneas couldn't bear their fury, looming large
Above them as he rushed up with his leveled spear.
Liger shouted at him,   580
"These horses that you see? They are not Diomedes'.
We're not on Phrygia's plain. This chariot's not Achilles'.
Here, war and life will end, for this is where you'll die!"

Mad Liger's far-flung words. The Trojan won't reply
In kind though, for he heaves his lance at all their forces,   585
As Lucagus leans toward the blow, flogging his horses.

He plants his left foot hard, to set himself to fight;
The piercing spear comes out the lowest rim the bright
Shield boasts; there on his left, the weapon gores his thigh.
Thrown from the chariot, he spills where he will die.   590

With bitter words, the great Aeneas speaks: "It seems[9]
No simple fear accounts for how your chariot team's
Retreated, Lucagus, no shadow of your foe.
It's you who leapt from churning wheels and let them go."

Words done, he seized the car. The wretched brother who   595
Had fallen too, held out imploring palms: "By you
Your Trojan hero's self; by him your parents bore:
Great Man, I beg your mercy; let me live once more."
He went on begging as Aeneas said, "You'd other
Words just now. Die. Brother should keep faith with brother." 600

Then with his blade, he laid the soul bare where it hid.
Over the plain, these were the deaths the Dardan did,
As he went raging like a torrent or a black
Tornado. Finally, Ascanius broke back
From camp with all who'd beaten off the failed attack.   605

Meanwhile, unprompted, Jupiter addressed his queen:[10]
"My sister Juno—my dear wife—it's clear you've been
Correct: your views on Venus show your judgment's keen.
She gives the Trojans might; it's not by their own hands,
Despite bold spirits long inured to war's demands."   610

Submissive Juno answered: "Fairest husband, why
Upset me with your stringent dictates? Heartsick, I
Obey, but fear. If love between us were a tie
Strong as before—as it should be—you'd not deny
Me this, Almighty One: snatch Turnus from the fight,   615

Safe for his father Daunus. Otherwise, you might
As well allow his death, to pay the Trojans' rage
With guiltless blood! But he is of our lineage,
Pilumnus' heir, four generations. Often he
Would load your limen with his generosity."   620

The King of High Olympus's reply was brief:
"If your plea for that doomed man is a reprieve
From present death, then—understand me well—I so
Command. *Save* Turnus from his fate. I'll let him go,
Though just so far—no more. But if in what you plead   625
You hide the wish to change the course of war, you feed
A vain hope that is pointless, for I'll do no more."

And Juno, all in tears, cried out, "But what if your
Heart granted what your tongue won't—Turnus safe from war?
Right now, he's either doomed though innocent, or else   630
I'm wrong. Oh, I'd prefer that these were only false
Fears mocking me; that you—who can!—would change your mind!"

When she was done, she came from heaven like the wind,
All wrapped in cloud and driving heaven's rack before
Her as she sought the Laurentines encamped for war—   635
The Ilian ranks. Then from the massive mist she made
A wraith, Aeneas-like, armed with a Trojan blade[11]
(A monstrous prodigy). She forged a shield and crested
Helmet for his god-like head, in which there nested
A phantom tongue with mindless words. It walked the way   640
Aeneas did, and flittered like the forms (men say)
Of death, or dreams that take the senses for their dupes.

The phantom flaunts itself before the front-line troops,
Taunting Turnus with its words . . . and spears that miss.

Turnus charges, hurling *his* spear with a hiss   645
From distant range; the phantom turned and took to flight.
Then Turnus, thinking that Aeneas fled the fight,
Was crazed enough to cling to that pathetic dream.
"Where to, Aeneas? What about that wedding scheme?
I'll give you all the earth you sought across the seas!"   650
Blade drawn in hot pursuit, he loudly hunts what flees,
But he can't see: winds bear his glory far away.

By chance, its gangplank down and ladders dropped, there lay
Now tethered to a high rock-pier, the ship that King
Osinius had sailed from Clusium. Hot to fling   655
Its "frightened" self down some dark hole, the airy thing
That seems Aeneas fleeing, leaps, with Turnus amply
Fast behind, who springs across the steep-pitched ramp,
Unstoppable. He's at the prow when Saturn's daughter
Snaps the hawser, shoves the ship across the water,   660
Fast receding. Then the wraith no more holds back,
But soaring up, dissolves inside the black cloud rack.
Meanwhile, Aeneas challenges his missing foe
To fight, while countless men receive their fatal blow,
And rescued Turnus rides the storm across the waves.   665

Confused, he looks back (less than grateful for what saves
Him), raising hands and voice to heaven: "Mighty god,
You thought that I earned *this*, the sentence of your rod?
Where am I bound? From *what*? What punished me with flight?
And why? How will I ever get back to the fight?   670
Or will I never see Laurentium's walls again,
And those who went where my flag went, my valiant men?
Have I left them to vicious death? Then vile crime lies
On me, who sees them falling, hears their groans and cries!
What should I do? No pit, no matter what its size,   675

Gapes wide enough to suck me down. Winds, pity me;
Let rocks and reefs be mercy's kind calamity.
I, Turnus, beg you. Let some ruthless sandbanks swallow
Me, where Rutuli and Rumor cannot follow."

That said, he wavers, this way, that way, in his mind—   680
If he should run right on his sword, half-crazed, half-blind
With shame, and bare his ribs, and drive cold steel deep in,
Or plummet to the waves, and swimming, try to win
The winding shore, to charge the Teucrians in the field.
Three times he tried each course; three times she would not yield, 685
Great Juno, stopping him from pity. Now held back,
He rides the favoring waves and tides and cuts the wrack,
Borne on to Daunus' ancient town—his father's town.

But meanwhile, warned by Jove, Mezentius fought on,
Attacking Teucrians in all their jubilation.   690
The Tyrrhenes closed their ranks in raging concentration,
All their hate and missiles hurled at that one man
Alone, who—like a crag that dares the sea's great span,
And fronts the raging gale winds, naked to the deep,
Suffering the force and threat of sky and sea to keep   695
Itself steadfast—still stood.

                        And then he killed: the son
Of Dolichaon, Hebrus; Palmus, on the run;
And Latagus. (He'd spotted Latagus, and smashed
His mouth and face with one great hillside rock, then slashed
Through Palmus' hamstring, and had left him there to twitch   700
In vain. Lausus he gave the dead man's armor, which
Would guard the shoulders, then the plumes to top his crest.)

Phrygian Evanthes next, then Mimas, Paris' best
Friend, whom Theano bore to Amycus the night

That Cisseus' daughter, *fascis*-gravid, showed the light   705
Of day to Paris. Paris lies where his forebears
Lie, Mimas on Laurentine shores where no one cares.

A boar that pine-treed Vesulus for years has hid,
Or one Laurentian marshes' stands of reeds have fed,
When driven from the hills by snapping hounds, will halt   710
Before the nets to snort, and no one has the salt
To beard the bristling beast, but from a distance throw
Insults and spears. The cornered boar's undaunted though.
He whips this way and that, gnashing his tusks and shaking
Lances from his hide. That's how the men were quaking   715
At Mezentius—men with good cause to hate
Him. No one meets him naked blade to blade. They wait,
A safe spear-throw away, and offer billingsgate.

Greek Acron, out of ancient Corythus, had come,
An exile, with his marriage not yet whole. When from   720
Far off Mezentius spots him, knee-deep in the fight—
Blue-plumed, in red robes that his bride had thought to plight
Him—in Mezentius plunges, mad to fight (the way
A starving lion prowls the high breaks, crazed for prey
From hunger, roaring from its maw if it should see   725
A frightened doe or big-racked stag that turns to flee.
Lording, it guards the gory guts with bristling mane;
The foul jaws boast their scarlet stain.).

Then hapless Acron's heels are hammering black ground
As he goes down, gasping for breath. From out the wound,   730
Blood stains the splintered spear. Mezentius will not deign
To kill Orodes as he runs. He won't be slain
By unseen lance thrown by Mezentius at his back.
That killer ran to *face* the one he would attack,
And man-to-man, prevailed by strength, not trickery.   735

Straining to pull his spear, foot on his enemy,
He calls out, "Men, Orodes lies here, no small part
Of all this war!" And they cry out in taking heart.
Orodes, though: "Whoever you may be who've killed
Me, I will be avenged, for soon they will be stilled,   740
Your boasts. My fate is yours, and *your* blood will be spilled
Here."

       Rictus-stiff with rage, Mezentius sneered, "Now die!
Great Jove the Judge says when I breathe *my* final sigh."
And then he pulled the spear from dead Orodes' breast.
Upon those eyes come iron sleep and lasting rest;   745
The living day dies down in death's eternal night.

Caedicus slays Alcathous. Hydaspes' fight
Is ended at Sacrator's hand. Then Rapo kills
Parthenius and tough Orses. Messapus now stills
Clonius and Ericetes, who's Lycaon's son.   750
(One lies beside his now unbridled horse, and one
Had come on foot.) The Lycian Agis, too, was killed
By Valerus, the heir of experts, just as skilled.
Nealces did for Salius who'd slain Thronius—
Nealces' lance struck home, his bolts insidious.   755

Now grief and death were equals, both the lethal Mavors',
And killing matched with dying were his bloody favors,
Victors like vanquished (neither ran). The gods were saddened
By all this balanced, useless rage in men death-maddened.
Here, Venus watches; there, Saturnian Juno sees.   760
Amidst those thousands, fury is Tisiphone's.

And now Mezentius, threatening with his hefty lance,
Storms down the field, the way Orion's steps advance
Through Nereus's deepest waters. (On he strides,

Cutting his way, with shoulders high above the tides. 765
Or else he hauls an old ash from some mountain height,
Walking the earth, his head cloud-hidden from our sight.)
Mezentius, heavily armored, stalked the field that way.

Far off, Aeneas sees him in the ranks' array
And runs to meet Mezentius waiting, firm and fearless, 770
To fight his great-souled enemy. His mass is peerless.
His measuring eye works out how far his spear must go:
"May this right hand—my god—now help me as I throw!
Now, Lausus, you yourself—and this I vow—shall be
The trophy, in *his* armor, of my victory 775
Over Aeneas—spoils that bandit's corpse will yield."

He launched a hissing spear that grazed Aeneas' shield
Then pierced the nearby fair Antores in the side.
(Antores—Hercules' friend from the Argolid.
He'd joined Evander, settling in a Latian town. 780
Now cursed with bad luck, by another's wound struck down,
Dying, he saw sweet Argos in the sky's high blue.)

Righteous Aeneas throws his spear, which bores right through
Mezentius' convex shield of triple bronze and folds
Of triple linen-braided bull's hides, till it holds 785
Fast in the groin, force spent. Aeneas, as it catches,
Exults to see Tyrrhenian blood; the hero snatches
His hip-side sword and runs hard at the man he's shaken.
Lausus groans at the wound his much-loved father's taken,
The awful sight of which makes tears roll down his cheek. 790
(And here, your brutal death, boy, means that I must speak,
If times to come will credit what you did—the facts
So glorious—remembering you and all your acts.)
His father hobbled over ground he had to yield,
And helpless, dragged Aeneas' lance stuck in his shield. 795

That's when the son rushed in, plunging into the fray
Just as Aeneas poised above the man he'd slay,
And caught that sword edge in his shield. The brief delay
Allows his friends to race up with an awful shout
To help the father, shielded by his son; dragged out,   800
He's safe beneath their storm of javelins that beat
Aeneas back. *He* rages, safe in his retreat.

Sometimes the storm clouds pour down catadoups of hail,
As every ploughman, every husbandman, turns tail
And flees the fields. The pilgrim finds some makeshift shelter   805
Under a riverbank or rock against the welter
Of the rain that pelts the land, so all may go
About their work again when sun returns.

                                  Just so,
Spears everywhere—a missile shower. Aeneas bides
His time, threatening Lausus. "O Lausus," he chides,   810
"Why such a rush to ruin? You dare more than you can.
Your filial love has made you rash."

                                Still, the young man
Reared up, crazed to fight, till the Dardan's fury, fanned,
Surged ever-higher, and the Parcae took in hand
Lausus' last threads: Aeneas ran his heavy blade   815
Right through the stripling's gut, hilt-deep. And there it stayed
(The point drove through the shield, too light a thing to match
His threats). They filled with blood the soft gold tunic which
His mother'd woven, as the soul flew through the air
To join the Manes and to grieve the body there.   820

But when Anchises' son looked on that dying face—
A face so strangely pale—he saw in Lausus' place
His filial love—a countenance that was his own.

His hand held out, deep pity made Aeneas groan:
"What can love's duty help me grant, unlucky son,   825
To one with such a heart, for all that you have done?
Keep what you've loved—your weapons—and if you're concerned,
Your fathers' long-dead shades will see your corpse returned.
And let this be some solace for your death, poor man:
You die by great Aeneas' hand." Then he began   830
Rebuking Lausus' men, and lifted him from where
The blood-soaked mire fouled that prince's lovely hair.

Meanwhile, on Tiber's banks, his father washed his wounds,
Then leaned against a tree-trunk, resting where his bronze
Helmet hung and his armor crushed the grass. Some hand-picked
    men   835
Stand round the weary prince who fights to breathe again;
He rubs his neck and lets his kempt beard drape his chest.
He asks and asks for Lausus, sends at his behest
A squad to call him back—a worried sire's command.
Already, though, that soldier's sobbing funeral band   840
Were bearing lifeless Lausus on his shield, a great
Man, victim of a greater wound. That seer of fate,
Mezentius' heart, already knew what he'd been sent.

White hair dirt-fouled, two hands raised to the firmament,
He clings to Lausus' corpse, then cries out to the blue,   845
"Did love of life possess me so that I let you,
My son, face harm a parent should have battled through?
I *fathered* you! And do I live because you died,
Because you took such wounds? The exile has been tried;
I'm guilty to the core. The deep wound's like a flame!   850
My son, my crime has brought dishonor on your name.
Once driven by their hatred from my fathers' throne,
I long have owed a reparation mine alone.
In any form of death, my life's what I must pay.

Right now, I live. I have not left the light of day,   855
But leave I will!"

                And as he speaks, he rises on
The wounded leg, though almost all its strength is gone,
And valiant still, commands his mount be brought. The source
Of all his pride and solace is this conquering horse
He's always ridden. Speaking to the grieving steed: 860
"Rhaebus, we have lived long, if any mortal breed
Can claim that word. This day, you'll either bear away
Aeneas' head and bloody spoils, making him pay
For Lausus' pain, or you will die with me, if force
Carves no way out. For I believe, most gallant horse,   865
You'll champ no stranger's bit, nor let a Teucrian sit
You."

      Done, he mounted as he always had, then fit
Two hefty, steel-sharp lances to his hands. Bronze lit
His helmet, with its bristling horsehair crest. He charged
Into the killing, as in that one heart there merged   870
A torrent made of madness, grief, and shame.

                      And then
He shouted "Aeneas!" again, again, again.
Aeneas knew the voice. He prays exultantly:
"So let it be, Great Father-God; so let it be,
Apollo! Let the fight begin!"   875
The words were done. With leveled spear, he's moving in.

But then Mezentius: "Savage! You can't scare me, now
My son is dead (the only way that I know how
You could have shattered me). I'm not afraid to die
Now, nor do I pay heed to any god. Since I   880

Am here for death, stop talking. Let these presents be
Your first from me."

               He spoke, and struck his enemy,
Landing first one spear then another, circling wide.
But none of them could pierce the golden boss they'd tried.
Leftward, he circled thrice the man who stood his ground,   885
Then hurled his lances. Thrice that Trojan dragged around
His bronze shield sprouting giant lances triple-thick.

Then, irked that this is dragging on; that he must pick
His buckler clean of spears; hard-pressed on foot to fight
A horse;—he weighs his move, breaks free at last, and right   890
Between the charger's eyes, he slings—and plants—his spear.
The animal rears up, hooves battering the air,
Then throws its rider. Tangled in that form, the horse
Falls headlong, shoulder wrenched by the terrific force.

Trojan—and Latian—shouts set fire to the skies.   895
Aeneas, sword unsheathed, stands over him and cries
Out words like these: "Where's powerful Mezentius' pride
Now—all his wild heart?" That Tyrrhenian replied,
Eyes heavenward, wits barely set, with gasping breath,
"My taunting enemy, why threaten me with death?   900
To kill me is your right; I knew that for a fact
When I came here to fight. And Lausus made no pact
Between us. This is all I ask, a victim's plea:
Entomb me in the earth. My people look on me
With hate-filled rage that hems me in. Protect me from   905
Them: give my son and me, I beg you, one shared tomb."[12]

He spoke—then took deep in his throat Aeneas' sword.
So life went out, and down his breast the blood-wave poured.

Book XI

And then Aurora rose and left the sea behind.
Aeneas, though black griefs are battening on his mind
("Bury your comrades," sorrow says), begins to pay
The gods his victory vows, as Eos breaks the day.
Lopping its branches off, he propped a big oak bole   5
(Dressed up to be a victory trophy) on a knoll
Votive to you, great War God. Boasting armor stripped
From Prince Mezentius, it shone; the bright blood dripped
From crests tied on. So were that warrior's broken spears
And battered breastplate hung (twelve times it had been
    pierced).   10
Aeneas tied the bronze shield on the left and hung
The ivory-handled sword around the "neck."

                                        Among
His whole glad band of brothers then, the high words ring:
"We've done great things, my men; fear nothing chance may bring.
These are the first spoils taken from a haughty king: 15
Here is Mezentius, made by my own hands! What calls
Us now is King Latinus and his city walls.
Now make your hearts and weapons ready; gird for war.
Then when the gods above us give the signal for
Our camp to raise our flags and march, nothing will slow   20
Us down—no faltering or fear when we must go.
Till then, let's bury those who've died, each fallen friend—
Those Acheron respects when heroes meet their end.
So go," he says, "and give these souls their final due;
They bled to win this Latian land, these happy few!   25

But first, send Pallas' body to Evander's city
Of grief. Though he was plainly brave, death showed no pity,
But stole his life and sank it in a bitter end."

So weeps Aeneas, tracking back to where his friend[1]
Is laid, a lifeless corpse, upon the threshold. There,   30
Agèd Acoetes, once the one assigned to bear
Parrhasian Evander's arms, now watched above
The foster-child who claimed his grieving guardian's love.
There, all the Trojans and their servants stood around,
The mourning Ilian women with their hair unbound,   35
As always.

      When Aeneas entered through the doors,
They beat their breasts and raised their voices to the stars—
A mighty wail. The palace rings; the sorrow roars.
And as he sees the pallid face and pillowed head
Of Pallas, and the patent wound that gouged in red   40
That polished breast a dread Ausonian spearpoint bled,
Aeneas speaks, in tears: "So you're the wretch," he said,
"Whom happy Fortune envied—whom she'd not let see
My realm to come? And she begrudged me you? To be
A victor riding to Evander? This was not   45
The pledge I made when he embraced me, sent me out
To win an empire, warning of the fear he bore
(The foe were brave—a people tempered hard by war).
Perhaps, deceived by hope, he's promising right now
To heap the altars with his offerings—a vow   50
In vain, while we, in grief, attend his lifeless son,
Whose debts to any god above are paid and done.
Poor man, to watch your son's cruel funeral! Our great
Return is *this* then? *This* the triumph they await?
Is *this* my solemn pledge? At least, Evander, you   55

Won't see a son who died with shameful wounds—one who
Will make you want to die because your son 'pulled through.'
Ausonia! What a stay you've lost—Iulus, too!"

His tears complete, he has men raise the sad dead form,
And sends, a thousand-chosen-soldiers-strong, a quorum   60
Of mourners who'll attend the final rites and take
Upon themselves the father's tears. Sadly, they make
Cold comfort for such giant grief, a father's due.

And quickly weaving wicker ribs were others who
Piled oak twigs and arbutus shoots. The bed they made,   65
A cushioned bier, was tented in a leafy shade.
It's here they lay the boy high on his rustic bed—
Soft violet, or hyacinth that hangs its head,
A flower that a virgin's fingers plucked, but one
Whose grace and radiance haven't faded in the sun,   70
Though Mother Earth no longer gives each needful gift.[2]

Aeneas then brought out twin purple robes (both stiff
With gold). Sidonian Dido wove him these, glad in
The work of her own hands once, plaiting gold in thin-
Spun threads through warp and weft. In sorrow now, he drapes   75
One over Pallas as a final honor, shapes
It so it keeps the hair from burning. Then he heaps
A slew of battle spoils won from the Laurentines
And orders that they be marched out in long sad lines.
He added swords and steeds stripped from the enemy,   80
Then bound behind their backs the hands of those that he
Was sending to be offerings to the Ghostly Souls,
Sparging the fires with blood. The leaders carried boles
Hung with the arms of enemies, their names nailed on.
Acoetes, led in staggering grief, his hope all gone,   85

Fists pounding bruises on his chest, nails tearing at
His face, falls full upon the earth, his length laid flat.

Then came the chariots that Rutulian blood had pied,
And then the warhorse Aethon, trappings laid aside,
Walks mourning; down his cheeks, tear after giant tear. 90
Though conquering Turnus claims the rest, some bear the spear
And helmet. Sad lines follow, Teucrians the first,
Tyrrhenians next, and then Arcadians, arms reversed.
With all his comrades passed and marching far ahead,
Aeneas stopped and sighed. These are the words he said: 95

"I'm called from here to meet this same grim fate of war
With other tears. Great Pallas, hail for evermore,
And for eternity, farewell." Then, no more words.
He walked into the camp whose walls he had turned towards.
And now ambassadors came from the Latian city; 100
Beneath the shade of olive boughs, they begged for pity.
They asked their bodies back—men cut down on the plain
And lying there. They begged a grave for soldiers slain,
For who could battle with the dead, bereft of day?
Why not spare men who might have given brides away 105
Or been guest-hosts?

           The good Aeneas grants what they
Have asked—he must—then speaks the words he has to say:
"Latians, what undeserved misfortune tangled you
In such a war, that now you flee our friendship? Do
You beg a truce for dead kin Fate has given Mavors? 110
I'd gladly see the *living*, too, share peace's favors.
Had Fate not granted me this place, I'd not have come.
Your folk are not our foes; your king had spurned us from
Him, thinking Turnus' sword would be the one to trust,
But Turnus meeting death—*that* would have been more just. 115

If he would end this war by force, and drive us out
Then he should fight me with these arms. Removing doubt,
The gods or someone's right hand would have granted life.
Go burn their corpses now who perished in this strife."

Astounded—silent—when Aeneas' speech is done,   120
They look around at one another, every one,
Till Turnus-hating Drances[3] speaks—an older man
Who strives to heap rebuke on Turnus all he can:
"O man of Troy, in glory great, yet greater still
In war, my praises fail, though high as heaven's sill!   125
Which stuns me more—your justice or your fighting skill?
Yes, what you've said, we'll tell our town. And yes, we will,
If Fortune shows us how, ally you to our king.
Let Turnus find new friends. Think what a marvelous thing—
To raise the massive walls that Destiny commands,   130
By shouldering stones to build New Troy with our own hands!"
They roared unanimous assent when he was done,
Then set twelve days of truce, with peace their guardian.
Latians and Teucrians roamed wooded hills as one,
All safe. The high ash rings to the resounding two-   135
Edged axe. Men cut the pines that scrape the stars. Nor do
They stop, as wedges split the cedar and the oak,
And mountain ash weighs down the wains that creep and croak.

Now Rumor flew its grievous omen to Evander,
Filling the palace and the city of Evander—   140
Rumor, that had just whispered, "Pallas' arms have won"
To Latium. The Arcadians, as they long had done,
Rushed torches to the gates. The road out scintillated
With ranks of flames that kept the far fields separated.

The mourning Phrygian column meets and joins them. Then,   145
Just as the women, by their houses, spied the men,

Grief set the city blazing with its shrieks and clamor.
But nothing known to man can hold back King Evander.
He bursts through all the mourners, falls on Pallas' bones,
And when the bier's set down, embraces them and groans.   150

The grief will barely let his throttled voice be heard:
"O Pallas, this was not your promise, for the word
You gave your father was to wage this war with care.
How sweet a first fight's honor tastes, I was aware;
How great could be a young man's pride in arms, I knew.   155
Oh, these were your first fruits of youth, the training you
Went through, and of a war so near; of prayers no god
Would hear! O blessèd Queen, to have been spared the rod
Of sorrow such as this by your own death! But I,
However, have outlived my fate: a son to die   160
Before his father! Would that I had marched with Troy's
Allies and died by some Rutulian spear! My boy's
Cortège! Oh, that *my* name were mourned, not Pallas' name!
And yet your treaty, Teucrians, will not make me blame
You, nor that we are friends. My white hairs brought this on.   165
And though death came too soon, I'm glad, despite you're gone,
You led the Teucrians into Latium, where the dead
Volscians lie in thousands, Pallas. For indeed
I deemed you worthy of no finer rites than these
Righteous Aeneas and the Tyrrhene companies   170
And captains have performed here. Those whom your right hand
Dealt death to bring great trophies. Turnus, you would stand
Here, too, a vast trunk hung with all your vanquished arms,
Had age and strength matched both of you on equal terms.
But should my sorrow keep the Teucrians away   175
From war? Go! Tell their king exactly what I say:
If I last out this hateful life, with Pallas gone,
It's that I know *you* know your sword-hand owes a son
And father Turnus' death. This is the only way

Your fate and worth have. While I see the light of day   180
No joy is mine (*nec fas*). I wish to give my son
In deepest Dis the word of what you will have done."4

Now Dawn's light called all men to see their work begun.
Aeneas Pater now, now Tarchon, built their pyres
On the crescent shore. Here, customary fires   185
Burnt the bodies there, as underneath dead kin
The flames go up; skies turn to smoke they're wrapped up in.
Three times, men bronzed in brilliant arms go round the flames;
Three times, on mounts, to honor their dead comrades' names,
They ride in circles round the fires, wailing their cries.   190
Tears wash the earth; tears wash the armor where it lies.
Men's clamor and their trumpet blasts ascend the skies.

Some feed the blaze with spoils they've stripped from Latians killed:
Helmets, rich swords, with reins and chariot wheels all spilled
Onto the flames, while others throw in gifts well-known   195
To dead men: shields and spears that missed when they were thrown.
Death eats the sacrifice of kine from all around,
As bristling, throat-cut boars, with flocks the knives have found,
Are bled to feed the fires. All down the sandy ground,
Men watch their comrades burn. They guard each charred death-
     mound.   200
No one can bear to leave the site till dew-soaked night
Brings on a sky of star-nailed, scintillating light.

Disconsolate Latians, too, just like the Teucrians, build
Their countless fires. Some of those so lately killed
Are borne off to the nearby fields, some corpses buried.   205
Yet other grieving houses take in dead, shield-carried.
The remnant—piles of carnage no one numbers—are
Gone up in smoke, sans any honors. Broad fields, far
And wide, are thick with pyres that compete in burning.

Then chilling shadows left the heavens at third dawning.   210
Bones are raked from ashes by the men still mourning.
Their dead friends wear Italian soil; the warm earth falls.

Meanwhile, within rich King Latinus' city walls,
The greater part of giant grief assaults the air.
Here, mothers and their sons' now doleful consorts; there,   215
The heart-crushed sisters and the orphaned sons, are cursing
This war and the marriage Turnus was rehearsing.
They argued he, and he alone, should use his sword
To settle this, who claimed all Italy for reward.

Then bitter Drances weighs in: only Turnus is   220
To fight. But at the same time, many friends of his
Speak out against this, challenging in varied phrases,
Defending Turnus. Hard-won spoils and fame's great praises
Argue for him, and the queen's name covers him.

Amidst the blazing-hot contention, look! The grim   225
Ambassadors top even this. The dread reply
From Diomedes' city: nothing garnered by
So much expense and effort—not by gifts nor gold
Nor by intense entreaties. Latium has been told:
Find other friends, or sue for peace from Ilium's prince.   230

Even Latinus sinks beneath these dire events.
The ire of the gods—and new-dug graves—convince
Him that Aeneas has been blessed by heaven's hand.
And so he calls his council by a king's command,
Gathering the realm's great men within the towering gates.   235

They streamed on toward the palace through the crowded streets.
Latinus, first of those convened, and *primus*, seats
Himself amidst them as he knits a troubled brow.

Those back from the Aetolian town he orders now
To tell of everything—full answers, each in turn.   240
All tongues fall silent as the council strains to learn
What the obedient Venulus begins to say.

"O countrymen, we made our journey, all the way
To Diomedes' Argive camp. We live to tell
You that we grasped the hand by which great Ilium fell.   245
(Iapygian Garganus' conqueror, he came
To found Argyripa, which took his fathers' name.)
When we had entered and were given leave to speak,
We offered gifts and said what we had come to seek.
We told him who we were, where from, and who had fought   250
To win our kingdom; by what cause we had been brought
To Arpi. Listening calmly, Diomedes spoke:⁵
'Of Saturn's old Ausonia, you're the blessèd folk.
What Fate has lured you in to fight this dubious war?
With swords, we raped the Ilian fields (and I ignore   255
What battles tortured us below those walls; the brave
Men drowned by Simois), and for those crimes we gave
Ourselves to every grief; we suffered everywhere,
Men ripe for even Priam's pity. Know: that pair—
Minerva's dreadful star and the Euboean cliffs;   260
Caphereus' vengeance. Atreus' Menelaus drifts
Far off from Troy, an exiled man, to Proteus' Pillars.
Ulysses looks on Aetna's Cyclopean killers.
And Mycenean Agamemnon, too, who led
Achaea, scarcely home: his vile wife struck him dead.   265
He conquered Asia, but Aegisthus lay in wait.
Idomeneus' house fell! Should I tell the fate
Of Neoptolemus's realm? How Libya's sands
Hold Locrians? How heaven grudges me my land's
Altars, my longed-for wife, and lovely Calydon?   270
Now omens hunt me, horrible to look upon:

Turned birds, my perished comrades sought the sky or went
To haunt the streams (O gods—my people's punishment!).
They fill the cliffs with tearful cries—a destiny
I should have seen would come, when my insanity   275
Instead incited me to do the goddess harm;
Steel blade in hand, I wounded Venus in the arm.
So no—don't spur me on to fight this war. Since Troy
Met ruin, Teucer's race and I are done. No joy
Inheres in memories of all that misery.   280
Take your homeland's gifts you thought to give to me
To *him*—Aeneas. I've withstood his killing spear
And fought him hand-to-hand. Believe me when you hear
The way he dwarfs his shield; the whirlwind when he throws
That spear. Had Ida made two like him for our foes,   285
The Dardans would have reached to Inachus's gates
And Greece's cities would have grieved contrary fates.
For all those years we spent at Troy-the-Stubborn-Walled,
The hands of Hector and Aeneas had us stalled,
Delaying victory for fully ten long years.   290
Both were courageous spirits skilled with swords and spears,
Aeneas first in reverence. Ally with him
The best you can, but never try to vie with him.'
Most noble King: you've heard what that king had to say,
And his advice about this lacerating fray."   295

The envoys barely done, a mixed-up murmur started
From the lips of scared Ausonians, like a parted
River balked by rocks (the pent-up current mutters
From its neighbor banks that echo plashing waters).

Then all the restless minds and jabbering tongues grew still.   300
The throned king speaks, invoking the celestial will:
"Latians, I wish we'd settled this most vital matter
Earlier. In times like these, it would be better
Not to have to meet; the foe's before our gates.

My countrymen, we war against our very fates,   305
Fighting a race loved by the gods—unconquerable men
No warfare tires. They won't give up, not even when
The battle's lost. You counted on Aetolian friends?
Give up. *You* are your one frail hope. See how it ends?
What's left of everything we planned is crushed. It lies   310
In ruin in your hands, before your very eyes.
I blame no single man; the most brave hearts can do,
You did. This war has drained the fight from all of you.
Now I will tell you what I have decided we
Should do. I will be brief, so listen carefully.   315
The Tuscan river runs beside my ancient land
Stretching to sunset—to Sicania and beyond.
Auruncans and Rutulians are sowing hopeful seed,
Ploughing its obdurate hills; their flocks and cattle feed
On the harshest slopes. Let all these piney heights   320
Be Teucrian in friendship. Yielding them just rights,
Taking them in as countrymen, we'll forge a treaty.
If that's what's in their hearts, come let them build their city.
But if their minds are set on grabbing other land
And other nations, leaving our own soil behind,   325
Then let's build twenty ships—Italian oak—or more,
If they can man more; all the wood's beside the shore.
Let them specify design, and name the number;
We'll give them bronze and shipyards, shipwrights, all the lumber.
There's more: I want a hundred noble envoys bearing   330
The offer of this pact—our best-born Latians—carrying
Olive branches, weights of ivory, and gold.
My royal throne and robe, too—signs of all I hold
As king. Consult now, and resuscitate our state
Grown so exhausted."

                              Drances stood up then, irate   335
And hostile as before—one Turnus' glory stung
(The bitter goad of hidden envy). Tart of tongue,

A lavish spender somewhat slow to wield a blade,
He dazzled with the sort of arguments he made
In council, fierce in faction. From his high-born mother   340
He'd achieved his status—not his nothing father.
Now he piles up words and aggravates their anger:

"Great King, you ask advice when all can see our danger
Is clear and needs no words, for all admit they know
What we require. They simply fear the saying so.   345
Have Turnus let *us* speak; his braggadocio,
With all its ill-starred leadership and half-crazed ways
Has sunk our city deep in grief and brought the days
Of many captains to an end. (And yes, despite
His death threats, I will speak!) He's certain of his flight   350
Route, so he fights the Trojans, using spears to fright
The gods. As for the Dardan nation, one more thing
Should be the gift that you command, most gracious King
(And don't be frightened off by any threatening man):
Wed your daughter to a prince, as fathers can—   355
Some great one worthy of her, bringing lasting peace.
But if our fear prevents this, plead that Turnus cease;
Beg him to surrender all his 'rights' to king
And country. Turnus, you're the font of everything
Poor Latium's borne. Why throw our people in harm's way   360
So often? War is not the answer. All we say
Is just give peace a chance—and show a sign, so we
Can see it's sure. You think that I'm your enemy,
And that's a charge from which I do not mean to hide,
But foremost, I'm your suppliant. Oh, set your pride   365
Aside and pity us. Give way! Defeated, we
Have seen our fields laid waste; Death drives us to one knee.
Or if you crave renown—if you're that fiercely souled,
Or dazed by what a palace dowry means—be bold
Then! Trust yourself to face the enemy. For why   370

Must we, the 'worthless,' strew the fields? Why must *we* die,
Unburied and unwept, so Turnus has a bride
That's royal? But Turnus: if you've any strength or pride—
Any of your fathers' fighting blood inside
You—brave your challenger then; do not hide." 375

The words of Drances now set Turnus' soul on fire
He groans from deep down in his heart, then vents his ire:
"Drances, it's always true, when fighting calls for men,
That you're just full of words—and first to show up when
The senate's called. This chamber needs no fulsome speech 380
From you. Your words come big when you are out of reach
Of enemies, behind our walls—when blood's not to
The moat-tops yet. Then thunder smartly, as you do,
Drances, and call *me* coward when *your* hand has piled
Up mounds of Teucrians, and strewn the battlefield 385
With trophies everywhere. What living bravery
Can do, you're free to try! To find the enemy
Is easy: look around! On every side, they wait.
Shall *we* go out to fight? Why do you hesitate?
Or does your blowhard's tongue hold all your appetite 390
For war—your tongue and flying feet?
I, *beaten*? Who can rightly say I've met defeat
When he can see the Tiber red with Ilian blood,
Evander's house and heirs laid low in Latian mud,
And his Arcadians all disarmed? Both Bitias 395
And giant Pandarus, whom I sent down to Tartarus
With thousands more—all on one day—did not think so,
Though I was ringed by the revetments of the foe.
So 'war is not the answer'? You're demented! Sing
That tune about the Dardan's life and everything 400
You own. Keep scaring others with your fear. Yes, shower
Praise on twice-defeated men; Latinus' power,
You mock! Now Myrmidons, and even Tydeus' son,

Tremble at Phrygian arms? Achilles the Larissean?
When Aufidus flows back from Adriatic waves!   405
He says my 'threats' are threats that no one like him braves
And lives. This clever nothing thinks his 'fear' makes me
A terror. But your life? My hand will let it be.
Don't shrink back. Let your coward's heart reside in state.
Now, father: back to you and to your great debate.   410
If all our fighting men no longer have your trust;
If we are doomed; if one lost battle means we're dust;
If Fortune can't re-trace her steps: then let us sue
For peace with useless hands. Oh, if we could renew
Our famous courage, though! That man would be to me   415
Most blessed in all his suffering, who not to see
Such sights, had bitten earth and bought death finally.
But *if* we still have means—resources and the men
Who still can say their manhood stands intact—and when
The peopled towns of Italy support us still;   420
And *if* to win their glory Trojans had to spill
Rivers of blood (they've died, too, and the storm of war
Has struck us all), then why give up in shame before
We even start? Why quake before the trumpets sound?
Time's often healed catastrophes. The years come round   425
Once more to work things new, and Fortune, mocking men,
Revisits, just to set them on firm ground again.
So the Aetolian and his Arpi won't help us.
Messapus will! And fortunate Tolumnius,
And all those sent by many folk. Honor will come   430
To Laurentines and all the best of Latium.
And there's Camilla, too, the mighty Volscians' pride,
Leading her bright bronze squadrons, riding on our side.
But if the Teucrians would challenge me alone
And you agree; and if I'm Latium's stumbling stone;   435
Then Victory is so far from having fled my hand
In hatred so that I would spurn a hope so grand,

I'd brave him had he slain Achilles and he were
All cased in that man's armor, made by Mulciber.
I, Turnus, brave as any of my father's line,   440
Here vow my life to you, and to my bride's Latinus.
Aeneas wants just me? That more than suits me fine!
And if the gods are angry, then I pray it's *I*,
Not Drances, who appeases them; that *I* will die,
Or if there's glory, I will win it all."

                      And then . . .   445
Debate. Aeneas, though, struck camp and moved his men.
Now look: a runner moils the royal halls as he
Comes racing in; the town, as frightened as can be,
Panics. For Teucrians and Tyrrhenes, keen to fight,
And swooping from the Tiber's plain, were now in sight.   450

At once, the shaken-hearted commons, terrified,
Are spurred to rage as if a shock had been applied.
Their fists up-raised, the young men call for arms; "to arms!"
Men cry. Sad fathers weep.

                  To deafening alarms,
A clamor fueled by discord now assaults the skies   455
On all sides, just the way swans burst with honking cries
Beside Padusa's fish-filled stream, in raucous coves,
Or crows in murders roost at will in mast-high groves.

"So be it, fellow citizens," cried Turnus, seizing
The moment. "Call your quorums. Sit around then, praising   460
Peace while armies come to take your throne!" He said
No more, but spurning that great corridor, he fled.

"Volusus!" Turnus shouts. "Call out the Volscians,
And muster for the quick-march all Rutulians.

Coras, with Messapus and your twin, dispose   465
The cavalry. Some, guard the gates against our foes;
Others, man the heights. The rest, come armed with me
Wherever I command."

                    The walls are instantly
Re-manned on every side. Dismayed by what may come,
His plans in ruin, Latinus flees. No running from   470
Himself, though, as he rues rejecting Ilium's prince
As son. The kingdom has been paying ever since.

Some trench before the gates or take up stones and stakes.
The silver trumpet calling war now snarls and shakes,
As motley circles formed by mothers and their sons   475
People the walls. The trial to come is everyone's,
The queen's, as well. With women trailing her in bands,
She scales the fortress heights where Pallas' temple stands.
Gift-laden, she ascends, Lavinia at her side,
Eyes down in shame for all the men who will have died.   480

The women reach the shrine and fill it with incense,
Then from its threshold, utter prayers that are intense:
"Tritonian Virgin, great in war and weapons, shatter
The Phrygian pirate's spear with your own hand, and flatten
Him in the dirt. Lay him out prone below our gates!"   485

Hot Turnus arms for battle he anticipates
With zeal. His flashing breastplate is already on,
Bristling with brazen scales. His gold greaves—how they shone!
With weapon buckled at his side, and brow still bare,
He races from the heights. There is no time to spare,   490
For wild with courage, he has braved the enemy
Already in his heart—a horse without a rein,
Unstabled, free, and master of the open plain,

Who either breaks for pasture and the waiting mares,
Or, used to plunging in some stream he favors, tears   495
Off at a gallop, with his head held high, while neighing
In joy, as on his neck and back his mane is playing.

Camilla⁶ rode to meet him with her Volscian force
In tow, and when the queen dismounted from her horse,
Her cohort followed suit; on cue, they leap down, too,   500
And stand their ground.

                Camilla speaks; her words are few:
"Turnus, if any trust is earned by bravery,
Then here's my word: I'll meet Aeneas' cavalry,
Riding to face those Tyrrhene horsemen all alone.
Allow this hand to try war's dangers on my own,   505
While you, with infantry, stay back and guard the town."

Transfixed by this amazing girl, Turnus replied,
"O Italy's great maid, not even if I tried
To could I thank you half enough. But since your soul
Outshines all ours, come fight with us to win our goal.   510
Aeneas, rumor says—and scouts confirm—has sent
Light cavalry to sweep the plain. He's insolent
Enough to steal a march across the ridges, down
Through lonely mountain trails to sneak-attack the town.
I'll trap him, though, there on the forest-vaulted track   515
Where troops will block both ends, so there's no turning back!
You'll face the Tyrrhene cavalry (Messapus and
The Latian troops will be with you—Tiburtus' band
As well). But it is you who must assume command."

When done, words like these urge an allied victory.   520
Then Turnus moves out, marching toward the enemy.

There is a dog-leg valley fit for trickery
In war—for cunning tactics. Hemmed in on both sides
By walls of dark, dense leaves: a track the forest hides.
That crooked trail has only one way in, and where   525
The lookouts stand, high up, flat ground lies hidden there—
The perfect cover for concealing troops that fight
From either side, attacking from the left or right,
Or if they make a stand and roll huge boulders down.
Here Turnus rushes, by a set of paths well-known,   530
To set his trap in treacherous woods. He lies in wait.

Meanwhile, Latona's daughter, sitting in high state,
Addressed swift Opis, one of her sorority's
Sacred virgins, giving voice to words like these—
Sad words: "O virgin girl, Camilla's off to war,   535
Cruel war, wearing my arms in vain. She means more
To me than anyone, and this is not a new
Love with me, nor a sudden sweetness I've come to.
When Metabus was overthrown and lost his crown
For tyranny, he fled Privernum's ancient town   540
Amidst that rebel war, taking his infant child
With him, changing her name, as both were now exiled.
Casmilla was her mother, and the girl became
Camilla. Daughter at his breast, he fled, his aim
A lonely forest ridge. But weapons waited there,   545
With Volscian battalions vulturing everywhere.
Mid-flight, he sees . . . the Amasenus! In full spate,
It's cresting to its banks from rains huge clouds create.
About to swim it, he holds back: the child. She's dear
To him, that burden that he loves. Checked by this fear,   550
He quickly sees that he must take one desperate chance:
The warrior ties his daughter to the knot-thick lance
Of oak he happens to be carrying. With craft,
Wrapping her in a cork tree's bark, he binds the shaft

And infant tight, Camilla balancing the haft.   555
Then hefting it, he cries out, 'Virgin daughter of
Latona, goddess of the woods: a father's love
Now consecrates this child to you. And as she flees
Through hostile air, yours is the spear she grasps first. Please
Make yours what I commit to the capricious breeze.'   560
Prayer done, he draws his arm back, then lets fly the spinning
Shaft, as poor Camilla arcs across the dinning,
Rushing river on that whistling missile. Then
Metabus, hard-pressed, hemmed in by hostile men,
Leaps, swims, and wins the other bank, where from its ground 565
He plucks his gift to Trivia—the babe, spear-bound.
No town would take him in beneath some sheltering roof,
Nor would his fierceness yield to one; he stood aloof,
Passing his life with shepherds in the mountains, where
He quartered with the savage beast deep in its lair.   570
And there he fed his child, at a mare's udder tips,
With milk squeezed from the teats onto her tender lips.
As soon as she began to take her baby steps,
He put a sharp lance in her hands and from her shoulder
Hung a bow and quiver. Barely grown much older,   575
For trailing robe and golden hair-clasp on her head,
Infant Camilla donned a tiger skin instead.
Even then, at that young age, her small hand hurled
Toy spears. Around her head, the smooth-thonged sling was whirled
To bring down the white swan and the Strymonian crane.   580
Mothers in Tyrrhene towers wished—but wished in vain—
She'd be their son's wife. Pleased with Artemis alone,
The chaste girl lives to make all warlike arms her own.
She stays a maid. I wish this war had let her be;
That she had left these Teucrians alone. For she   585
Would be my darling still and of my company.
Come, Opis, nymph. Since she is driven on by Fate,
Leave Heaven and find the borders of the Latian state,

Where omened armies clash, and from this quiver take
A deadly arrow of revenge with which to slake   590
My thirsting rage should someone injure her. Then make
Italian, Teucrian, repay me their same share
Of blood! Thereafter, in an empty cloud, I'll bear
The poor girl's body and her untouched arms to where
They can be buried in her own land's tomb."

                                      She spoke.   595
And Opis whirred down through the ether, a black cloak
Of wind around her.

                        Meanwhile, Trojan troops draw near
The walls. Etruscan chiefs and cavalry appear,
Arrayed in numbered squads. Warhorses neigh and ramp
Across the fields; tight-reined, they fight the bits they champ,   600
Swerving left and right. The plains of battle blazed
With bristling steel, as everywhere the spears are raised.

But massed against them: Messapus, with Latians known
For speed—and Coras, with his brother. Camilla's shown
Up too, that virgin with her troops opposing, drawn   605
Up on the plain. Arms reach back, thrust, and brandish spears
And lances. Marchers burn and snorting steeds grow fierce.

Now both sides pause, within a spear's throw, then . . . attack.
Shouting, they charge; their horses cannot be held back,
As javelins rain from every side, from everywhere,   610
Blizzard-like, their masses blackening the air.

Now fierce Aconteus and Tyrrhenus charge at one
Another with their spears. A crash! Both are undone,
With horses' breastbones shattered as these two collide—
The first to fall. Aconteus, hurtled from his ride—   615

A thunderbolt or catapulted stone—is thrown
Far off. The air receives the last breath he'll have known.

Quickly, the Latian ranks break, and they flee, their shields
Thrown back. Toward town, they race their mounts across the fields,
With Trojans chasing, as Asilas leads his men   620
Almost up to the gates. The Latians once again
Cry battle as they wheel their horses' heads around;
The Trojans race away, free-rein, across the ground.

(It's how the sea-waves rush in, one-by-one, on toward
The land, and overrun the rocks in racing shoreward.   625
The foaming breaker drowns the inland sands, its crest
Withdrawing with the sucked-up stones that were at rest,
Now tumbling. Sands go dry, with shallows in retreat.)

Twice, Tuscans pinned the Rutuli; yes, twice they beat
Them back against the walls: a rout. Their backs defensed   630
By shields, they run—shields Tuscan bows now shoot against.
But at the third clash, lines locked up, and each man aimed
At someone. Soldiers died with corpses, and the maimed
Men groaned, as butchered riders bathed in human gore
And rein-fouled horses' blood. Blood—there was always more.   635

Orsilochus's lance, hurled horse-ward out of fear
Of Remulus, then struck below that charger's ear.
The steel stuck, maddening the beast, who could not bear
The wound. Chest reared, he thrashes out, so that, thrown clear,
His rider rolls to earth.

        Huge, brave Herminius,   640
Massive-bodied, giant-limbed, and Iollas,
Catillus kills. Herminius' shoulders bare, his hair
A tawny shawl, he laughs because no wound can scare

Him. He is giant in his armor. But a spear
Pierces it, killing him, a man who knows no fear.　　645
Black blood is streaming and swords clanging as they deal
Out death. Men seek a shining end from wounding steel.

With one breast bare, Camilla raged through all this slaughter,[7]
A quiver on her shoulder—Amazonia's daughter,
Now brandishing a battle-axe, now letting go　　650
A javelin shower. Diana's golden battle-bow
Is clattering on her back, so even when she's chased
Hard by the foe who makes her wheel her horse in haste,
She swivels in the saddle, shooting as she goes.

And Tulla and Larina, virgins whom she chose,　　655
Are with her—and Tarpeia, with her axe of war.
And the Italides (Camilla chose them for
Her special glory—servants good in war or peace).
Such are the blazon-armored Amazons of Thrace
When by the feeder-streams of Thermodon, they ride　　660
In ranks next to Hippolyte, or at the side
Of Mars' Penthesilea, back from war. Their cries,
Beside her chariot, are lifted to the skies
With half-moon shields.

　　　　　　　　　Fierce girl, who's first, who's last you shear?
How many strew the earth, the victims of your spear?　　665
Euneus, Clytius' son, is first. His undefended
Chest her long pine shaft runs through, and he is ended,
Falling, gushing blood. He feasts on dusty gore,
Dying, twisting on his wound, and is no more.

She brings down Pagasus and Liris, too, the one　　670
Grabbing his wounded horse's reins as he's undone,
The other reaching his bare hand out on the run

(They die as one). To these she adds Hippotas' son,
Amastrus. Leaning back, she hunts Harpalycus,
Demophoon, and Cromis, spearing Tereus.   675
For every spear sent spinning from her hand, a Phrygian
Fell.

    The hunter Ornytus, on his Iapygian
Mount, is strangely armored, as she sees him ride,
Far out of range, broad shoulders in a bullock's hide,
His warrior's head protected by a wolf's huge maw.   680
Inside its gaping mouth, the white fangs line each jaw.
He brandishes a rustic's spear while riding tall
Amidst the ranks, a full head higher than them all.

She caught and pierced him (easy work in that melee),
Then loomed above him ruthlessly, with this to say: 685
"Tyrrhenian, did you think we were some forest prey?
Our woman's weapons now have proved you wrong: that day
Has come. But still your share of fame will not prove small.
Tell your ancestors' shades Camilla caused your fall."

She kills Orsilochus and Butes next, a pair   690
Of giant Teucrians, as Butes gets it where
Breastplate and helmet meet—where Butes' neck shines white,
And where his shield hangs from his left arm. She, in flight—
Chased by Orsilochus in widening curlicues—
Eludes him, spiraling in: who was pursued, pursues.   695
Then, rising up with battle-axe, she slices through
His armor, then his bone. There's nothing he can do
But beg. The gashes drench his face with warm, wet brains.

And now an Aunian soldier from the Apennines,
Seeing Camilla, reined up short, afraid to die   700

(A real Ligurian . . . while Fate would let him lie).
And when he sees he can't escape her wrath by running
Or some feint, he turns his mind to craven cunning,
Concocting this—a stratagem of wily lies:
"Queen, where's the glory when a warrior relies   705
On a strong horse? Don't ride away! Come down and trust
In hand-to-hand combat. Fight fairly, in this dust.
You'll soon learn who's a fraud with all her blowhard boast."

When he was done, she flared—she raged—at what he'd said.
Shucking her horse, she faces toward him, blade to blade,   710
On foot, with naked sword and plain shield, unafraid.
But certain that his trick had worked, at once he flicked
His reins, and raced off at a gallop as he pricked
That charger with a pair of spurs of roweled steel.

"Ligurian fool, your bragging is to no avail;   715
Now watch the putrid ruses of your homeland fail.
You won't reach wretched Aunus by your trickery,"
Camilla cries, and with breakneck celerity
She blocks the horse's path and head-on, grabs the reins,
Wrestling him off. His hated blood burns with the pains   720
Her vengeance takes. She's Phoebus' bird, fast-falcon-light
(It swoops down from a cliff to snare the dove mid-flight
Inside a cloud, then claws the heart to make it die.
Heartsblood and shredded feathers flutter from the sky).

The sower of the gods and men, though, throned on high,   725
Sits seeing everything with his Olympian eye.
Jove rouses the Tyrrhenian Tarchon to the fight,
Goading his rage; the Maker's spur is far from slight.
So Tarchon rides amidst his wavering men and tries,
In all that blood, to spur them with his furious cries,   730
Hoping to rally his retreating squads to battle.

"Reluctant Tyrrhenes! What has caused your hearts to rattle
With such fear, O you who are immune to shame?
One woman's all it takes to hunt you down like game?
Why bother with these spears and swords in feckless hands?   735
You're quick to *bedtime* fights . . . at Venus's commands.
And when the flute announces Bacchus' dance, you're there.
Well, wait for wine-cups and the feasting table's fare
(Your passion and your pleasure), while the favoring seer
Reports the omens and the rich fat victims call   740
You to the groves."

             Then spurring to the free-for-all,
Prepared to die, he storms toward Venulus, to wrest
Him down from off his horse, and clasp him to his chest
With just one hand. Then off with Venulus he hies,
As all the Latians watch. An uproar rocks the skies.   745
Over the battlefield, like lightning, Tarchon flies,
Bearing arms and the man. And then he breaks the tip
Off Venulus's spear, searching where he can rip
Him open with a lethal wound, as both men fight,
With Tarchon's hand around his throat, might against might.   750

Picture a tawny eagle soaring at some height:
The snake it's caught is trapped in clinging claws and twisted
Feet—a wounded serpent coiling and resisting,
Its upraised head still hissing as its scales are bristling.
With crooked beak, the eagle tears its struggling prey;   755
The air is battered as the pinions flap and flay.
That's how exultant Tarchon bears his prize away
From the Tiburtians.

             Modeling him, Maeonia's men
Attack. Then fated Arruns starts to try to pen
The fast Camilla in. With devious javelin   760

And cunning skill, he tries to find some cheap way in.
Wherever she is charging in her fury, he's
Behind her, sneaking up in silent stealth, as she's
Victorious or just back from some single fight.
That's where he hides and quickly pulls the reins up tight.   765
He looks all round for some way in, now there, now here,
While in his tireless hand he shakes his perfect spear.

By chance, Cybelus' sacred priest called Chloreus
Shone from afar, his Phrygian armor glorious.
He spurred his sweating charger on (a horse whose hide   770
Wore for defense what gold-clasped bronze scales could provide).
He shone in foreign purple hues, a blazing show,
Shooting Gortynian arrows from a Lycian bow.
On his shoulder hangs that golden bow. Bright gold's
That seer's helm, his crocus mantle's rustling folds   775
Of linen tied with yellow gold. His tunic showed
An Asian needle—leggings, too.

                                        Picked from the crowd
Of battling men, it's Arruns that she singles out.
The huntress means either to hang his Trojan gear
And gold on some great temple wall, or else she'll wear   780
It all herself. She's chasing with a rage that roils,
Recklessly, through the ranks, in female lust for spoils,
When Arruns, from his ambush, brandishes his lance.
He prays like this to heaven, for now's his chance:

"Sacred Soracte's guard, O greatest god, Apollo: 785
The pinewood blazes for *us*—chief of all who follow
You. Our faith is strong; for us, the fire's fed.
We walk on piled-high embers; through the flames we're led.
Almighty one, destroy her; she offends our eyes.
My weapon waits. I want no trophy, seek no prize   790

From her defeat—no spoils. Some other epic act
Will bring me fame. Just let her die when I've attacked
This scourge, and I'll go home bereft of glory."

                                        Half
The prayer that Phoebus heard, it happened he'd vouchsafe
Within his heart; the random winds received the other half.   795
So Arruns killed Camilla by his ready hand,
But did not live to see once more his native land.
The whirlwind headed south with Arruns' hopeless prayer.

So Arruns sent his missile whistling through the air,
And all the Volscians turned keen eyes toward the queen,   800
Who heard no sound and felt no wind. Nor was it seen—
That weapon plunging from the sky—until it sank
Its spear point deep within the target. There it drank
Camilla's virgin heartsblood from her naked breast.

They rushed to save their queen, her comrades, sore-distressed,   805
While Arruns, glad and yet more fearful than the rest,
Sped off with mixed emotions, trusting in his spear
No more, Camilla's arms a threat he would not dare.

A wolf adding a bull or shepherd to his kills
Will head at once to hide deep in the trackless hills   810
Before bloodthirsty spears can find him out. He knows
The reckless thing he's done, and toward the woods he goes,
His drooping tail tucked quivering beneath his gut.
That's just how frightened Arruns, glad to run, next shut
Himself from sight: he plunged into the army's ranks.   815

The iron point's stuck deep, although Camilla yanks
With weakened hands (it splits the ribs, down in the wound).

She sinks back, drained of blood; her lifeless eyes have swooned
In chilling death. Her fresh blood-color drains away.

And breathing out her life, there's something she must say   820
To Acca, that most faithful of Camilla's peers—
The true partaker in her dying leader's cares:
"Dear Acca, I've prevailed till now. This bitter wound,
Though, drains my life, and shadows darken all around.
Escape now! Race to Turnus with these last commands: 825
To take my place and scourge the Trojans from our lands.
Farewell."

          And having said this, she let loose the reins,
Which slipped to earth. Then bit by bit, the icy pains
Stole her from her flesh. She bowed her lifeless head
And neck, which death had now. Like her, her arms fell dead   830
To earth. She moaned. To Sheol, her bitter soul now fled.

Truly *then* an outcry struck the stars of gold.
Camilla gone, the battle raged and swelled and rolled.
In one great mass, Evander's troops of Arcady,
The Teucrians, and Tyrrhene chiefs surged like the sea.   835

Now Opis, Trivia's sentinel, long seated high
Up on a peak, has calmly watched men kill and die.
But when, amidst the distant fight, she chanced to spy
Camilla, maimed by grievous death, she loosed a sigh
And spoke out words like these, that came from far down deep: 840
"O virgin, you have paid too steep a price—too steep—
For challenging the Teucrians in war! It's done
Your life no good to worship Dian all alone
In trackless woods, or wear our quiver on your back.
Still, she will see there is no honor you will lack,   845
Now at the last of death. Nor will your downfall be

Unknown throughout the world. There'll be no infamy
Of death left unavenged. Whoever desecrated
You will pay death's price."

         A mound lay ilex-shaded—
A tomb below a mountain that stood towering.   850
(It was Dercennus's, an old Laurentian king.)
Here lovely Opis comes down, leaping to alight,
And from the high-built royal barrow catches sight
Of Arruns gleaming in his armor, puffed with pride.
She cried, "Why stray so far afield? Come, turn aside.   855
Come here and die. Camilla's death has merited
This. May not you, too, win Diana's arrowhead?"

So Opis. Then the Thracian goddess drew a feathered
Shaft from her gold quiver. Her bow's horns came together
As she arched its full length with a rage-fueled grip.   860
And then, with leveled arms, her left hand to the tip,
Her right hand pulled the bowstring back to reach her nipple.
Exactly then, as Arruns heard the hissing air
And whistling shaft as one, the arrow pierced him there.
His friends knew nothing, leaving him in dust unknown.   865
Gasping on the earth, he gave his final groan
As Opis flew up to the sky.

         Camilla's light-
Horse first, and then Rutulians, take to scattered flight.
Yes, even brave Atinas. Scrambled chiefs in rout,
Along with men un-captained, wheel their mounts about   870
And race to seek safe city walls that shut them out.

No one can stop the lethal Teucrian attack;
No one—no weaponed troops—can keep the Trojans back.
With unstrung bows, the men retreat for all they're worth,

As hooves of fleeing horses shake the crumbling earth.   875
Toward city walls, a cloud of smoky dust rolls on.
Along the ramparts, mothers scream. All hope is gone.
Their women's cries assault the air; each beats her breast.

Rutulians raced on; the first ones through, hard-pressed,
Were all jammed up among the ranks inside, in flight,   880
And met a wretched death. Their native walls in sight,
There on the very verge, their houses in plain view,
They gasped away their lives as lances ran them through.

Some shut the gates—no pathway for their pleading friends,
Who closed their lives with the most miserable of ends: 885
Those rushing toward the swords, those fighting at the gates.
Before their wailing parent's eyes, some meet their fates
By pitching headlong into ditches, having been
Shut out. Some blindly race (they give their mounts free rein)
To pound on city gates that iron bolts defend.   890

Seeing Camilla, rampart mothers now contend
Who is the fiercest (patriotism points the way).
Weak arms hurled missiles down. In haste, they grabbed what lay
At hand: charred stakes instead of steel; tough oaken poles.
They vie who'll be the first to die atop the walls.[8]   895

Meanwhile, in the forest, Turnus hears about
The bitter outcome: Acca tells him of the rout—
The Volscian troops destroyed; Camilla dead; the foe
Advancing, killing all before them as they go;
The evil luck of war; the panic in the town.   900

Raging Turnus leaves the ambush, rushing down
The hillside (cruel Jove demands it), bursting from
The woods. Just at the plain, he sees Aeneas come

Riding up the ridge. That leader races through
The pass, emerging from the thick-grown forest, too.   905

Both race to reach the walls with all their forces, just
A plain apart. That's when Aeneas sees the dust
Like smoke ahead, a short way off. He catches sight
Of the Laurentian troops. Then Turnus sees those forces:
Aeneas is in arms! He hears the snorting horses   910
Of the foe, the tramp of marching feet that follow.

They would have fought at once had not rose-red Apollo
Been already at the Spanish ocean deeps
His weary team now washes in. Day ebbs; night seeps
Across their city camps. They dig in hard, for keeps.   915

Book XII

W<small>HEN</small> T<small>URNUS</small> <small>SEES HIS</small> L<small>ATIANS CRUSHED</small>—<small>ALL THEY'VE BEEN</small>
 <small>THROUGH</small>;
Their setbacks in the war; his sacred promise to
His men unkept; himself their gazes' mark—he blazes
With a grim and smoldering rage that almost crazes.

A Punic lion, run through by some brigand's spear,   5
At last will rise to battle, proud and free from fear,
Shake his mane, and break the shaft sunk deep inside,
Then roar with blood-stained mouth, defiant in his pride.

So Turnus fires his heart as he confronts the king,
His fury swelling like a storm-cloud billowing: 10
"In Turnus you will find no cowardly delay,
No cause for Trojans to go back on what they say!
I'll fight him! Move the marriage pact and wedding day
Ahead, Father. Either that Asian runaway
Will buy his Tartarus by my right hand (let Latians   15
Watch!), and I alone will save us from our nation's
Shame, or else he'll win Lavinia for his bride."

Latinus, calm in equanimity, replied,
"Young Turnus, Greatheart: by as much as you excel
In stalwart courage, all the more would I do well   20
To think through every outcome cautiously, with care.
You hold your father Daunus' kingdoms and your share
Of conquered towns, and I possess good will and gold.
Now Latium and Laurentium's virgins are extolled
For their nobility. So let me say this trying   25

Thing, stripped free of guile. Plant these few words, undying,
In your heart: all gods and men forbade that I
Should let my child and any earlier prince ally.
Defeated by my love for you, and for my kin,
And by Amata's tears, I lost all thought of sin,   30
Snatching Aeneas' bride away, raising foul swords.
Well, Turnus, now you see the sum of our rewards.
These are my war-trials, but the worst still fall on you.
We're beaten badly—twice. It's all that we can do
To maintain hope. Our blood still heats the Tiber's stream,   35
And all along the endless plains, our white bones gleam.
Why do I hem and haw? What madness makes me dream?
If I'm prepared to sue for peace with Turnus dead,
Then why not end this war with him alive instead?
Italian and Rutulian kin: What would they say   40
If you should die (the Fates forbid!) as I betray
You while you court my daughter? Think of war—its changes . . .
And mischances, too. Ardea now estranges
Your agèd father, far away. Pity him so!"

The words had no effect on Turnus' fury, though;   45
It blazed up higher, the cure far worse than the disease.
When he could speak, his answer came in words like these:
"Great lord: that care you feel for me, I ask you please,
For me, set it aside, and let me barter fame
For death. I, too, can shower spears. No sword is lame,   50
In my right hand, either. The wounds I dole out bleed
As well. His mother will desert him in his need,
Who cloaks herself in shade and clouds his coward's flight."

The queen wept though, foreseeing how that pair would fight.
She clung to fiery Turnus, half-prepared to die: 55
"By any love you bear me; by these tears that I
Believe may touch your heart—(My life's last, grieving hour
Draws hope and peace from you alone. Latinus' power

And honor lie with you. Our tottering house relies
On you.)—don't fight with him. Whoever lives or dies,   60
Turnus my son, your battle-fate awaits me, too.
I mean to leave this hateful light behind with you.
I'll be no prisoner, with Aeneas for a son."

Lavinia's cheeks burned when her mother's words were done,
And drenched in tears, they blushed with kindled fire. Shame   65
Was spread across her glowing face, which seemed aflame.
Her virgin features showed the color one might see
When crimson dye has stained white Indian ivory,
Or lilies mixed with roses wear a pinkish cast.[1]

Love roils him as his gaze is on her—fixed, steadfast.   70
Briefly to Amata, longing even more
To fight: "O mother, please—don't send me off to war
With tears or omens as I leave. My fight will be
A brutal thing, and as for death, I am not free
To stop it. Idmon, take the Phrygian tyrant these   75
Unwelcome words: as soon as morning's dawning sees
Aurora in her scarlet car, and turns the sky
To Punic red, let Trojans and Rutulians vie
No more, but all lay down their weapons. You and I
Will duel for Lavinia. One of us will die."   80

When he was done, he went back to the palace, where
He called his horses to him. As they snuffed the air,
He shared their joy. (Orithyia's gift—an honor—to
Pilumnus. Whiter than snow, like the wind they flew.)
Their eager drivers stroke each deep-resounding chest   85
And comb their flowing manes.

                    Then Turnus clads his breast
In stiffened gold and pallid bronze, fitting his crest
Of crimson to its horns, with sword and shield. (Vulcanus

The Fire God had made that very sword for Daunus,
Turnus' father, dipping it, red-hot, in Styx.)   90
Next, striding to the middle of the hall, he picks
Up, with an iron grip, a hefty spear that's propped
Against a giant pillar. Turnus, when he'd stopped
Auruncan Actor cold, had won it.

                                        Now he shakes
It till it shivers. And this is the speech he makes: 95
"You've never failed me, spear, and this is now the day.
Great Actor's once, you're Turnus's. Oh, let me lay
It low—that Phrygian eunuch's body. I will tear
His breastplate off and drag his curling-ironed hair
All through the dust it drenches with its myrrh."

                                        Driven   100
To a frenzy, he's aflame. His eyes are giving
Sparks off as his whole appearance flashes fire.
He's like a bull before a battle: ever-higher
Climbs his fearful bellowing. He tries his ire,
Horns slashing at the air. He charges at a tree,   105
Mock-battling, or paws the ring sands savagely.

Meanwhile, Aeneas, fierce too, in his arms—a debt
To Venus—calls up manly valor he would whet,
And glad the war might end by pact (so it appears),
He comforts friends and settles anxious Iulus' fears.   110
Teaching of fate, he orders them to take his firm
Demands straight to the king, to bring the war to term.

The day's new dawn has barely lit the peaks (that time
When Helios's horses leave the waves and climb,
Flaring their nostrils as they snuff the morning light),   115

When Trojans and Rutulians mark the battle site,
Below the city's massive ramparts, then prepare
Their hearths and mounded altars for the gods they share.
Some bring hot coals and water from the spring: they wear
Priests' aprons, and vervain is wreathed about their brows.   120

Ausonian soldiers armed with spears march out in rows,
Pouring from the crowded gates. The Trojans and
Tyrhhenians stream out opposite, their swords in hand,
Their armor every different kind, as if the bitter
War called out. The captains, too, bravely glitter   125
In gold and purple as they race among their many
Thousands: Assaracus' Mnestheus, brave as any;
Asilas and Messapus, Neptune's son, the horse
Tamer.

    The sennet sounding, each man has recourse
To his ground, and props his shield with planted spear.   130
Then women, weak old men, and unarmed folk appear
Upon the battlements. They rush out eagerly
And throng the towers and the lofty gates to see.

But Juno, from the crest known by its Alban name
Now (though back then a hill of no account or fame   135
Or glory), saw Laurentine troops as she looked down,
And Trojan ranks as well, and King Latinus' town.

At once, one goddess to another, turning, she[2]
Addressed Prince Turnus' sister, genius-deity
Of lakes and singing rivers (Jupiter had given   140
These because she'd lost the maidenhead he'd riven):
"Nymph dearest to my heart, and glory of the rivers,
You know that of all Latian girls, it's you alone

Whom I've preferred of all who've mounted to the throne
Of mighty-hearted Jove, and I've enskied you, my   145
Juturna. Learn the grief you'll be afflicted by—
In case you should blame me. Whenever Fate agreed
Latium would thrive, I guarded Turnus in his need—
The city, too. Now I foresee a fighter who
Will meet a stronger fate, as violence comes due.   150
This pacted duel is something I can't look upon.
But if you dare do more for Turnus, then go on;
It's fitting. Maybe good will come when bad has gone."

Juturna'd barely done when tears streamed down, hands beating
Her lovely breast not once, but three—four—times repeating.   155
"This is no time for tears," Saturnian Juno cries.
"Run to the fight, before your brother Turnus dies.
Save him! Or stir the ranks to break this treated truce;
I back your daring"—and having urged her thus,
She left her troubled, doubting, suffering, and passive.   160

Meanwhile, the kings ride out, Latinus in a massive
Four-horse chariot (twelve rays, a golden crown,
Circle his brows—sign of the Sun-god he comes down
From). Turnus drives a snow-white team, shaking two spears
With broad steel blades.

                              Across the battlefield appears   165
Aeneas, leader of, ancestor of, Rome's race.
He comes with starry shield and arms from heaven, the place
Beside him filled by his Ascanius, Rome's bright
Next hope. Meanwhile, a priest in robes of purest white
Leads in a boar shoat and an unshorn sheep together   170
To the blazing altars where he stakes their tether.
Both heroes turn to see the sun that's rising now,
Sprinkle the salted meal, and from each victim's brow,

Cut off some hairs, then wet the altars with libations
From their cups.

        These are Aeneas's orations,   175
With his sword drawn: "Be my witness, Sun; this land
As well, for which I've suffered all a man can stand.
And mighty Jove; and Juno, whose kind favors
Now at last I beg, and you, renownèd Mavors,
Father, bending war to your divine decree.   180
I call on floods and founts and all the majesty
Of heaven, and the powers of the huge blue sea:
If Fate should give Ausonian Turnus victory,
Then we'll go to Evander's town; so we agree.
Iulus will leave this land forever. Nor will we   185
Draw swords on you again; from this you shall be free.
But if it falls that Mars grants victory to me
(As I think most likely—and may it so be,
Great gods), I won't set Teucrians over Italy.
Nor do I seek a kingdom. Let both nations live   190
Unconquered, swearing peace. Your gods and rites I'll give
You freely. Let Latinus keep his arms and be
My father, granted all his wonted power. For me,
The town my Teucrians build shall bear Lavinia's name."

So swears Aeneas first. Latinus does the same.   195
Raising his eyes, he lifts his right hand to the sky.
"I swear, Aeneas, by those same things you swear by:
Earth, sea, and stars, and by Latona's twins; by two-
Faced Janus and by Dis's shrines. Great Father who
With lightning sanctifies all treaties, hear me now.   200
I touch the altars. Gods and fires between us, be
My witness of this truce that never Italy
Shall break, no matter what. No force shall turn aside
My will—not if it drowns the land in ocean's tide;

Not if in Tartarus, the heavens melt—just as   205
This scepter, cut forever," (for by chance he has
It in his hand) "torn from the lowest forest bough,
And stripped bare of its parent branch, and yielding now,
Forever, all its leaves and scions to the knife,
Will never, sheathed in craftsman's fine-wrought bronze, show life   210
In Latian elders' hands, or leaf itself to shade."

With words like these they seal the treaty they have made
Before their leaders' eyes, then slit the offerings' throats
In fiery rites. Ripping the guts from sheep and goats,
They heap the altars high with platters heavy-fraught.   215

To the Rutulians, though, the duel had seemed, they thought,
Unfair, and they were worried, fearful, and morose—
Especially when they'd seen the mismatched men up close.
And Turnus' steps are soft; his people's fears compound.
Meek at the altar site, his eyes are on the ground,   220
And making matters worse—his pale cheeks and young frame.[3]

Juturna, Turnus' sister, saw doubt spread. To tame
It, as the people's minds began to waver, she
Appeared as Camus in the ranks, god-secretly.
(Camus—whose lineage was renowned; whose father's name   225
Was glorious; who'd won himself a warrior's fame.)

She comes amidst the troops, knowing what she must do,
Sowing rumors. These are the words men listen to:
"Rutulians, don't you blush to risk one life for many
When our massive strength makes us the match of any?   230
See all the Trojans and Arcadians here, with fate-
Advanced Etrurian troops who offer Turnus hate:
Were only half of us involved, it's even odds,
While Turnus would ascend in glory to the gods

Whose altars he has vowed his life on. He'll live on   235
In story, while our pride and country both are gone.
We'll serve proud masters—we who here sit idly by."

The young men stir to words like these, their spirits high—
And higher yet, as murmurs spread throughout their lines
(Even the Latians change, as do the Laurentines).   240
Those who had lately hoped for safety and a stay
Of battle, long for weapons now. The truce, they pray,
Will fall apart. They pity Turnus' unjust fate.

Juturna adds to what she means to aggravate
By showing in the sky the most foreboding sign   245
Italian minds can view: an omen that's malign.
Jove's golden eagle,⁴ flying through the raddled sky,
Is chasing shore-birds letting loose a clanging cry
In their ranks, when like a thunderbolt he lands
To snatch the leading swan with greedy, crooked hands.   250

Before the rapt Italians' eyes, the birds wheel round
In clamorous flight (*mirabile dictu*) and hound
Their raptor in a cloud, through air. Their wings then pall
The sky, till driven by their mass, he lets it fall—
The swan, un-clawed—and flies away high through the cloud.   255

When the Rutulians see this sign, they raise a loud
Hurrah. The omen makes an uproar of their shout,
Their hands spread wide. Augur Tolumnius cries out
(He is the first): "This is—yes, *this*—what I have prayed
For. I accept the god-sent sign. Now wield the blade   260
With me—with *me* to lead, you luckless people like
Weak birds some alien frightens, waging war—a shrike
Along your shores. He'll soon turn tail and sail away

Far down the sky. To save your king, form one array,
Defending him who has been rapt from you for prey."   265

He spoke, and charging at the foe, let go his spear.
The sure and hissing cornel shaft then split the air.
At once, as one, the phalanxes cry out; hearts roar
In awful tumult, hotter than they've been before.
The lance flew where, by chance, nine handsome brothers   270
Stood in its path. They were one faithful Tuscan mother's—
Boys she'd borne Gylippus back in Arcady.
It caught one—gleaming-armored, handsome as could be—
Mid-waist, the place a stitched and buckled belt abrides
The stomach and the buckle locks the joining sides.   275
The spear runs through him; lays him on the yellow sand.

But set aflame with grief, his brothers' gallant band
Draw swords, or some snatch iron spears or blindly rush
In. Laurentine troops charge *them*. Trojans and a crush
Of Agyllines and painted-armed Arcadians flood   280
In, countering the attack. One passion, that of blood,
Now rules them—fighting to the death with sword and mail.

They've stripped the altars bare, as falling spears assail
Them and, from storm-cloud skies, cold steel comes down like hail.
The kraters and the hearthstones snatched, the king has fled   285
With all his conquered gods. The treaty now is dead.
Others harness their chariots or leap up on
Their horses, waiting, each man with his weapon drawn.

Messapus, hot to break the pact, comes galloping
Up, frightening Aulestes, who's a Tuscan king   290
In kingly gear. That wretch, in his retreating, stumbles;
Tangled, he hits a waiting altar as he tumbles.

So mad Messapus charges with a giant lance,
And on his high horse, strikes. Aulestes has no chance.
He begs, but this is how Messapus vaunts: "He's done					295
For. Since the gods need noble victims, here is one!"

Italians crowd in, while the corpse is warm, to strip
It. With a charred torch from an altar in his grip,
Then Corynaeus smashed Ebyso's face. (The blow
Scorched one who'd thought to lay that Corynaeus low.)				300
His thick beard flares and smells; he's stunned. His blazing foe
Then grabs his hair with one hand, and with bent-back knee
Dug in, brings down Ebyso. Then with his still-free
Sword-hand, he stabs him.

							Podalirius, with blade
Bare, towering, chased the shepherd Alsus as he made					305
A dash through showering front-line spears. But Alsus now
Swings back and axes through his hunter's chin and brow,
Drenching the armor with the splatter-patterned gore.
Harsh iron sleep weighs down the eyes; he sees no more,
Does Podalirius, except for endless night.							310

But good Aeneas, head bare, stretching out his right
(And swordless) hand, called loudly to his furious men:
"Where are you running? Why this sudden tumult then,
This rage? Stand down! We have agreed already; terms
Are set: and I alone may rightly take up arms.							315
Let me! Don't be afraid. I'll prove with this right hand
The pact is good—already Turnus is un-manned."[5]

Amidst words such as these, amidst such cries, look now:
An arrow flew against him, hissing from some bow.
Shot whirling by what hand, there is no way to know,					320

Nor who—some chance? a god?—had earned such great renown
For the Rutulians. The credit goes unknown,
Since no one bragged he'd caused Aeneas' injury.

When Turnus sees Aeneas exit hastily,
His captains rattled, he kindles with hope that's new.   325
He calls for arms and horses, proudly leaps into
His chariot, and takes the reins. So many brave
Men in his chariot's path are hastened to the grave!
Scattering scores half-dead, or crushing infantry
Under his wheels, he palls with spears all those who flee.   330

As blood-stained Mavors, by the Hebrus' chilly streams,
Swashing his buckler madly and igniting flames
Of war, lets loose his frenzied chargers to out-race
The South and West winds down the plain, and farthest Thrace
Groans to pulsing hoofbeats while Black Terror's form—   335
And Treachery's and Wrath's—the god's attendants, storm,
So Turnus, fast as that, now whips his steeds that steam
With sweat. Right through the fight they trample foes, that team—
Wretched, slaughtered men. Where pounding horse hooves land,
They splutter blood and kick up gore all mixed with sand.   340

Then Sthenelus and Thamyrus and Pholus all
Were killed, two close, one far. Imbrasus' boys both fall,
Glaucus and Lades, at a distance—sons he'd reared
In Lycia and had given matching arms; they feared
No fight, up close or mounted on a wind-swift horse.   345

Elsewhere, Eumedes rides into the fight full-force.
Famous in war, he was old Dolon's son; named for
His father's father, he recalled, in skill at war,
That Dolon who for spying on the Greek camp dared
To name Achilles' chariot as his reward.   350

But Tydeus' son gave something else to pay his claim
Who dares and dreams no more about Achilles' team.

When Turnus saw Eumedes far across the plain,
He sent a lance to chase him down the space between
Them, then reined in his team and pounced on that half-dead   355
Man. Foot upon Eumedes' neck, he tore the blade
Out of Eumedes' hand and buried it inside
The bloody throat, then vaunted over him in pride:
"Trojan, see Hesperia's fields you thought you'd win
Through war? Now stretch out; measure what you're lying in—   360
Their prize who test my sword. See how their walls begin!"
Avenging then his good dead friend, he speared Asbytes,
And killed too, one thrown by his charger: Thymoetes.
Then Chloreus died, and Sybaris, and also Dares.
Thersilochus fell, too.

             The way the North Wind roars   365
His gales on the Aegean (breakers pound the shores),
And Boreas' winds drive cloud wracks down their scudding path,
So Turnus scythes whole columns where he cuts his swathe
(Ranks run). Against his impetus, the wind is pressed.
His headlong chariot creates a streaming crest.   370

Phegeus, knowing Turnus' charge must be resisted,
Leapt in the chariot's path, and with his right hand twisted
Aside the racing horses' jaws, which foamed their bits.
Still clinging to the yoke, he's dragged. The spearhead hits
Him in his open flank and bites the two-ply mesh   375
Of mail. There where it's struck, it grazes Phegeus' flesh.

Shield up, though, Phegeus lunged at Turnus with his blade
As his defense. But then the spinning axle laid
Him low, knocked headlong by the chariot wheel and hurled

To earth. Then Turnus, hot to kill his victim, whirled   380
His sword, slicing between the helmet's lower rim
And Phegeus' breastplate. Earth accepted head and him.

While Turnus' victories turn the plains blood-red and grim,
Achates, Mnestheus, and Ascanius are leading
Aeneas, limping, into camp. He's struggling, bleeding: 385
At every other step, he leans hard on his spear.
Raging, he strains to pull the broken arrow clear.
He calls for what will help—relief that is most near:
To sword-cut deep to find the arrowhead and send
Aeneas back to fight.

                    Now Phoebus' dearest friend   390
Came close—Iasus' son, Iapyx.[6] He'd received
Apollo's own gifts once. (Seer Phoebus had believed
Himself in love, and gladly given one his skills:
His augury, his lyre, and the shaft that kills.)
But hoping to put off his dying father's doom,   395
He chose to study herbs, and how he might assume
A healer's ways and humbly practice quiet arts.

Aeneas, in a crowd of men with grieving hearts
(Iulus, too), is chafing bitterly, his spear
His massive prop. No sorrow touches him, no tear.   400

The old physician, robe rolled back Paeonian style,
Works fast with Phoebus' potent herbs of healing, while . . .
There's no effect. To no effect, he tugs and tugs
The shaft, gripping its buried iron barb with tongs.
Luck fails him, though, and all Apollo's power shows   405
Itself no use, while more and more, cold panic grows.
All down the plains, disaster looms: it seems the sky
Is propped by dust, as horsemen charge and arrows fly,

Plunging down on the camp. Up goes the awful cry
From fighting men: struck down by raving Mars, they die.   410

Venus sees his cruel pain, and shaken, she
Alights on Cretan Ida, plucking dittany.[7]
A plant with downy leaves, it bears a purple flower.
Even wild goats are known to make use of its power
When winging arrows strike their flanks.

                                        Then Venus carried   415
This down, her face all masked in veiling mist. With varied
Magic medicines, she steeps the dittany whole
In water. Then she pours it in a shining bowl
And sprinkles panacea and ambrosia juice.

Agèd Iapyx, unaware, now put to use   420
This liquid in the wound, and suddenly all pain
Was gone, all bleeding stopped. Without the slightest strain,
The shaft came out; his strength came back as good as new.
"Quick! Bring Aeneas' weapons here! What's wrong with you?"
Iapyx cries. He is the first to stir the men   425
To valor, so they'll rush to join the fight again.
"It was no man, Aeneas, you were made well by—
No human healing hand or art. It was not I.
Some greater god has saved you for brave deeds untold."

Aeneas, mad for battle, greaved both shins in gold,   430
And scorning all delay, hefted his spear to fight.
Shield strapped on at his side, and breastplate tied back tight,
Despite he's cased in steel, he hugs Ascanius.
And through his vizor, kisses him, beginning thus:
"Learn bravery from me, my son, and work that's true;   435
Learn luck from others. My sword is defending you
In war now; it will lead you to life's best rewards.

Remember, when you reach what you've been growing towards,
Aeneas and your uncle Hector. Don't forget,
They stirred your soul by the example that they set."   440

His speech done, he rushed out the gate in all his might,
Shaking a giant spear. With him, rushing to fight,
Went Antheus and Mnestheus; none would remain.
They stream from camp in throngs, which turn the plain
To blinding dust. The trampled earth shakes in their train.   445

From his revetment, Turnus saw them come. So too
Did the Ausonians see them, and chill ran deep through
Their bones. Juturna was the first Latian to hear
And recognize the sound. She fled in abject fear.

Aeneas draws his storm-dark troops across the plain.   450
The way the weather breaks and clouds armed full of rain
Charge inland, and the wretched farmers' hearts can see
It come, and shudder at the ruin of every tree,
And havoc in the crops, and all's catastrophe
As death-winds race ahead to bring their blasts to shore: 455
That's how the Rhoetean leader drives his ranks before
Him toward the foe. His men mass at his side for war.

Osiris falls before the sword of Thymbreus,
Epulo to Achates, Arcetius falls to Mnestheus,
Ufens to Gyas. Then the man of augury,   460
Tolumnius, died, who'd launched against the enemy
The first spear.

            Then a cry goes up. Rutulians flee
In dust clouds all across the fields. Aeneas will
Not kill them as they run, nor does he deign to kill

The infantry or cavalry or slingers. One   465
Man is his goal; he's tracking Turnus, on the run
Through choking dark. He challenges none but Prince Turnus,
Which terrifies his maiden sister, so Juturna
Knocks down Turnus' charioteer Metiscus. Far
Behind she leaves him, fallen from her brother's car,   470
And with the flowing reins in hand, she takes the place
Of all that is Metiscus: arms, form, voice, and face.

Think of a soot-dark swallow darting through some lord's
Great banquet house. It wings high up in halls, then hoards,
For squawking young, the dinner's crumbs and fallen orts.   475
It twitters now by marsh lands, now in vacant courts.
And so Juturna, horse-drawn through the hostile host.
Flying in her chariot, she crissed and crossed
The plain, now here, now there, to show her brother at
His triumphs—but not single fight. No, *far* from that.[8]   480

To get to Turnus, though, Aeneas tracks her courses,
Doubling back, and shouts his challenge through the forces
Scattered round. Each time he sees his enemy
And tries to catch those horses in their circuitry,
Juturna turns, and wheels the chariot about.   485

God! What to do? Madly he tries to think things out,
Now this way and now that, wave-tossed by shifting cares.
Messapus, then, who had by chance two steel-tipped spears
His left hand hefted, stalked him like some hunted game.
He leveled one, then slung it with near-perfect aim.   490
Aeneas stopped, crouched back behind his shield, and dropped
Down on one knee. But still the flying javelin topped
His helmet crest, and knocked its very plume-tips free.

His anger flames then, goaded by the treachery.
Seeing the far-off war-car of his enemy,   495
Swearing by broken treaty altars, and by Jove
As witness, finally, into the fight he dove.
Now backed by Mars, he's wreaking carnage on the plain—
Wild slaughter—as he gives his murderous wrath full rein.

What god could tell us of such awful, blood-drenched things,   500
Or sing so many deaths that outraged Fortune slings—
Dead captains Turnus kills, the Trojan hero kills,
By turns, along the plains? And Jupiter—he wills
That races bound to live in endless peace some day
Should clash like this?[9]

                            Aeneas, finding in his way   505
Rutulian Sucro (first to stall the charge), now drives
His sword deep through the side (that's where the ribbed heart lives
And death comes quickest).

                            Turnus throws down from his horse
Amycus, then Diores, brothers in his course.
He stalks on foot to kill one with his yards-long lance,   510
The other with his sword, stopping a doomed advance.
And from his car, he hangs each severed, blood-drenched head.

Cethegus, Tanais, and Talos all are dead
In one attack Aeneas launches. Then he's done
For Thebes' Onites, one who was Peridia's son.   515

Next, Turnus kills two Lycian boys dear to Apollo,
And then Arcadian Menoetes, loath to follow
War from birth—in vain. His humble home and living
Had been near the fish-filled Lerna's streams. The giving

Favors of some lord, he never knew—just hired   520
Land his father farmed.

                             Like dry woods sparks have fired
In crackling laurel thickets, or like streams that roar,
And with destruction in their wakes, race toward the shore,
Both Turnus and Aeneas, far from being slow
To crash on through the fight, wreak havoc where they go.   525
It's *now* their anger surges up from deep inside;
It's *now* that they're invincible, hearts bursting wide;
It's *now* they scourge the battlefield with all their strength.

Murranus boasts of his ancestors, of the length
Of all his ancient line, on back through Latian kings.   530
Aeneas, though, now knocks him down, the rock he flings
A thing that tumbles him beneath the yoke and reins.
The wheels roll over him; the horse hooves shred his veins.
Now uncontrolled, they smash his corpse repeatedly.

Turnus meets roaring Hyllus's ferocity   535
By leveling his lance at that gold-ribboned brow
And piercing Hyllus' helm—and brain—with one sure throw.

Bravest Greek, Cretheus: your hand could not delay
Turnus. Cupencus, priest: no god hid you away
Against Aeneas' coming, for you set your breast   540
Just where his sword swung, but your bronze shield failed that test.
And Aeolus: Laurentian plains saw you fall, too,
All sprawled back, broad upon the ground. What could you do
But die, whom Argive phalanxes could not lay low—
Even Achilles, source of Priam's overthrow?   545
Here lay the boundaries of your death: your house beneath
Lyrnessian Ida . . . and the grave Laurentian heath.

Then all ranks turn to battle—all the Latians, all
The Dardans. Mnestheus and Serestus heed the call,
As do the horse-taming Messapus, the brave man   550
Asilas, and the Tuscans, and Arcadian
Evander's troops. All strain to do all that they can.
In this great war, they fight on with no lull or rest.

Now in his mind, inspired by the loveliest
Of mothers, came this thought: Aeneas should attack   555
The city walls—bring sudden ruin. On the track
Of Turnus, hunting him through Latians he's struck down,
He sweeps his gaze this way and that, and sees the town
Still free from savage war—unharmed, in peaceful quiet.

Quickly he forms a grander plan, and means to try it.   560
He calls his captains, Mnestheus, brave Serestus, and
Sergestus. On a mound, with all the Teucrian band
Surrounding him (their shields and spears still ready), he
Stands in their midst and cries out, "Now listen to me!
Move fast as I command. We've Jupiter to back   565
Us! No delays because of this abrupt attack.
This day, I mean to raze that cause of war, the seat
Of King Latinus' realm, and burn it in defeat,
If conquered, they won't yield to our hegemony.
Can I sit idle till their Turnus fights with me,   570
Deigning to duel again, though beaten once before?
Countrymen: he alone began this evil war.
Bring torches—quick!—and we'll reclaim the pact with fire."

He'd spoken. All then form a wedge. Their hearts aspire
To match his, and they move against the town as one.   575
In moments, flames and ladders can be seen. Some run
To smash the gates in as the first defenders die,

While others hurl black lances that darken the sky.
Aeneas, in the lead, implores the gods. He stands
At the walls accusing Latinus. With raised hands,   580
And crying out, he says that he's been *forced* to fight
Again, the treacherous Latians *twice* not in the right.

Strife billows up among the fearful polity:
Some beg to yield the city—that the gates swing free
For the Dardans. The king's dragged to the ramparts. Some,   585
In arms, now rush the parapets to guard their home.

It's like a shepherd tracking bees: he finds the rock
They're hiding in and fills it with an acrid smoke.
The fearful hive swarm through their waxen camp, and honing
Their anger, buzz and teem and make a horrid droning.   590
The black stench rolls all through that apiary lair;
The rocks hum blindly as the fumes invade the air.[10]

But more misfortune struck the weary Latian race
And shook the grieving city to its very base.
When Queen Amata, from her palace, sees the foe   595
Atop the walls, the city's roofs on fire, but no
Rutulian lines, no troops of Turnus, fighting back,
The frantic queen thinks he has died in some attack,
And anguished and distraught at once, she wails that she
Alone's the guilty cause of this calamity.   600
She screams out frenzied words of grief, prepared to die,
And rips her purple robes apart to loop a high
Beam with a lethal noose.[11]

          So when the dread word reaches
The wretched Latian women, first Lavinia scratches
Her pink cheeks, tears her golden hair, and loses all   605

Control (her retinue does, too). Through every hall
The lamentations ring. From here, the awful woes
Spread through the town, as spirits sink. Latinus goes
About in robes all looped and windowed; ragged; torn.
Stunned by his wife's fate (and his town ruined and forlorn),   610
He fouls his white locks in a cloud of filthy dust,
And chides himself repeatedly for how unjust
Has been the treatment of the Dardan man who might
Have been his son.

               But meanwhile, far off in the fight,
Turnus is chasing stragglers—ever slower, less   615
And less glad for his horses' battlefield success.
A breeze then brought him there a mingled, clamorous cry
Filled full of unknown dread—a town about to die
In abject chaos; sounds that reached his pricked-up ears.
"God, what great grief now shakes the walls? What clamor rears   620
Up from the far-off city?"—these his words as he
In frenzy yanks the reins and pulls up short.

                       When she
(Juturna), still Metiscus' twin, and guiding yet
The car and team, hears this, she says to Turnus, "Let
Us hunt down Ilium's sons, where victory shows the way.   625
Others can fight to save our home. Meantime, while they
Fight back, Aeneas kills Italians. Seize the day,
And we will cruelly slay the Trojans. Never yield!
Your kills and battle honors garnered on this field
Will match his own before you quench your deadly thirst."   630

Then Turnus: "Sister, I knew who you were the first
Moment you slyly overthrew the truce and tried
To fight this war. And still there's no way you can hide
Your godhood. Tell me who it was who wished that you

Descend Olympus for this work. Was it to view 635
Your hapless brother's awful death? What can I do?
What fate can guarantee security for me?
I saw Murranus fall before my eyes as he
Called out my name. There's no one left who's dearer than
He was. A mighty wound laid low a mighty man. 640
And luckless Ufens fell, lest he should see our shame;
The Trojans have his corpse and armor all the same.
Shall I live through the razing of our homes—the one
Disgrace that's left—and leave the taunts of Drances un-
Avenged? Shall I turn tail? Shall Latium see me run? 645
Is death so bad a thing? O Shades below, be kind!
For all the gods above have put me from their mind.
I will go down to you a stainless soul and free
Of guilt. I will be worthy my great ancestry."

He'd barely done when Saces rushed past on a sweat- 650
Flecked mount, straight through the enemy (an arrow'd hit
Him in the face). He calls by name on Turnus as
He passes: "Pity us! You're all our homeland has!
Aeneas thunders as he threatens to throw down
Italy's highest citadel and raze the town. 655
Right now, brands rain down on our roofs. The Latians look
To you, all eyes. Latinus mutters: friends forsook
His realm. Whom should he call his sons? Whom should he lean
On? Even she who was most loyal to you, Queen
Amata, killed herself to flee the light of day. 660
Atinas and Messapus only still hold sway
And rally at the gates. Beside them, dense troops stand—
A crop of bristling steel, drawn swords in every hand—
While in your car, you race across deserted land."

Stunned and bewildered by these pictures of disaster, 665
Turnus stood mutely staring. Shame rose ever-faster

In that single heart—insanity gone sad,
And consciousness of what worth is, and love stung mad.

But when those shadows fled, and light dawned in his mind,
He turned his blazing eyes to view the walls behind,   670
And from his chariot saw the wide-walled town. See how
A twining spire of flame engulfed a tower now,
And eddied skyward stage by stage—a tower he
Had fashioned with the jointed beams of carpentry
And set on wheels and given walkways in the sky.   675

"*Now*, sister! Now Fate wins. No putting off, for I
Will go where cruel Fortune and the gods demand.
I mean to meet Aeneas fighting hand-to-hand;
To bear death's bitterness. You'll see my shame no more.
I only beg, before I'm mad, let madness war."   680

Then quickly he jumped from his car to earth, and tore
Through hostile spears. He leaves his grieving sister, breaking
Through the foe with all the lightning speed he's making.

It is as if a storm-torn mountain crag has crashed
Headlong down-slope, when some torrential tempest's washed   685
It free, or it's come loose in tedious time. It tumbles
In a mighty somersaulting rush and rumbles
Down, with stones and trees and men all swept before
It.

   That's how Turnus rushes to the town, through gore
And broken ranks, where earth is drenched in all that war   690
Is best at—blood and spears and shrieking. Signaling
By hand, he shouts, "Rutulians, cease firing!
You Latians, too. Stop now! No spears! What Fate may bring
Me here is only mine. Better my sword alone

Decides this. For your broken truce, *I* will atone."   695
Then all drew back and left him there on open ground.

But patriarch Aeneas hears and turns around
At Turnus' name. He leaves the walls and leaves the high
Fortress. Without delay, he puts his war-work by,
And loudly clangs his arms, exulting in his joy.   700
He's vast as Athos, vast as Eryx, or as vast
As Father Apennine himself when he roars fast,
Through shimmering oaks, and proudly lifts his snowy head
Skyward.

    In earnest now, all turned their eyes and shed
Their arms—Italians, Trojans, and Rutulians who   705
Now held the ramparts or with rams were crashing through
The gates. Latinus, too, is stunned that men like these,
Born worlds apart, should try their animosities
By single-handed combat.

    When the plain was clear
And open, each man came on, letting go his spear   710
While yet still far away. They sprinted into battle
Raising shields—in armor clanging with a rattle
Of bronze. Earth groans. And then repeated sword-strokes clash
And clash again—a blend where skill and fortune mesh.

You've seen two bulls in lethal battle, charging head   715
To head on Sila or Taburnus' heights? In dread,
Their drivers fall back while the whole herd stands there mute
With fear, and heifers low in wonder: Which huge brute
Will rule the groves? Which mighty bull will lead the cattle?
Each wounds the other as they charge in gruesome battle,   720
Goring with their butting horns and sluicing blood
Down neck and shoulders. Bellows thunder through the wood.[12]

That's how the Daunian hero and Aeneas clash
Their shields. They fill the heavens with the deafening crash.
Then Jupiter himself, with balanced scales, set weights   725
For both men, who were destined to such different fates—
Which scale sank to death, and which one's fight was doomed.[13]

Now Turnus, sure that he was safe, sprang up, assumed
Full-body height, and raised his sword . . . and struck. Just then,
The fearful Latians and the anxious Trojan men   730
Cried out, both armies fever-pitched. But Turnus' blade
Snapped halfway through the violent blow. Failed and betrayed,
The fiery warrior ran faster than the East Wind
When he saw the weird hilt in his naked hand.

(They say when he first climbed up in his car in haste   735
To fight, his father's sword was left behind, misplaced
Or missed. Metiscus' sword had been snatched up instead,
Which served him well . . . as long as straggling Teucrians fled.)
But then the man-made sword was shattered at first stroke
On Vulcan's god-made shield. Like brittle ice, it broke.   740
Now, glittering fragments of it litter yellow sand.

The frantic Turnus ran across that blood-soaked land,
Now here, now there, while weaving ever-maddening
Circles, Trojans on all sides, in a choking ring.
A vast fen here, steep ramparts there: both hem him round.   745

Aeneas does no less, despite the arrow wound
That slows his knees, which now are weakened and refuse
Him speed. His foe is panting; hotly he pursues,
Stride-for-stride—a hound who howls and hunts a deer
Trapped by a riverside, or choked by panic-fear   750
Of crimson feathers, of the snare that terrifies,

And of the high stream-bank, as back and forth he flies
A thousand ways.

        The Umbrian, though, sticks close, with gaping
Jaws. Now! He has him *now*, but . . . still the stag's escaping.
Snapping jaws—so close!—bite down on empty air.   755
An uproar rises, truly. Pools and banksides share
The tumult that assaults the heavens' frame.

Even fleeing, Turnus chides those called by name—
Rutulians—and clamors for the sword he knows.
Aeneas warns those who'd come near: quick blows,   760
Quick death, and ruin for the town. His quaking foes
Will see their city razed!

        Wounded, he presses on.
They circle round five times, re-tracing where they've gone,
This way and that. For here is no athletic prize,
No measly thing, but whether Turnus lives or dies.   765

By chance, a bitter-leaved wild olive had stood here,[14]
Faunus's own—a tree old sailors would revere.
When saved from drowning, they would gift that shrine
By hanging garments votive to the Laurentine
Divinity. The Teucrians though, had hauled away   770
The trunk (there would be no exceptions) so that they
Could war on open ground.

        Here stood Aeneas' spear,
Fixed in the sinewed root (sheer force had borne it there).
The Dardan bent to tug the weapon out and catch
The fleeing man for whom—on foot— he was no match.   775

Then Turnus cried out, in his truly frantic fear,
"Pity me, Faunus, I beg you, and Earth most dear.
If I have honored you and kept that liturgy
Aeneas' sons have fouled with war, then don't set free
That lance's steel."

        It worked, that heartfelt, pious plea: 780
Aeneas, though he wrenched and wrestled hard and long,
Couldn't pry back that stump's hard bite; it was too strong
And stubborn for him.

        While he yanks and fiercely strains,
The Daunian goddess comes up (once again she feigns
Being Metiscus) and gives Turnus back his sword.   785
But Venus, seeing that that bold nymph had restored
Her brother's blade, came down enraged, and tore the spear
Out of the olive trunk. Now armed and free of fear,
Both stand: one trusts his sword, the other man looms there
With lance. Both, breathless, wait on Mars as they prepare . . . 790

And golden-clouded Juno waits: How will they fare?[15]
She looks down as Olympus' mighty king speaks: "Wife,
What will the end be now? What's left after such strife?
You know (and you admit) Aeneas will be sent
To highest heaven, raised up in the firmament.   795
Here in these chill clouds, what's your hope? What's your intent?
Could it be *fas*[16] when mortals wound a deity,
And gods return that sword (Juturna! What could *she*
Achieve without you?) so that vanquished Turnus might
Regain his strength? Bend to my will: give up this fight, 800
Lest silent grief consume you now, lest sadness grip
You often and I hear it from your honeyed lip.
All this is *done*. You've harried Trojans wide and far.
You've scarred a royal house and kindled evil war,

Injecting grief in sacred wedlock. Now, no more.   805
I will not let it be."

                    So Jupiter averred;
So humbly the Saturnian goddess spoke this word:
"Great Jove, because I knew the way you'd have it be,
I left the Earth and Turnus, though reluctantly.
Elsewise, you wouldn't see me on this cloud-wrapped chair,   810
Alone, enduring good and bad. I'd be down *there*,
In battle, fire-wreathed, to lure the Trojans in
To death. I helped Juturna help her brother win,
It's true, and sanctioned even more for his life's sake.
But archer was a role I did not bid her take.   815
I swear this by the Styx's fatal fountainhead—
The only name the gods above swear by with dread.
Yes, now I yield to you; I leave this hateful killing.
But for the greatness of your line, if you are willing,
I beg—and for your kin (no law of Fate forbids):   820
When soon they come to peace, with happy grooms and brides
(Amen!); when soon they join by laws and pacts; don't make
The native Latians change their ancient name to take
The name of Teucrian or Trojan. It's my prayer
They keep their language and the kind of clothes they wear.[17]   825
Let Latium live. Let Alban kings still reign. And may
The valiant Roman race of Italy hold sway.
Troy is fallen. Troy and her name should stay that way."

She heard the heavens' smiling All-Creator say,
"Truly, you *are* Jove's sister, Saturn's other child.   830
Such waves of wrath, deep in your heart, have surged and roiled!
Come. Calm this needless anger you have stirred within.
I grant your wish quite willingly as I give in.
Ausonia's sons shall speak their fathers' speech and think
As always, keeping their name. Teucrians shall sink   835

Into the mass, their laws and rites a gift from me.
I'll have all speak the Latian tongue. A progeny
Mixed with Ausonian blood will rise, which you will see
Surpass both gods and mortals in its piety.
No race will match them as they worship you."

                             As she   840
Agreed, the glad Queen Juno calmed her angry mind.
Departing from the sky, she left her cloud behind.

This done, the Father deeply ponders something other:
He's set to take Juturna from her warring brother.
Men say twin-sister plagues—the Ones That Mortals Dread,[18]   845
Whom Night untimely bore at once and wreathed each head
Tartarean Megaera-like in snakes, with wings
Wind-swift—wait by Jove's throne, and on that cruel king's
Threshold. That's where they whet what being sickly brings—
Namely, the fears that terrify. They do this when   850
The monarch of the gods decides to wreak on men
Disease and awful death, or curse some guilty town
With war.

          From high above, he sent one quickly down,
To meet Juturna for a sign, by his command.
She streaks to earth, a whirlwind flying to the land.   855
An arrow fired through a cloud, shot from the bow;
A lethal and envenomed shaft a Parthian—no,
A Parthian or Cydonian—looses, deadly past
All cure (unseen, it hisses through the shade that fast):
That's how Night's racing daughter sped to earth.

                       And when   860
She spots the Ilian battle lines and Turnus' men,
Suddenly she shrinks to look like that small bird

That perched on lonely roofs and tombs, is often heard
Among the shadows late at night in eerie singing.[19]
Then right at Turnus, back and forth the fiend goes winging,   865
Screeching in his face. Her wings tattoo his shield.
Melted with fear and dread, his buckling knee-joints yield.
His hair's on end; his voice sticks in his throat; he's numb.

Distraught Juturna heard the Dread One's wing-beats come
While still far off. She tears her hair. Nails claw her face,   870
Fists beat her breasts, in cruel, disfiguring disgrace:
"Turnus, how can your sister ever help you now?
What misery's left for suffering me? Can I—oh, *how*?—
Extend your life by art, or fight a prodigy
Like this? Now—now—I quit the field. Don't frighten me,   875
Ill-omened birds; I'm terrified as I can be.
I know your lethal wing-beats and proud Jove's decree.
And *these* are my reward for my virginity?
Not left to die, condemned to live eternally?
At least then I might end such pain, and at his side,   880
Pass through the shades with my poor brother. Deified?
I, deified? Would anything of mine be sweet
Without you, brother? What earth-fissure could secrete
Me so far down, a goddess in the Manes' place?"
She stopped, and with a grey cloak, hid her grieving face.   885
The goddess groaned and plunged deep in the river race.

Aeneas comes on, brandishing his tree-sized spear,
And raging deep within his heart, begins to jeer:
"What? More delay now? Turnus, why still more retreat?
Not in a race, but up close, in someone's defeat—   890
That's our battle. *Be* every shape; *use* all your skill
And might and courage. *Try* to fly, if that's your will,
Up to the stars. Or seek earth's hollow prison."

Shaking
His head then, Turnus cried, "Hot words don't set me quaking,
Braggart, but Jove and the gods do." No more to say,   895
He looked around and saw a huge rock where it lay
By chance there in the field—a giant, ancient stone
For boundary, so litigious seed might not be sown.
Twelve hand-picked men like those our world knows now just might
Have heaved it to their shoulders. Turnus rose full-height   900
Though, quickly lifting it, and just as hard as he
Could throw it, hurled that boulder at his enemy.

But Turnus, moving, running, throwing, does not know
Himself—or raising that great stone he tried to throw.
His knees give in; cold turns his blood to ice. That stone   905
Though, fails to ride the arc through which it has been thrown.
Dropping from empty air, it lands no blow, but lies
There spent.

                Sometimes, at night, in dreams, when leaden eyes
Succumb to torpid sleep, we try in vain to make
Our urgent way, but weakly fall and cannot take   910
Another step. Tongues fail us, and the strength we've known
Deserts our bodies. Words and voices all are gone.

That's how the dire goddess blocks whatever way
Brave Turnus tries to go, as shifting visions play
Across his mind. He looks at the Rutulians and   915
His city, faltering in fear, for death's at hand,
And he cannot be saved. There's no strength left to fight,
No chariot or sister-charioteer in sight.

Pausing, Aeneas shakes his fateful weapon. Seeing
His chance from far off, he lets go with all his being.   920
Stones shot from catapults will never roar so loud.
Never do such huge crashes burst a thunder-cloud

With lightning. Like some jet-black cyclone flies the spear,
Bearing dire death. It drills the outer sphere
Of seven folds of shield, and through the breastplate rim,   925
Hissing, it penetrates the thigh . . . and buckles him.
Great Turnus, on his knee, sank down beneath the blow.
Rutulians groaned as one, and hills echoed their woe,
While everywhere, the woods sent back the sound.

                                       His eyes
Downcast in supplication, hands held out, he cries: 930
"I've earned this. *Show* no mercy; *seize* your chance. But if
There's hope your heart can be touched by a father's grief
(For in Anchises, once, you had a father, too),
Then pity Daunus's old age, I beg of you,
And give me—or my lifeless body, should that be   935
Your will—back to my people and my family.
You've won; Ausonia's seen my vanquished, outstretched hands.
Wed Lavinia; hate no more!"

                        Aeneas stands
Armored, fierce, with glinting eyes. He holds back, swayed
By Turnus more and more, moved by the speech he's made . . .   940
Till he detects young Pallas' luckless sword-belt, stone-
Bossed, shoulder-high on Turnus, and to all, well-known.
So Turnus wears the baldrick of his now-dead foe—
The man he wounded, drove to earth, and there laid low.[20]

But when his eyes fix on that spoil, that memory   945
Of cruel grief, Aeneas burns ferociously:
"Shall you escape me in the spoils of someone who
Was mine? It's Pallas—*Pallas*—sacrificing you
With this. With your own guilty blood, now you will pay!"
And as he speaks, he drives his sword in all the way,   950
Till Turnus' chill limbs slacken[21] at the lethal blow.
Groaning, his bitter soul fled to the Shades below.[22]

Notes

Book I

1: **I.2.** In order that Rome might be founded, Aeneas must arrive in Italy. This is his destiny and the city's, and the plot of the epic revolves around the difficulties of the hero in achieving this end. Not all things are predetermined in the *Aeneid*, notably Dido's death at IV.696. See too Jupiter's declaration of neutrality at X.112–13, "Let Fates do what they may." The ultimate connection of Fate to the will of Jupiter is a tricky matter. To some degree, Virgil has Homer in mind: in the *Iliad*, Zeus wonders whether he ought to alter Fate but Hera indicates the other gods would disapprove were he to do so.

2: **I.5.** "Unrelenting Juno" will in fact, at long last, be forced to yield by Jupiter (XII.818), but not before she causes Aeneas, the Trojan refugees, and others a great deal of grief. The contest between Jovian order and Junonian chaos is one of the epic's primary dynamics.

3: **I.8.** For the archaic epic poets Homer and Hesiod, the invocation of the Muse was a genuine call for inspiration. Virgil's calling upon the Muse, however, is strictly a literary convention, for he has been clear since the first line that it is "my poem," an explicit translation here of *cano*, "I sing." Virgil will call upon the Muses again at several other points in the *Aeneid*.

4: **I.10.** The word translated here as "righteousness" is *pietas*, from which the customary epithet of Aeneas as pious is derived. His dedication to the will of the gods is Aeneas's defining characteristic, and perhaps makes him resemble an Old Testament figure more than a hero from a Homeric epic.

5: **I.52–75.** The episode of Aeolus, the king of the winds (depicted by Homer in *Odyssey* Book Ten), is modeled by Virgil after another Homeric scene from *Iliad* Book Fourteen, in which Hera (Rom. Juno) bribes the god Hypnos (Rom. Somnus; Sleep) with the promise of a beautiful nymph.

6: **I.92–96.** "They're three and four times blessed who rendered up / Their lives as Trojan fathers watched them from some wall." Aeneas's opening words in the *Aeneid* are ones of utter despair. His knees buckle the first time we see him, just as Turnus's knees will in the *Aeneid*'s final lines (XII.951). Diomedes, "Tydeus' son," will himself in Book XI remember the encounter with Aeneas (XI.252–93).

7: **I.125.** Neptune, patterned after the Greek god Poseidon, has sensed the disturbance in the waves from below and rises to see what is happening. He instantly recognizes Juno's hand in the events, but trains his anger on the winds and their king.

8: **I.148–56.** In Homer, epic similes often compare human activity to natural phenomena. The first epic simile of the *Aeneid* notably inverts this tradition by associating the calming of the storm to an authoritative orator. The noble figure calming the mob to whom Neptune is compared is derived from an anecdote told of Cato the Younger.

9: **I.198.** "We few—till now, unhappy few." The translation here deliberately aligns Aeneas's encouraging words to his crew with the famous Saint Crispin's Day speech from Shakespeare's *Henry V* (Act 4, Scene 3).

10: **I.255.** The knowledge of the glorious fate in store for Aeneas seems to bring a smile to the lips of the gods. Aware of the hero's future, Jupiter smiles here upon Venus as a show of reassurance. Herself knowing, Venus will smile at Juno's later stratagems (IV.127), even as Jupiter will smile at his wife when she ultimately submits to his will (XII.829).

11: **I.282.** The toga was the distinctive dress of the Romans, as Jupiter notes here. See note at XII.825.

12: **I.314–417.** Venus, in disguise as a local hunting woman, relates to Aeneas the story of Dido, sometimes called Elissa. Though derived from older Greek sources and perhaps even from Phoenician material, Dido becomes in Virgil's hands one of the greatest female figures of world literature. Later depictions of Dido are found in Ovid, Shakespeare, and opera as well as on contemporary Tunisian banknotes and even modern video games (e.g., *Civilization V* and *VI*). She will in death be reunited with her Phoenician husband Sychaeus (VI.473–74), but the affair with Aeneas in Book IV is perhaps one of the greatest tragic romances in epic poetry.

13: **I.364–65.** *Dux femina facti*, the Latin phrase here translated as "a brilliant action which is / A woman's," has long been employed to praise powerful women. On medals issued to commemorate the Spanish Armada's defeat in 1588, for instance, the phrase appears as a tribute to Queen Elizabeth I.

14: **I.393–400.** Venus indicates that twelve Trojan ships have survived the storm by the appearance of twelve swans escaping from an eagle's attack. Swans were long held sacred to Venus, and she (or her Greek counterpart, Aphrodite) is often depicted in their company in ancient art. The swans thus stand for the followers of her son, Aeneas.

15: **I.430–36.** In this famous simile, the workers busily building the city of Carthage are compared to bees. Virgil's knowledge of bees was extensive, and the entirety of Book Four of his *Georgics* was dedicated to a description of their origin and care. The souls of those yet to be born will be likened to bees in the Underworld (VI.708) and a swarm of bees will augur Aeneas's arrival to Italy (VII.64).

16: **I.455.** Aeneas and his comrade Achates, hidden within a cloud provided by Venus, enter Juno's temple and here ironically first feel a sense of comfort. Within the temple are depictions of scenes from the Trojan War—the scene patterned after *Odyssey* Book Eight, in which Odysseus hears a bard sing a tale about himself and must wipe his eyes.

17: **I.462. *lacrimae rerum.*** Quite literally, "the tears of things," but the deep sadness inherent in the words is almost beyond articulation, as is shown by the translation's refusal to put the words into English. As he recognizes all these moments of his life in this foreign setting, Aeneas is overwhelmed with emotion.

18: **I.630–31.** "Not immune to woe, I learn to ease the toil / Of others." This line, in the original Latin—*Non ignara mali, miseris succurrere disco*—has served as the motto of various first responder and medical service units.

19: **I.657.** Venus is here called Cytherea (as she was earlier, I.257, and will be called elsewhere in the epic), in reference to her cult site on the Aegean island of Cythera. According to Hesiod's *Theogony*, the goddess was born off the coast of this island in the sea foam formed from the severed genitals of the god Uranus that his son Cronus had tossed into the sea.

20: **I.664.** Venus addresses Cupid as "My son," and impresses him craftily into service to aid the situation of her other son, Aeneas, by causing Dido to fall madly in love with him.

21: **I.741–46.** Why Virgil here depicts Iopas, the bard, singing a song of cosmic creation is a matter of some literary debate among Virgil scholars. Dido will be more interested in hearing about the heroics of the Trojan War.

BOOK II

1: **II.2–13.** Deep silence pervades the telling of the Trojan story, from the hush that falls over the room as all eyes turn to the hero, to Aeneas's own characterization of the tale as a "grief beyond /All telling" (II.3–4). When he concludes his narrative, it is Aeneas who will end "in a stillness" (III.718).

2: **II.7–8.** The Myrmidons and Dolopians fought in the Trojan War first under Achilles and then his son, Pyrrhus. The Ulyssians are soldiers of Ulysses, the Latin name for Odysseus.

3: **II.21.** Tenedos is an island, now called Bozcaada, just off the coast of Asia Minor that indeed "lies just in sight" of Troy.

4: **II.49.** "Whatever gift Danaans bring, I doubly fear." *To fear Greeks bearing gifts* has been a proverb ever since Virgil wrote these lines, quite at odds with *Do not look a gift horse in the mouth.*

5: **II.79.** Sinon, a name derived from the Greek verb *sinomai*, "to make mischief, do harm," had been featured in earlier post-Homeric epics and in a lost play of Sophocles. He represents the truly Odyssean (Ulyssean) element of the Trojan War, the reliance on trickery and disinformation.

6: **II.167.** The Palladium was a wooden cult image of Minerva, upon which the safety of Troy and later Rome was believed to depend, which Sinon maintains was stolen by Odysseus (Ulysses) and Diomedes (here called Tydides, meaning "son of Tydeus," on which see note at I.92–96). According to later myth, the Palladium will end up in Rome under the special protection of the Vestal Virgins.

7: **II.214–25.** The death of the Trojan priest Laocoön and his sons by the serpents was famously depicted in an ancient statue, now on display in the Vatican Museum, that had been described by Pliny the Elder and was rediscovered during the Renaissance.

8: **II.271.** Aeneas has a nighttime vision of the great Trojan hero Hector, who appears as he had been when he was killed and his body violently abused by Achilles, as described by Homer in *Iliad,* Book Twenty-two.

9: **II.295.** The Penates, together with the Lares, were representations of household gods held in high reverence by the Romans. It is a cult by Virgil projected on to the ancient Trojans, as the Romans' putative ancestors. An old laurel tree shades the Penates of Priam's castle (II.515) and Anchises carries their family's Penates as they flee Troy (II.718). In Crete, the Penates will appear to Aeneas in a dream and urge him to seek Italy (III.148).

10: **II.342–44.** Coroebus was a Trojan warrior engaged to the prophet Cassandra, cruelly destined never to be believed. The god Apollo had compensated her with the gift of prophecy after raping her, but punished her for refusing him (see note on Juturna at XII.138–46). She will be carried off as a war-prize by Agamemnon and witness the destruction of Agamemnon's house, as depicted famously in the play by Aeschylus entitled *Agamemnon.*

11: **II.423.** "The first to note our shields and bogus arms." With his comrades, Aeneas has hastily put on Greek armor. The issue of the clothing he wears will arise again in Carthage in Book IV, and what clothing the Trojans should wear will be stipulated by Juno in Book XII.

12: **II.470.** Pyrrhus, also called Neoptolemus in the tradition (though not by Virgil, because it did not fit the meter of his poem), was the son of Achilles born on the island of Skyros. In other depictions, he displays a noble character—notably in Sophocles's play *Philoctetes*—but here he is villainous and implicitly compared to a snake.

13: **II.549.** A "quidnunc" (from the Latin for "what now?") is an English word meaning "a gossip," first coined by Richard Steele in *The Tatler* (1709).

14: **II.558–59.** According to the ancient commentator Servius, Virgil's depiction of Priam's ultimate fate is based on the death in 48 B.C. of Pompey the Great, whose body was tossed onto a beach after his head had been cut off for presentation to Julius Caesar.

15: **II.569–88.** The authenticity of the so-called Helen episode is a much-debated controversy in Virgilian scholarship. It is not found in the earliest manuscripts but is quoted by the fourth-century commentator Servius. The events described here are at odds with Deïphobus's account in the Underworld, on which see note at VI.512–29.

16: **II.683.** The "tongue of fire" doing no harm that appears on Ascanius's head is a sign of divine favor. A similar fire will alight on Lavinia's hair (VII.73–80). The brow of Augustus, the descendent of both Anchises and Lavinia, will be graced with two such flames on Aeneas's shield (VIII.680–81).

17: **II.722–25.** The iconic image of Aeneas carrying his father on his shoulders and leading his son by the hand appeared on coins of Julius Caesar as a pointed allusion to his claim of divine ancestry.

18: **II.771–90.** Aeneas's wife Creusa had been lost in the confusion, but here she appears as a ghost to him to encourage him in his flight. Her loss, while tragic, allows the hero to be involved later with Dido in Carthage and then Lavinia in Italy.

19: **II.780.** *Fas* is a Latin word meaning "speakable" or, more fully, "permitted by the gods to be spoken." It carries with it a sense of obligation and authority, even as its negative, *nefas*, is considered blasphemous and unholy.

BOOK III

1: **III.24–68.** Polydorus, the youngest son of Priam and Hecuba, had been entrusted to King Polymestor of Thrace for protection during the Trojan War. The story had famously been told by Euripides in his tragedy the *Hecuba*. Meant to be Troy's "saving remnant," Polydorus was instead murdered by the king for the Trojan gold that had been sent along with him. The surreal element of the bleeding myrtle tree plucked by Aeneas is Virgil's own invention, and was copied by Dante in Canto Thirteen of *Inferno* for his depiction of the Wood of the Suicides.

2: **III.73.** The unnamed "sacred, dearly cherished isle" mentioned here by Aeneas is, in fact, Delos, though it is later called Ortygia, "Quail Island" (III.124). Sacred to the god Apollo, whose birth here was described in the *Homeric Hymn to Delian Apollo*, the island was long associated with oracles such as this one, unfortunately misunderstood by the Trojans.

3: **III.104.** Although the interpretation of the oracle given by Anchises is mistaken, the poet's purpose in this Cretan detour may be to draw a greater connection with Jupiter who, as an infant, was hidden on the island from his father Saturn's murderous intentions. Like the chief god, the Trojan exiles arrive to Crete when they are weak and helpless but will emerge from it eventually to achieve worldwide domination.

4: **III.148.** On the Penates, see note at II.295.

5: **III.225.** The Harpies (whose name is derived from the Greek verb *harpazein,* "to snatch") are monsters with women's faces and the bodies of birds of prey who recall the Sirens of the *Odyssey* as well as the Furies. Virgil particularly has in mind their depiction in Book Two of Apollonius of Rhodes's Hellenistic epic *Argonautica,* where they continuously assault the blind seer Phineus as he attempts to eat.

6: **III.245–57.** The character of the chief Harpy, Celaeno, is Virgil's invention. Her prophecy about the Trojans' eating their plates, although terrifying when uttered, will come to amusing fulfilment when they arrive in Italy (VII.108–17).

7: **III.274–88.** Virgil conflates here the promontory on the island of Leucas with that of Actium on the mainland, some thirty miles north, as he will do again in his description of the shield of Aeneas. The geographical imprecision is influenced by a desire to link Aeneas closely with the site of Augustus's great naval victory over Mark Antony and Cleopatra in 31 B.C., on which see note at VIII.675–713.

8: **III.293–352.** Although there was a real city of Buthrotum (modern-day Butrint in Albania), the entire episode of the Little Troy established by Helenus and Andromache is both uncanny and heartbreaking. Traumatized by the war and its aftermath, they re-create in pathetic detail the home they have lost and can never regain, a symbol of incapacitating nostalgia.

9: **III.309.** Upon seeing Aeneas, Andromache is described as "zero at the bone," an apt adaptation of Emily Dickinson's famous reaction to seeing a snake in her poem "A Narrow Fellow in the Grass" from 1865. In the Latin, Andromache's incomprehension is indicated by a sudden change from quick dactylic rhythm to more laborious spondees.

10: **III.340.** Andromache is much damaged by her wartime experiences, having witnessed the deaths of both her husband Hector and son Astyanax and been forced into slavery as concubine to Pyrrhus. In Buthrotum, she seems particularly unable to find any sense of closure, as perhaps this unfinished line is intended to demonstrate.

11: **III.374–462.** Helenus, a minor Trojan warrior in the Homeric tradition, plays a significant role in the *Aeneid* as the husband of Andromache and ruler of Buthrotum after Pyrrhus's death. His long prophecy here recalls those given to Odysseus by Circe in Book Ten of the *Odyssey* and Tiresias in Book Eleven, but also includes details of Roman sacrificial practice. As Hector and Creusa had during the fall of Troy, he too tells Aeneas to seek Italy, though unlike them, he is not a ghost but a living figure inspired by Apollo.

12: **III.523–24.** "Italy!" The land so long sought and still even now out of the Trojans' grasp is mentioned three times in this couplet, a sign of the excitement felt by the exiles to claim their promised land.

13: **III.537–43.** The omen of the four white horses presages both war and peace, Anchises suggests. The Roman reader would recall that white horses, four in number, customarily led the chariots of triumphing generals to the temple of Jupiter Optimus Maximus.

14: **III.595–654.** The castaway Achaemenides, a character of Virgil's invention, reveals himself to be a sailor abandoned by Ulysses on the island of the Cyclopes. His story is reminiscent in some ways of the lying Sinon's tale (II.77–144), but the Trojans' ability to look past this resemblance is a mark of their merciful nature.

15: **III.656.** Aeneas and his men see Polyphemus whose encounter with Odysseus in Book Nine of the *Odyssey* was as well-known a tale in Virgil's day as it is in our own. That Virgil considers Polyphemus not an unsympathetic figure, despite his monstrosity, is suggested by the pastoral care he affords his sheep (III.660–61).

BOOK IV

1: **IV.2.** The astute reader will note how often Dido's growing passion for Aeneas is described in terms of fire imagery, from "burning in liquid fires" here to "the embers of that old flame" (IV.23) and elsewhere. All of these references foreshadow with grim irony the queen's death on the suicide pyre (IV.642–65).

2: **IV.34.** In contrast with Dido's high-minded resolve, Anna provides a more down-to-earth interpretation of her sister's burgeoning feelings for Aeneas. The frank materialism of Anna's argument is parodied, though only slightly, in the story of the Widow of Ephesus related in Petronius's *Satyricon*.

3: **IV.72–73.** In this epic simile, Dido is famously compared to a deer wandering "through Dictaea's glen" on the island of Crete. It is from this mountain that the herb dittany is gathered by Venus when Aeneas is wounded (XII.412–15). The queen, however, like the deer to which she is likened, will find no salve for her injury.

4: **IV.86–89.** The depiction here of Dido as being incapable of balancing her private life with her public role as queen in charge of building a new city has come in for justifiable criticism.

5: IV.**90–128.** The interlude here shows Juno and Venus engaged in a game of strategy against one another that involves the passions and lives of the human protagonists. Dido, while incapable of resisting this divine interference, will know enough to complain against Juno (IV.372–73) and even accuse her of premeditation (IV.608). Outplayed by Venus, Juno will be somewhat caustically called *omnipotens*, "mighty," by Virgil by the book's end (IV.693).

6: **IV.127.** On Venus's smile here, see note at I.255.

7: **IV.165.** The phrase "Dido and the Trojan prince" is nestled in the center of the verse, as the pair is nestled in the center of the cave. The Latin, *Dido dux et Troianus,* intermingles the word order still more suggestively.

8: **IV.171.** For calling her arrangement with Aeneas a marriage (here, and at IV.315–16), Dido has been accused of willful self-deception, which the fact that Juno, the goddess of marriage, was present with witnesses at its consummation (IV.166–68) has done little to diminish. Mercury will call Aeneas "uxorious" (IV.266), recognizing him as a husband perhaps facetiously, but perhaps not. Some forms of cohabitation, despite the lack of formal ceremony, were observed as valid marriages in ancient Rome.

9: **IV.172–88.** Virgil's description of Rumor here is a justly famous instance of personification. In her rush forward—for Rumor is characterized as yet another example of irrational female behavior in the *Aeneid*—she does not lose strength, as runners ordinarily do, but perversely gains it. With her many heads and eyes "as numerous as her plumes," Rumor is an evil-looking bird-woman monster like the Harpies or Sirens, though ultimately more destructive than either.

10: **IV.198–218.** Iarbas, mentioned earlier by Anna (IV.37), is a non-Punic North African king and suitor of Queen Dido. He is presented as powerful in terms of his martial prowess and, as the son of Hammon (the North African Jupiter), possessing mighty familial connections. The bitter complaints to Jupiter, together with his many sacrifices, touch his father's heart.

11: **IV.238–78.** Hermes (the Greek name used sometimes in this translation for metrical reasons instead of Mercury) is modeled by Virgil after the image of the messenger-god in *Odyssey* Book Five, who directs Calypso to release Odysseus from her grip: that this implicitly makes Dido equivalent to the powerful kidnapping goddess seems rather unjust.

12: **IV.283–95.** Generations of readers have cursed Aeneas for his failure to break the bad news to Dido personally. While it is true that Jupiter through Hermes commanded the hero to leave, even as God gave orders to Moses in the Book of Exodus, failing to speak with Dido about his heartbreaking decision is blameworthy. That he is leaving against his will (IV.361) is no exoneration.

13: **IV.302–4.** Dido is likened here to a Maenad, a female worshipper of Bacchus. The fearsome activity of this cult is memorably portrayed in Euripides's masterpiece *The Bacchae*. On Mount Cithaeron, noted here, the Theban king Pentheus (mentioned at IV.469) is killed by his mother in a Bacchic frenzy.

14: **IV.385.** Though Dido promises that her "ghost will chase [him]," there is no indication that Aeneas is haunted by her afterward. In fact, she refuses even to acknowledge him when they meet in the Underworld (VI.469).

15: **IV.393.** Here, for the first time in Book IV, Virgil calls Aeneas *pius*, "good," a sign evidently of authorial approval for the hero's obedience to the gods, no matter the personal cost.

16: **IV.436.** This perplexing verse, as the renowned *Aeneid* scholar John Conington once wrote, is "well known as the most difficult in Virgil." See John Conington, ed., *P. Vergili Maronis Opera. The Works of Virgil, with a Commentary*, Vol. 2, Aeneid I–VI, 3rd ed. (London: Whittaker and Co. George Bell and Sons, 1876), 302.

17: **IV.441–46.** The comparison of Aeneas to an aged oak tree, with branches extending as high as its roots are deep, is notable. Epic similes in Homer often compare elements of the natural world with physical activity: just a little earlier, for example, the hardworking Trojans have been likened to ants (IV.402). Here, however, it is Aeneas's ethical struggle that calls forth the analogy to a mighty oak. Readers will note in the *Aeneid*, and throughout Virgil's work, many affectionate references to trees, too numerous to list here but worthy of sustained study.

18: **IV.461–62.** The owl, in antiquity as today, is often thought a bird of ill omen because of its nocturnal nature and uncanny "dirge-like song."

19: **IV.528.** While not particularly un-Virgilian in sound or sentiment, this line is believed by scholars not to be authentic.

20: **IV.569.** In this verse, *femina est mutabile* ("Women always change in all their ways"), Virgil once again codes chaos and instability as particularly feminine in nature.

21: **IV.631–62.** The depiction here of Dido's suicide, about which so much insightful scholarship and so many significant works of art have been produced, can hardly be overestimated for its power and pathos. In a true Virgilian synthesis of the literary and political, the scene is patterned after both the tradition of heroines' deaths in Greek tragedy and the account of Cleopatra's suicide after the defeat at Actium, on which see note at VIII.689. In Book One of his *Confessions*, Saint Augustine claims to have wept more over the death of Dido than he did for himself.

22: **IV.696.** Dido's death was "not by fate," the poet states. On fate, see note at I.2.

23: **IV.700–5.** Iris has been dispatched by Juno to cut a lock of Dido's hair, so as to allow the queen to enter the Underworld. A figure drawn from Homer, Iris is closely associated with the rainbow, and in one of the earliest illustrated manuscripts of the *Aeneid*, the *Vergilius Romanus* of the fifth century A.D., the rainbow billows like a veil above her. Where Mercury conveys messages for Jupiter, Iris is dispatched to carry out Juno's will.

BOOK V

1: **V.12.** The helmsman Palinurus, mentioned early in this book, will feature prominently at its end when his death is characterized by Neptune as a necessary sacrifice (V.815). Aeneas will see him in the Underworld in Book VI in a scene inspired by Odysseus's encounter with Elpenor in *Odyssey* Book Eleven.

2: **V.66.** In Aeneas's announcement to "sponsor Trojan games," Virgil again couples a Homeric prototype with Roman politics. Achilles's funeral games for Patroclus were depicted in Book Twenty-three of the *Iliad*, and many of the scenes in this book are drawn from that Homeric source. In addition, the poet has in mind the quadrennial Actian Games, instituted by Augustus in 28 B.C. in commemoration of his defeat of Cleopatra and Mark Antony at the Battle of Actium and staged at nearby Nicopolis.

3: **V.84–90.** The ominous appearance of the snake from Anchises's tomb in fact is an unexpectedly good omen, unlike the serpents who had killed Laocoön and his sons at Troy (II.216–25) or the snake associated with Alecto when sent to incite Amata and Turnus (VII.329).

4: **V.113–24.** The ship race here is modeled after the chariot race of *Iliad* Twenty-three, though it alludes as well to the regatta celebrated at the Actian Games. We should imagine each of the ships to have a decorative figurehead corresponding to its colorful name. Virgil uses this scene, furthermore, to establish mythological Trojan genealogies for the noble Roman families of the Memmii, the Sergii, and the Cluentii.

5: **V.241–42.** Cloanthus's prayer is answered by the harbor god, Portunus. The temple to this god, still standing today in Rome near the Tiber River, was doubtlessly known to Virgil.

6: **V.252–57.** Depicted on the first-prize cloak given to Cloanthus is the "royal boy" of Troy, Ganymede, whose abduction and subsequent honoring by Jupiter is specifically held against the Trojans by Juno at I.28–29.

7: **V.328–38.** At this critical moment in the footrace, Nisus slips in the gore of sacrificed victims, perhaps shed by the cattle killed nine days before (at V.101). Virgil has in mind here the moment in *Iliad* Twenty-three when Ajax somewhat comically slips in the dung of the victims. The substitution of blood at this moment points ahead to the self-sacrifice of Nisus on behalf of Euryalus at IX.425–50.

8: **V.401–21.** Entellus displays the *caesti*, "boxing gloves," once owned by Eryx, who was killed when fighting against Hercules. Although Entellus does not wear these in the match, the reference anticipates the great symbolic fight between Hercules and the monstrous Cacus at the site of Rome, narrated at VIII.205–67. The only known pair of boxing gloves from antiquity was discovered at Vindolanda, a fort on Hadrian's Wall, in 2018.

9: **V.521–28.** The sudden comet-like appearance of Acestes's arrow during the archery contest is another instance of divinely sanctioned fire, on which see note II.683.

10: **V.545–603.** At Aeneas's urging, Ascanius and the young Trojan men engage in the "rousing war games" (V.585), known historically as the *Lusus Troiae* and staged by Julius Caesar, Augustus, and other emperors on ceremonial occasions.

11: **V.618–43.** On Iris, the goddess of the rainbow, see note at IV.700–5. At Juno's bidding, she arrives disguised as the aged Beroë to provoke the Trojan women to burn their ships, even as she will later be sent to incite Turnus (IX.1–24).

12: **V.636.** On Cassandra, see note at II.342–44.

13: **V.654.** It is worthwhile to note that the Trojan matrons are *ancipites*, "dubious." Uncertain as they may be about the imperial prospects pursued by pious Aeneas and the other male characters, the women are not immediately won over by Iris's rabble-rousing. The difference between "this land and Italy" (V.656) is unclear to them.

14: **V.722–40.** After urging Aeneas to follow Nautes's advice (V.704–18), Anchises tells his son to seek him in the Underworld. Virgil here adapts Circe's advice to Odysseus in *Odyssey* Book Ten to travel to consult with the dead Tiresias.

15: **V.741–43.** Aeneas calls after his disappearing father here in the same anguished way that he had called after his disappearing mother at I.406–9.

16: **V.815.** On Palinurus, see note at V.12.

Book VI

1: **VI.2.** The passageway into the Underworld is here represented as being at Cumae, in the promised land of Italy. What purports to be the Sibyl's cave is still a tourist destination in the modern town of Cuma near Naples.

2: **VI.10–12.** The Sibyl of Cumae, whose name we learn is Deïphobe (VI.34), is a priestess of Apollo and the epic's most authoritative mortal woman. Like Cassandra, on whom see note at II.342–44, her prophecies are associated with a frenzied possession by the god. In his Fourth *Eclogue*, Virgil had attributed to this Sibyl the prophecy about the birth of a messianic boy, interpreted by early Christians as a reference to Jesus. The Sibyl is much depicted in the later tradition, notably by Michelangelo near the center of the Sistine Chapel ceiling, and referred to specifically in the inscription of T. S. Eliot's *The Wasteland* (1922) by way of a quotation from Petronius's *Satyricon*.

3: **VI.14–33.** Aeneas's viewing here of a work of pictorial art is meant to recall the passage in Book I, where the hero had encountered images of the Trojan War in Juno's temple, on which see note at I.455. Daedalus, we are told, has carved these scenes from his own life story. Hired by the king of Crete, Minos, to build a labyrinth in which to imprison the Minotaur—the monstrous child of his wife, Pasiphaë—Daedalus then escapes by constructing a pair of wings and flying away from the island. The story is told by Ovid in Book Eight of the *Metamorphoses*.

4: **VI.31–33.** Daedalus's sorrow over Icarus perhaps anticipates the passage about the death of the young Marcellus near the book's end, on which see note at VI.883.

5: **VI.83–97.** The Sibyl's prophecy of "grim wars" (VI.86) and "a new Achilles" (VI.89)—all of which will begin in earnest after Book VI—introduces the epic's second half, the transition from what the classicist Brooks Otis called the Odyssean to the Iliadic *Aeneid*.

6: **VI.111.** On Aeneas's carrying of Anchises, see note at II.722–25.

7: **VI.120–21.** Though many of the descents to the Underworld are made by heroes, Virgil had depicted at length the *katabasis* by the singer Orpheus in Book Four of his *Georgics*. Through his artistry, Orpheus hoped to recover his dead wife, Eurydice. At the very last moment, he turned around to make sure she was there, against the express wishes of Pluto. In Virgil's hands, the failure of Orpheus takes on a tragic dimension that can be felt in his depiction of Aeneas throughout Book VI.

8: **VI.123–24.** As Charon will recollect later (VI.392–93), both Hercules and Theseus descended to the Underworld, about which see the following note at VI.129–30. The grumpy ferryman is depicted in Canto Three of Dante's *Inferno*, as well as on Michelangelo's *Last Judgment* fresco behind the high altar in the Sistine Chapel (circa 1540).

9: **VI.129–30.** The descent to Avernus (see note at VI.242) is "no trouble," but the return is difficult. Like Odysseus, who visited the land of the dead in Book Eleven of the *Odyssey* after which this book is modeled, Aeneas too makes an epic *katabasis*, descent into and return from the Underworld. In the Apostles' Creed (A.D. 390),

Jesus is likewise said to have "descended to the dead" and risen again. In the *Divine Comedy* (1320), Dante will be accompanied on his visit to Hell and Purgatory by the figure of Virgil, though the pilgrim will emerge alone into Paradise.

10: **VI.138.** Proserpina, the Roman name for Persephone, is the wife of Pluto who notoriously abducted her. She is "Hell's Juno" in that she reigns with her husband over the Underworld as Juno reigns with Jupiter over the sky.

11: **VI.141–47.** The meaning of the golden bough, one of Virgil's most memorable symbols, has tantalized generations of interpreters with possible meanings, though none is certain. The important multivolume work of anthropology by Sir James G. Frazer called *The Golden Bough* connects Virgil's symbol with the weird rites of Diana at Aricia, while others think the poet may be referring to myths connected to the mistletoe. Whatever its ultimate meaning, the bough's power is clear, and Charon will cower before it when the Sibyl brandishes it before his face at VI.406. Aeneas will lay the bough on the threshold of the Elysian Fields at VI.636–37.

12: **VI.162–74.** Misenus, a trumpeter in the Trojan retinue, has died and must be buried before Aeneas can proceed. Like Palinurus, on whom see note at V.12, his fate is derived from the figure of Elpenor in Book Eleven of the *Odyssey*. The name of Misenus is thought to be commemorated in the Bay of Naples's northern headland, Cape Misenum, as noted at VI.234–35.

13: **VI.190.** Like swans (on which see note at I.393–400), doves are sacred to Venus. In Greek art, Aphrodite is often portrayed with an accompanying dove.

14: **VI.210–11.** In Latin, the bough is described as *cunctantem*, "delaying," when Aeneas breaks it off. Some scholars, with differing interpretations, find this hesitation to be at odds with the Sibyl's instruction that "it will come off in your hand with perfect ease" (VI.146).

15: **VI.242.** The poet gives a learned etymology here for Avernus, the volcanic crater-lake thought to be the entrance to the Underworld, from the Greek *a-*, "without" and *ornis*, "bird." The lack of birds by the lake is theoretically connected to its sulfurous smell. The line is rejected by some textual critics as not original with Virgil but an interpolation.

16: **VI.264–67.** On the invocation of the Muse, see note at I.8

17: **VI.337.** On Palinurus, see note at V.12.

18: **VI.417.** Cerberus, the three-headed guard dog of the Underworld, was famously carried off by Hercules as his final labor. A memorable monster, Cerberus is depicted in numerous works of art and literature. In J. K. Rowling's *Harry Potter* series, the three-headed hound is amusingly called Fluffy by Hagrid.

19: **VI.431–33.** Together with Rhadamanthus who presides over Tartarus (VI.566–79), Minos is "Styx's magistrate" determining the fates of the dead. Homer had already named Minos to this role in *Odyssey* Book Eleven, but Virgil makes him more of a Roman magistrate. On Minos's backstory as king of Crete, see note at VI.14–33. Dante builds on this Virgilian description of Minos for his own portrait of the infernal judge in Canto Five of *Inferno*.

20: **VI.450–77.** Dido's portrait in the Underworld is modeled after that of the Homeric hero Ajax. Feeling disgraced when the arms of Achilles have been awarded to Odysseus rather than himself, Ajax committed suicide, as depicted by Sophocles in his tragedy named for the hero. Still angry even in the afterlife, Ajax refuses to speak to Odysseus in Book Eleven of the *Odyssey*. In like fashion, Dido turns away from Aeneas in silence, and there are few who do not think he has richly earned this coldest of cold shoulders.

21: **VI.494.** Deïphobus, one of the sons of Priam, was the second Trojan husband of Helen after the death of Paris.

22: **VI.512–29.** The behavior of Helen before the Trojan Horse was described with equal bitterness by her Greek husband, Menelaus, to Telemachus over dinner in *Odyssey* Book Four. This story told by Deïphobus appears to be inconsistent with the Helen episode of Book II, on which see note at II.569–88.

23: **VI.540.** At this point, the Sibyl points out that one branch of the road leads to the damned in Tartarus and the other to the blessed in Elysium. The idea is derived from Plato's dialogue the *Gorgias*. The translation here "Two roads diverge within this wood" consciously evokes the famous lines from Robert Frost's "The Road Not Taken" (1916).

24: **VI.555–73.** The souls of those damned to Tartarus by Rhadamanthus (on whom see note at VI.431–33) are whipped by the Fury Tisiphone, who will later appear in the Trojan war against the Rutulians (X.761). Some of those punished in Tartarus had been mentioned in *Odyssey* Book Eleven, notably Tityus and Ixion.

25: **VI.617.** On Theseus, see note at VI.123–24.

26: **VI.638–78.** Elysium, the land of the blessed souls, is mentioned by Homer in *Odyssey* Book Four as the final resting place of Menelaus and Helen but is influenced by another Greek conception of the afterlife, the Isles of the Blessed.

27: **VI.645–47.** On Orpheus, see note at VI.120–21.

28: **VI.667.** Musaeus, a mythical figure connected with Orpheus, will lead Aeneas and the Sibyl to Anchises.

29: **VI.715.** The waters of the Lethe provide a calming forgetfulness to those who drink from them, allowing souls to return to the world purged of their memories, as is related in the Myth of Er from Book Ten of Plato's *Republic* (though the river is not named there).

30: **VI.724–51.** In crafting Anchises's long response to Aeneas's question about souls (VI.719–22), Virgil engages in a grand synthesis of Stoic beliefs, Orphic mystery cult elements, and Platonic ideas of the soul's reincarnation, in the poetic idiom of Lucretius's *On the Nature of Things.*

31: **VI.756–853.** The Parade of Roman Heroes elaborated here by Anchises is justly famous, pointing backward to Jupiter's prophecy to Venus in Book I and ahead to Aeneas's shield in Book VIII. It has not gone without criticism: in "Secondary Epic" (1959), the British poet W. H. Auden condemns the anachronism of this "Roman history in the future tense," and chastises Virgil as a propagandist, writing, "Behind your verse so masterfully made / We hear the weeping of a Muse betrayed." The numerous figures mentioned come from different points of the Roman past and are not presented in strict chronological order.

32: **VI.777.** On Romulus, see note at VIII.343–44.

33: **VI.786.** Concerning the Magna Mater, see note at IX.82.

34: **VI.789–807.** Virgil's patron, Augustus, is singled out for particular honor by Anchises in what is perhaps the most obsequious portion of the Parade of Heroes. The final settlement of the Roman civil wars and the consequent *Pax Romana* were celebrated by many artists of the Augustan Age. That the epic is not consistently pro-Augustan is a widely held critical opinion.

35: **VI.826–35.** The souls of Pompey the Great and Julius Caesar are noted, with Anchises lamenting that they are father-in-law and son-in-law. Caesar's daughter, Julia, had been married to Pompey from 59 B.C. until her death five years later. The war between them, which ended with Caesar's victory, was the subject of the epic poem, *Pharsalia,* by Lucan in the first century A.D.

36: **VI.847–53.** This epilogue to the Parade of Heroes, addressed not to Aeneas but specifically to the Roman reader (VI.850), outlines in broad ideological terms the imperial responsibilities of the *Pax Romana.*

37: **VI.883.** The handsome youth with downcast eyes whom Aeneas inquires after is Marcus Claudius Marcellus (42–23 B.C.), the beloved nephew of Augustus and, but for his early death, a likely successor to the throne. The depiction of the doomed young man is steeped in pathos, and legend has it that when Virgil read this passage aloud at the court, Marcellus's mother Octavia fainted. A 1787 painting of this scene by Jean-Joseph Taillasson hangs in London's National Gallery. Marcellus is the last figure in the Parade of Heroes, which thus ends not on a triumphant note but far more dolefully.

38: **VI.893–901.** The twin Gates of Sleep are described here: true dreams pass through the Gate of Horn, while false dreams pass through the Gate of Ivory. Penelope had described the Gates of Sleep in *Odyssey* Book Nineteen. In a book full of wonderful moments and mysterious symbols, Virgil's decision to have Aeneas and the Sibyl pass through the gate of false dreams is the final enigma. The effect, evidently, is like that of drinking from the Lethe (see note at VI.715): when Aeneas takes up the shield, he will not recognize the figures on it (VIII.730), though some of them he surely must have seen during the Parade of Heroes.

Book VII

1: **VII.1.** Virgil indicates that the busy port of his day named Caieta, now the modern city of Gaeta (home to a large NATO naval base), was in fact named in legendary times for Aeneas's nurse.

2: **VII.37.** As he begins the second part of his epic, the poet invokes Erato, traditionally considered the Muse of love poetry, in imitation of Apollonius of Rhodes, who had invoked this Muse in beginning the affair of Jason and Medea in his *Argonautica*. Virgil will invoke the Muses again later in the book (VII.641). On invocation of the Muse, see note at I.8.

3: **VII.47–49.** Faunus is a prophet whose advice his son, King Latinus, will consult and unwisely repeat (VII.81–106) and then be reminded of afterward (VII.254–58, 368–69). The trunk of his tree will hold fast the spear of Aeneas in the decisive battle against Turnus, XII.766–87.

4: **VII.64–70.** On Virgil's employment of bee imagery, see note at I.430–36.

5: **VII.72.** Here, readers get their first glimpse of Lavinia, the princess destined by Fate for Aeneas and from whom the Roman race will derive its origin. Her name has been prominent as an adjective synonymous with the promised land of Italy since I.1, though she herself is presented as being as dull a character as Dido is compelling. In her novel *Lavinia* (2008), Ursula K. Le Guin imagines the princess speaking for herself about Virgil, "who brought me to life, to myself, and so made me able to remember my life and myself, which I do, vividly, with all kinds of emotions, emotions I feel strongly as I write, perhaps because the events I remember only come to exist as I write them, or as he wrote them" (p. 3). As she adds, "But he did not write them. He slighted my life, in his poem."

6: **VII.73–80.** On ominous fire, see note at II.683.

7: **VII.108–17.** On the prophecy that the Trojans would consume their plates together with their food—the first Italian pizza, or possibly focaccia—see note at III.245–57. There it was Celaeno who delivered the prophecy, not Anchises as here (VII.123).

8: **VII.169–94.** The description of Latinus's enormous colonnaded palace is perhaps meant to recall the temple of Jupiter Capitolinus in Virgil's own day.

9: **VII.212.** Ilioneus is the first Trojan to address Latinus, just as he had been the first to address Dido at I.521. Virgil is clearly aligning the episodes in order to draw a connection between the epic's first and second halves.

10: **VII.286–91.** Juno spies the Trojans "from a great height," in a moment inspired by Poseidon's seeing Odysseus as his chariot flies through the air in Book Five of the *Odyssey*. As in Book I, she is determined to somehow prevent Aeneas's success in Italy and goes to a henchman, here the Fury Alecto, to carry out her dirty work.

11: **VII.312.** Sigmund Freud famously used this line in Latin, *Flectere si nequeo superos, Acheronta movebo*, as the epigram to his seminal work, *The Interpretation of Dreams* (1899).

12: **VII.324.** Juno's chosen agent of chaos is the Fury Alecto, a figure of utter discord who will incite to war Queen Amata (VII.341–405), Turnus (VII.406–74), and Ascanius's dogs (VII.475–99) in turn. The snaky imagery that characterizes her aligns her with other important serpents in the *Aeneid* (e.g., those attacking Laocoön, II.205–28).

13: **VII.389.** On female madness and Bacchic imagery, see note at IV.302–4.

14: **VII.477–503.** Ascanius, while hunting, kills a remarkable *cervus*, "stag," hand-raised by Silvia, the daughter of Latinus's chief herdsman, Tyrrhus. The scene recalls the epic simile describing Dido and Aeneas as a deer and unknowing hunter (IV.71–73). Ascanius's innocent mistake provides Alecto with the pretext for inciting the Italians to war against the Trojans.

15: **VII.601–28.** The so-called Gates of War on the Temple of Janus, the two-faced god of doorways, were left open during times of war. In his monumental funerary inscription, the *Res Gestae* (sec. 13), Augustus claimed to have closed these gates three times to signal victorious peace. Virgil here projects this ideological practice on Italy's legendary prehistory; Jupiter had already spoken of it to Venus, I.293.

16: **VII.641.** Here the poet calls again on the Muses for inspiration, as he had earlier in the book at VII.37, to offer a listing of Italian heroes that the scholar W. Warde Fowler called a "Gathering of the Clans." Such lists, called an epic catalogue, are a feature of epic poetry, most notably in Book Two of Homer's *Iliad*.

17: **VII.647.** Of the numerous enemies pitted against pious Aeneas, it is significant that the very first of these should be "blasphemous Mezentius," the exiled Etruscan king called in Latin *contemptor divum*, "scorner of the gods." When he confronts Aeneas in battle, Mezentius will call upon "this right hand—my god"

(X.773), further evidence of his impious nature. Though Evander will present him as an archetypal tyrant (VIII.481–95), a more nuanced picture emerges from his behavior in battle in Books IX and X. The very evident mutual love between Mezentius and his son Lausus (see especially X.789–832) further adds to the complexity.

18: **VII.761–70.** In Euripides's tragedy the *Hippolytus*, the title character is unjustly accused by his stepmother, Phaedra, of attempting to seduce her; for this reason, he is cursed by his father, Theseus, and killed by his own horses. According to later legend (recounted by Ovid in Book Fifteen of the *Metamorphoses*), Hippolytus was restored to life by the agency of the goddess Diana. In this new life, he is called Virbius, although the Virbius mentioned here as a warrior is *not* the reanimated Hippolytus, but his son.

19: **VII.785–92.** The triple-crested helmet of Turnus features the Chimaera, the infernal hybrid monster mentioned in the Underworld (VI.288). His shield depicts the legend of Io (the daughter of Inachus, a river-god in Argos), who was raped by Jupiter. He subsequently turned her into a cow in hopes of hiding the matter from Juno, but she found out and set the many-eyed Argus over her as guard. Ovid tells her story in Book One of the *Metamorphoses*. Io is the ancestor of numerous heroes, including Perseus and Heracles. Amata had already indicated that Turnus's genealogy could be traced back to this myth at VII.371–72

20: **VII.803.** On Camilla, see note at XI.498.

Book VIII

1: **VIII.31.** Tiber, the ancient river-god crowned with reeds and wearing a grey cloak, appears to Aeneas as he sleeps by the bank. On one of the reliefs of Trajan's Column, the river-god Danube is likewise depicted as having reeds in his hair. The god of the river will a little later be called *caeruleus*, "blue," at VIII.64, although the Tiber itself is customarily thought to be *flavus*, "yellow" on account of its muddiness. As a sign of his favor, Tiber will hold back the swell of his river to allow the Trojan ships safe passage (VIII.86–93).

2: **VIII.40.** On the Penates, see note at II.295.

3: **VIII.43–46.** The river-god here points out to Aeneas that he will soon come upon a great sow with thirty piglets, the favorable sign prophesied by Helenus as indicating the hero's place of ultimate rest (III.390–93). The Trojans in fact see the sow at VIII.80–85.

4: **VIII.100.** At the future site of Rome, the settlement established by King Evander is called "an unexalted realm." Here the two exiled figures come together to join hands (at VIII.169), on the unassuming location from which the grand city and worldwide empire will arise. Later (VIII.362–66), Evander will invite Aeneas into his "humble royal house."

5: **VIII.110.** As the Trojan ships are sighted on the river, Evander's son, Pallas, makes his initial appearance in the epic. The name of Pallas is to be associated with Pallanteum, the Arcadian homeland of Evander (as Tiber explains at VIII.51–54), as well as with the Palatine Hill, near where Evander's community is located. The first epithet used of Pallas, *audax*, "bold," helps to characterize the young man as noble and rash, an ancient version of Hotspur from Shakespeare's *Henry IV Part 1*.

6: **VIII.185–279.** Evander recounts the foundation legend of the Ara Maxima (the "Mightiest" altar, as it is translated at VIII.271), which involves the mythic battle of Hercules and Cacus. Ancient commentators noted how Evander, *eu andros*, signifies "good man" in Greek, and that his counterpart is called *Cacus*, a name meaning "evil." Whether these etymologies were in Virgil's mind is difficult to say. The Roman historian Livy had depicted Cacus simply as a ferocious local shepherd, not a fire-breathing monster. For Virgil, the struggle between Hercules and the native Cacus is meant to prefigure the battle of the invading Trojans against the indigenous Rutulians.

7: **VIII.343–44.** The grotto of the Lupercal, the Wolf's Cave, is traditionally connected with the location where Romulus and Remus were fostered by a *lupa*, she-wolf, as noted on the shield at VIII.630–34. The place is also associated with the unrestrained primitive festival of the Lupercalia (represented on the shield at VIII.662), which was celebrated each February in the Roman calendar.

8: **VIII.357.** On Janus, see note at VII.601–28.

9: **VIII.370–406.** Venus's address to Vulcan here is a recasting of Hera's seduction of Zeus from *Iliad* Book Fourteen, a scene already referred to in the Aeolus episode, on which see note at I.52–75. Venus is seeking from her blacksmith husband new armor for her son by Anchises.

10: **VIII.481–95.** On Mezentius, see note at VII.648.

11: **VIII.515.** Pallas here is entrusted to Aeneas. See Evander's prayer later at VIII.574–82. In the same way that Patroclus's death in the *Iliad* brought on the culminating clash between Hector and Achilles, so the death and despoiling of Pallas (X.439–509) will prompt the final duel of Turnus and Aeneas in Book XII.

12: **VIII.608–731.** The shield of Aeneas, one of the epic's greatest set-pieces, is modeled after the shield of Achilles, described at length in Book Eighteen of the *Iliad*. As is Virgil's poetic practice throughout the *Aeneid*, this Homeric prototype is reimagined in terms of Augustan ideology. The shield depicts numerous significant moments from Rome's history, some already recounted in the Underworld by

Anchises. A number of the scenes mentioned on the shield were in fact represented in reliefs on the (probably) contemporaneous frieze of the Basilica Aemilia in the Roman Forum. W. H. Auden was critical of the ideology of the Parade of Heroes and the shield, on which see note at VI.756–853.

13: **VIII.635.** The legend of the Sabine women—who, when invited to Rome to watch the ceremonial games, were abducted by the Romans as wives—was recounted also by Livy and Ovid, and appears on Roman coinage issued in the early first century B.C.

14: **VIII.646–52.** In the early years of the Republic, Rome was besieged by the Etruscan king Lars Porsenna. Horatius Cocles defended the city by taking a heroic stand on the Sublician Bridge against Porsenna's invading forces. Cloelia was a Roman woman who, given as a hostage to the Etruscans as part of a subsequent peace treaty, escaped from their camp and heroically swam across the Tiber, for which she was honored with an equestrian statue.

15: **VIII.652–61.** The sack of Rome by the Gauls in 390 B.C., though perhaps more fiction than fact, left a long imprint on the Roman imagination. A prominent story concerns the former consul Marcus Manlius Capitolinus, who was awakened to the invasion by the honking of Juno's sacred geese (themselves represented in flustered agitation on the Basilica Aemilia frieze).

16: **VIII.668.** Lucius Sergius Catilina—Catiline, as he is known in English—was a Roman patrician who, disappointed by his failure to obtain the consulship, led a conspiracy to overthrow the republican government in 63 B.C. His plot was exposed by the consul Marcus Tullius Cicero, whose four orations against Catiline mark a high point of Roman oratory.

17: **VIII.671.** Marcus Porcius Cato—called Cato the Younger, in English—valiantly opposed Julius Caesar in the Civil Wars, and committed suicide in 46 B.C. For his courage and dedication to the Republic, he was admired even by his political opponents. "The conquering cause pleased the gods, but the conquered cause pleased Cato," wrote the poet Lucan in his epic poem about the Civil Wars (*Pharsalia* 1.128). In later tradition, Cato became a symbol of Stoic virtue, and Dante—much influenced by this line of the *Aeneid*—imagines him as the just guardian of the approach to Mount Purgatory (*Purgatorio* 1.31–75).

18: **VIII.678–82.** On Augustus, see note at VI.789–807. The twin flames by his head recall those of Ascanius (II.683) and Lavinia (VII.73–80), on which see note at II.683.

19: **VIII.689.** Cleopatra VII, "Antony's Egyptian 'wife'" and the last of the Ptolemaic rulers of Egypt, famously committed suicide rather than be taken captive after the defeat at Actium. One of the most celebrated women of classical antiquity, she has been the subject of portrayals in literature, drama, and the visual arts too numerous to mention. "Age cannot wither her, nor custom stale / Her infinite variety," Shakespeare wrote fittingly of her in *Antony and Cleopatra* (Act 2, Scene 2). On the shield of Aeneas, she offers an archetype of female chaos that brings her into close association with both Juno and Dido.

20: **VIII.675–713.** As the reader can easily determine from its central place on the shield, no event occupied a more critical part of Augustan ideology than the Battle of Actium. On September 2, 31 B.C., the naval forces of Mark Antony and Cleopatra were decisively defeated by Octavian and the last of the Roman civil wars was consequently brought to an end. Whether the wide-scale commemoration of this event is rightly considered an act of state propaganda is a matter much debated by scholars.

21: **VIII.730–31.** Here at the end of second book of the *Aeneid*'s second half, Aeneas takes up onto his shoulder the representation of his descendants' future, even as he had taken up the Trojan past in the figure of Anchises at the end of Book II, on which see note at II.722–25. He does not seem to recognize any of the figures on it, despite being shown the Parade of Heroes in Book VI, on which see note at VI.893–901.

Book IX

1: **IX.13.** On Iris, see note at IV.700–5.

2: **IX.69–79.** As he had been ordered by Alecto at VII.431, Turnus attempts to burn the Trojan ships, an action associating the Rutulian hero with Hector, who burnt the Achaean ships in Book Sixteen of the *Iliad*. To make the allusion more explicit, Virgil even calls upon the Muse (IX.78), as Homer had in that episode.

3: **IX.82.** The goddess Cybele, named at IX.108, had her origin on Mount Ida in Phrygia. The title "Berecynthian" is a learned reference on Virgil's part to a native people of this area. Also known as the Magna Mater, "Great Mother," Cybele was worshipped in Rome after her cult statue had been brought there for ritual reasons during the Second Punic War.

4: **IX.117–21.** After the ships' transformation into nymphs, they are seen again at X.219–47. This passage may be the *Aeneid*'s most flamboyant, for which Virgil has not escaped criticism. Ovid himself listed this metamorphosis as an example of overly indulged poetic license (*Amores*, 3.12). Perhaps in keeping with the poetic extravagance, the reference in this translation to the "mermaids singing each to each" is a borrowing from T. S. Eliot's "Love Song of J. Alfred Prufrock" (1915).

5: **IX.122.** Some manuscripts incorrectly insert a line here from elsewhere in the epic (X.223) to fill out what has been deemed an incomplete description of the metamorphosis.

6: **IX.128–59.** Turnus's blatant attempt to recast the signs from the gods and fate itself as somehow favorable rather than obviously unfavorable is an act of audacity, if not outright blasphemy along the lines of Mezentius, on whom see note at VII.648.

7: **IX.176–223.** Nisus and Euryalus have already been seen in the footrace of the funeral games in Sicily (see note at V.328–38), a scene heavily foreshadowing the warriors' heartbreaking deaths later on.

8: **IX.182.** Older scholarship had temporized about the meaning of "Their love was one," suggesting a mutual passion for battle, but it is clear that the bond between Nisus and Euryalus is a romantic one. Like Jonathan and David in the Hebrew Bible, their shared devotion is "passing the love of women" (2 Samuel 1:26). In crafting this relationship, Virgil has in mind Achilles and Patroclus from the *Iliad*, as well as the historical Sacred Band of Thebes.

9: **IX.185–86.** Nisus's question here—"does each man make his desire / His god?"— touches on a central Virgilian question about fate, about which see note at I.2.

10: **IX.314–445.** The Virgilian night raid is modeled after the sorties described in *Iliad* Book Ten of both the Trojan warrior Dolon and the Greek warriors Odysseus and Diomedes.

11: **IX.435–37.** One of the most moving similes in the *Aeneid*, the likening of Euryalus's drooping head to a poppy is informed both by Homer and the Roman lyric poet Catullus. In *Iliad* Book Eight, the warrior Gorgythion's head had been compared to a cut poppy, as here. In Poem 11, Catullus employed the image of a dying flower at the edge of a field as a symbol of his romantic heartbreak. The long association of poppies with the death of young warriors continues in John McCrae's World War I poem, "In Flanders Fields," where "the poppies blow/ Between the crosses, row on row." The commemorative wearing of red poppies on Remembrance Day in the British Commonwealth and, in the United States on Memorial and Veterans Days, is likewise connected with this tradition.

12: **IX.446.** In this apostrophe, the poet directly addresses Nisus and Euryalus and promises that as long as Rome stands and his poetry is read: *Nulla dies umquam memori vos eximet aevo*. Translated as "No day shall erase you from the memory of time," these words are inscribed on the wall of the National September 11th Memorial & Museum in New York City in letters forged from the steel wreckage of the World Trade Center. Some scholars have criticized the use of the quotation, noting that though the "you" of the monument is addressed to the victims of the attack; Nisus and Euryalus more closely resemble the terrorists who carried the attack out. Readers will decide for themselves whether the pathos inherent in Virgil's verse justifies divorcing it from its immediate context.

13: **IX.473.** On Rumor's flight, see note at IV.172–88.

14: **IX.481–97.** The lamentation of Euryalus's mother, among the saddest passages of the *Aeneid,* draws on the mourning of Andromache for Hector in *Iliad* Book Twenty-two and of Anna's reaction to the death of Dido (IV.672–85). Euryalus had specifically asked that she not be informed of his involvement in the raid (IX.283–92). Her particular cry, "I followed you by sea / And land for *this?*" (IX.492–93), is suffused with bitterness because she alone (as we read at IX.217) had followed Aeneas's army to Italy rather than remain in Sicily in Book V.

15: **IX.525–29.** On invocations of the Muse, see note at I.8. Calliope is considered the most important of the Muses. Here the so-called Iliadic *Aeneid*, with its many scenes of heroic combat, begins in earnest.

16: **IX.815–18.** Why the river-god Tiber (on which see note at VIII.31) should here rescue Turnus, despite an allegiance to the Trojans, is a matter not fully resolved by literary critics.

Book X

1: **X.1–18.** The Olympian Council here is rendered in imitation of various such meetings of the gods in Homer, notably *Iliad* Book Eight.

2: **X.111–13.** On the matter of free will and determinism touched on by Jupiter's remark, see note at I.2.

3: **X.163.** The catalogue of allies brought from Tuscany is preceded by the invocation of a Muse, as it had been for the Italian heroes, on which see note at VII.641.

4: **X.220–47.** These are the nymphs who had been transformed earlier by Cybele, on which see note at IX.117–22. Cymodocea speaks on behalf of all of them.

5: **X.284.** The old Roman proverb "Fortune favors the brave!" was quoted by Pliny the Elder when, as a fleet commander, he sailed toward Pompeii during the eruption of Mount Vesuvius in A.D. 79. With various wordings, it appears as a motto for a range of athletic teams and military units.

6: **X.439.** The water-nymph Juturna, sister of Turnus, here makes her first appearance in the epic, though she will play a greater role in Book XII (see note at XII.138–46). In the Roman Forum, there was a pool sacred to her close to the Temple of Castor and Pollux.

7: **X.441–89.** The death of Pallas at Turnus's hands is patterned after Hector's killing of Patroclus in Book Sixteen of the *Iliad*. The boasting of Turnus, however, is far more arrogant than that of his Homeric prototype. Turnus's wishing that his father, Evander, could watch Pallas be killed associates the Rutulian warrior with Pyrrhus, who killed Polites while Priam watched (II.526–44).

8: **X.495–509.** The removal of Pallas's belt as a trophy by Turnus will be the immediate cause of the Rutulian hero's own death by Aeneas (XII.941–44).

9: **X.591.** It is striking that, in the midst of this frenzied attack on the Rutulians, an elaborate working out of the shame he feels for failing to protect Pallas, Aeneas is called *pius*, here translated as "righteous." He will again be called *pius* when hurling a spear at Mezentius (X.783) and when he has killed Lausus (X.830). Bloody vengeance is a part of Aeneas's duty to the gods, the Roman poet indicates with some grimness. See note at IV.393 on the cost of piety.

10: **X.606–27.** The exchange between Jupiter and Juno here once again touches on the role of fate and its mutability, on which see note at I.2.

11: **X.637.** One of the more bizarre episodes in the battle books of the *Aeneid*, the figure of the phantom Aeneas is ultimately based on a similar moment from Book Five of the *Iliad*, where Aeneas is rescued from Diomedes.

12: **X.895–906.** In this final exchange between Mezentius and Aeneas, it is the former whose noble acceptance of death in combat draws our admiration. In his boasting Aeneas here seems petty, and we never do learn whether he honors his enemy's dying request for a common tomb with Lausus.

Book XI

1: **XI.29–81.** The funeral of Pallas is inspired to some degree by that of Patroclus in the *Iliad*. In *Falling Asleep Over the Aeneid* (1948), Robert Lowell dreams that he is Aeneas at this funeral before the imagery slides into memories of his uncle's funeral during the American Civil War.

2: **XI.68–71.** As had been the case with Euryalus, the poet likens the death of young Pallas to a flower, on which see note at IX.435–37. The question "Where have all the flowers gone?", as the lyrics of Pete Seeger's antiwar song go, is in keeping with this tradition.

3: **XI.122.** "Turnus-hating Drances" is a Rutulian politician and the bane of Turnus throughout the debates of Book XI. He is later said to be a brilliant speaker though somewhat venal, who from "his high-born mother / He'd achieved his status—not his nothing father" (XI.340–41). It is likely that Virgil here is depicting a *novus homo*, "new man," a type of politician in Rome who had risen to prominence due to his talents rather than his lineage. The most notable of these in the late Republic was Marcus Tullius Cicero, though whether Virgil is casting aspersions on him indirectly is hard to say. The portrait of Drances is likewise derived in some part from Thersites, the ugliest man of the Greek army, who disparages Agamemnon in *Iliad* Book Two.

4: **XI.158–82.** In Evander's mourning for Pallas, Virgil alludes to Priam's lament over Hector in *Iliad* Twenty-four. We might also compare the Arcadian king's wish to have taken his son's place in death (XI.163) with the grieving words of King David in the Hebrew Bible, "O my son Absalom, my son, my son Absalom! Would God I had died for thee, O Absalom, my son, my son!" (2 Samuel 18:33)

5: **XI.252–93.** According to later tradition, Diomedes, the Greek warrior whose heroism is memorably depicted in Book Five of the *Iliad* (some of which is recounted here), had settled after the Trojan War in Argyripa in northern Italy. An embassy had been sent to him at VIII.9–17, but he refuses to engage again with Aeneas (who remembers the encounter himself with "Tydeus' son, greatest Danaan of them all," I.96).

6: **XI.498.** Camilla, the virgin warrior princess of the Volscians, comes to Turnus as an ally. An Italian version of the famous Amazon warrior Penthesilea, her backstory is filled out by Diana in conversation with the nymph Opis (XI.535–95). Like Aeneas, she too is an exile (XI.542). A character entirely of Virgil's own creation, Camilla represents an admirable female character with many courageous achievements on the battlefield. Her death, however, will be caused by a "female lust for spoils" for the Phrygian armor of Chloreus (XI.782), though Virgil softens this condemnation by suggesting that she may have wanted to dedicate it as a trophy to Diana.

7: **XI.648.** According to folk etymology, the word "Amazon" derived from *a-ma-zon*, "without a breast," giving rise to the idea that the warriors cut off a breast in order to better hold their bows. The artistic tradition does not bear this interpretation out, although Amazons are often depicted with a single bared breast (not always the right one, as indicated here for Camilla).

8: **XI.891–95.** Inspired by Camilla's noble death—she speaks not of herself but of the cause in her dying words (XI.823–27), the Rutulian women are newly filled with patriotism and strive to defend their walls from Trojan attack.

BOOK XII

1: **XII.64–69.** In a book filled with so many volatile moments, there is something admirable about the quiet modesty of the princess signified by her blush here. On Lavinia, a lackluster character who is nevertheless the object of great devotion and destiny, see note at VII.72. She never speaks, and so the meaning of her famous blush here is mysterious, subject to any number of interpretations. As Keats once wrote, "There's a blush for won't, and a blush for shan't, / And a blush for having done it; / There's a blush for thought, and a blush for nought, / And a blush for just begun it" in "O Blush Not So!" (1818).

2: **XII.138–46.** On Juturna, see note at X.439. The poet notes here that she has been sexually violated by Jupiter, and in return has been granted the "rapist's gift" of immortality, just as Cassandra had been given prophetic powers by Apollo (see note at II.342–44).

3: **XII.201–21.** For all his previous bluster, Turnus here wordlessly reveals his dread at the coming conflict. In contrast with the blushing Lavinia, Turnus grows pale, as both Dido (IV.499) and Cleopatra (VIII.709) had before their suicides. We are reminded in these lines, too, of the age difference between the seasoned Trojan warrior and the young Rutulian.

4: **XII.247–56.** The omen sent by Juturna of an eagle unsuccessfully attacking a flock of swans encourages the augur Tolumnius to break the truce. He has been misled by Juturna into thinking the swans represent the Rutulians, but Virgil is in fact alluding to the omen in Book I, on which see note at I.393–400.

5: **XII.311–17.** Aeneas, although he is called "good" (*pius*) here, fails to control his soldiers, or, at any rate, has the opportunity to control them taken away by the arrow by which he will be suddenly wounded (XII.319). Perhaps we should contrast this moment with the simile of the honorable statesman in Book I, on which see note at I.148–56. Aeneas's question—*Quo ruitis?* "Where are you running?" (XII.313)—is undoubtedly meant to echo the opening of Horace's *Epode 7*—*Quo, quo scelesti ruitis?*— a famous lament about the Roman civil wars. That Virgil does seem to think of this battle as civil war is implied in his direct address to Jupiter at XII.503–5.

6: **XII.391–410.** Iapyx, the aged doctor known only from this passage, is like his patient a model of filial devotion, who attempted "to put off his dying father's doom" (XII.395). The hero's wound is beyond his ability to heal, however, and requires the supernatural intervention of Venus in the next passage. Iapyx's attentive treatment of Aeneas is illustrated in a well-preserved wall painting from Pompeii.

7: **XII.412–15.** Dittany, an herb famed in antiquity for its anesthetic qualities, was native to Crete's Mount Dicte, on which see note at IV.72–73. In a learned allusion to this Virgilian scene, a magical potion called "essence of dittany" is used to heal various battle wounds in J. K. Rowling's *Harry Potter* series.

8: **XII.473–80.** This memorable simile of a swallow flying through a great house seems to have been adapted by the Venerable Bede in Book Two of his *Ecclesiastical History of the English People* (A.D. 731), where the human soul's time on earth is likened to the flight of a bird on a winter's night through a royal banquet hall.

9: **XII.503–5.** On the poet's lament to Jupiter, see note above at XII.311–17.

10: **XII.587–92.** The angry hive of this simile ought to be contrasted with the peaceful bees of the simile in Book I, see note at I.430–36.

11: **XII.603.** Amata hangs herself, as do various queens in Greek tragedy, notably Jocasta in Sophocles's *Oedipus Rex* and Phaedra in Euripides's *Hippolytus*.

12: **XII.715–22.** This epic simile of Turnus and Aeneas in combat is drawn from Virgil's own elaborate description of a bullfight from Book Four of the *Georgics*. There, the bulls battle over a heifer, as here the warriors fight for Lavinia's hand, although the larger matter of which of the two will rule is also at stake.

13: **XII.725–27.** The image of Jupiter holding up scales to indicate the fate of the combatants is drawn from Book Twenty-two of the *Iliad*. In an improvement to this epic motif, Milton indicates in *Paradise Lost* that the scales did not sink to indicate Satan's defeat but rather, because of his lesser value, "quick up flew, and kickt the beam" (4.1004).

14: **XII.766–87.** Aeneas's spear is lodged in the tree trunk dedicated to Faunus, the native Italian god favorable to the Rutulians, on whom see note at VII.47–49.

15: **XII.791–842.** Jupiter, at long last, demands that Juno accept Aeneas and his fate, and she of her own accord renounces the "savage indignation" (I.11) that has been her motivating force throughout the poem. The scene is meant to parallel Jupiter's reassurance to Venus in Book I (I.228–97).

16: **XII.797.** On *fas*, see note at II.780.

17: **XII.825.** In renouncing her anger, Juno stipulates that the Trojans must lose their language and, significantly, "the kind of clothes they wear." Their descendants, consequently, will not wear Trojan attire but rather be "the togaed Romans," as Jupiter had predicted at I.282.

18: **XII.845.** Juno's obedience assured, Jupiter now moves ahead with grim efficiency to finish off the last resistance to the Trojans' fate. Whether "the Ones That Mortals Dread," *Dirae* in Latin, are to be distinguished from the Furies is a matter of scholarly debate, though their fearsome nature is beyond doubt.

19: **XII.862–64.** The creature here is evidently an owl, such as the one that haunted Dido, on which see note at IV.461–62.

20: **XII.941–44.** On Pallas's belt, see note at X.495–509.

21: **XII.951.** On the buckling of Turnus's knees, see note on Aeneas at I.92–96.

22: **XII.945–52.** The combat between the Trojan and Rutulian heroes now finds its final resolution in Aeneas's angry slaying of Turnus. The cultural background to this moment is rich and multilayered: It is difficult not to see, for instance, a broad allusion to the civil war between Octavian and Mark Antony, explicitly referenced on the shield of Aeneas (VIII.685), although the victory of the hero from the East over the defender of Italy is sternly ironic. From Homer, we can recognize the duel of Paris and Menelaus in *Iliad* Book Three and, even more significantly, the death of Hector at Achilles's hands from *Iliad* Book Twenty-two. But whereas in

Book Twenty-four, Homer had depicted Priam's noble act of humiliation before his son's killer and Achilles's act of graciousness, Virgil ends the *Aeneid* here without resolution. In the fifteenth century, Maffeo Vegio wrote a thirteenth book of the *Aeneid* to tie up what some consider to be the loose ends of the epic, but perhaps Virgil's abrupt conclusion is not a literary failing but an intentional political commentary.

Selected Glossary

This glossary includes names of most persons, divinities, and places as well as many distinctive cultural, mythological, or historical terms mentioned in the *Aeneid*. It also glosses various foreign or uncommon words and phrases (most of them from Latin) found in the translation. Synonyms, demonyms, and adjectival forms of names are also sometimes provided. Entries for Roman deities often give the names of equivalent Greek deities within square brackets.

Abas (1): Trojan chief. I.121

Abas (2): Greek warrior. III.287

Abas (3): Etruscan ally of Aeneas. X.170

Acamus: Greek warrior. II.264

Acarnania (adj.: Acarnanian): region of west Greece. V.299

Acca: Camilla's most trusted companion. XI.821

Acesta: city founded by Aeneas in Sicily. V.718

Acestes: Trojan who became a king in Sicily. I.195

Achaea (adj.: Achaean): part of the northern Peloponnese. By extension, another word for Greece. I.242

Achaemenides: comrade of Ulysses, abandoned by him on the island of the Cyclopes. III.614

Achates: Aeneas's most trusted companion. I.121

Acheron: one of the five rivers of the Underworld. VI.107

Achilles: greatest Greek hero of the Trojan War. Slayer of Hector who was in turn slain by Paris. I.30

Acoetes: servant of Evander and then companion of Pallas. XI.31

Acragas: city of Sicily. III.703

Acrisius: king of Argos, father of Danäe, and grandfather of the hero Perseus. VII.372

Actium: promontory of western Greece, site of a famous victory by Octavian (the future Caesar Augustus) over Antony and his lover, the Egyptian queen Cleopatra in 31 B.C. VIII.675

Actor (1): Trojan warrior. IX.500

Actor (2): an Auruncan warrior. XII.94

Adamastus: father of Achaemenides. III.614

Adrastus: king of Argos killed at Thebes. VI.480

Adriatic: sea off the east coast of Italy. XI.405

Aeacid: descendant of Aeacus, great-grandfather of Pyrrhus. VI.841

Aeacus: grandfather of Achilles. III.296

Aeaea (adj.: Aeaean): island of the witch Circe. III.386

Aegaeon: One of the hundred-handed giants. X.564. Another name for Briareus. VI.287

Aegean: the part of the Mediterranean Sea between Greece and Asia Minor. III.74

Aegis: Minerva's magic breastplate. III.544

Aeneadae: name given by Aeneas to a settlement in Thrace. III.18

Aeneas: son of Venus (thus, "goddess-born") and the Trojan prince Anchises. Leader of the Trojan survivors who sail to Italy. I.92

Aeolia: island near Sicily, kingdom of Aeolus. I.51

Aeolian: pertaining to a group of islands near Sicily that includes Aeolia. VIII.417

Aeolid: descendant of Aeolus—e.g., Ulysses, rumored in Greek tragedy to have been the son of Sisyphus, and thus grandson of Sisyphus's father, Aeolus (1). VI.529

Aeolus (1): god of the winds, whose kingdom is Aeolia. I.52

Aeolus (2): various less important mortal Greeks and Trojans of this name, e.g., XII.542

Aethon: horse of Pallas. XI.89

Aetna: volcano in Sicily. III.554

Aetolia (adj.: Aetolian): district in north Greece, home of Diomedes; also used for his home in Italy. X.28

Agamemnon: king of Mycenae, brother of Menelaus, commander in chief of the Greeks at Troy. III.55

Agathyrsians: people of Scythia (southeast Europe). IV.146

Agenor: Phoenician king, brother of Belus, descended from a family originally of Argos in Greece. I.338

Agrippa: friend of Augustus. VIII.682

Agylla: Etruscan city. VII.651

Ajax: Greek hero of the Trojan War, also known in mythology as Ajax son of Oïleus, or Ajax the Lesser; he was punished by Minerva for violating her temple. I.42

Alba (Alban): Alba Longa. I.7

Alba Longa: city founded by Ascanius near the future site of Rome and closely identified with it. I.272

Albula: early name for the river Tiber. VIII.332

Albunea: mountain in Latium, which stands over a famous spring also called Albunea. VII.83

Alcanor: Trojan, father of Pandarus (2) and Bitias. IX.673

Alcides: descendant of Alcaeus; also called Hercules. V.414

Alecto: one of the three Furies; virgin of Cocytus. VII.324

Aletes: Trojan chief. I.121

Allia: river north of Rome, called "Fate-cursed" because of a Roman defeat by the Gauls in 365 B.C. VII.718

Aloeus: father of two giant sons who piled up mountains to attack Zeus. VI.582

Alpheus: river near Olympia in Greece that supposedly ran under the sea to Sicily. III.694

Altars, the: a rock reef south of Sicily. I.109

Amasenus: river in Latium. VII. 685

Amata: wife of Latinus. VII.344

Amathus: a town in Cyprus. X.51

Amazons: race of female warriors. I.490

Amphitryoniades: Hercules, stepson of Amphitryon. VIII.213

Amphrysian, the: a Thessalian river associated with Apollo and, by extension, with his priestess the Sibyl of Cumae. VI.398

Amsanctus Vale: valley in Italy with an entrance to the Underworld. VII.564

Amyclae: town on the coast of Latium. X.564

Amycus (1): famous boxer. V.373

Amycus (2): various Trojans of this name, e.g., I.221

Anchises: Trojan prince and father of Aeneas. I.618

ancile **(Latin)**: a sacred shield from heaven. VII.188

Ancus: early king of Rome. VI.815

Androgeos (1): Greek warrior. II.371

Androgeos (2): son of King Minos of Crete. VI.20

Andromache: wife of Hector, later married to the Trojan Helenus. II.456

Anius: king of the island Ortygia (Delos) and priest of Phoebus. III.80

Anna: Dido's sister. IV.9

Antandros: town near Troy. III.6

Antenor: Trojan leader who settled in northern Italy and founded Padua. I.241

Antheus: Trojan warrior. I.182

Antiphates: Trojan warrior, son of Sarpedon. IX.697

Antony: Mark Antony, a rival of Octavian's defeated by him at the Battle of Actium in 31 B.C. VIII.685

Antores: Greek from Argos who came to live in Pallanteum. X.778

Anubis: jackal-headed Egyptian god of the Underworld. VIII.698

Apennines: range of mountains running north and south through central Italy. XI.699

Apollo/Phoebus: son of Jupiter and Latona; sun-god and twin brother of Diana/Trivia. II.121

Aquicolus: a Rutulian. IX.684

Araxes: river in Armenia. VIII.728

Arcadia, Arcadians: mountainous area of southern Greece; colonists from Arcadia founded Pallanteum on the site of Rome before the Trojan War. V.300

Arcens: a Sicilian. IX.582

Archippus: king of the Marruvians in Latium. VII.752

Arcturus: the star Alpha Boötis, one of the brightest in the sky. I.744

Ardea: capital city of the Rutulians. VII.411

Arethusa: nymph pursued by the river-god Alpheus. III.696

Argiletum: area in Rome. VIII.345

Argive (adj. and noun): Greek. II.178; II.259

Argos: city in south Greece and, by extension, Greece itself. I.24

Argus (1): hundred-eyed guard of Io. VII.791

Argus (2): a stranger murdered at the place later called Argiletum. VII.346

Argylla: Caere, town in Etruria. VIII.478

Argyripa: a town in southern Italy, later called Arpi. XI.247

Aricia: site north of Rome of a famous temple of Diana; personified as a nymph, mother of Virbius. VII.762

Arisba: a town near Troy. IX.264

Arpi: city in Italy, founded by the Greek Diomedes. VIII.10

Arruns: Etruscan ally of Aeneas. XI.759

Artemis (adj.: Artemisian): Diana. XI.582

Ascanius: son of Aeneas and Creusa; also called Iulus and, until the fall of Troy, Ilus. I.267

Asia: Asia Minor. II.194

Asilas (1): Rutulian archer. IX.572

Asilas (2): Etruscan prophet and ally of Aeneas. X.175

Assaracus: early king of Troy who was grandfather of Anchises and great-grandfather of Aeneas. I.284

Astur: Etruscan ally of Aeneas. X.180

Astyanax: son of Hector and Andromache. II.458

Athesis: river of northern Italy. IX.681

Athos: mountain in north Greece. XII.701

Atinas: leader of the Rutulians. XI.869

Atlas: giant who held the sky on his shoulders. I.741

Atreus: king of Mycenae and father of Agamemnon and Menelaus. II.416

Atrides: the sons of Atreus, Agamemnon and Menelaus. I.458

atrium (English loanword from Latin; pl.: atria): open-air architectural space such as those often found in ancient Roman homes. II.484

Atys: Trojan youth. V.568

Aufidus: river that bisects Apulia. XI.405

Augustus Caesar/Caesar Augustus/Octavian: great nephew as well as adopted son and heir of Julius Caesar. He took the title Augustus after defeating Antony and Cleopatra at Actium. First emperor of Rome. VI.792

Aulestes: Etruscan ally of Aeneas. X.207

Aulis: port in eastern Greece where the Greek fleet left to sail to Troy. IV.425

Aunus: Ligurian ally of Turnus. XI.717

Aurora [Eos]/Dawn: personification of dawn. IV.6

Auruncan (adj.: Auruncan): member of an early people of Italy, who lived south of Rome. VII.206

Ausonia, Ausonian: Italy, Italian/Hesperia, Hesperian. III.170

Auster [Notus]: god and personification of the South Wind. II.111

Automedon: Greek leader. II.477

Aventine: one of the hills of Rome. VII.660

Aventinus: son of Hercules and the priestess Rhea. VII.655

Avernus: lake and its surroundings near Cumae (modern-day Cuma, in Italy) whose air was thought to be deadly to birds and where lies an entrance to the Underworld. III.443

Bacchus (adj.: Bacchic) [Dionysos]/Liber: god of wine, son of Zeus and the Theban princess Semele. I.734

Bactra: capital of Bactria, Asiatic land near India. VIII.688

Baiae: town near Cumae. IX.710

Bebrycia (adj.: Bebrycian): country in Asia Minor. V.373

Bellona: Roman goddess of war. VII.319

Belus: Phoenician king, brother of Agenor and father of Dido. I.621

Benacus: lake of north Italy and its personification from which the river Mincius flows. X.205

Berecyntian: of Berecyntus, mountain in Phrygia where Cybele was worshipped. IX.82

Beroë: old Trojan woman, impersonated by the goddess Iris. V.620

Bitias (1): bibulous member of Dido's court. I.738

Bitias (2): Trojan warrior, brother of Pandarus (2), who was killed by Turnus. IX.672

Bola: Italian city. VI.776

Boreas: god and personification of the North Wind. X.351

Briareus: one of three giant brothers with a hundred hands and fifty heads. VI.287

Brontes: a Cyclops. VIII.425

Brutus: Lucius Junius Brutus, founder of the Roman Republic, who killed his sons for treason (not to be confused with Marcus Junius Brutus, an assassin of Julius Caesar). VI.818

Butes (1): famous boxer. V.372

Butes (2): servant of Anchises, then companion to Ascanius. IX.647

Butes (3): Trojan killed by Camilla. XI.690

Buthrotum: city in Epirus in northwest Greece (modern-day Butrint in Albania). III.293

Cacus: fire-breathing giant son of Vulcan. VIII.195

Caeculus: ally of Turnus and son of Vulcan. VII.678

Caedicus: wealthy Latin. IX.360

Caeneus: mythical girl who changed into a man and then back into a woman. VI.448

Caere/Argylla: former home of the Etruscan king Mezentius, against whom his people revolted and whom they exiled. VIII.597

Caesar: Roman imperial title derived from a family name of Caius Julius Caesar and of his adopted son Octavian (Augustus Caesar). I.286

Caicus: Trojan warrior. I.183

Caieta: city on the Italian coast near Rome, named for Aeneas's nurse. VI.900

Calchas: prophet of the Greeks in the Trojan War. II.101

Calliope: a Muse. IX.526

Calybe: priestess of Juno. VII.419

Calydon: city on the west coast of Greece, home of the famous hunter Meleager. VII.306

Camerina: city of Sicily. III.700

Camers: Rutulian warrior. X.563

Camilla: virgin warrior who is leader of the Volscians and ally of Turnus. VII.803

Camillus: conqueror of the Gauls in the fourth century B.C. VI.825

Campania (adj.: Campanian): region southeast of Latium; its main city is Capua, from Capys (1). X.145

Caphereus: promontory on the island Euboea, where much of the Greek navy was shipwrecked on their return from Troy. XI.261

Capitol: the Capitoline Hill in Rome. VIII.348

Capitoline: the capitol in Rome. VI.836

Capreae: the island Capri, near Naples. VII.736

Capys (1): Trojan warrior after whom the Campanian city of Capua was named. I.183

Capys (2): king of Alba Longa. VI.768

Carians: people of southwest Asia Minor. VIII.724

Carinae: a section of Rome. VIII.362

Carmental: gate in Rome near the shrine of the nymph Carmentis. VIII.339

Carmentis: a prophetic nymph, mother of Evander. VIII.336

Carthage: a Phoenician colony in North Africa and Rome's great rival during the Punic Wars. 364–146 B.C. I.13

Casmilla: mother of Camilla. XI.543

Caspian, Caspians: of the Caspian Sea in Asia and the area around it. VI.798

Cassandra: virgin daughter of Priam, prophetess whose predictions were destined not to be believed. Slain by Ajax, son of Oïleus. II.247

casus belli **(Latin)**: cause of war. VII.553

Catiline: Roman aristocrat who tried to seize power in 63 B.C., but was prevented and executed. VI.668

Catillus: ally of Turnus from Tibur. VII.671

Cato: early Roman statesman. VI.842

Caucasus: mountains between Europe and Asia. IV.366

Caulonia: Greek colony in Italy. III.554

Celaeno: Harpy with prophetic powers. III.211

cenotaph (English, from Latin): empty tomb, or memorial to a deceased person whose corpse lies elsewhere. VI.505

Centaur **(1)**: ship commanded by Sergestus in the funeral games for Anchises. V.121

Centaur (2): a race of mythical beasts with the body of a horse and the head and arms of a man. VI.287

Ceraunia: Sicilian promontory. III.506

Cerberus: multiheaded dog who guards the entrance to the Underworld. VI.417

Ceres [Demeter]: goddess of vegetation, sister of Jupiter. II.715

cestuses (English, from Latin): ancient gloves for boxing or fighting. V.364

Chaon: son of Priam. III.336

Chaonia, Chaonian: most northwest part of Greece. III.292

Chaos: personification of the Underworld, as well as of the unlimited void at the beginning of the world. IV.511

Charon: ferryman who carries souls of the dead across the river Styx. VI.298

Charybdis: whirlpool monster on the south side of the strait between Italy and Sicily. III.420

Chimaera (1): fire-breathing three-bodied monster killed by the hero Bellerophon. VI.288

Chimaera **(2)**: ship commanded by Gyas in the funeral games for Anchises. V.118

Chloreus: priest of Cybele and ally of Aeneas. VII.768

chori **(Latin, from** *choros***, split into)**: split into halves. V.560

choros **(Latin)**: kind of dance. IV.145

Circe: witch goddess who bewitched Ulysses's men in the *Odyssey* and made Picus a woodpecker. III.386

Circus: a place for Roman games. VIII.636

Cisseus: king of Thrace and father of Priam's wife Hecuba. V.536

Cithaeron: mountain near Thebes in Greece. IV.303

Civic Oak: source of leaves for a crown for those accomplishing great deeds in the civic realm. VI.772

Clarian: of Claros, a city in Ionia and center of the worship of Apollo. III.360

Clausus: Sabine prince and ally of Turnus. VII.706

Cloanthus: Trojan warrior and commander of the *Scylla*. I.221

Cloelia: a Roman girl captured by the Etruscans who escaped and swam across the Tiber. VIII.651

Clonus: artist who made the sword-belt of Pallas. X.499

Clusium: Etruscan city. X.167

Cnossian: of Cnossus (Knossos); Gnossian. Also, an inhabitant of Cnossus, home of King Minos of Crete, site of the Labyrinth, as well as of his brother, Rhadamanthus. III.115

Cocles: the famous Roman Horatius who held a bridge against the Etruscans. VIII.650

Cocytus: one of the five rivers of the Underworld. VI.132

Coeus: a Titan, son of Earth and brother of Enceladus and Rumor. IV.179

Collatia: Italian city. VI.774

Cora: Italian city. VI.776

Coras: Greek who founded Tibur in Italy with his brothers Catillus and Tiburtus. VII.670

Corinth: city in southern Greece, conquered by the Romans in 146 B.C. VI.837

Coroebus: Trojan warrior, in love with Cassandra. II.342

Corybants: cymbal-clashing priests of the Asian mother goddess Cybele. III.111

Corynaeus (1): Trojan priest. VI.228

Corynaeus (2): Trojan warrior. XII.299

Corythus: Etruscan town. III.170

Cosae: Etruscan city. X.168

Cossus: Roman general. VI.842

cothurnus (English from Latin): a kind of high boot. I.337

Crete: large island south of Greece, home of King Minos and the Labyrinth. III.104

Cretheus: Trojan musician. IX.775

Creusa: wife of Aeneas. II.563

Crinisus: river-god of Sicily. V.38

Cumae/Cumaea: town between Rome and Naples, home of the Sibyl and entrance to the Underworld. III.442

Cupavo: Ligurian warrior, son of Cycnus. X.187

Cupid [Eros]: son of Venus and god of Love. I.658

Cures: Sabine city, home of Numa and Tatius. VI.811

Curetes: inhabitants of Crete, including its priests of Jupiter, who protected him there in his infancy by clashing cymbals to drown out the sound of his crying so Saturn wouldn't know he was there. III.131

curule (English loanword from Latin): high office, authority. III.452

Cybele [Rheia]: mother goddess of Asia (Phrygia), recognized by the Romans as the Great Mother. III.111

Cybelus: mountain of Asia Minor sacred to the goddess Cybele. XI.768

Cyclades (adj.: Cycladic): Aegean islands south of Athens. III.127

Cyclopean/Cyclopian: of the Cyclopes, one-eyed giants. VIII.419

Cyclops (pl.: Cyclops or Cyclopes) (1): member of a race of one-eyed giants of Sicily, in particular, Polyphemus. I.202

Cyclops (2): laborers in the forge of Vulcan. VI.631

Cycnus: Ligurian king who changed into a swan while mourning for Phaëthon. X.189

Cydonian: from Cydon, a city in Crete. XII.858

Cyllene (adj.: Cyllenian): mountain in Arcadia, birthplace of Mercury. IV.256

Cymodocea: sea-nymph. X.225

Cymothoë: a sea-nymph, daughter of Nereus. I.144

Cynthus (adj.: Cynthian): mountain on the island Delos, birthplace of Apollo and Artemis. I.498

Cyprus: large island in the eastern Mediterranean Sea. I.622

Cythera: island favored by Venus. I.681

Cytherea: Cytherean: a name for Venus (from Cythera, one of her favorite islands). I.257

Daedalus: famous inventor, architect, and designer; builder of the Labyrinth in Crete. VI.14

Dahae: Scythian people from beyond the Caspian Sea. VIII.728

Danaan: Greek. I.96

Danäe: mother of Perseus; she went to Italy and founded the city of Ardea, Turnus's capital. VII.410

Dardania, Dardans, Dardanians (adj.: Dardan, Dardanian): Troy, Trojans, descendants of Dardanus. I.495

Dardanidae: sons of Dardanus, Trojans VI.83

Dardanus: son of Jupiter and Electra, ancestor of the Trojan kings. III.167

Dares: Trojan boxer in the funeral games for Anchises. V.368

Daunian: Rutulian, from Daunus, an ancestor of Turnus. VIII.146

Daunus: father of Turnus. X.616

Dawn: Aurora, personification of dawn. I.751

Decii: two father and son consuls named Decius, both famous warriors. VI.824

Deiopea: a nymph, attendant of Juno. I.73.

Deïphobe: the Sybil of Cumae; the seer of the Amphrysian; prophetess and priestess of Apollo and Hecate. VI.34

Deïphobus: son of Priam, who married Helen after the death of Paris. II.311

Delian, the: a name for Apollo, from his association with Delos. III.162

Delos, Delian: Aegean island also known as Ortygia, birthplace of Apollo and Diana/Artemis. IV.145

Demoleos: Greek warrior. V.260

Dercennus: old king of Laurentium. XI.851

Diana [Artemis]; also Dian/Trivia/Phoebe: daughter of Jupiter and Latona, twin sister of Apollo, huntress goddess, goddess of the moon and closely identified with Hecate. I.499

Dictaea (adj.: Dictaean): mountain in Crete. III.171

Dido/Elissa/Dido-Perdita: queen of Carthage, originally from Phoenicia. I.299

Didymaon: an artist. V.360

Dindymus: mountain in Asia Minor connected with the worship of Cybele. IX.618

Diomedes: Greek hero who fought Aeneas in the Trojan War and who later settled in Italy, founding Arpi. I.752

Dione: mother of Venus. III.19

Diores: Trojan aristocrat. V.297

Dirae [Erinyes]: the three Furies, goddesses of retribution and guilt. IV.473

Dis: Hades, god and personification of the Underworld; see also Elysium, Tartarus, and Styx. IV.703

Discord [Eris]: Roman goddess of strife. VIII.702

Dodona: site of the oracle of Jupiter in northwest Greece. III.466

Dolon: Trojan spy in the Trojan War, father of Eumedes. XII.347

Dolopians (adj.: Dolopian): members of Achilles's troops from Dolopia, in Thessaly. II.7

Donysa: small Aegean island. III.126

Doric: Greek. II.27

Doris: sea-goddess and mother of the Nereids. III.74

Doryclus: Greek from Epirus and husband of Beroë. V.620

Doto: a Nereid nymph. IX.102

Drances: Rutulian leader and speaker opposed to Turnus. XI.122

Drepanum: city on the west tip of Sicily. III.707

Drusi: famous Roman family that included Livia Drusilla, wife of Caesar Augustus. VI.824

Dryope: a forest nymph. X.550

Dryopes: people of northern Greece. IV.146

Dulichium: island of the Ionian Sea. III.270

Dymas: Trojan leader. II.342

Earth: personification of the earth, mother of all. IV.166

Egeria: Latin nymph associated with Diana whose groves provided a hiding place for the resurrected Hippolytus. VII.763

Electra: daughter of Atlas and mother of Dardanus; also one of the Pleiades. (Not to be confused with Electra daughter of Agamemnon and Clytemnestra.) VIII.135

Elis: area of Olympia in the western Peloponnese. III.695

Elissa: Dido. IV.335

Elysium: home of the blessed in the Underworld. V.735

empyre, the (archaic English): the highest heaven. X.144

Enceladus: son of Earth and brother of Coeus and Rumor; a giant who fought against Jupiter. III.578

Entellus: Sicilian boxer. V.387

Epeus: Greek leader, builder of the Trojan Horse. II.265

Epirus: the northwest region of ancient Greece. III.292

Epytus: Trojan leader. II.341

Erato: Muse of poetry. VII.37

Erebus/Pluto/Orcus/Dis: god and personification of the Underworld; see also Elysium, Tartarus, and Styx. IV.26

Eridanus: river in Hades's Elysium associated with the Po. VI.659

Eriphyle: woman of Argos who forced her husband to go to war and was killed by her son Alcmaeon. VI.445

Erulus: king of Praeneste who had three lives and three sets of arms and was son of the goddess Feronia. VIII.562

Erymanthus: river and mountain of Arcadia in Greece where Hercules captured a wild boar. V.449

Eryx (1): son of Venus and half-brother of Aeneas, who settled in Sicily. V.24

Eryx (2): mountain in Sicily. I.570

Etruria (adj.: Etrurian): the Etruscan lands north of Rome. VIII.494

Etruscan: of Etruria, an area north of Rome. VIII.480

Euboea: second-largest Greek island, which sent colonists to Cumae in Italy. VI.2

euhoe **(Greek)**: cry of joy used by the devotees of Bacchus. VII.389

Eumedes: a Trojan, son of the spy Dolon. XII.346

Eumelus: a Trojan. V.664

Eumenides: Furies. IV.469

Euphrates: river of Mesopotamia. VIII.726

Eurotas: river of Sparta; a city in south Greece. I.498

Eurus: god and personification of the East Wind. I.139

Euryalus: Trojan youth, beloved of the Trojan Nisus. V.294

Eurypylus: Trojan messenger. II.114

Eurystheus: king of Mycenae, master of Hercules during his labors. VIII.292

Eurytion: Lycian archer. V.495

Eurytus: father of Clonus. X.499

Evadne: wife of Capaneus who died on his funeral pyre. VI.447

Evander: Parrhasian Evander: Greek king who, before the Trojan War, led colonists from Greek Arcadia to found Pallanteum on the future site of Rome; the founder of Rome's fortress. VIII.51

Fabii: early Roman family with many famous leaders, especially Fabius Maximus (nicknamed "Cunctator," the "Delayer," for strategically delaying battle with Hannibal). VI.845

Fabricius: Roman consul, famous for his honesty. VI.844

Faith: Roman goddess of fidelity. I.292

fane (archaic English): temple. II.166

fas **(Latin)**: speakable, in the godly sense. II.780

fasces: English loan word from plural of *fascis*. VI.818

fascis **(Latin)**: a firebrand or rod, usually part of a bundle (fasces) that symbolized authority and was used ceremonially in ancient Rome. X.705

Fates: the Parcae, three goddess sisters who spun, measured, and cut the thread that determined a person's life span. I.39

Faunus [Pan]: grandson of Saturn and father of Latinus, he became a god of the woods and meadows. VII.47

Feronia: Italian goddess, sometimes associated with Juno. VII.800

Fidena: Italian city. VI.773

fons et origo (**Latin**): source and origin. VII.50

Fortune: Fortuna, personified goddess of chance, often similar to Fate. II.79

Forum: the center of Rome, an open area with temples, colonnades, and public buildings. VIII.361

Furor: personified Rage or Madness. I.295

Fury, Furies (1) [Erinyes]: three goddesses of retribution and guilt. III.330

Fury, Furies (2): another name for the Harpies. III.252

Gabii (adj.: Gabine): Italian city. VI.773

Gaetuli, Gaetulian: tribe of north Africa. IV.40

Galaesus: old, rich, and peaceful Italian. VII.535

Galatea: a Nereid nymph. IX.103

Ganges: river of India. IX.29

Ganymede: Trojan prince, loved by Jupiter (more than his children by Juno). I.28

Garamantian: of the Garamantes, a people of Libya. IV.198

Garganus: mountain ridge in Apulia. XI.246

Gauls: tribes living in what is now France, perennial enemies of early Rome. VIII.655

Gela: river and city of Sicily. III.702

Gelonian: Scythian people who lived in what is now Ukraine. VIII.725

genius: a place's or person's attendant spirit or deity. V.95

gens (**Latin**): family. VI.580

Geryon: three-bodied or three-headed warrior killed by Hercules during his tenth labor. VI.289

Getae: a tribe of Thrace. III.36

Glaucus (1): prophetic sea-god. V.823

Glaucus (2): shade of a Trojan warrior, the son of Antenor. VI.483

Glaucus (3): Trojan killed in a charge by Turnus. XII.343

Gnosian: of Gnosius [Knossos], city of Crete, home of King Minos. V.306

Gorgons: Medusa and her two sisters; they had snakes for hair and turned men to stone with their eyes. II.615

Gortynian: of Gortys, a city in Crete. XI.773

Gracchi: plural of Gracchus, name of two famous Roman statesmen. VI.842

Gradivus: name for Mars. III.35

Graviscae: Etruscan town. X.184

Great Bear, the: the constellation Ursa Major. I.745

Grynean: of Gryneum, town in Asia Minor with an oracle of Apollo. IV.345

Gyaros: Cycladic island. III. 77

Gyas: Trojan leader and, in the funeral games for Anchises, pilot of the *Chimaera*. I.221

Gylippus: an Arcadian. XII.272

Hades/Pluto/Erebus/Orcus/Dis: god and personification of the Underworld; see also Elysium, Tartarus, and Styx. IV.387

Haemon: a Rutulian, son of Mars. IX.685

Haemonides: priest of Apollo and Diana. X.537

Halaesus: son of Agamemnon and Briseis, who emigrated to Italy and became an ally of Turnus. VII.724

Hammon: North African Jupiter and father of Iarbus. IV.198

Harpalyce: a princess of Thrace, the northeast region of Greece. I.316

Harpy, Harpies: mythical monsters, half-bird and half-woman. III.211

Hebrus: a river in Thrace. I.317

Hecate: Underworld goddess, closely identified with witchcraft, crossroads, and Diana. IV.510

Hector: greatest Trojan hero in the Trojan War. I.99

Hecuba: wife of Priam and mother of Hector. II.502

Helen: stepdaughter of the Spartan king Tyndareus and wife of the Lacedaemonian king Menelaus who eloped with the Trojan prince Paris (thus starting the Trojan War). She married Paris's brother Deïphobus after Paris's death and betrayed him to the Greeks. I.649

Helenor: Trojan warrior. IX.544

Helenus: son of Priam and slave to Pyrrhus who took Hector's widow (and Pyrrhus's slave-wife) Andromache as his wife after Pyrrhus tired of her. III.295

Helikon: Greek mountain, one of the homes of the Muses. VII.641

Helorus: river of eastern Sicily. III.699

Helymus: Sicilian leader. V.73

Hercules [Herakles]: also Alcides or Amphitryoniades; hero known for his great strength and accomplishment of twelve great labors. Son of Jupiter and the mortal woman Alcmena. III.551

Hermes: Mercury, son of Jupiter and Maia, messenger of the gods. IV.238

Hermione: daughter of Helen whose pursuit by Pyrrhus drove the jealous Orestes to kill him. III.328

Hermus: river of Asia Minor. VII.721

Hesione: sister of Priam. VIII.158

Hesperia: Italy: Italia: Ausonia. I.530

Hesperides: nymphs who guard a paradise garden with a magic golden apple tree. IV.484

Hipocöon: Trojan archer. V.492

Hippolyte: Amazon queen and mother of Hippolytus. XI.661

Hippolytus: Virbius (2) and son of Theseus who died and then was brought back to life in Italy by Diana. VII.761

Homole: mountain in Thessaly. VII.675

Hours, the: goddesses of the seasons and time. III.512

Hyades: the constellation "Rainy Ones." I.745

Hydra: nine-headed monster killed by Hercules in his second labor. VI.576

Hylaeus: a Centaur. VIII.294

Hypanis: Trojan leader. II.342

Hyrcania (adj.: Hyrcanian): a region near the Caspian Sea. IV.367

Hyrtacus (1): a Trojan archer, the father of Hipocöon. V.492

Hyrtacus (2): a Trojan, the father of Nisus. IX.177

Iaera: mother of Pandarus (2) and Bitias (2). IX.673

Iapygian: from Apulia, a region of southern Italy. XI.246

Iapyx (1): Trojan physician. XII.391

Iapyx (2): place in southern Italy. VIII.710

Iarbas: North African chief and suitor of Dido. IV.37

Iasius: son of Jupiter and Electra and brother of Dardanus; a forefather of Troy. III.168

Iasus (1): father of Palinurus. V.843

Iasus (2): father of the physician Iapyx. XII.391

Icarus: son of Daedalus. VI.31

Ida (1) (adj.: Idaean): mountain in Western Anatolia near Troy; also called Phrygian Ida. II.697

Ida (2): mountain of Crete where Jupiter was raised. III.105

Ida (3): a Trojan huntress and perhaps the mother of Nisus IX.177

Idaeus (1): charioteer of Priam. VI.485

Idaeus (2): Trojan warrior. IX.500

Idalia (adj.: Idalian): mountain of the island Cyprus. V.760

Idalium: mountain of the island Cyprus. I.682

Idomeneus: warrior of Crete who fought on the Greek side in the Trojan War and settled in Italy. III.121

ignis fatuus **(Latin)**: will-o'-the-wisp. VI.61

Ilia: another name of Rhea Silvia, mother of Romulus and Remus. I.273

Ilian: Trojan. I.97

Ilione: oldest daughter of Priam, king of Troy. I.653

Ilioneus: Trojan chief. I.120

Ilium: Troy. I.457

Illyria: the region on the east side of the Adriatic Sea, across from Italy. I.243

Ilus (1): a name of Ascanius used before the fall of Troy. I.268

Ilus (2): early king of Troy. VI.651

Ilus (3): a Rutulian. X.400

Ilva: island off the Etruscan coast. X.173

Inachus: first king of Argos and river-god. VII.287

Inarime: an island near Cumae. IX.715

Indian: inhabitant of India. VI.795

Ino: woman of Thebes who was changed into a sea-goddess. V.823

Inus's Fort: Castrum Inui, a city in Latium. VI.775

Io: daughter of Inachus and princess of Argos who was loved by Jupiter and changed into a cow by jealous Juno. VII.790

Ionian Seas: the part of the Mediterranean Sea between Italy and Greece. III.210

Iopas: Carthaginian singer. I.741

Iphitus: Trojan leader. II.436

Iris: goddess of the rainbow and Juno's messenger. IV.695

Italus: mythical king of Italy. VII.178

Ithaca, Ithacan: Ionian island, home of Ulysses. II.104

Iulus: son of Aeneas and Creusa; also called Ascanius. I.267

Ixion: criminal who tried to rape Juno, punished in the Underworld on a fiery wheel. VI.601

Janus: ancient Italian god of thresholds who had two faces, one looking one way, the other the opposite way. VII.180

Jove (adj.: Jovian): Jupiter, king of the gods, as well as brother and husband of Juno. I.43

jugeri **(Latin; sing.:** *jugerum***)**: unit of measurement used by the Romans for area; roughly 233' x 116' (British imperial). VI.596

Julius: a family name of Caius Julius Caesar, who was supposedly descended from Iulus, and which was taken by his great-nephew and adopted son Octavian, the emperor Augustus (C. Julius Caesar Octavianus). I.288

Juno [Hera] (adj.: Junonian): Saturnian Juno, jealous wife and sister of Jupiter, enemy of Troy and patroness of all enemies of Troy. I.5

Jupiter [Zeus]: Jove, king of the gods raised on Crete's Mount Ida, as well as brother and husband of Juno. His power is limited only by the Fates. I.223

Juturna: water-nymph, sister of Turnus. X.439

Kids: the constellation Haedi. IX.668

Labyrinth: the maze built by Daedalus in Crete to imprison the Minotaur. V.489

Lacinian: of Lacinia; location in south Italy of a temple of Juno. III.552

Laconia: region of Sparta. II.601

lacrimae rerum (**Latin**): literally, the tears of things. I.462

Laertes: father of Ulysses [Odysseus], according to Homer. III.273

Laocoön: Trojan priest of Neptune [Poseidon]. II.41

Laodamia: wife of Protesilaus who died with her husband. VI.448

Laomedon: king of Troy, father of Priam. III.247

Lapiths: people of Thessaly in northern Greece who fought the Centaurs. VI.601

Lares (**sing.: Lar**): like Penates, idols of guardian household gods; also, these gods themselves. I.68

Larissa: city of Thessaly associated with Achilles's birthplace. II.198

Latian: Latin, of Latium. I.110

Latinus: king of Laurentium, whose daughter Lavinia married Aeneas. VI.891

Latium (**adj.: Latian, Latin**): territory in central Italy including Rome and bordering the Tyrrhenian Sea where the Trojans came to settle. Founded by Saturn in exile, and so named because he had lain low and safe there. I.2

Latona [**Leto**]: goddess and mother of the twins Apollo and Diana by Jupiter. I.502

Laurentines (**adj.: Laurentine, Laurentian**): people of Laurentium. VI.892

Laurentium (**adj.: Laurentian, Laurentine**): city in Latium near Rome, ruled by King Latinus. VII.343

Lausus: noble son of Mezentius and ally of Turnus. VII.649

Lavinia: daughter of Latinus, Italian wife of Aeneas. IV.236

Lavinium (**adj.: Lavinian**): city in Latium near Rome founded by Aeneas and named for his Italian wife. I.3

Leda: mother by Zeus of Helen. I.652

Leleges: a people of Asia Minor. VIII.726

Lerna: marsh south of Argos in Greece; home of the monster Hydra. VI.288

lèse-majesté (**French**): crime or offense committed against a sovereign power. I.231

Lethe: river of forgetfulness in the Underworld. V.855

Leucaspis: Trojan chief. VI.334

Leucata: Ionian island. III.274

levin (**archaic English**): lightning. IV.269

Liber: Bacchus Liburnia; Illyria. VI.804

Libya (**adj.: Libyan**): territory in northern Africa to the west of the Nile. I.22

Licymnian: of Licymnia, a town of Argolis in Greece. IX.546

Liger: Latin who taunts Aeneas and is killed by him; brother of Lucagus. IX.572

Liguria, Ligurian: Italian region northwest of Etruria. X.186

Lilybaeum: promontory on west tip of Sicily. III.706

Lipare: the island of Aeolus. VIII.416

Little Bear, the: the constellation Ursa Minor. I.744

Locrians: people of northern Greece who founded a colony in southern Italy. XI.269

Lucagus: brother of Liger, killed by Aeneas. X.575

Lucifer: the Morning Star. II.802

Lupercal: cave in Rome where the pastoral Lupercalia festival was celebrated, supposedly brought there from Arcadia before the Trojan War by King Evander. VIII.343

Luperci: priests of a fertility cult. VIII.662

lustrum (English loanword from Latin): a period of five years, from a Roman purification ceremony that took place on such interval. I.283

Lycaeus: mountain in Arcadia where Pan was worshipped, and whose name and that of Lupercal (a cave in Rome that Virgil claims was named after it), were believed to be related to the words in Greek and Latin for wolf. See Lupercal and Pan. VIII.344

Lycaon (1): swordsmith of Crete. IX.304

Lycaon (2): father of the Trojan warrior Ericetes. X.750

Lycia (adj.: Lycian): large peninsula on the south coast of Asia Minor. I.113

Lyctian: of Lyctus, a Cretan city. III.400

Lycurgus: king of Thrace. III.14

Lycus: Trojan warrior. I.222

Lydia, Lydian (1): kingdom of Asia Minor, thought to be the original home of the Etruscans. VIII.479

Lydian (2): synonym for Etrurian, by association with the supposed original home of the Etrurians. II.783

Lyrnessian: inhabitant of Lyrnessus, a town near Troy. X.128

Machaon: Greek leader and physician who was concealed within the Trojan Horse. II.264

Maenad: frenzied follower of Bacchus [Dionysos]. IV.302

Maeonia (1): region of Lydia. IV.216

Maeonia (2): Etruria, since the Etruscans were supposedly descended from the Lydians. VIII.500

Maeotians: a people from near Lake Maeotis (Sea of Azov) in Asia and the area around it. VI.799

Maia: daughter of Atlas and mother by Jupiter of Mercury. I.298

Malea: most southern point of mainland Greece. V.193

Manes (Latin): spirits of the honored dead who watch over and are sacrificed to by the living. VI.896

Manlius: Roman hero who was awakened by the sacred geese and saved the Roman citadel from the Gauls. VIII.654

Manto: prophetic nymph, mother of Ocnus. X.199

Mantua: northern Italian city, near Virgil's birthplace at Andes. X.198

Marcellus (1): Roman general who fought against Carthage and the Gauls. VI.855

Marcellus (2): adopted son of Caesar Augustus who died at the age of nineteen. VI.874

Marica: a nymph, mother of Latinus. VII.48

Marruvian: of the Marsi, a people of Latium. VII.750

Mars [Ares]/Mavors/Gradivus: Roman god of war and agriculture. I.274

Marsian/Marruvian: of a region in Latium inhabited by the Marsi. VII.758

Massicus: Etruscan ally of Aeneas. X.166

Massylian: of the Massyli, a people of north Africa. IV.132

Mavors/Mars: Roman god of war and agriculture. III.13

Maximus: Fabius Maximus, nicknamed "Cunctator" for the delaying tactics he used against Hannibal. VI.846

Medon: Trojan warrior. VI.483

Megaera: one of the Furies. XII.847

Megara: city in Sicily. III.689

Melampus: father of Cisseus and Gyas and friend of Hercules. X.320

Meliboeans: inhabitants of town of Thessaly in northern Greece. III.401

Melite: sea-nymph. V.825

Memnon: king of Ethiopia and ally of Troy, killed by Achilles. I.489.

Menelaus: king of Sparta, brother of Agamemnon, husband of Helen. II.265

Menoetes (1): Trojan helmsman of the *Chimaera* who competes in the funeral games for Anchises. V.160

Menoetes (2): Arcadian warrior killed by Turnus. XII.517

Mercury [Hermes]: son of Jupiter and Maia, messenger of the gods. IV.222

Messapus: Etruscan ally of Turnus. VII.691

Metabus: king of Privernum who went into exile with his daughter Camilla. XI.539

Metiscus: charioteer of Turnus. XII.469.

Mettus: Alban king who broke a treaty with Rome and was torn apart by two chariots. VIII.643

Mezentius: disgraced Etruscan king of Caere against whom his people revolted and whom they exiled; father of Lausus and ally of Turnus. VII.647

Mincius: river and river-god of northern Italy and son of the lake-god Benacus. X.205

Minerva [Athena]: also Pallas, Tritonia; virgin goddess of wisdom and war. II.31

Minio: Etruscan river. X.183

Minos: mythical king of Cnossus in Crete and husband of Pasiphaë who became a judge of souls in the Underworld. VI.15

Minotaur: half-bull, half-man son of Queen Pasiphaë of Crete and a bull. VI.25

Misenus: Trojan trumpeter. III.239

Mnestheus: Trojan leader. IV.288

Monoecian: of Monoecus, a city in northern Italy. VI.831

Monster-of-the-Sea [Brine]: ship piloted by Mnestheus in the funeral games for Anchises. V.117

Morini: Belgic tribe of northern Gaul that lived near the English Channel. VIII.727

Mother of All Nations: Cybele, mother of the gods; mother goddess of Phrygia, in Asia Minor VII.139

Murranus: Rutulian warrior. XII.529

Musaeus: prophet and singer of Thrace. VI.667

Muse: one of nine goddesses of poetry and the other arts. I.8

Mycenae: city in southern Greece; home of Agamemnon, the Greek commander in chief at Troy. I.285

Myconos: Cycladic island. III.76

Mygdon: father of Coroebus. II.343

Myrmidons: soldiers of Achilles from Thessaly. II.7

Nar: river north of Rome. VII.516

Narycian: of Naryx, a city of southern Italy. III.399

Nautes: old Trojan prophet. V.704

Naxos: Cycladic island. III.125

***nec* (Latin)**: nor. XI.181

Nemea: city near Argos, site of Hercules's first labor, to kill the Nemean Lion. VIII.295

Neoptolemus: son of Achilles; also called Pyrrhus. II.263

Neptune [Poseidon]: god of the sea, son of Saturn and brother of Jupiter and Juno. I.124

Nereids: sea-nymphs, daughters of Nereus. V.239

Nereus: a sea-god, father of the Nereid nymphs. II.420

Neritos: Ionian island near Ithaca. III.271

Nesaea: sea-nymph. V.826

Night: night personified as a goddess. II.251

Nile: river of Egypt. VI.800

Nisus: Trojan warrior who loved the Trojan Euryalus. V.294

Nomads (adj.: Nomad): Numidians; tribe of north Africa. IV.40, VIII.724. At III.101, "nomads" is used as a common noun.

Nomentum: Italian city. VI.772

Notus: god and personification of the South or Southwest Wind. III.268

Numa (1): Numa Pompilius, legendary lawgiver of early Rome. VI.812

Numa (2): Rutulian casualty. IX.454

Numa (3): member of Turnus's troops. X.562

Numanus Remulus: Rutulian married to Turnus's sister. IX.592

numen (Latin): divine favor, will, protection, or presence. I.447

Numicius: river in Latium. VII.150

Numidians: Nomads. IV.40

Numitor (1): king of Alba Longa. VI.768

Numitor (2): a Rutulian. X.342

Nysa: mountain in Asia where Bacchus was raised. VI.804

Ocean: mythical river that encircles the world personified as a god. I.125

Ocnus: son of the Sybil Manto and the Tuscan river and founder of the city Mantua. X.198

Oebalus: ally of Turnus. VII.733

Oechalia: city of King Eurytus in northern Greece, conquered by Hercules. VIII.291

Oenotria, Oenotrians: people of southern Italy. I.532

Olearos: Cycladic island. III.126

Olympus: highest mountain of Greece, home of the Olympian gods. I.223

Opheltes: father of Euryalus. IX.201

Opis: attendant of Trivia/Diana. XI.533

Orcus: Hades, the Underworld. II.400

Orestes: son of Agamemnon, he killed his mother Clytemnestra and, later, Pyrrhus. III.330

Orician: of Oricia, a port town in Illyria. X.136

Orion: constellation named for a mythological hunter. I.535

Orithyia: wife of Boreas, the North Wind. XII.83

Orontes: a chief from Lycia. I.113

Orpheus: mythical prophet and musician who tried to rescue his wife, Eurydice, from Hades. VI.120

Ortygia (1): island in the Cyclades archipelago also known as Delos. III.124

Ortygia (2): island near Sicily. III.694

Oscan, Oscans: very early people who lived east of Latium. VII.730

Othrys (1): father of Panthus. II.321

Othrys (2): mountain in Thessaly. VII.675

Pachynus: promontory of Sicily. III.429

Pactolus: river of Asia Minor famous for its gold. X.142

Padua: city of northern Italy founded by Antenor. I.247

Padusa: a canal off the Po river. XI.457

Paeonian: medicinal; from the god of medicine Paeon. XII.401

Palaemon: Ino's son who was changed into a sea-god. V.823

Palamedes: Greek warrior at Troy who had outwitted Ulysses [Odysseus] by exposing his scheme to avoid serving in the war and who in turn was framed by Ulysses for committing an act of treason, falsely accused, and executed. II.81

Palatine: the most important of Rome's seven hills. IX.9

Palicus: son of Jupiter and a nymph, worshipped in Sicily. IX.585

Palinurus: pilot of the fleet of Aeneas. III.201

Palladium: image of Minerva that served a defensive purpose for the city of Troy and was stolen from her temple there by Ulysses and Diomedes. II.167

Pallanteum: city in Italy founded by the Greek (Arcadian) migrant King Evander and named after his ancestor Pallas (3) on the future site of Rome. VIII.54

Pallas (1): son of Evander who is killed by Turnus. VIII.104

Pallas (2): title of Minerva. I.41

Pallas (3): ancestor of Evander. VIII.51

Pan: Arcadian god of the woods also known as Lycaean Pan, since he was worshipped at Arcadia's Mount Lycaeus. VIII.345

Pandarus (1): Lycian archer who wounded Menelaus in the Trojan War. V.496.

Pandarus (2): Trojan warrior, brother of Bitias and grandson of Jove. IX.672

Panopea: sea-nymph, daughter of Nereus. V.240

Panopes: Sicilian athlete. V.301

Pantagia: river in Sicily. III.689

Panthus: Trojan leader and priest of Apollo. II.319.

Paphos: a city in Cyprus. I.415

Parcae: the three Fates. I.22

Paris: Trojan prince who judged the beauty contest between Juno, Minerva, and Venus. He later ran off with Helen, the wife of Menelaus, inciting the Trojan War. I.26

Paros (adj.: Parian): Aegean island, famous for its marble. III.126

Parrhasian: Arcadian. VIII.344

Parthenopaeus: Greek warrior killed at Thebes. VI.479

Parthians: people of central Asia continually at war with the Roman Empire. VII.607

Pasiphaë: wife of King Minos of Crete and mother of the Minotaur. VI.25

Pater (Latin): father or forefather. I.582

Patron: Greek athlete. V.298

Pelasgian, Pelasgic: of an ancient pre-Greek-speaking people of Greece. I.624

Peleus: father of Achilles. II.549

Pelias: Trojan leader. II.436

Pelops: Greek mythical hero for whom the Peloponnese ("island of Pelops") is named. II.195

Pelorus: promontory of Sicily. III.411

Penates: like Lares, idols of guardian household gods; also, these gods themselves. II.295

Peneleus: Greek leader. II.426

Penthesilea: Amazon queen and ally of Troy, killed by Achilles. I.490

Pentheus: king of Thebes in Greece, who opposed the religion of Bacchus [Dionysos]. IV.469

peplum **(Latin)**: a ceremonial robe. I.481

per saecula saeculorum **(Latin)**: for ever and ever. VI.235

Perdita (Latin): Lost One, a name by which Dido addresses herself (rendered in the translation by the compound name Dido-Perdita). IV.541

Pergamum (1): the citadel of Troy and, by extension, Troy itself. I.466

Pergamum (2): city in Crete named by Aeneas for Troy. III.134

Periphas: Greek leader. II.477

Perseus: historical king of Macedon and supposed descendant of Achilles who was conquered by the Romans. VI.841

Petelia: city founded by Philoctetes in southern Italy. III.402

Phaeacia, Phaeacians: Ionian island, now called Corfu. III.291

Phaedra: wife of Theseus who loved her stepson Hippolytus and killed herself. VI.445

Phaëthon (1) [Helios]: a name for the sun-god. V.104

Phaëthon (2): son of Phaëthon (1) who perished after losing control of his father's chariot in the sky. X.190

Phegeus (1): Trojan prize-bearer. V.263

Phegeus (2): Trojan killed by Turnus within the Trojan camp. IX.765

Phegeus (3): Trojan warrior beheaded in attack on Turnus's chariot. XII.371

Pheneus: town in Arcadia. VIII.165

Philoctetes: Greek warrior who possessed the bow of Hercules. III.402

Phineus: king of Thrace who was tormented by the Harpies. III.212

Phlegethon: personified river of fire, one of the five rivers of the Underworld. VI.265

Phlegyas: king of the Lapiths who burned Apollo's temple. VI.619

Phoebe: a name for Diana and the moon. X.215

Phoebus: Grynean Phoebus, a name for Apollo. I.329

Phoenicians: people of western Asia from what is now mainly modern-day Lebanon who settled Carthage. I.442

Phoenix: Greek leader. II.763

Pholoë: slave girl from Crete. V.284

Pholus (1): a Centaur. VIII.294

Pholus (2): a Trojan. XII.341

Phorbas: Priam's son, killed in the Trojan War. V.842

Phorcus: sea-god. V.240

Phrygia (adj.: Phrygian): a kingdom of Asia Minor. I.182

Phrygian: of Phrygia and, by extension, Trojan. I.182

Phthia: region of Thessaly in Greece; kingdom of Peleus, father of Achilles. I.284

Picus: son of Saturn and grandfather of Latinus. VII.49

Pilumnus: grandfather of Turnus. IX.4

Pinarii: family of priests of Hercules. VIII.270

Pirithoüs: king of the Lapiths who went to the Underworld with Theseus. VI.393

Pisa: Etruscan city (modern-day Pisa). X.179

pius **(Latin)**: devoted to the will of the gods, righteous, pious; an epithet for Aeneas. I.377

Plemyrium: promontory of Sicily. III.693.

Pluto [Hades]: also Erebus, Hades, and Dis, god and personification of the Underworld; Styx's king; see also Elysium, Tartarus, and Styx. VII.327

Polites: son of Priam. II.527

Pollux [Polydeuces]: son of Jupiter and Leda, twin brother of Castor (the twins are the Gemini). VI.122

Polyboetes: Trojan priest of Ceres. VI.484

Polydorus: son of Priam, killed in Thrace. III.45

Polyphemus: a Cyclops and shepherd, blinded by Ulysses. III.641

Pometii: Italian city. VI.775

Pompey: son-in-law and ally of, then opponent in Civil War of, Julius Caesar, by whom he was defeated at Pharsalia. He escaped to Alexandria, where he was beheaded. II.558–59 note

Populonia: Etruscan coast town. X.172

Porsenna: Etruscan king who tried to make Rome take back exiled King Tarquin. VIII.646

Portunus: sea-god, patron of ports. V.241

Potitius: priest of Hercules. VIII.269

Praeneste: city east of Rome. VII.679

Priam (1): king of Troy during the Trojan War; father of Hector, Paris, Cassandra, and many other children. I.458

Priam (2): grandson of King Priam of Troy. V.563

Privernum: town in Latium. XI.540

Procas: king of Alba Longa. VI.767

Procida: small island near Cumae. IX.715

Procris: jealous wife killed by her husband Cephalus. VI.445

Proserpina/Proserpine [Persephone]: wife of Pluto [Hades] and queen of the Underworld. IV.698

Proteus: shape-shifting sea god sometimes called a king of Egypt. XI.262

Proteus's Pillars: an eastern Mediterranean counterpart of some kind to the Pillars of Hercules of the western Mediterranean. XI.262

Punic/Phoenician: Carthaginian. I.20

Pygmalion: brother of Dido and king of Tyre. I.347

Pyracmon: a Cyclops. VIII.425

Pyrgi: Etruscan town. X.184

Pyrgo: nurse of Priam's children. V.644

Pyrrhus: son of Achilles, also called Neoptolemus. II.470

Quercens: a Rutulian. IX.684

quidnunc (neo-Latin): a gossip or talebearer. II.549

Quirinal: most northern hill of Rome. VII.187

Quirinus: deified Romulus. I.292

Quirites: the inhabitants of Cures as well as an old name for the Sabines, later used for the combined Sabines and Romans. VII.710

Remulus (1): a Latin from Tibur. IX.361

Remulus (2): other name of the Rutulian Numanus. IX.592

Remulus (3): Rutulian thrown from his wounded horse. XI.637

Remus (1): brother of Romulus. I.292

Remus (2): Rutulian whose armorer is among those killed by Nisus. IX.330

Rhadamanthus: brother of Minos and a judge of the dead in the Underworld. VI.567

Rhamnes: Rutulian king and prophet. IX.325

Rhea: mother of Aventinus by Hercules. VII.660

Rhesus: prince of Thrace and ally of the Trojans, killed when he arrived at Troy. I.470

Rhine: river of central Europe. VIII.727

Rhoetean: of a promontory near Troy. III.108

Rhoetus (1): Marsian ancestor of Anchemolus. X.389

Rhoetus (2): Rutulian warrior killed by Euryalus. IX.345

Rhoetus (3): Rutulian warrior killed by Pallas (1). X.399

Ripheus: Trojan leader. II.341

Romulus: founder of Rome, brother of Remus, son of Mars and Rhea Silvia. I.275

Rumor: personification of rumor, gossip, news. I.532

Rutuli, Rutulians: Latin people whose king was Turnus. I.266, VII.318

Sabaeans: a people of Arabia. I.417

Sabethis: nymph who was mother of Oebalus. VII.734

Sabine: of the Sabines, a people of the mountainous area northeast of Latium. VII.666

Sabinus: mythical king of the Sabines. VII.178

Sagaris: Trojan slave. V.263

Salamis: island in the Saronic Gulf near Athens. VIII.158

Salii: dancing priests of Mars. VIII.285

Salius: Greek athlete. V.298

Sallentia: Calabrian town in southern Italy invaded by Idomeneus. III.401

Salmoneus: Greek king who imitated Zeus and was punished. VI.585

Samé: Ionian island near Ithaca. III.271

Samos: island of the east Aegean Sea, famous for the worship of the goddess Juno. I.16

Samothrace: island of the north Aegean, near Thrace. VII.208

Sarpedon: son of Jupiter, king of Lycia and ally of the Trojans, killed by Patroclus at Troy. I.100

Saturn (adj.: Saturnian, Saturnine) [Kronos]: father of Jupiter and Juno and founder of Latium, where he settled after being overthrown and exiled by Jupiter, and of which he was ruler during the Golden Age. I.569

Scaean: famous gate of Troy. II.613

Scipio: family name of several famous leaders in Rome's wars against Carthage. VI.842

Scylaceum: promontory of southern Italy. III.553

Scylla (1): hybrid sea-monster, a woman above and dolphins and dogs or wolves below, which is perilous to sailors and, like its counterpart Charybdis, associated with the strait between Italy and Sicily. I.200

Scylla **(2)**: ship piloted by Cloanthus in the funeral games for Anchises. V.123

Scylla (3): a kind of monster at the doors of the Underworld. VI.286

Scyrian: of Scyros, an Aegean island associated with Neoptolemus. II.479

Selinus: city of western Sicily. III.705

Serestus: Trojan leader. I.612

Sergestus: Trojan warrior. I.510

Serranus: Roman consul who fought against Carthage. VI.844

Sibyl: a prophetic priestess, usually Deïphobe, the Sibyl of Cumae. III.444

Sicania, Sicanians (adj.: Sicanian): Sicily, from a people of Latium who later migrated to Sicily. III.692

Sicily: large island south of Italy. I.35

Sidon: city of Phoenicia. I.613

Sidonian: of Sidon, famous Phoenician city; Carthaginian. I.446

Sigea, Sigean: promontory near Troy. II.313

Sila: forest in southern Italy. XII.716

Silvanus: old Italian god of farmers. VIII.602

Silvia: daughter of Tyrrhus. VII.487

Silvius: son of Aeneas and Lavinia, king of Alba Longa. VI.763

Silvius Aeneas: king of Alba Longa, who waited fifty years to rule. VI.769

Simois: river of Troy. I.100

Sinon: Greek who betrayed Troy. II.79

Sirens: half-woman, half-bird goddesses of music and death. V.864

Sirius: the Dog Star, which rises at the hottest part of summer. III.141

Sleep [Hypnos]: Somnus, the god of sleep. V.838

Sol [Helios]: the Sun personified as a god. I.568

sopor **(Latin)**: deep sleep. II.254

Soracte: mountain north of Rome. VII.696

South Wind: Auster [Notus] personified South Wind. I.108

Spartan: of Sparta, a city of south Greece. I.316

Spio: sea-nymph. V.826

Spolia Opima **(Latin)**: armor and weapons taken from the corpse of a slain leader by a conqueror after one-on-one combat. VI.856

SPQR: Roman acronym for *Senatus Populusque Romanus*, meaning the "Roman Senate and People." VIII.680

Steropes: a Cyclops. VIII.425

Sthenelus: Greek leader. II.261

Strophades: group of islands in the Ionian Sea. III.209

Strymonian: of Strymon, a river of northeast Greece, home of many cranes. X.264

Styx (adj.: Stygian): chief river of the Underworld; also, by extension, the Underworld itself, Pluto's kingdom. V.855

sua sponte **(Latin)**: of one's, or their, own accord. VII.204

Sulmo: father of four sons taken alive by Aeneas to be sacrificed at the funeral of Pallas. IX.412

swale (English): a hollow. III.111

Sychaeus: Dido's dead husband. I.343

Symaethus: river of Sicily. IX.584

Syrtes: Syrtis. V.51

Syrtis: treacherous area off the north coast of Africa. IV.41

Taburnus: Italian mountain range. XII.716

Tarchon: Etruscan ally of Aeneas. VIII.505

Tarentum: city founded by Hercules in southern Italy. III.551

Tarpeia (adj.: Tarpeian) (1): a traitor to Rome executed on the Capitoline Hill at a place that came to be known as the Tarpeian Rock. VIII.347

Tarpeia (2): warrior in Camilla's troop. XI.656

Tarquin: one of two kings of Rome by this name, who was expelled for tyrannical rule. VI.817

Tarquitus: young Latin, son of the nymph Dryope. X.550

Tartarus (adj.: Tartarean): the Underworld, or that part of it reserved for special criminals. IV.244

Tatius: king of the Sabines. VIII.637

Tegea (adj.: Tegean): city of Arcadia in south Greece. V.299

Teleboan: of the legendary colonists of Capreae. VII.736

Telon: father of Oebalus. VII.735

Tenedos: island (modern-day Bozcaada) near Troy. II.21

testudo: military formation with a covering of shields, like a tortoise shell, to protect soldiers beneath. II.442

Teucer (1): Greek warrior, son of Telamon and brother of Ajax. III.108

Teucer (2): forefather of the Trojans and early king of Troy who migrated to Asia Minor from Crete. I.235

Teucrian, Teucrians: Trojan, Trojans, from Teucer (2). II.459

Teuton: of the Teutons, a migratory tribe who settled in Germany. VII.741

Thalia: sea-nymph. V.826

Thapsus: island east of Sicily. III.690

Thaumas: father of Iris and the Harpies. IX.5

Thebes: city in Greece. IV.470

Themillas: Trojan warrior. IX.578

Thermodon: a river of Asia Minor flowing into the Black Sea. XI.660

Thersilochus: Trojan warrior. VI.483

Theseus: greatest mythical king of Athens, he killed the Minotaur and escaped with help from the princess Ariadne. VI.30

Thessandrus: Greek leader. II.262

Thetis: sea-goddess, mother of Achilles. V.825

Thoas: Greek leader. II.264

Thrace, Thracian: most northeast region of Greece, home of Orpheus. III.15

Thybris: Italian king after whom the Tiber River was supposedly named. VIII.330

Thymbran: of Thymbra, city sacred to Apollo near Troy; by extension, Apollo himself. III.85

Thymoetes: Trojan leader. II.33

Tiber: river of Rome. I.13

Tibur, Tiburtians: city near Rome. VII.630

Tiburtus: founder of Tibur and brother of Catillus and Coras. VII.672

Timavus: river in northern Italy. I.244

Tiryns: Greek city near Mycenae where Hercules stayed during his labors. VII.662

Tisiphone: one of the three Furies. VI.555

Titan Sun: a personification of the sun. IV.119

Titans: family of giants overthrown by Jupiter. VI.725

Tithonus: husband of Aurora. IV.585

Tityos: giant punished in the Underworld for trying to rape Latona. VI.595

Tmarian: of Epirus. V.620

Tmarus: a Rutulian. IX.686

Tolumnius: Rutulian priest. XI.429

Torquatus: consul who executed his son for disobedience. VI.825

trabea (**Latin**): formal garment of elite Romans worn for ceremonial functions. VII.188

Trinacria, Trinacrian: Sicily, Sicilian. I.197

Triton: sea-god whose legs end in fish tails, a merman. I.144

Tritonia (adj.: Tritonian): name for Minerva. II.172

Trivia (adj.: Trivian): name for Diana shared with Hecate, with whom she is closely identified. VI.13

Troilus: Priam's youngest son. I.474

Troy, Trojan: city on west coast of Asia Minor, conquered by Greece in the Trojan War. I.1

Tullus: Tullus Hostilius, early Roman king who punished Mettus. VI.813

Turnus: Italian hero, king of the Rutulians, and prime antagonist of Aeneas. VII.55

Tuscany (adj.: Tuscan; also Tyrrhenian/Etrurian/Etruscan): the area of Italy north of Rome. X.164

Tydeus: Greek warrior killed at Thebes who was father of Diomedes. I.96

Tyndareus: wife of Leda, stepfather of Helen. II.572

Typhoeus (adj.: Typhoean): a monstrous giant killed by Jupiter. I.665

Tyre: with Sidon, one of the two famous cities of ancient Phoenicia. I.13

Tyrian: of Tyre, a Phoenician city; by extension, Carthaginian, since Carthage was a Phoenician settlement. I.302

Tyrrhenian: Etruscan, Tuscan. VII.43

Tyrrhus: game warden of King Latinus. VII.485

Ucalegon: Trojan leader. II.312

Ufens (1): Latin ally of Turnus. VII.744

Ufens (2): a river in Latium. VII.801

Ulysses [Odysseus]: important Greek leader in the Trojan War, from the island Ithaca. II.44

Ulyssian: any member of Ulysses's troops. II.8

Umbrian: of Umbria, a region of Italy north of Latium and east of Etruria, known for its hunting dogs. XII.753

Umbro: Marruvian priest, snake charmer, and healer who was an ally of Turnus. VII.752

vates **(Latin)**: seer. III.463

Velia: port city in Italy. VI.366

Velinus: a lake in Sabine territory. VII.517

Venilia: mother of Turnus. X.76

Venulus: messenger of Turnus. VIII.9

Venus [Aphrodite] (adj.: Venusian): Cytherea: goddess of love, mother of Aeneas by the Trojan Anchises. I.228

Vesta [Hestia]: goddess of the hearth. I.292

Vesulus: a mountain in Liguria. X.708

Virbius (1): name of Hippolytus's son, an ally of Turnus. VII.761

Virbius (2): name taken by the resurrected Hippolytus while living incognito in the groves of Egeria. VII.777

Volcens: a leader of the Latin cavalry. IX.370

Volsci, Volscians: a people of Latium. VII.803

Volusus: Rutulian, herald of Turnus. XI.463

Vulcan (adj.: Vulcan) [Hephaistos]: god of fire and metallurgy associated with the north Aegean island of Lemnos. II.311

Vulcania: island near Sicily, home of Vulcan and his forges. VIII.422

Vulcanus: Vulcan. XII.88

Xanthus: river of Troy. I.473

Zacynthus: Ionian island. III.270

Zephyr: god and personification of the West Wind. III.120

Adapted from *The Aeneid: A Prose Translation*, translated by Richard Caldwell (Focus © 2004), and reprinted by permission of the publisher.